GIVE YOUR HEART TO THE
BARROW

GIVE YOUR HEART TO THE

BARROW

BLUEBEARD'S SECRET
BOOK 3

SARAH K. L. WILSON

PUBLISHED BY SARAH K. L. WILSON, 2022

This is a work of fiction. Similarities to real people, places, or events are entirely coincidental.

GIVE YOUR HEART TO THE BARROW

First Edition. March 1, 2022

Copyright © 2022 Sarah K. L. Wilson

Cover Art by Kristen De Palma

Written by Sarah K. L. Wilson

www.sarahklwilson.com

They say you should write with just one reader in mind.

For this book, that reader was Melissa Wright who puts up with me calling her at eight in the morning to ask what kind of cheesecake to make for Christmas (she doesn't even like cheesecake) and then gasp, "Orioles, Melissa! The answer is orioles!"

PENSMOORE

SALAMOORE

ROURANMOORE

AYYADMOORE

OARAMOORE

PTOLEMOORE

ILKANMOORE

MORAVIDMOORE

MORTAL LANDS

CHAPTER ONE

The Law of Greeting stole me away. The machinations of man brought me back, torn from the Wittenhame and dragged – ragged and bloody – back to the washed-out world of mortals. I had no say in the first and less in the second, caught as I was like a leaf tumbling on the surface of the river, swirling and bobbing in the grip of a mighty current. But so it is with the great stories. They create their own currents, forge their own streams, and we poor mortals are ever subject to them as the tide to her mistress moon.

"I'm so sorry, I'm so sorry," my brother's harsh sobs echoed, and faded, and then returned a long time later with other voices joining his. I was cold – so, so cold – as I lay shivering on the hard ground, but not nearly as chilled as my husband must be in his place beneath the greedy sea.

I saw him in my mind's eyes, his blue beard and bright cat's eyes under the swirling depths, his flushed cheeks turning pale and then blue, his teardrop of blood washing from the planes of his lovely face, the fish snatching at his hair and clothes, as he was pinned to the pillar, immobile, trapped.

It was not for myself that I moaned when they lifted me into a carriage with concerned voices. Not for my own fate banished back to this plain mortal world that brought tears slowly leaking from my heavy eyes. They brought me to a close dark room filled with whispers and worry but it was not for my own self that I sought when my consciousness was snatched and returned and snatched again.

It was for him that I searched in every whisper of speech I heard, in every gentle touch, in every small glimpse of a face. It was for just one more glimmer of him, one more of his words passing like fine silk through the ring of my mind, one more sweetly bitter kiss searing my lips like fresh ginger.

But none of these attended me. Nothing at all tended me except the cold hands of mortals, the plain speech of plain people, thrall to the whims of nature and time. As I grew well again, it was only their faded faces and pale food that greeted me, seeded though it was by generosity and charity.

From the first, the sea called to me. Any open window meant the echoes of her moaning voice – so like the one echoing forever inside of me. I learned to listen for it beneath the sounds of the household around me. For if I could not touch my husband again, I could at least listen to that which touched him and caressed him daily in his grave.

Eventually, my broken body healed and grew strong again, to the great relief of Lady Greatspur who had graciously taken me into her home and ensconced me in the chambers of her long-deceased daughter. I pleased her with my quiet manner and my willingness to embroider every cloth she put before me as I convalesced in her home. I ate little, spoke less, and kept my hands very busy – a credit, she said, the sign of a good wife and lady, and didn't my brother need that right now in his sister, what with the chaos in the capital?

But though my hands worked busily, and my manners worked even harder, it was the sea I was listening for in every space where the good lady drew a breath and paused her musings. It was the sea I watched for in glimpses through the windows. I was as attuned to it as a mother with a new babe, noticing its every mood and whim and bending myself to it.

I waited patiently, biding my time until the first day that I could sit unaided and cross the room without assistance. That night, I crept from the lady's great house, passing the doors of those who slumbered with as much silence as the specter on my shoulder. No matter that I was in the mortal world, she lingered still, wrapped around my shoulders, waiting for the moment where she could morph from spectral collar to guardian and snatch the words from my mouth. For a wonder, none of the mortals around her seemed to see her there. It was just the two of us who knew she shared my silent vigil.

I stepped out onto the stones, my bare feet feeling every slippery surface, every snatching grassy caress of a dull empty land. I slipped toward the call of the sea, careless to how rocks bit my feet or cold stung my skin. The moment my toes met the freezing water, I ran over the glazed rocks and threw myself into the sea. What did I think I would find within? Did I think I would hear his voice? Did I think I would find some strange magic that would bear me to his side? Did I expect that the sea would bargain with me?

If I expected any of that, I was wrong. Gravely, sorely wrong. For nothing greeted me but *nothing* – a great raw roaring nothing as if my very life had been hollowed out as one hollows a wooden bowl and scraped down to the narrowest shape that can still hold a soul.

I returned to the grim estate eventually, hiding my misadventures with a hasty bath beside the well and hanging my clothing by the fire to dry. When questioned, I claimed a fever had taken me, soaking me in sweat. And after the chill of the night, I was just as feverish as I claimed, and worry filled the glances and words of those around me as they had when I first arrived.

The fever passed as all mortal things do, and when it did, I tried twice more. The first, in a small fishing boat I stole from the shore. I discovered nothing except that I was very bad with oars and not nearly as strong as I'd hoped.

Of my husband and my life, nothing was left to me.

On the last time that I slipped out to the sea in the night, I arrived with fury and acceptance and the words of a funeral on my lips.

The wind howled, blustering along the shore with the violence to stir clouds of sand and bursts of sea spray up into the air in swirling specters dancing over the landscape in murderous frenzy. There could be no more perfect atmosphere for what I was to do there.

I sank to my knees on the sand, the dark of midnight clinging to me like a second specter and with no one to witness what I did but the wailing wind, the sober moon, and my grim spectral companion.

"You loved drama and murder." I spoke my memorial to Grosbeak. If he were here, he'd be insisting on a better funeral than this. He'd be insisting that I do the impossible and find some way to go down to him in the depths and draw him back. "You were a friend both kind and terrible, and in your jests and screams I washed up on shoals of kindness."

There. It had been said.

I spread my fingers on the sand and sank my weight into my

palms, wetting my lips to speak funereal words for my husband. It had been three weeks since we were found on the edge of the sea.

Three mortal weeks could be decades in the Wittenhame. He could be long dead, his tumbled bones half-hidden by sand and memory, his people scattered, and his lands razed.

Or, it could be mere minutes for them, and even now he could be gasping under the sea, his lungs filling with choking black water as the sea sucked his life from him and forced him unwillingly into her embrace. And even now when I spoke the words over him, I could be speaking his death when still he clawed for a last scrap of life.

And I couldn't do it.

I couldn't.

I broke down as I had not yet broken, wailing my sorrow in a terrible harmony to the crash of the waves and the cry of the wind. I cried and cried until I thought, perhaps, that I had cried an ocean large enough to fight the sea for him, a salty jhinn to champion my cause and rise up to bear my standard.

But in the end, dawn rose as my husband did not, mocking his submersion with her flagrant ascent, and no champion emerged but a battered fisherman troubled to find me not far from his nets and distraught beyond human ken. He put me on his donkey and rode me to the Lady's house where dark murmurings filled every corner and kind hands put a hot drink in my hands, tucked me in a warm bed, and whispered that the Lord Savataz's sister had lost her wits.

It was from that miserable stupor that I emerged the next morning to find the house in an uproar.

Lady Greatspur entered my room with trepidation just before noon, clutching a black gown to her chest and worrying at her lower lip as if I were the lady here and her the poor wretch dragged in by an ancient mariner.

"Lady Izolda," she said timidly. "Can you dress yourself, my girl?"

I could not have found a kinder hostess. I sank deeper into the blankets thinking of the night I had hidden in a ball from my new husband in just such a bed.

The lady crept to my bedside and if I had been more in possession of myself, I would have been shocked by how she – a lady of Pensmoore – sank to her knees so that her face was not far from mine, and she could whisper to me.

"We ladies have little power over ourselves, Izolda of Savataz." She paused, listening for a moment, and then shook her head and spoke again. "And you have clearly suffered a great loss. Doctor Ryvataz believes you to have lost your wits and he will tell your brother so – indeed he already has told him in the missive he sent, and you brother is riding here with great urgency – and this on the verge of his coronation."

Coronation? That made me sit up and push the hair from my face with heavy hands.

The lady was nodding. "Indeed. After a bloody struggle and a bloodier peace agreement, your brother is to be crowned king of Pensmoore. The wars have taken and taken, and to find a living lord of Pensmoore capable of managing the nation – well, the kingdom has rejoiced that he is returned to us. Surely, my girl, you must realize how desperate things are for us that we rejoice to have a second son of Northpeak to reign."

I nodded, my voice too thick to speak, but the nod seemed to encourage her.

"And that is why I am here. For I see before me not a deranged woman lost to sense, but a woman in deep grief as I was when my daughter was taken by the fever while not yet thirteen." Her lip trembled at that, and I reached out to take her vein-crossed hand in mine and the look in her eyes was steel and purpose. "So now, listen to me, and I will tell you what I would have told her if she had lived to lose all she loved. Grief honors our lost. The greater the flow of it, the greater the heart that once held love. And yet, you must take back possession of yourself, or find yourself locked away in a madhouse and what tiny freedom you have left stripped from you.

"So now, heed my words. Dry your eyes. Fix your hair. Put on this gown I have brought – one of my own. I have done you the dignity of choosing black. And when you are dressed, and coifed, and shut away inside, you will act the perfect lady again and you will embroider, and you will listen, and you will be a great boon to your brother and your nation, and whatever this great grief is, you will let it take you within, but never without, for if you do not learn to bridle it and force it to hand, then you will be ridden by it and lose what little hopes you still have."

And her words were sensible and wise and so I opened my swollen lips and spoke with my thick tongue.

"Thank you."

By midday, my brother was upon the household with a grand stamping retinue of men and horses. They arrived in the first squalling snowfall of the season, their breath and pride puffing out in white gusts.

Svetgin was pleased to see me well and dressed in muted black, my hair drawn back sharply from my face, and as unadorned as a proper widow ought to be. He praised Lady Greatspur and took me off with him immediately once his party was refreshed at her table.

"I'm to be crowned tomorrow," he confided in me in the carriage. "And I will be counting on you for your help, sister, in securing my reign."

And I had smiled a tiny, serene smile and kept my face and hands as calm as Lady Greatspur had advised me, but my heart rolled and broke as the sea within me, and the roar of the ocean filled my ears and mind and did not let me go.

CHAPTER TWO

I claimed very little from my royal brother after the coronation – only a room in his tiered castle, an occasional place at his table and in his counsels, and a royal horse.

He certainly received the best end of the bargain as I worked tirelessly to secure him the support of his military, to secure his borders, to reestablish trade, to calm impassioned nobles and impassion calm ones. I was for him everything a sister of a king could be and handy with a pen and ledger besides.

I ate with care, careful not to miss meals after those first few months. I dared not see the land starve for my grief, but the rain and snow never seemed to let up – changing what crops we grew and how we built. I could not prevent that, for though I could force myself to eat for the sake of the land tied to me, I could not dam my tears.

Despite my careful attention, I had grown to hate Pensmoore as one hates a sister who has stolen the affection of one's betrothed. I hated her success because it was bought with the death of my love. I hated her peace, for it was bought with my pain.

I was not a fool. I knew all this was only possible because the Game of Crowns had shifted. War was constant south of our borders. Constant and growing, encompassing everyone else –

even Ayyadmoore was overrun, and we shipped much of our surplus grain and meat to them in aid and compassion – or so we told the people. In actual fact, the longer she held out, the longer it would be before enemies crawled over our border like a swarm of grasshoppers eating all there was to consume as they had with her. We bought ourselves time with every barge of grain that sailed, with every lowing cow that was driven over the bridge, with every piece of gold sent to her relief.

I alone, of all Svetgin's counselors, saw what that meant. I, alone, understood our reprieve was temporary, that war would come when the powers that ruled from on high remembered we were here.

It mattered not. My brother, my fellows on his council, and even my own self would be dead long before the patterns I saw came to fruition. I fought now – against them and for Pensmoore – only for a memory. I fought for the memory of my mother's eyes and my father's smile and the thought that both would shatter if I did not keep safe what they had entrusted to me.

I did not forget those who had died for me in this faded mortal world, and I steered my brother toward patronage not only of Northpeak's stables – ensuring our cousin who stood now as landholder would have enough ready coin to keep up our parent's legacy, but also toward the stables of Lord Danske who had so nobly died in defense of my honor. His successor – his steward as no living relative could be found – honored me with the gift of a horse along with horses we purchased for the army.

The horse, I adored. He was a gorgeous black stallion pronounced unfit for riding, for he was too spirited and too nervous. A mere glance at him shot my heart through with pained nostalgia for he was precisely the horse my father would have chosen. He danced at the smallest sound, balked at orders, tried to throw anyone but me, and was altogether too large and too expensive for a stable in the city.

I doted on him, giving him apples when he bit the fingers of the stable hands, preparing his hot mash myself, and pressing my pale forehead to his dusky one. The people of Pensmoore City called me horse-mad and referred to him as my prince so much that I began to call him so, myself.

"And how are you today, Horse Prince?" I murmured to him, gratified that no one bothered us this morning.

To the dismay of Svetgin and his men alike, I – Princess of Pensmoore though I was – rode him to the sea every month. I would have ridden out more if I dared, but the journey was a three-day ride and though I stayed with Lady Greatspur, I spent one of those days and nights every month riding up and down the shore looking, looking, looking for my lost love until I thought my heart had grown numb from it. And yet, I could not stop. What if one day his body washed up with none but the old fishermen to find and bury him? That, I could not allow. What if I heard a cry and he still lived, clawing his way across the sand in need of succor and care? What if he perished after so long, due only to my failure to come to him?

The rumors among the people that Northpeak's sister was Wittenbrand-touched were only confirmed by my behavior, and there was much feigned pity for him, but only raised noses for me. I did not care. I was more than happy to be the Mad Princess. It suited me inside even if on the surface I was carefully composed, neat as a fresh-baked roll, and always draped in stainless black or forbidden blue.

"Please, Izolda, please," Svetgin begged me the first month. "Cease in this madness. Stay in the castle and help me. Marry well and help me forge an alliance."

"Twice you have married me off for the benefit of Pensmoore, and twice the choice has circled back and bitten you on the nose," I warned him in icy tones. I had not found renewed affection for my brother. Living with him was like wearing clothing from my girlhood – it did not fit anymore and did not suit me, king though he was.

He hissed at my words, but he could not declare my strike untrue. Eventually, he agreed. "Then I shall marry, and you must stay to help me tally the numbers, repair the fences, and keep this kingdom from falling into the brink."

For seven years it had been so. Svetgin married well and sired a pair of sons and a big-eyed daughter whose beauty and sly charm rivaled her mother's.

And for seven years, my heart beat only pain and my hands worked busily for the benefit of others. I scribed and tallied, scored and listed, inspected and ordered, investigated and counseled, and each month I rode out to the sea on my grand, foolish stallion with the blazing hooves.

Seven years was not enough time to make me forget. It was not enough time to dull the agony of my loss even a fraction. My brother's gifts – mink stoles, golden trinkets, and soft velvet cloaks which I gave to the orphanage as often as I was gifted them – did not ease the feeling of claws snagged in my soul. Not one bit. My place as a princess felt no more real nor meaningful than the games I played with Svetgin's small children, and if I had beauty of any kind, it had long fled as my eyes grew ringed in purple shadows.

"Time heals all wounds," Svetgin said sagely last year. Svetgin made a good king. The people all agreed on that, calling him Svetgin the Bountiful. But he was a terrible counselor. Time healed nothing, it only amplified everything as echoes amplify a noise until it was all I ever heard ringing in my heart.

And so, once more, I set out for the lonely shores of the coast of Pensmoore in my black riding habit, wrapped up against the bitter squalls that haunted the shores. My specter wrapped around my face, an ever-present reminder of the world I'd lost.

I'd tried once to access the Wittenhame through a colossus as Vireo had told me was possible. I'd tried to cajole the specter into helping me, but she had denied me any help and in the end, I left home emptyhanded and broken-hearted. There was no access there for mortals on their own. The only scrap of Wittenhame left to me was the specter on my shoulder and her mute judgment.

When we stopped in a village, I tried to tell a peddler on the road about the conspiracy between Coppertomb and Tanglecottt just to feel the ghostly hand grip my jaw and force me to swallow the words. It comforted me to have my spectral jailer with me – one tiny piece of the Wittenhame kept with me.

We left the village, turned off the road, and wended our way through the waist-high grasses that rimmed the well-worn trail to Yellow Squall Bay. Prince shook his head, jingling the reins, desperate for the freedom he'd come to expect, and I slipped from his back and pulled the well-oiled tack from his head, freeing him. He waited only long enough for me to mount again, our time-shaped practice. This time, I gripped his flowing black mane and clung tight, lying flat over his neck as he reared and then plunged down the path. The autumn air rushed through my lungs, spiced with an icy edge and fragrant with the death of leaves and the tang of mushrooms.

Anyone with sense would panic at a nervy stallion given his head and racing toward the cliffs along Yellow Squall Bay, but I never had and never would. Once you'd lost everything, losing your life seemed of little consequence. I loved the way the wind plucked and tore at my long hair as it became unraveled from its pins and streaked out behind me, long as my history. And as all proper decorum unwound around us, something tight unwound in my chest and flapped loose, trailing us, snapping and screaming in our passage. Sometimes I thought that our souls were like that, riding white-knuckled on the perilous ride our bodies forced upon them.

We galloped through the November winds, dancing through little whirlwinds carrying the lightest dusting of early snow – just enough to nip at our skins and remind us we would be soon assaulted by Lord Winter but not enough to freeze us. Until, at last, red-cheeked and winded, we settled into the dogged pace of those determined to cover ground.

I rode with my eyes on the shore, on the querulous bottle-green waves, on the white froth. I scanned the flotsam washed ashore – great viridescent weeds with bulbous boles, half-desiccated fish carcasses, shells and rocks that gleamed from a distance but would prove to be valueless upon inspection, and timbers that had been adrift so long they'd been leeched of color, kin to the mortal world adrift on the tides of fate.

The song of the sea that never let up in my heart erupted again, loud and long and aching. I wondered, for what must have been the thousandth time, why I combed this beach over and over when Coppertomb could have set us down anywhere. I might not be near where Bluebeard was drowned. I might not be where the confrontation had taken place. I might be on the other side of the world.

And yet, my heart was buried with my husband, drowned with him in his watery grave, buried with his body so certainly that if it had been sliced open, seawater would have flowed out with the blood.

True to my new nature, I hunted and sought and refused to bend even now, seven years from the time I'd last seen him.

No one else roamed along the ragged shore. Sometimes there were birds.

The first few times I went, Svetgin had irritably sent soldiers along to watch me. Occasionally, I saw a fisherman or clam digger from afar. Eventually, they all stopped taking notice of me. My comings and goings were of no more importance than the wax and wane of the moon.

Which was why Prince reared when the grass in front of us moved against the wind, as suddenly and uncertainly as if an uncanny hand shook it.

He neighed his horsey displeasure, coming down hard on the bank, front feet stomping like weapons, just in time to shy back from a pair of figures that emerged from the grass. They did not paw upward as if they had lain in wait but revealed themselves from the air, as if they had just been rendered visible. A third emerged a heartbeat later.

That was too much for Prince. He screamed, reared again, and this time I could not hold on and I was thrown into the grass while he tore away, shaking his equine head as if he could dislodge a spectral rider.

If my three visitors cared, they did not show it. The center one adjusted his ragged doublet and held out to me a small token in his palm.

"Frost! Yarrow!" he cried as if he'd forgotten they were right beside him. "She does not match her image!"

"I believe that is your token, Lord of the Wittenhame," I said, collecting myself and getting to my feet. My voluminous skirts rustled stiffly and the light widow's veil I usually wore was gone – blown away in the excitement.

"The ruler of Moravidmoore," one of the pair whispered to him and the Wittenbrand looked from me to the piece and back again.

My heart thundered harder than the sea as I took a step forward, drawn to them as a moth to the flame. For here, in front of me, were living people once more, bright and bonny – even the hoary Marshyellow – and alive as none of the mortals I lived my days with ever could be. The attraction of them drew me ever forward, even as I knew they were made of blades and poison rather than blood and flesh.

"But we came for her, we did," Marshyellow muttered to himself. "She is … she lives. She is."

"She's the wife of the Arrow, now lover to the Sea," one of them whispered to him and I hoped that "lover to the sea" was a euphemism because jealousy rose in my heart as a fire rises when oil is thrown on its fury.

"Oh, yes!" Marshyellow said and his fey eyes lit with excitement. The little token vanished and if he'd used sleight-of-hand then I would do best not to underestimate him because his actions were firm and sure. "Bargain with me, mortal wife of the Arrow. That's why I'm here. To see if you'd like to taste a sweet bargain."

And, with all my heart, I found that I did.

CHAPTER THREE

"A place, a circle. Frost!" Marshyellow muttered. A bubble appeared in the corner of his mouth. Even the Wittenbrand could become disgusting when tossed upon the surf of ages, and yet this flotsam fae still commanded the respect and service of his men.

Grave in face and action, Frost and Yarrow trampled a neat circle in the waist-high, cream-colored grass. It lay down tidily for them, and once the perfect circle was crafted, they took up their places again on either side of the raving Lord of the Wittenhame – two halves of a whole, two mirror images. They wore their single braid on opposite sides of the head, the other side shaved. They wore their leather straps and buckles opposite to one another and their clothing was divided down the middle. One side fawn brown, the other pale cream, and these, too, were mirrored. What made a powerful creature like a Wittenbrand choose not only a life of service but to be formed so much to it that they styled themselves as pieces rather than as men?

I regarded them surreptitiously but when I caught the eye of Yarrow by accident, the pure murder in his eye chilled me, rippling through my body. My very fingertips vibrated until he released my gaze.

Well then. They were not playing pieces. More like tigers

strolling along on twin pieces of string while a babe pointed and burbled. They were me with Svetgin – tolerant, dutiful, capable. They cared for the cause over the man. There was a lesson in that, if I could find it.

Marshyellow settled himself in the center of the flattened circle, sitting cross-legged, his worn palms held on his knees as if he were to soon receive a gift. He turned his face up, eyes closed, hoary eyebrows twisting into their own uncanny pattern.

Frost jerked his head to me, and I realized I was meant to sit opposite their Lord.

I took my time finding my place. It's not easy to sit cross-legged in skirts – not even wide ones – without getting insects inside them. The grasses crunched and hissed with my movements like little bones snapping under my weight instead of plant stalks.

Marshyellow's eyes snapped open the moment I was still.

"A bargain I offer, a pledge between souls, for the jockeying of position and the fanning of coals."

Whatever had taken his mind had not taken his poetic ability. But I had not spent these years as a mortal negotiator without learning a few things myself.

I spoke my own poem, and if it wasn't as fine as his, at least it had the benefit of rhyming. "A pact beneficial to both of us two, is what I'll consider, that neither will rue."

His laugh put me in mind of a raven. It screeched out between throaty coughs, leaving him swaying, smiling, a little breathless. His leashed tigers didn't so much as flinch.

Above us, snow clouds gathered in roiling charcoal and Prussian blue, an ominous sign if ever one could be.

"Make your offer, Prince of the Wittenhame," I said smoothly, and his grin turned toothy.

To my horror, I saw his teeth had been sharpened to points and they were stained – not the brown and yellow of age but a maroon as if he feasted regularly on uncooked flesh.

I kept my face blank and careful. It was impractical to bargain with the Wittenbrand and yet I found I could not prevent myself from leaping into his offer. I wanted nothing more than to return to their untamed world by any means I could find.

His devil grin widened further, and he spoke each word as if it were a boiled sweet he was turning over his tongue.

"For the winning of a key, a hazard for a watery captive's release, would you wager a season to your enemy, your hand to a friend?"

He winked when he was through and I prodded the offer carefully in my mind, twisting it one way and then the other looking for holes, for hooks, for what might turn and bite me.

I was thoroughly sick of being proposed to. I did not wish to marry again. But did he know that I would do anything to free my husband – even that? I did not know. I watched him guardedly, but he let nothing slip from behind his mask of madness,

Carefully, I countered.

"For the winning of a key, a hazard for the release of my heart's conqueror," I began.

He'd been right in guessing what might tempt me to bargain with him, but I wanted to be specific. I didn't want the key to *any* captive's release. I wanted the key to *this* one's release.

"I would give this hand of mine in its current form."

There. I wasn't available to marry but I'd submit to whatever ceremonies or transfers of wealth he desired if only for this. But I'd need to sweeten the pot for him to accept a variance in what he asked for.

"Binding to it now all that was bound to you and offering to you its many skills."

There. I offered him skills – I had some a Wittenbrand could use – and if I'd worded that correctly his two guardians would not be able to harm me because they would be bound due to their loyalty to him. I could smell my own fear sweat as I carefully wove my counter-offer. Negotiating with the Wittenbrand was more dangerous than walking over beds of burning embers or through halls of spitting snakes. A viper or a fire could only kill you once.

And now to make up for the season I would not give him, because never again would I give one of my days willingly to anyone other than my lord Bluebeard.

"And I will forswear all vengeance by my own hand on the taker – both now and always."

He snickered and it was so close to Grosbeak's snicker that it made my heart swell with pain.

"A clever counter. A clever…" His eyes went glassy. "Did I make a mortal again?"

Frost leaned down to whisper in his ear and Marshyellow's vision sharpened once more. I did not like the smile he turned on me – all hungry bright eyes, sharp red teeth, and wild, unkempt hair.

Little sizzling streaks of fear ran down my spine as he looked me up and down, winked, and said, "Done, done, and done. You'll find your key on the water's edge."

And then he snapped his finger and my left hand flared with such blinding pain that it took all my self-control to hold back the blackness that threatened to take me, as Marshyellow produced a single silver key, turned it in the air, and then vanished through the door he'd made to the Wittenhame with his tigers on his heel.

One of them looked back at me before the door had closed and the derisive glee in his eyes sent terror whooshing down my spine. I followed his gaze to my hand, resting on my lap.

What I was seeing wasn't possible.

Breathe, Izolda. Measured breaths. Controlled. One. Two. One more.

I blinked. And blinked again.

But still, when I looked at the hand in my lap, the flesh ended abruptly at my wrist, smooth, as if healed naturally, leaving a hand that wore no flesh at all. I lifted it, crooked a finger, and then had to catch my breath as my skeleton palm and finger responded exactly as a flesh and blood hand would.

My hand.

He hadn't meant marriage at all. He'd meant my actual hand.

I was still swallowing down bile when a watery cough sounded from the edge of the water.

I did not hesitate. I leapt to my feet, stumbling through the high grass, sliding when I reached the sandy bank, afraid to catch myself with my skeleton hand. What if it broke? How easy did finger bones snap?

But my mind was caught up in a dream of hope, soaring and bold, desperate in hope. Was it him? Could it be that he'd be returned to me with only the loss of a single hand needed to secure his release? Would I be in his arms in moments, kissing his lovely face and drawing him from the water?

He had promised to shower me in kisses like rain. No, Izolda. Don't get ahead of yourself. But I couldn't breathe. My thoughts snapped and sparked with excitement.

I scrambled over the dunes, following the sound of coughing, as confusion overtook me. I couldn't see him, couldn't find him. My breath came in sobs and gasps as excitement turned to panic. Twice, I fell, slipping in the sand and surf, recovered myself, and ran again, my heavy skirts wet and dragging. If my mangled hand was less effective, I did not notice.

I tore down the beach, tripping on my skirts as thunder cracked the sky in two. Lightning danced between banks of clouds like the laughter of the Wittenbrand.

The coughing was close, deep, echoing, and full of power. It sounded from behind that large, whitened drift log. I scrambled over it, heart in my throat.

There was no body. I clawed through the surf, a mad thing, as if I could drag something from nothing in the swell of the tide.

Something croaked from behind me.

"I'd expected madness and mortal foolishness, but this takes the cake, Lady Arrow."

I spun and he was there. Not *him*. Not my beloved husband. But rather the bodiless head who had been my friend for so long.

I threw myself to my knees, not giving a thought to the icy fingers of the November sea, and scooped him up, choking on a sob.

"Careful now, careful. I'm still made of flesh, rotting and poxy though this severed head may be!"

His skin was swollen and bleached, far too pale even for a dead thing, his lips so blue they were almost green, and something had chewed off one of his ears. Seaweed twisted through his tangled black hair – and there, amongst it, was a golden key on a chain. *My* golden key to the Room of Wives.

I yanked it free and threw the chain around my neck. A hand for a key. That had been the bargain. And yet this was both less and more than what was promised.

"My husband," I said through thick lips. When had my teeth started chattering like that?

"Him whose side was wounded, and hands pierced through?" Grosbeak's lip curled derisively.

"The very one," I agreed. "Does he yet live?"

His pause was filled with thunder. Above us, the storehouse of heaven opened. Snow fell heavy as goose down, melting as it touched water and land with equal abandon.

"He lives," Grosbeak said and something like hope burned through me, hot and quick and nauseating.

Hope is a torturous thing. It wrenches one from despair just long enough to allow one to take a breath before plunging her back beneath the icy waters. If it wasn't for those breaths, it would be easy to let ice claim the soul. Easy to let surrender swallow the struggle. But hope – cruel mistress that she is – is not satisfied with so neat an ending. Like a house cat with a tiny prisoner, she wants only to torment the soul again, and again, until it dies from a burst heart.

"He still dwells beneath the waves, though for how long he can stave off the advances of death, I do not know. He is to that old inevitability as a maiden in her first season of society – so desirable as to not be ignored," Grosbeak said, "I would have thanked you to leave me there at his side."

"You would?" I asked, surprised out of the terrible gnawing wretchedness that came at his word. I had not the return of a husband. I had only a key to it. And even the key was a puzzle.

"I told you I would fall in love with a mermaid and so I had," he said, sniffing.

"A mermaid who allowed half your ear to be eaten away?" I asked wryly.

But his nonsense had brought me back to my senses. I had a key. I had some way to free Bluebeard, if I could just figure out what it was. The first step was not to freeze to death on the shore.

"Who's to say she didn't nibble it herself?" Grosbeak asked coyly.

I stood, wrapping my skeletal fingers through his tangled hair and carrying him away from the sea.

"And what will you do now, mortal girl?" he asked through chattering teeth.

"I will take you home with me, tattered trophy," I said as I caught sight of a black stallion galloping toward us along the beach. "And you will tell me everything that has happened these past seven years that you have been at the feet of my husband."

"Seven years?" he asked, stunned.

"Yes."

Prince arrived in a flurry of hooves and snow. He stopped before me, snorting, head bent in apology.

"You should be sorry," I scolded him. "It was cruelly done to leave me with those creatures."

The horse snorted again and tried to take a bite out of Grosbeak's hair. I held my prize higher and off to one side and calmed my stallion with my other hand, leaning my forehead against his.

"No luck today, my friend," I whispered to him. "We must head back home."

"No luck? Is that what you say upon our reunion. I would have thought you would be starved for my company after seven long years. Seven! Why, you're old now!" Grosbeak looked horrified.

"I'm twenty-six," I said coolly, mounting Prince and grabbing a fistful of his mane as a handhold.

I very pointedly did not look at my left hand. How would I hide it? What excuse would I make for it in the Court of Pensmoore? I shivered at the thought of being caught with such a hand.

"Like I said, ancient," Grosbeak told me. "Meanwhile, I was only beneath the sea for two days."

"Two days?" my gaze snapped to his. "You fell in love in two days?"

He laughed, a terrible creaking laugh, arrested suddenly by a fit of coughing and then he spat out a bright silver minnow, crossed his eyes, and grew greener before finally saying, "Did you forget us, Izolda? Did you laugh at our demise? Your Bluebeard won't like the sound of that."

"Tell me everything about him," I demanded as I kicked Prince into a gallop and the snow puffed up around us in furious clouds. "Can he survive much longer? How can he be freed?"

"No," Grosbeak said coolly.

"No, he can't survive?" I asked, feeling colder than any snow could ever make me.

"No, I won't tell you," he said, instead, sounding irritable. "I promised I would not and some of us still keep our promises, you terrible solemn thing."

CHAPTER FOUR

Our ride home was wild and woeful. The storm grew worse with each passing moment as if it had declared war on our very selves. I determined to declare war back.

I rode to where the tack had been left and awkwardly fitted Prince with it, cooing to him and calming him with my flesh hand while the skeletal one worked. He did not like the feel or scent of it and shied away if it touched his body. I didn't blame him. Twice, when I tried to brush my hair back with it, I froze at its cold touch against my face. The feeling left me ill and wretched.

"Lost a hand, did you?" Grosbeak asked. "And I missed seeing it. Tell me you traded it for something of equal value, at least."

"I'm beginning to suspect I did not," I said coolly.

I was almost grateful that the storm lent me little time to fuss over it. I needed a warmer cloak and gloves. I was soaked through and the wind bit with long teeth. And yet I felt a sense that I must return to the capital as soon as possible. If my Bluebeard lived, then I must formulate a plan to get him back. I had new tools – my Wittenbrand guide and a key to a single Wittenhame room. Perhaps it was not enough, but it was more than I'd had these past seven years. I would not waste this gift now that it had been granted.

"Where are we going?" Grosbeak asked as soon as I had Prince tacked again, my living knuckles red and fingers clumsy with cold.

"We'll ride to Lady Greatspur's home, where I will beg a fur cloak and gloves," I told him as I mounted, settling my skirts and balancing his head in front of me. "Did you shake that fly problem?"

"Even flies must fly the flag of defeat when presented with a league's depth of seawater," he grumbled. "But I was not ready for the enthusiasm of crabs. The creatures torment me yet."

I reached into his hair to remove a sand-colored crab the size of my thumbnail. I flicked it away with disgust. His sojourn – short though it may have felt to him – had left its mark.

"I'll have to leave you in a tree somewhere while I beg for clothing," I said grimly as Prince began to walk. "It will be hard enough to hide a ruined hand, never mind the head of a corpse."

"The hand is hideous. Were I offered such, I would have refused."

"At least I have a hand," I said tightly. Would my husband think the same when he saw it? Would he shudder at the sight of me and rear back from my touch?

I hadn't thought of that.

I held the imposter up before me and flexed the fingers. The sight sent shivers through my jaw and an uncomfortable feeling blossomed in my mouth like biting into meat only to find a sliver of arrowhead within.

"If you think to make me jealous with those diviner's tokens you now call fingers, think again. I'm perfectly happy to be free of hands if the alternative is *that*."

"Tell the truth, at least," I scolded.

"I don't like trees and I won't be left in one," Grosbeak said miserably. "I have not been in good humors of late, Izolda. You ought to have turned your attentions much sooner to freeing me. Seven years! Teeth of the Gods, that's a long time. The sea does not agree with me."

"Clearly." My mind was absent, watching our trail. It was hard to see it in the swirling snow. My heart was also absent, drifting out across the turbulent waves, wondering if beneath their emerald furor my husband gulped and gasped in briny breaths.

"Besides which," Grosbeak continued, "the nattering of a lovelorn swain is hardly the type of entertainment I'd bargain for and yet I could not stop my ears to it. I tried coaxing the crabs into them, but you can see that was a disaster."

I paused, and Prince halted with me, his movements easily conforming to mine. "Lovelorn?"

My heart skipped a beat, warming in my chest. I couldn't breathe. Something was trapped in my throat.

"Don't you dare look like that," Grosbeak said darkly. "One of you is bad enough. If I must deal with two, I will need ichor smoke, a chest of cherry-pit brandy, and at least a dozen mermaids."

"What can you possibly offer mermaids when you're nothing more than a rotten head?"

"Your lack of imagination does you a disservice."

Lovelorn. His choice of word echoed in my mind all the way to Lady Greatspur's house.

I likely should have asked for the cloak and gloves. I was

no natural-born thief. And I knew the lady well enough to be certain that I would have been given them with a generous smile and a reminder to mention her to the king. But as the gale grew louder, wailing all around me, blocking sight of the tree where I'd tied Prince and hung Grosbeak from a branch, I changed my mind. There was no certain way to hide the hand. Not without gloves. And I knew the layout of the house completely. I knew Lady Greatspur would be taking tea at this time in the afternoon and with the storm afoot, her servants would be hunkered down within, attending only to those chores that kept them inside.

Sneaking in and out through the kitchen door in the back proved to be as easy as I'd hoped and I was soon back with Grosbeak, hands tucked into leather gloves and a warm fur cloak wrapped around me. And if I felt guilt, it was nothing compared to the pressing need to be home with quill in hand and parchment before me to solve this mystery.

"Tell me how to free him," I begged my newly returned friend.

"I will not."

"Then tell me he can hold on a little longer." My jaw was tight.

"He'll likely expire before the next dawn. I will not mourn his passing."

"So cruel. You're sure it was only two days to you?"

"I'm sure of nothing. Perhaps it was two centuries, and I was too enamored of soft lips, sleek hair, and the iridescence of scales to know otherwise. And as for cruelty, it is my greatest asset, and I would no more abandon it than I would abandon this year's fashions if I were offered them. Which I have not been, I'll remind you."

The cloak kept the worst of the wind from biting me and was bulky enough to hide Grosbeak inside it and none would be the wiser. Perhaps I could make a sling and carry him like a child.

"You'll do nothing of the sort!" he said when I put it to him. "*That* is not fashion at all."

"Perhaps, I will anyway, if you do not tell me how to free my husband," I said tightly. Inside my thoughts buzzed like flies, untamable with excitement, while also edged with irritation. Everything conspired against me now that I had a tool to get him back. The hand. The storm. The one I'd called friend. Everything.

I turned Prince into the wind, found the road, and urged him to a gallop. He tossed his glorious head, arrogant in the face of driving snow and blinding wind, and ran as if his mind were kin to mine.

"I told you I made a promise. 'She'll try to come here,' he told me in one of his long monologues. 'I'll have your vow not to lead her here, Grosbeak.' I tried to ignore him. Trust me, I had affairs of my own to conduct." He paused and then snickered. "I said, I had affairs of my own – "

"It wasn't funny the first time you said it."

"If it isn't funny then why should I bother telling the rest?" He was almost more snappish than I was.

I made a sound of disgust, but I wasn't sure if he could even hear me over the rising wind and the pounding of Prince's dish-sized hooves striking the cobbled road. We were riding through the nearby village, the wind swirling at our backs, the tang of snow in our noses, and the church bells of the town clanging intermittently in a discordant rhythm to the thunder above.

Night had fallen, deep, luscious, and filled with broken

dreams in the form of stars.

"Ha. Ha," I said eventually to get him talking again. It came out in a wooden imitation.

"I'll take that," Grosbeak said sourly. "At any rate, he pressed me. 'Your vow,' he said to me. 'Not a word spoken to her of how to free me or what she must do.'"

"What I must *do*? Then it's up to me somehow?" I pressed.

His answering snap was sharp. "I'd forgotten how witless mortal girls were, but it seems you'll remind me with every breath. Did you not hear I made a vow? Besides, forget the sea. There's no drama to be had there. We were awash in sea and fish and nothing of interest. Take me instead to where mortals sup and drink and we shall celebrate my return in proper style."

"Did the vow include gestures?"

"Had I hands, I'm sure it would. As it stands, it matters not. Is there no succor in this frozen land of yours?"

"Did it include winks, hints, or puzzles?"

"It did not. Words were the only thing ripped from my jaw. But though you seem enthusiastic, you should know that I know no language of winks, I mislike puzzles, and consider hints a fool's errand. And I did not much warm to the method used on be to extract this extraneous vow and I will have my revenge on it in this life or the next. So, enough of this ghastly talk and find me a stuffed pheasant and some oranges or it will be the worse for everyone."

"We can work with that," I said firmly, ignoring his request for food. We would have to work with it. Right now, it was all I had.

"I do not plan to work at all. We Wittenbrand are well known for toiling not nor spinning."

"When I'm through with you, old friend," I said, threateningly, "I'll have worked you so long and hard, you'll claim my firstborn as wages."

He sounded forlorn when he answered. "I fear I cannot. He bound me from that, too, when he heard me devising a trick with the help of my harem under the sea."

That closed my mouth with a click. We were riding through a second town already. Usually, I would stop to spend the night here, but Prince's feet were full of fire and my heart was galloping with him.

"A harem?"

"Indubitably."

The gates loomed ahead, we sped through, kicking up snow as the guards scattered, cursing us as we passed.

"As in, more than one?"

"It's impossible to have a harem of only one."

"More than one mermaid fell for your charms under the sea?"

The town was empty, the streets clear, the small diamond-paned windows of the homes and inns lit with dancing marigold light.

"Your lack of faith offends me." He sounded truly hurt.

"Your lack of charms should offend all. I do not believe a word you are telling me."

He clicked his tongue irritably. "You bring to the surface all the salt of the sea, mortal girl. Must I remind you that your imagination is insufficient?"

"Must I remind you that your bodily form is the same?"

And to my surprise, he laughed, a horrible throaty, chesty laugh that should be impossible for a man with no chest. It fell into wheezing as we thundered through the gate on the other side of the town, riding for the capital as if our heels were being dogged by mist lions.

"Did he know you were coming to me?"

"It would break my vow to tell you."

"Did he send a message?"

"Anything he would say would be whimsical nonsense and we both know how you hate that."

I clenched my jaw, clutched the reins to my chest with my living hand, and tried to keep from shattering as the memory of that first ride with my Bluebeard howled through me with more force than any winter storm, and this time, I let the loneliness and pain of his loss howl on and on and I did not try to gather it in. Not when it might fuel his return.

CHAPTER FIVE

Riding through the night seemed like a fine thing to do and one would think it would shave a full day from a journey but that only worked in fairytales and stories. In actual fact, I had a flesh and blood horse, and while he was high in spirit and brim-full with energy, he was also a living thing.

By morning, Prince was slow and tired. I dismounted to lead him into Brackenstown, a hamlet just outside Pensmoore City. From this point, the roads would be filled with travelers and lined with hawkers, wayside stops, patrols, army posts, and any number of things that would slow a traveler and draw all eyes on her – especially when the one journeying was the King's mad sister.

I chose, instead, to stable Prince for the day, pay an exorbitant price to have him fed and rubbed down, and hurry to hide in the inn's best room before anyone would wonder why I was hunched inside a fur cloak and wearing gloves when the sun was bright in the sky as a new penny. There were some things I liked about being Svetgin's sister. Not needing to wait was certainly one of them.

My breath frosted the air as a yawning serving girl lit my fire, ignoring my protests that I could do it myself. Two men and three more maids filled a steaming bath and left a plate of breakfast, and not a word I said deterred them. Royalty must be treated a certain way, even royalty that everyone whispered was mad as a Wittenbrand and possibly just as dangerous.

I fought a maid off my cloak when she tried to take it to hang up for me.

"But Lady Princess, it needs to dry," she protested.

"I will keep the cloak on, thank you," I said coolly, clutching it closed with my flesh hand. I'd tucked the skeletal one inside the cloak and it was tangled around Grosbeak's drowned head. I could only imagine what any of these mortals might say if this poor girl succeeded in ripping the fur from me and saw what I clutched against my belly.

"But Princess, the —"

"I keep the cloak."

They fled before the fire in my eyes, likely to start more rumors about the ill-mannered wildness of the princess, and I bolted the door, stuck a chair under the handle, and set Grosbeak on it.

"Princess?" he asked in a drawl, eyebrow raised. "What a complicating occurrence. Do tell me it comes with perks."

"They made Svetgin king," I said, feeling my face flush as I hung the fur coat over another chair by the table to dry. My dress was a ruin. I had more in my saddlebags, but none so fine as this one.

"That quivering mortal? The weeping one? They made him king? You did not speak out against him, saying unto them how he had sold you twice and found the short end of the bargain each time?"

"If I had, they would have applauded him for it and made him king all the sooner," I said dryly, turning his head around so I could undress.

"I'll never understand mortals. A bad bargain made is all you need to besmirch you with the Wittenbrand."

"And an attempted murder gone awry is all that's needed to sever your head and leave you a mortal's pet."

"Touché. That hit strikes hard."

I was just as tired as my horse. My mind had bubbled all night with daydreams of riding to my husband's rescue and dragging him up from under the sea while he still lived. They had only been daydreams. Each plan I tried to concoct involved knowing where he was imprisoned. Marshyellow might know. But I'd have to get to him first. Grosbeak knew, but would not tell, and I doubted I could torture it from him since anything I might threaten to do had already been done to him.

I looked back and forth between him and the hot bath, considering.

"You can't drown information out of me," Grosbeak said snidely. "I've been underwater for so long it's made me twice the weight."

I made a moue of agreement.

Mixed generously with my new relief that my husband yet lived was the terrible, gnawing anxiety that he may die at any moment and my very mortal-ness – the slowness of my horse, the frailty of my body – was preventing his rescue.

"I don't know why you turn me around," Grosbeak grumbled as I spun him quickly in place. "It's hard to speak with my head facing the wrong way."

"Yes, but it's easier for me to bathe that way."

My ruined dress was off quickly, my flesh hand running over the long twisting red scar on my side before I dropped into the steaming bath and worked to clean my hair. My bone fingers tangled in the long strands, and I had to pick them free with my living hand as if I was cleaning a comb.

I shuddered as I regarded the foreign limb, dead and horrifying where the pink of my flesh ended suddenly at the wrist and gave way to ivory digits. It would be a very miserable life if I spent it blanching every time I saw my own hand. I should simply accustom myself to it and move on. I tried to do just that, focusing instead on cleaning myself. I smelled of sweat and horse and the sea.

If I arrived at the palace rumpled and unwashed, there would be questions and I must avoid questions until I decided what to do about Grosbeak.

I would be keeping him – of course. He was my one link to the Wittenhame and it was possible he would slip and let out a clue even if he was trying to avoid it. Perhaps the key was to find those mermaids – if they existed at all.

He was not easily disguised.

"Perhaps, I should keep you in a shrouded cage," I said, considering. "I could claim I had acquired a bird from afar. One that speaks."

"The indignity!" he hissed. "I won't stand for it."

"You don't stand at all, and that is the problem. Perhaps a large satchel."

"And breathe leather all day? What will you say next? A basket for bread? A barrel for fish? No, you must hang me from a pole as you did before, so I can see properly."

The warm bath was not soothing me, but rather making my stomach swim. I left it, dressing in a crumpled black dress from my saddlebags – the only other one I'd brought, and it was damp at the edges – and then turning him around.

"If I do that, they'll pack me away to a nunnery and I'll be imprisoned for the rest of my life with a bunch of chaste women nursing the sick and copying scrollwork."

"That's an option?" his eyes lit.

"It's not as fun as you seem to think. Scrollwork is very fiddly business," I said wryly. "I need a way to keep you hidden and I can't wear heavy furs forever. Perhaps your mermaids have a suggestion. We could ask them."

"Ha! You misjudge if you think me so easily fooled, mortal princess. I know a coy womanish plan when I hear one. Not winkling the secret out from me, you think to rob my oysters of the pearl."

I shook my head and fell silent. I had played my hand too early. Best to focus for now on how to get him into the palace. After that, I'd have time to work on his cooperation.

But when I'd eaten and fallen into the bed, I still had not come up with a solution that was not ridiculous. Sleep took me and I woke to sunset and the sound of drinking in the inn below.

"Time to ride, unworthy princess," Grosbeak said with a snicker. "Do you wear a crown?"

It took bare moments to gather my things and hide him in my cloak. "I do not wear a crown. I'm known as the Mad Princess."

He nodded sagely. "Then they won't mind when it seems you

talk to yourself. Convenient."

"When we arrive at the palace, I will need to speak to my brother," I said coolly. "And then I will get to work discovering how I may return to the Wittenhame and how I will fetch my husband back. You'd best spend the ride considering how you'll help with that."

"Easy. I will not help you. I will, in fact, do everything to hinder you until he has breathed his last and no one but the Bramble King himself could bring him back to life."

Acid churned in my stomach.

"And if you were wondering, I would guess his time is measured in moments, not hours, so if you were thinking of taking a terrible risk, you shouldn't be wasting so much time."

My face flushed hot at that, heart pounding hard in my breast.

I took a last look in the mirror. My hair was settled and braided, my face and dress clean. The specter sat sadly on my shoulder as she always did, sending her mournful, shivery gaze over the room as if I might spill my confidences to it if not for her guardianship, and my huge fur cloak – bear, I thought – covered the drowned head of Grosbeak.

"You'd best consider if you'd like to spend the rest of your immortal life thrown down the hole of the castle garderobe. If you fail to help me rescue him, that is where I'll put you."

He was mercifully silent after that, even when I reached the common room of the inn and inspiration struck.

The Whiskeylamp Inn catered to a noble clientele and seated around a table to one side was Lady Sergaz of Cliffmeadow and her two daughters. In tune with the latest style, the lady had a leather satchel at her feet, the nose of a ferret peeking out of it.

He was silent for the brief conversation and negotiation. Silent, as I left the inn with one highly prized ferret and the extremely fashionable bag that held him slung over one shoulder. I could wear this bag in court, and no one would notice, provided I fed the ferret.

He was not silent when I turned the corner of the inn, slunk into the alley, and stuffed his head into the bag.

"You're mad!"

"So, they tell me."

"What is this thing in here with me? Oh, Bramble King above, it bites! Stop it! That's my nose. My nose! Izolda!"

I cuffed the bag. "Both of you make yourselves silent. We have a horse to mount and a night journey before us."

Fortunately, few nobles depart as the sun is setting, even though our roads are safe for travel. Prince was saddled and stamping almost before I finished requesting it. I sprang onto his back, stretched my fingers in my gloves – one hand fit them better than the other – and took up the reins before the grooms so much as blinked.

We trotted boldly from the stable, cantering onto the street, and galloping down the road, ignoring the icy blast of the wind and the slick frozen puddles in our path, as if we were the heart of winter freed upon the north.

"I hate the cold," Grosbeak said from within the bag. "If you think this will make me talk, you can think again."

I said nothing, giving Prince his head and reveling in the freedom of traveling at speed as we flew through the cold, morphing into one spiritual creature, horse and rider, purpose and action, two halves of one whole. Riding was the last joy afforded me, and I clung to it as a child clings to a beloved toy. This time, it was not enough. It could not ease the gnawing in the center of my belly.

Too late, the sound of hooves on cobbles told me. *Too late. Too late.*

"Ferrets are not a legal form of torture." Grosbeak's voice muffled for a moment. "And this one reeks of something terrible."

We cycled from a gallop to a trot and then a walk and then up to a gallop again, shifting from one to the next as Prince required it.

"At least tell me this creature has a name," Grosbeak said eventually.

"The lady called him 'Honey,'" I said, "for his sweet temperament."

"Sweet? She called this hellion sweet?"

"Oh, I think you'll find he's sweet compared to me if you continue to deny me what I most want," I said in my most honeyed tones. I thought you said you were my pet and not the Arrow's and yet I see none of that sworn allegiance. But I will take pity on you and grant you one boon."

"Good. Let it be the death of this creature." His words were muffled, and the ferret yelped as if it had been bitten.

"I will not kill it. It has done far less to harm me than you have. I thought, rather, that I would let you rename it."

Grosbeak's yelp told me the ferret was giving as good as it got. Good. I'd hate to leave an innocent creature in that bag with him. Someone had carefully embroidered vines on the flap of the purse in a pattern known as a lover's knot.

"To name a thing gives it power," he muttered.

"To rename it puts it under your power," I countered.

"Wise," he said with a nasty twist to his words. "Perhaps that is how you wove your spell over your Bluebeard."

"Perhaps," I said lightly, but I hoped it was not true. I wanted nothing between my husband and me except what had grown up on its own. It would be a horrifying thing indeed to find your affections and loyalties were merely the product of glamor.

We rode some hours before he spoke again.

"Then I shall name it '*Look And Despair*' in hopes that it will do just that."

"I think it's a she," I said.

"You don't need to tell me."

We'd reached the gates of Pensmoore City and one of the guards held up a hand to me. I gently drew in the reins, bringing Prince up short.

"Princess Izolda Savataz of Northpeak now of Pensmoore City?" the guard asked though we both knew who I was.

"Is something urgent?" I asked instead.

"Your brother bid us give you this missive were you to arrive at this gate," the guard said with a hasty bow. It was just as cold for them as it was for me. My flesh hand was so numb from the cold that it couldn't have taken that slip of paper if it was required to save my life. To my surprise, the bone hand had no such trouble. I plucked the sealed note deftly from his hand, cracked the seal, and studied it.

My brother had been in a hurry when he penned it, but it was in his florid hand.

"Izolda. Urgent we speak. Come to the hole when you get this."

Something was awry in our kingdom. I felt a stab of cold run through me, but it was not dread, just impatience. I had not the time for this, not when I finally had the key to free my husband and a desperate reminder that his life was nearly forfeit.

"Trouble?" Grosbeak hissed.

The guard looked up sharply.

Irritated, I gritted my teeth and repeated, "Trouble, I'm afraid. Please burn the note for me."

I handed it to the guard and his face glowed with pride as he placed it on the glowing brazier meant to warm him on this terrible night.

At least someone was pleased. I turned Prince to the palace, hissing to Grosbeak as we rode, "If you speak where someone else can hear you again, the garderobe will look like the happier fate."

"Keep threatening me and see where that gets you. You're toothless as a sapped snake and just as venomous and I do not give you one solitary tremble."

CHAPTER SIX

I had thought to sneak up to the secret room my brother and I called "the hole" with little trouble, but the moment I rode through the palace gates I could smell the magic of the Wittenbrand. It clung to the frosted doorposts and rolled down the icy steps. It swept up in curls of temptation and trailed streamers of cinnamon-sugar desire down every cobbled path. It had not been there when I left this place five days ago.

My teeth set on edge, and I tasted metal as I dismounted a dancing Prince and offered him to the groom.

"Stallion seems wild tonight, princess," he'd said, biting his lower lip and looking over his shoulder.

I didn't answer him. He was just as edgy as the horse. All the staff I saw were, backs straight as pokers, movements jerky, eyes darting, dark Pensmoore uniforms pressed as if order could be restored by an iron. What in the world had happened here?

Whispers followed me – harsh and prickling.

I hurried up the steps, shushing Grosbeak as I went, and shedding the fur coat into the competence of a waiting maid. She flinched when the wet fur fell into her arms.

I could see why my brother had sent for me. Nothing short of renewed war could turn this well-oiled palace, this luxury of polished wood and woven fabrics, warm fires and the scent of pine, set amid snowy defensible rock, into the snappish threadbare place I'd returned to. Even the maid's bow was tight and shallow.

I didn't have time to so much as turn around, before my brother's wife swept down on me like a velvet and lace-clad hawk on a mouse.

"Sister," she said tightly, wrapping an arm around me. Her arm was shaking though her curls were tightly ironed.

My eyebrow rose without my intending it to. That she called me "sister" was a sign of deep distress.

"Has someone died?" I asked calmly. I bit the inside of my own lip. Could it be Svetgin? He had an heir in her son. She had no need to implore me for help. Her rule through him was secure.

"Not yet," she said ominously, and then she was hustling me down the hall so fast that my ferret bag smacked one of the corners. Grosbeak yelped and my sister by marriage hissed, "Quiet! You'll disturb the servants. They don't need to know that there is pain raining down on us, Izolda!"

I felt my eyebrows rising as a cold draft caught me from behind. My specter caught my eyes placing her silent finger to her chin, as curious as I was. Her eyes danced. Every denizen of the Wittenhame lived and breathed anticipation of violence. What terrified mortals was just the beginning of a fun evening for them.

"I think you should tell me what has happened, my queen," I said calmly. Seven years of this had at least taught me to keep myself under strict control.

The queen rolled her eyes at me. Another surprise. Usually, Emelina was the height of decorum in all situations. I had overheard her complaining that I was a disgrace with my direct words and informal addresses on more than one occasion. To have her throw that away was dire.

Again, I smelled the scent of the Wittenbrand in the air. Frost and cardamom and danger. I wanted more of it. I wanted to bury my face deep into it and never recover.

"I think we can dispense with titles today," Emelina said. Her eyes were red-rimmed. Had she been crying? "By tomorrow we may not have them. Or at least, I may not."

"Heaven forfend."

Her chin trembled, and now I really was worried.

Emelina hated me on principle. She had hated me from the moment her tiny feet touched our land and her perfect doll eyes had taken this country in and found only one thing wanting in it. She'd hated me from the moment her artful lips had formed their perfect smile and her slender finger its perfect crook as she drew my brother in and realized, to her chagrin, that it did not draw me in with him.

I did not care that she was lovely, fecund, rich, and of a royal bloodline. She was welcome to take the brother who had betrayed me and doomed my husband. Welcome to have the throne of the land that had sold me like cattle and shamed my parents despite it.

I thought, sometimes, that it might be my sanguine goodwill and indifference that bothered her most of all. She was the instigator of at least half the rumors of my madness. For my part, I contented myself with daydreams of her deposited in her royal robes and crown in the Wittenhame, shrieking at the horrors that awaited her.

But the more I refused to react to her jabs and barbs, the more she threw at me, whether in the service of close study or vent spleen, I could not have guessed.

That she was here now, crying where I could see it, was disturbing for both of us. It was the widow Princess Chasida, returned to us from Ptoolemoore where her royal husband died of a fever, who was usually in her confidence, not me. And yet here she was – on the verge of tears – sharing this with *me.*

The Wittenbrand. I forced myself to keep my face immobile. They must be at the root of this. The suspicion of it was enough to leave my senses tingling with a terrible mixture of fear and anticipation. There would be a riddle at the heart of this. There would be a way back *in.* If I was bold. If I recognized it.

It was no use. My heart was racing.

I tried to swallow down my hopes so they would not choke me but choke I did.

We hurried into a large reception room, empty of people but thick with trophies and the latest brocaded seating from Ptolemoore. Emelina had taken care to outfit every public room in the palace with the finest fashions of last season. It was I who had argued strenuously over the strain to our coffers, choked with more dust than gold after decades of war and deprivation. Now, Emelina slammed the inlaid door shut with no care at all for how the expensive carving shuddered and whirled to face me in the empty room.

"Izolda, you must save us. Please. If you care for me at all." My cold expression must have killed that speech before it finished. She changed tacks quick as a ship before a storm. "If you care for your brother, or his kingdom, and I know you must or why are you still here?" That was a point well taken. "You are the only one familiar with them and their whims."

It *was* the Wittenbrand. I knew it!

I could hardly catch my breath. Calm, Izolda. You must not rush in. You must wait for the opportunity.

But it was coming. I could feel it just on the edge of sight, coming to me. It left me aching with hunger.

"It must be you who settles them," Emelina said. "I don't know what I'll do. I just don't."

She dissolved into tears – ugly, gasping sobs that contorted her face like a gargoyle's – very much like the one she'd placed there in the corner, which had become a favorite of mine since it reminded me of a once-dear friend. The one currently muffling a giggle from within my leather satchel.

I found myself in the awkward position of having to allow her to weep on my shoulder while my specter pulled faces and leaned away. Drama, the creatures of the Wittenhame loved. Sentiment, they did not.

"What in all of Pensmoore and her many hills is going on, Emelina?" I asked as she wet the shoulder of my gown right through. But under my calm words, I was quivering.

"A lady of the Wittenbrand arrived tonight." She hiccuped between sentences. "She made demands. She says your brother must marry her."

"Ridiculous," I said, dryly. "He is married to you."

"She says he must put me away and disinherit our children, and if he doesn't –" Her wail swallowed the words.

"I'm afraid I didn't hear that."

Were those feet just outside the door? Was the time to act here already?

My mind was racing so fast it tripped over details.

Where had they put this Wittenbrand lady, and which one was it? This had to be about the Game of Crowns and Thrones. If one of them married Svetgin, then what? Would it rip the playing piece from my husband's grasp and disqualify him? If one of them was making a play to seize Pensmoore, then the game was still afoot, and my husband was still in it.

Still in it. My heart lurched and stuck.

Which meant we could still get him back. If I was just capable of finding and seizing the opportunity. I clenched my jaw and forced the words out.

"Explain, please, Emelina."

"She says that if he doesn't agree by tomorrow night, she will rip our children apart and feed them to her beasts," Emelina managed, choking on the words and on her sobs.

"Typical," Grosbeak muttered, no longer able to contain himself.

Emelina looked at my bag in alarm.

"What beasts?" I asked as if my bag had not spoken. But I already knew.

"The ones with four wings. Lions of the Mist, they were called."

Lady Tanglecott. I was warm right through with satisfaction.

This was her next move. And I was here to counter it.

"Take me to my brother," I ordered.

Like all palaces, the one in Pensmoore City had back stairs for servants and spies and so many hundreds of people that they were hardly secret, but the hidden ways were still faster than the main stairs where the nobility "chanced" upon one another day or night. It was to these passages that we fled, speeding up one set of steps and down another, through a series of turns, and then another, until we finally reached the hole.

Seven years ago, I would have been intimidated by Wittenbrand and bargains and royalty. Now, my mind was on what kind of bargain Lady Tanglecott might have offered, and whether there might be some way we could word it to trap her with her own schemes. I needed back into the Wittenhame. And she would be my way in.

My brother, it seemed, had found *his* solace in the jug. It was, all things considered, the worst place he could have gone to find it. We found him sprawled across a scarlet tufted chair, head thrown back and eyes glassy. On the table in the hidden room maps and documents were strewn with the haphazard look of a place that had been rifled for valuables. Doubtless, he had scoured them for a way out and found nothing.

My fingers twitched to touch the document in the center of it – one touching no other paper. It was written in gold script on a parchment so pale white as to be unnatural. A complicated, florid seal on gold wax with purple ribbons was fixed on the bottom of the page. That would be her proposal.

Not yet, Izolda, I told myself. Patience.

Volkov, Svetgin's general, sat opposite him, head in his hands. I did not think he was quite as drunk, but his eyes were just as red-rimmed, his breathing just as labored.

The merry tapestries hanging from the walls showing dryads dancing in the forest and great battles won mocked the desperate pair. Some of the candles around the room were still lit but the rest had burned to a stump and gone out hours ago. They must have started their hopeless vigil before night fell, and now they were still here when dawn was close to rapping on our doors.

There was more broken pottery in the corners and wet patches on the walls than I'd thought one raging man could make. Perhaps, I could still underestimate my brother in some things.

I did not judge them. I'd spent my share of nighttime vigils despairing of life. I'd bargained with myself back and forth and lost, just as he was doing now. But I didn't judge myself, either. Not when this might be my chance to be rid of all of that.

"You're drunk," Emelina cried. "Our family hangs in the scales and you're drunk!"

"What would you have me do, Lina?" Svetgin asked, his voice a pained croak. It sent me back to his sobs the night I'd lain cold and near death in his clutching arms on a lonely piece of coast. "I'll not watch our children ripped to pieces by beasts."

"Then you'll set us aside? Sent us to the countryside without name or protection – to what? Starve? Be sold to men with ill intentions? Shall I sell myself to feed them?"

"Don't be so dramatic, woman," Volkov said, his head still in his hands.

He said it in the way men do, with the calm knowledge that the things spoken of will never be their lot. But I found myself sympathetic to Emelina. Any woman could find herself in the same position in the blink of an eye, queen or scrub girl or mad sister of a king.

Svetgin straightened, finally facing his wife, his red-rimmed bleary eyes meeting her tear-filled ones. He quivered with helpless rage as bitter words dripped from his tongue.

"What would you have me do? What? Were I to slit my own throat before you, it would not save you now, nor them. I may choose to watch you die fast or slow, but that's all the choice left me, woman. You heard what she told us, and it's written in golden script if you wish to read the particulars for yourself."

"I think *I* will," I said calmly, striding past their agonized tableau and drawing two of the guttering candles closer so I could read the parchment laid on the desk as one lays an execution warrant.

"Written in her own hand," Grosbeak whispered from the leather bag as the ferret's head popped up over the edge of it. How had he made a hole in the seam? It hadn't been there when we started out, but I saw one of his terrible gleaming eyes light up as he watched from the inside of the bag.

The script was elegant and elongated as if to draw out the pain of the words.

To the Royal Blood of Pensmoore, on this eighth day of Gray in Pensmoore City, capital of Pensmoore, from the great Lady Tanglecott of the Wittenbrand, Princess of the Oak, Patron Saint of Ilkanmoore.

I present to you this formal offer. You will make all preparations and present yourself to me at midnight of the next full moon on the roof of your palace, renouncing the mortal world and all within it. For three days, you shall live in my home in the Wittenhame, and for three nights you shall warm my bed.

Failure to present yourself as proposed will result in the death of your loved ones who I will feed to my mist lions as is a fitting consequence for such defiance.

Failure to formally disentangle yourself from your mortal ties will result in the same.

If you fail to live through our sojourn in my home, I will inherit your lands, title, and sovereignty, and I will use your land and people as I please.

If, however, against all odds, you survive these appointed days and nights, you shall be returned to the mortal world and be free to resume your ties and loyalties as you wish. In my magnanimous bounty, I shall even grant you one other soul – of your choice, excluding my magnificent person – to bring back with you to those lands.

The bargain is made, with or without you. Present yourself or suffer the consequences.

The parchment was signed in an illegible overly ornamented swirl that I assumed was her name.

Behind me, bitter words were being exchanged, but my heart was in my throat as I reread it twice. This. This was my opportunity.

"It's a Three Night Bind," Grosbeak whispered to me from in the bag. He sounded gleeful. "A classic trap. It warms the heart to see her keeping up the traditions."

"Tradition?" I murmured.

"Certainly. Mortals have been offered the bargain many times before. Surely the tales remain of it in your world, too?"

"Has anyone survived to tell the tale?" I whispered back. I was only asking absently. My eyes were searching the letter for any detail I might be reading incorrectly. I couldn't afford a single misstep.

"One," Grosbeak said. "Luritan the Poet of Ilkansmoore saved his lover from the Wittenhame that way. She had been dragged away and hung in the lake upside down by her hair to drown endlessly for all eternity."

"How pleasant," I murmured.

"Marshyellow thought so. 'Twas he who placed her there. But when her lover was offered the Three Night Bind by Lady Wittentree, he took it in a heartbeat. Poet he was, but also prince, and she thought to snipe his lands from whoever was playing Ilkanmoore at the time – Antlerdale, I think – but in the end, she lost, and he fled the Wittenhame with his drowned lover."

I shivered. I was not sure that was a happy ending. For anyone.

"And the other times?" I asked.

"Mortals die easily. And then their lands are forfeit, and the Wittenbrand who thinks he is playing them as his pawn finds it gone and his game lost."

"Then I have guessed right," I murmured, "And if Tanglecott wins this Three Day Bind, then my husband loses this nation and his stake in the game. Which, I recall, is his very immortality."

"Yes," Grosbeak said, and he sounded so excited that I half expected his bag to quiver. Fortunately, the ferret was squirming around the top, disguising any movement. "Ouch! This must be her third move. And a very, very clever one at that. A classic. The Wittenhame will be abuzz with it."

"Why can she not just take the land without the Three Day Bind?" I whispered. Upon a fifth reading, I had found nothing in the letter I didn't see the first three times. My mind was nearly made up.

"Sovereignty can only pass by inheritance, the spoils of war, or marriage. She cannot inherit. Your Bluebeard beat them off in war – and though she can certainly go back to that and likely win, we both know she is allied to Coppertomb and his allotted lands for this game lie between hers and ours. Her best bet is to steal them by marriage."

"Marriage? This is not marriage. It's a brief kidnapping."

"In the Wittenhame, it amounts to the same."

"Your kind are very obsessed with marriage," I hissed. Behind me, my brother's wife had collapsed in a heap on the floor, sobbing hysterically.

"We like rules. They are fun to have because then you get to break them."

"What rules do you live by then, Severed Head?"

"Wouldn't you like to know?"

"My brother is already married," I pointed out, returning reluctantly to the point.

"But if he renounces all mortal bonds, he will not be." The nasty snickering began again. "Oh, I do so love drama. I wish I could watch this one play out in full. To be part of a Three Day Bind, ah could the afterlife truly be so good?"

"What if the person stolen were married to a Wittenbrand?" I asked him. I needed this last answer quickly. Things had devolved behind me. An earthen tankard crashed against the wall, and Svetgin was cursing so loudly it was a wonder I could hear Grosbeak at all.

"Well, it wouldn't count as a marriage then, that's understood. The rest of the bargain would still need to be fulfilled, and lands and lives still exchanged, but I do rather feel the audiences would find it a cheap trick. It's not as much fun as a marriage."

"Fun aside, it would still be binding?"

"I never put fun aside."

I shook the bag.

"Fine. Yes. Binding."

Well, then. I drew in a deep breath and turned just in time to step hastily aside and avoid a second flying tankard.

My brother cut off mid-curse, shocked to realize he'd almost hit me, and I took the opportunity to step forward and speak with an authority I did not feel.

"No one needs to be fed to lions or turned out to die of starvation. Not today, at least."

CHAPTER SEVEN

"No, not today," my brother said bitterly, collapsing back into his chair. He snatched a decorative egg from the table beside him – a gift from the court of Salamoore – tracing the gilding with a finger. "Tomorrow. Tomorrow she will return."

"Return? She is not here?" I asked and he finally met my eyes, and for just a moment there was a look of brotherhood there. No one in our land knew the Wittenhame nor the denizens within it the way we two did. Far from my tingling excitement, his eyes held only swirling horror.

"She will return when she comes for me on the roof tomorrow night. I'm not even to have your hasty wedding, Izolda. I'm to be snatched away like a callow youth stolen by a great monster." He ran a hand through his thinning hair. It was always strange to think he'd once been younger than me. Now, he was a man in his forties, and I was not yet thirty.

"You're of a dramatic turn tonight, Svetgin," I said coolly. On the floor, Emelina had collapsed into breathless sobs, trembling, but mercifully silent.

"I love it," Grosbeak hissed from his bag. "Drama. Misery. Risk. Mmmwaaa."

"Did your ferret speak?" Volkov asked, watching the creature frolic in the mouth of the bag with drunk wonder on his face. His blue eyes were alight, his mustache twitching.

I was spared having to answer when Svetgin cut him off.

"Of course, I'm dramatic, sister. I was there with you. I saw everything. I will not be pinned to a pole and made a target for throwing knives. I will not be wrapped again in dead spirits." He took a long drink. "I still feel their hands on me sometimes upon a night, still feel whispers and corpse-like caresses." Emelina shuddered as if absorbing his words. He did not modulate them for her sake. "I will not be led around like a trophy on a leash for her pleasure. I will not be degraded." He was bright red now. "I'm a man, not a beast. And I will not give up my lands or my people. I see only one solution." He snatched up his stein, stared at it miserably when he realized it was shattered beyond use, and then simply drank straight from the jug. "I must fall upon my sword – tonight – before she can come to claim me."

Emelina stopped sobbing, turning her wide eyes on Svetgin.

"The loyal wife. How touching," Grosbeak whispered as if this were all entertainment for his amusement.

How interesting that this was what made her *stop* sobbing.

"I swear, the ferret spoke," Volkov said staring at me blearily. His hand felt for the sword hilt at his waist wrapped in white silk and red ribbon.

"I think you forget, brother of mine," I said calmly, "that there is more than one royal in this palace."

My brother's eyes flicked sharply to his wife and to his credit, drunk as he was, he straightened in his chair, puffed out his chest, and said, "I will defend my wife and children to the last drop of my blood."

"Very noble, I'm sure," I murmured before saying more clearly. "Shall I remind you, Svetgin, that I am also of your blood? Royal, though the court may not like to admit it. Available, despite my marriage to the Lord Riverbarrow."

Svetgin shivered at that. We did not speak of Bluebeard. The mention of him still left my brother trembling with rage and then spewing up his breakfast all day. Our time together in the Wittenbrand had left acid wells in his heart and mind that if touched at all, overflowed in ill humors.

I made my voice firm and steady. "There is nothing in the missive that would disqualify me from taking your place."

"No!" The muffled protest was from my bag. "That spoils the whole thing! It should be a three-day marriage, not an empty human puppet theatre. Why drag me from the depths only to corrupt the epic of the ages before my rotting eyes?"

"I'll bring the ferret with me, of course," I added dryly.

"Well. Well. Front row seats to a Three Day Bind? You mollify my fury. I accept."

It was all I could do to roll my eyes.

"The ferret really did speak," Volkov said, pale as a ghost. He leapt up, lightning-fast, snatched the ferret from my bag, and dangled it before him by the scruff of its neck, peering into its eyes. "Speak, creature."

To Honey's credit – or what were we calling her now? Look and Despair. To Look and Despair's credit, she snarled and snapped at Volkov.

"If you don't mind, General," I said smoothly, "I'll keep my pet. I'll need him in the Wittenhame."

My blood hadn't pumped this fast in years. My cheeks flushed, blossoming of their own accord. My heart began to throb with song, building in my heart, layer on layer, as the familiar theme returned from the crypt it had been banished to. My feet itched to move. I was going back. Three Day Bind or Three Lifetime Doom, I did not care. I was going back. I could barely breathe.

"I should break the creature's neck," Volkov muttered. "It's witchcraft."

"It's so much worse than that. Trust me."

Volkov ran a hand over his face, ignoring my retort, and then thrust the ferret at me with a shake of his head as if he could shake away the memory. "The missive was addressed to the royal blood of Pensmoore, Savataz. I think she counts."

She. Like I was a breeding mare. Volkov always discounted my opinions and person. And no wonder. He was only a general because the good ones and the old ones were all dead. If they hadn't been, he'd still be a puppy of a lieutenant who only had his commission because his father was a minor noble and had bought it for him with a dozen good horses and a dozen bad.

He twisted his mustache between two fingers and watched me with glittering eyes, running a hand over his well-dressed chest as if to remind me of his rank. Most of the court was too dead to remember his past. The departure of my accurate memory would suit him perfectly.

I received Look and Despair back and dropped her into the bag. She popped up again, looking out. Beneath him, Grosbeak grunted.

Svetgin took the letter from my hand, his eyes not meeting mine. Shame burned hot in his cheeks. He read it – or looked like he was reading it. If I'd drunk as much as he had, I wouldn't be reading anything at all.

"It says the royal she takes will warm her bed," he said finally, miserably. "What do you say to that?"

"The wording is very specific. I must warm it. I could do that huddled in one corner with a knife in one hand and a cranky ferret in the other."

"It had better be me in the other hand or the deal is off," Grosbeak murmured. "It's front row seats or nothing."

"Witchcraft," Volkov whispered unsteadily. He reached for Svetgin's jug as if more alcohol would help his judgment.

"Your lands and title will be forfeit," Svetgin said, and I knew he was going to give in. He was just putting on a show for himself now.

"What lands?" I asked, spreading my hands.

He snorted.

I leaned forward, eyes steady. "And as to the title of Mad Princess, I have enjoyed it, but it does not well suit me. I don't gibber enough for the impressive role."

It was only in the silence that followed those words that I realized Emelina had quieted. She rose to her feet unsteadily.

"It says you'll renounce your mortal ties," she said, not hopefully, but challenging as if she didn't believe I'd do it.

"You keep assuming I will die in those three days," I said. But these words were making me nervous. It was my ties to Pensmoore that had made me doubly valuable to Bluebeard – more than anyone realized. That and my days. And I was gambling them both on my ability to survive the Wittenhame.

But either I took that gamble and found a way to free my husband before he died in the endless brine, or I lived out my moldering years here in the mortal world, slowly drying up until I snapped like old leather with the sure knowledge that I had been too late to save him.

I wasn't the self-sacrificing saint they thought I was. I wasn't doing this for my brother. I wasn't doing it in a fit of compassion for Emelina and her children. I was, very practically, killing a whole flock of birds with one arrow. If I could survive just three days – and nights, I should not forget the nights – in the home of Lady Tanglecott, then I could save my brother, his wife, their children, his kingdom, and so much more importantly, I could find a way to draw my husband back from the embrace of the sea. And I could go back to the Wittenhame.

If.

Svetgin blinked at me owlishly. Volkov's eyes were narrowed on the bag.

I could barely keep my hands from trembling with excitement.

Emelina seemed the swiftest on the uptake – maybe because she was the most sober.

"Then we're saved." Her voice was small. Barely more than a whisper.

"I can't offer you up a third time," Svetgin said, his face crumpling. "What kind of a man would I be?"

"What kind were you when you gave me to the Sword?" I asked acerbically. He'd never actually apologized for that. I wasn't entirely sure he was sorry. It had been justified. He'd had the right of it. In his mind, at least.

"An honorable man," he gasped, and Emelina trod carefully

over to him and put a hand on his shoulder.

"It's a practical solution," she said calmly, meeting my eyes a little fearfully as if she thought I might abandon this cause now that I saw it benefited her.

"You'll do this, then?" Svetgin asked me, his eyes thick with misery, as if even this salvation was worse than the original curse. And in a way it was, wasn't it? Would I not rob him of his manhood if I took this burden that was his to bear? "You'll take my place?"

And he looked like he was going to be ill. As if he both desperately wanted my assent, and also needed me to deny him.

"I will."

"Your oath on it. Double clasp."

I hesitated. If I took off my gloves, he would see my skeleton hand.

"No oath?" he asked, freezing now, his voice trembling.

I took a step back, carefully angling my body. "Come here and I'll give it."

I removed one glove, twisting just a little so his body would be between me and the other two. He joined me readily, hands already held out as I removed the second glove.

He froze at the sight of my skeleton hand, eyes wide with shock, I lifted a single eyebrow and he swallowed.

"Is something wrong?" Emelina's voice trembled.

"Nothing," Svetgin said hoarsely as he crossed his arms and I crossed mine and we clasped hands. He couldn't hide his wince at the feel of my bones between his flesh fingers.

"I swear on life and death to do what I have promised, to stand in your stead before Lady Tanglecott and the Wittenbrand," I said calmly.

"I accept your oath." His voice broke on the end and his eyes never left my hand until I'd covered it again.

His head hung like a whipped dog's when he turned from me, and Emeline wrapped an arm around him.

"You could build her a statue to honor her sacrifice," she said kindly.

"In the square?" he asked looking up at her with boyish hope.

I went ahead and rolled my eyes this time. "I won't require a statue."

"In silver?" Svetgin asked, leaning toward his wife. He looked exactly like a man who had spent the night drinking now that he was relieved of his burden.

"In any material you like, my love," Emelina said, leading him toward the door. He leaned heavily on her light frame, and I knew she couldn't help her satisfied smile. After all, she was getting everything she wanted – safety and position for herself and her children, no risk to her husband, and an annoying rival removed forever.

"Volkov." Svetgin's order was bleary as they reached the doorway. "See to my sister's well-being. We don't want anything to happen to her. Her sacrifice tomorrow will save us all. See to it she has whatever she wishes."

"Hold on!" I objected but he was already gone. Volkov took a step toward me, and I didn't like the calculated look in his eye. I seized the ferret from the bag and held it up toward him in the most threatening manner I could manage. "I think I'll be going to my rooms."

"Or we could chew his ears off." Grosbeak snickered nastily. "It's not fun feeling them ripped apart so slowly. Trust me."

Volkov swallowed three times and I was almost certain it was bile he was fighting down.

"I think that would be best," he said, when he could finally speak, staring at Look and Despair, his face green as my old enemy, the sea. "I'll place a pair of guards at your door and two more on the roof watching your window. You'll be safe until tomorrow night. Or tonight, I suppose, if dawn is already here. I can never tell in this accursed hidden room. Ask them for whatever you need, but please keep that demon in your bag. Pensmoore is cursed enough already."

I left with my heart in my throat. I was going to the Wittenhame. And all I had to do to win my husband back was just not die. I was reasonably sure I could manage that. I'd done it quite well for twenty-six years now. What were three more days?

CHAPTER EIGHT

In the inky midnight sky, the moon hung as a brass sliver just over the edge of the horizon as if someone had carved free the edge from a button and then tried to tuck it behind the hills for safekeeping.

I'd watched a moon just like it once with my mother before the Everburn feast in the dead of winter, only then, the two of us had scraped frost from a small, glazed window instead of standing on the palace roof. We had looked out over the slumbering hills where the herds of horses slept, silent before the great silence of a sleeping world. Now, I stood overlooking sleeping Pensmoore, its shops and smithies, warehouses and taverns, and inns and homes spread out all around me like a rumpled blanket after sleep. They were frosted with snow and wreathed in hearth smoke and in every one of them dwelled a living being who was counting on me right now, though they did not know it. What would my mother have thought of that?

Likely, she would have had a story for this, too. Not one about catching the firebird or riding the ice dragon, but one about a girl with a savage heart who was about to wrestle a blizzard into submission. I wished, for what might be the thousandth time, that I could see her again. Of all that I had lost, I missed her most of all.

I'd slept most of the day away. A person did that when they were truly exhausted. The sleep had been fitful and left me raw and edgy, as it did that when you weren't quite exhausted enough to block out fear of what came next.

Grosbeak's loud snoring had not helped.

I had refused the many gifts Svetgin offered through the afternoon, taking only a large black wolf cloak trimmed with rabbit, an embroidered woolen overcoat, and a pair of thick black boots. If I had to wait on the palace roof at midnight, at least I was dressed for it.

"You should have killed the general before we left. You saw how he was watching you like a goat staked out for wolves. It's a fool who leaves a living enemy behind him," Grosbeak muttered for the ninetieth time. "Also, the ferret stinks."

I was resting against a parapet, grateful that while much of the roof was peaked and shingled in cedar to shed the snow, Pensmoore still had battlements.

"She said midnight," I hissed, though why I was whispering was anyone's guess. No one else was here. I'd refused the escort. Why should they freeze up here with me? If she even arrived this decade, she'd be on time for the Wittenbrand – and besides, I didn't want to give her options. She was bound to be upset when she realized it was me here. Best to leave her with no other mortal she could snatch in my place.

I clung to her too-pale missive as if it were a ticket of passage. It was, in a way. A ticket to opportunity.

"Did you know they stink?" Grosbeak pressed.

"Everyone knows that." I wiggled my frozen toes and focused again on the errant moon. Did it belong with the silver stars?

They seemed an unmatched set. As unmatched as me and the elegant Tanglecott. How would she collect me from way up here? I'd made my way out onto this part of the parapet from a window, but we did not keep it clear in winter and with this ice and snow, one misstep would send a girl falling straight to her death in a way that even the encrusted snow and dancing lights of the city could not charm from my head.

Below, the sound of song drifted up. I did not begrudge Svetgin his merrymaking. But laughter and song did not fit my mood. Anxiety suited me more. Could I live three days in the Wittenbrand surrounded only by those most hostile to me? I'd barely survived last time and that was with help.

Grosbeak growled in his hiding spot. "Ferrets don't taste like food, either. I tried it. Nasty thing."

That explained some of the noises coming from the bag, but since neither of them was dead, I hoped they'd sorted out their differences.

"I know not why you have chosen to doom us both back to hell, Izolda, but I must admit I relish the thought. To be back in the action. To once more watch the princes fight and dance over mortal souls. Ah, but I have missed it."

Something fluttered in the air above me and I looked up to see a small bird battling the gusty wind. Was that an orange breast I saw? It was too late in the year for an oriole, and yet this one flew, battered and rolled by the wind, clutching something in one clawed foot that fluttered madly in the gusty wind.

"You act as though you were beneath the sea for an age, and yet you tell me it was a mere two days," I said wryly. My toes were so frozen I could not feel them and the skin on my cheeks was tight and sore. How was that summer bird flying in this weather?

"Yes," Grosbeak said as if it were a curse. "Days! Days out of the game. Who knows how many moves we've missed?"

The bird fell from the sky so suddenly that I gasped, certain he'd been shot with an arrow or died of the cold before my eyes. He fell, spiraling bonelessly, and I lunged forward to catch him in outstretched hands. My gasp caught in my throat as he looked up at me, his feathers ruffled by the icy blast of the wind. The bird chirped sharply and thrust its laden foot at me. Gently, I took the scrap of parchment from him and then cooing, tucked him into the large pocket of my overcoat under the fur cloak. He could warm up there. Though he might want to fly away before I went to the Wittenhame. No mortal creature could survive there long.

The oriole snuggled in, tucking his wings around his little body and his beak to his breast. I unrolled the parchment and read.

In falls of dew and howl of wind, there comes the cry of eagle grim,

Along the falls, the black bear waits, his sober eyes survey the brim,

But fiercer still, the visage of the one who stole my heart and love,

For only she can bid me die and bid me watch her steps above

This terrible monstrosity still echoes in the empty plot

Where once dwelt rib and heart. I grasp yet still she lingers though I rot.

I felt the last blood rush from my face and extremities. These words. The voice behind them was as familiar as my own. I knew them though I knew not how I had received them. It was like receiving a letter from the dead.

Desperately, looking around as if I might be caught, I folded up the – what? Poem? Letter? Dare I say, *love letter*? – and tucked it inside my dress where it could sit next to my skin, my cheeks flaring hot.

"What's going on out there?" Grosbeak complained. "If there's drama unfolding I remind you that in my debt you are, and for that debt, you must pay."

"I'm not in your debt," I told him breathlessly as I coaxed the bird from my pocket and carefully set him in a nook at the base of the parapet. He shivered there, but better for him to shiver here than to die in the Wittenhame. Poor brave little soul to have brought this to me. But how had he found it? He was no sea creature, and he certainly was no diver. Could my drowned husband have sent him to bear this last present to me from some other place? And if he had, what did it mean? Was it a last goodbye?

I dared not dwell on it.

A sound like fabric being torn made my spine shiver and then the snow rose in a swirling gust, blocking out all sight of the roof and the city and even the brass sliver of moon.

As the snow settled silently, a carriage was revealed, hanging in the air as if it, too, were a moon and pulled by four harnessed snow lions, their wings extended and their eyes glittering with hatred. Rather than proper leather harnesses, the bonds holding them were merely wisps of smoky cloud. One of them snapped at me, barely held back by that meager binding. I danced to the side, almost losing my footing on the narrow battlement. Down at the end of the parapet was the carving of a cat just like that mist lion but without the wings – for all the help that good luck charm was providing now.

I swallowed my unease and gasped as the coachman bowed to me, revealing he had no head. His collar flapped around his absent neck like a tattered flag.

"I believe we've found your match, Grosbeak," I said, a little unsteadily.

His snicker was unsettling. "How rude. I'd rather eat a pair of golden scissors than be attached to *that*."

I felt my eyebrows rising, even more so as they trailed to the carriage.

It was a pumpkin.

Occasionally, the Pensmoore countryside will produce large pumpkins in strange oblong shapes, their bulk more fascinating than beautiful. As they grow, they seemed to pale, as if form and color could only be found in limited quantities and must be stretched and watered down to extend to the larger parts of the pumpkin. This pumpkin was not like those. Perfectly rotund, deeply, duskily orange, edged in frost and crusted snow, it was an imposing, ridged gourd. In the side of it, in lieu of windows, someone had carved a garish face that looked so much like Grosbeak that I almost pulled him free to compare the two.

A hand – lily-white, naked, bearing a single silver serpent ring – reached out the mouth of the pumpkin. I passed the letter to her, saying nothing.

"Ah," the cultured voice said, sounding satisfied as the hand withdrew into the pumpkin's mouth. The way she formed each word was sultry and seductive and I was utterly immune. "You've agreed, then? A Three Day Bind with a wager? Three enchanted nights and three spellbinding days – and if you still have your skin and your wits when you're through, you win your life back and one other besides. If you do not survive, then I gain your mortal fortunes."

Still, I remained silent. One false word and I might lose this chance.

"I bid your assent," she said, and there was hunger behind her cold words. "My oath is spoken, but now to bind us, you must speak your part. I will have it, royal. Do not forget the consequences if you do not agree to my generous terms."

My heart raced in my chest. This was it. My one chance. To take it, I would need all the cleverness and courage I'd ever possessed. I seized all my courage and held on tight.

"I assent," I said clearly. "Take me to your home, Lady Tanglecott."

"What is this?"

The carriage door was thrown open – the entire face of the pumpkin swinging outward to show the carved hollow of the interior where Lady Tanglecott sat. Strings of pumpkin flesh and smooth seeds the size of dinner plates swung from the coach ceiling.

She looked at me, aghast, her waterfall of golden hair seeming to stand almost on end and her eyes flashing bright. She hissed, her beautiful face turning viper-sharp.

"Wife of the Arrow. You were not the one sent for."

"Was I not?" I asked grimly. "Am I not a royal of this land? I'm the Mad Princess of Pensmoore – as royal as I am odd. Specificity is the friend of legal documents."

Her curses were like black diamonds, perfect and cutting.

Quickly then, before she could think of a way to wriggle out of her contract, I slipped into the carriage, dodged a swinging seed, and closed the pumpkin door behind me, my heart in my throat. This was my only chance, and I'd only get it if I rode in – white-knuckled though I might be! – and took it.

Pumpkin carriages are exactly as disgusting inside as one would think – even frozen ones. Strands of pumpkin flesh solidified in thick ropes where they ringed our seats, while the seats were constructed of rib cages shoved into the pumpkin flesh and frozen in place and then swathed in layers of deer hides, fur side up. To my relief, the rib cages also seemed like deer, though scraps of flesh still clung to them just like the scraps of flesh clinging to the pumpkin interior as if both were butchered by a careless hand – or possibly a hand wielded by a body with no head. I was more grateful than ever that everything was frozen.

Lady Tanglecott's mouth remained open at my boldness as I settled myself opposite her. The paleness of her face blushed the slightest dawn pink. She'd dressed to kill – if I was a man – in gossamer fabric so light I could see her every curve and valley under the folds of it. The edges shimmered when they caught the light and a cloak of sealskin sewn in luxurious strips cushioned her bottom and would hold back the cold if she but drew it around her. I did not want to know what my brother might have thought of this obvious enticement, were he here in my place.

Personally, I had no interest in the form of her body or what she was so obvious in offering with it – but I *was* interested in the key dangling from her neck on a golden chain. It was silver. I'd seen its kind before.

Lightning fast, I reached across from my bench, snaked my hand into her bodice, caught the key, and pulled it forth, twisting it in the air before she could open her mouth and scream.

The carriage juddered as if suddenly swept up in a blizzard, rolling hard to one side so we were thrown into the pumpkin walls. Thank goodness I had left the bird behind. The ferret shrieked with alarm. Half-rotted vegetable scent filled my nose despite the frost, and then we were righted as the nightmares seared across our minds, spinning us into madness, sifting us down to threads of persons, and reweaving madly like a grandmother intent on having completed gifts by Yearswatch Night.

"I'll wring your neck. I'll wring it!" I didn't know if the threat was Tanglecott or Grosbeak.

I was Izolda and not Izolda. My heart was buried in the sea. No, it was queen of the mountain. No, it was black as the night without stars. My family were there and then gone, dead a thousand ways and screaming in in my mind, on and on and on. My throat raced to catch up, my scream competing with the matching screams of Lady Tanglecott and Grosbeak, and then the carriage juddered again, and spun, end on end, so we were flung against opposite curved walls of thready vegetable. It struck something so hard we shuddered, spun, and then stopped abruptly.

When a pumpkin bursts, it falls into gory plant pieces and even a frozen one is no exception. Bits of orange flesh coated my face, hair, and wolf coat. More settled in wet pulp over Lady Tanglecott whose curses had grown more vicious.

My bag had spun away and sat now on its own shred of pumpkin as Look and Despair peeked out the top as if expecting a hail of arrows incoming. Beneath him, Grosbeak's string of curses melded in harmony with our lady kidnapper's.

I picked myself up from the tangle of rib cages and deer hide and pumpkin. The walls had fallen outward when the carriage burst apart and the roof with the long curling stem had fallen between Lady Tanglecott and I like a trophy for a game not yet played.

Who would win? I wondered.

We'd crashed into the sacred monument, the un-drawable arrow stuck into the rock before us. Only this time, there was no white marble altar – only a great lump of black, twinkling rock, and the white flames that once roared around the arrow were only caught by the corners of my eye when I turned my head, as if they had become specters.

This time, our arrival was not met with an unearthly chorus, but with the woeful beating of ominous drums, starting low and soft and slow so that I thought they were only the beating of my heart. Gradually, they gathered speed and sound until they produced in me a terrible foreboding.

And this was not the clearing in the forest where first I'd seen that arrow. I looked around me, bewildered by the clifftop we'd crashed upon. Scant grasses blew in the wind along a cliff's edge and in ragged patches nearby. Small tumbles of the same black rock were dotted across the grass, but the world below the cliff was naught but mist and treetops, and the world behind faded into fog in the same way.

"Three Days in my house," Lady Tanglecott said, spitting the words. "And Three Nights in my bed. This was the bargain."

"I read it," I said, boldly. And perhaps the madness had taken me this time because my heart was soaring. Every color was brighter, every sound clearer, every pain more focused. I was in the Wittenhame. It tasted like hot coffee after a night with no sleep.

"And you must survive each one," Tanglecott said, drawing

herself to her feet, flicking a piece of pumpkin from her cheek, and then gathering her swirling seal cloak around her.

"My life is not my own," I told her steadily. "It was bought with a price, and I will repay the buyer."

His words echoed in my mind, *This terrible monstrosity still echoes in the empty plot, Where once dwelt rib and heart.*

She laughed then, condescending and waspish. "You'll have a hard time fulfilling that bargain, mortal woman. You have my invitation, but you'll have to find my door to enter my house, and find my room to enter my bed, and I wish you luck in doing what no mortal ever has."

She snapped her fingers, and her four harnessed lions were suddenly there, their feet kicking up pumpkin debris and their four heads snapping in four different directions. She took up their reins, snapped the spectral threads within her palms, and they sped away and into the fog, somehow drawing her along behind them as if her feet were shod with runners from a sleigh.

And this time it was my turn to look around me fruitlessly. I had assumed she would take me to her house. I had guessed wrong.

"I have never liked pumpkins," Grosbeak said miserably. "They feel like they should be combined with beans and cinnamon and steaming milk, but I can't for the life of me decide why."

"That sounds utterly terrible," I said, scooping up his bag.

"I saw it in a vision of hell once," he said dreamily. "Perhaps I will open my own ale cart and sell them to the folk."

"You'd need hands for that," I said absently, turning in a circle and looking for tracks. Lady Tanglecott had left none. I was on my own.

"You'll be my hands for me. After all, you'll need to pay someone to tell you where Lady Tanglecott lives. And you'll have to offer me something valuable to get me to tell."

"What if I offered you a continued adventure?"

He cursed. "I'd hoped for more, but we've already established that you have a poor imagination. And I did promise your drowned husband that I wouldn't intentionally kill you."

"How sweet."

"I thought so."

CHAPTER NINE

"The question is not how you'll find her house," Grosbeak said as I finished picking shreds of pumpkin pith from our faces and hair, "but how you'll get in. She would not have dared you to try if she thought it easy."

I picked up the bag again and slung it over my shoulder. It was not winter in the Wittenhame, though it was night. A dusky breeze blew the small flowers of the hilltop, tussling them like curls, and the warmth was already melting the frozen edges of the pumpkin. The fog should have paled everything around us, but the colors were sharp and vivid, and my heart sang with anticipation at the sight of them.

I paused, taking a moment to stare at the silver arrow plunged into the stone. It seemed too normal, too average to be a portent of disaster and yet it drew me toward it – my gaze, my thoughts, even my feet.

Without meaning to, I was already pacing toward it when Grosbeak said, "We have but a few hours until day and then you'll need to be in her house. Not long to solve a puzzle, mortal girl, and you'll need all the time you can get."

"Is it far from Bluebeard's home?" I asked, holding my breath as I climbed the jagged back stone and reached delicately toward the silver arrow. I ran my fingers up the shaft. It trembled at my touch – or perhaps I trembled at its touch – and for a bare moment the song that had been sung here for my prince of the Wittenhame seemed to echo in a perfect note in the air or perhaps in my heart, tuned in such a way that my whole self vibrated with it. The fletching under my fingers' touch felt almost real for all that it was silver. On a whim, I gripped the shaft of the arrow and pulled.

"What is near? What is far?" Grosbeak intoned.

I hadn't expected movement, but to my surprise, I felt the tiniest shift in the arrow. My imagination, of course. I was too excited not to be seeing things. I was strung like a ready violin now that I was within the Wittenhame. It was as if it had robbed me of all my brightness these past seven years, leaving me pale and desolate while it stored up that vibrant emotion here in storehouses already brimming.

Perhaps that was why I couldn't help myself any more than I could have stopped Grosbeak from spewing obscenities and insults. I tried to pull the arrow again, face flushing hot at my own temerity.

The arrow did not move. It was locked solidly in the rock. Whatever response I'd thought I'd felt was mist and ashes.

Grosbeak snickered. "I told you no one gets it out, but oh no, you thought to prove we immortals foolish with your mortal might. And you're not just any frail mortal but a prematurely elevated lesser noble who spends the only time she has weeping and haunting the barren shores like a sad scrap of ghost because the man who kidnapped her lies under the waves. Pathetic."

I drew in a patient breath. I needed Grosbeak to guide me, or if he would not, then I needed to seek Bluebeard's house and if I could get in, I might consult his Wall of Wisdom to get answers.

That must be a last resort for me. It would take up valuable hours with no guarantee that the house would even let me in.

"How may I arrive at Lady Tanglecott's house, decapitated warrior?" I asked formally.

Grosbeak made a rude sound. "You've given your heart to the barrow, that's sure enough, but at least you kept your head. Get it? Kept your head?"

"It's not a very good joke," I said coldly. "And I asked you a question."

He looked away coldly, intoning as if he were speaking funeral rites, "Your head knows he's a bad bet, but your heart keeps saying otherwise."

"The way to the Lady's house," I demanded, refusing to acknowledge his japes.

This time he turned a look of vitriol to me. "You don't want to end up head-ed in the wrong direction."

"What I lack in imagination, you lack in a sense of humor," I said, crossing my arms. "Is there any end to this? Immortal, you may be, but who knows where you'll end up if I fail this Three Day Bind."

His tone turned to one of impatience as if I had interrupted his fun. "Just snap your fingers and think about what you love about Lady Tanglecott and you'll arrive immediately on her doorstep."

"And if there is nothing that quickens my heart about her?"

"Then you'll have to walk. There's a reason that almost no one uses that trick."

I screwed up my face and tried to think. I did love her sense of fashion. She looked gorgeous all the time. It was not a trait we shared. I concentrated on her pretty dresses and closed my eyes.

"Your efforts are pale as a twice-dead fish."

On the island of Burning Guilt, she'd been a fearsome thing as she made that secret contract to battle my Bluebeard. A hand snaked around my mouth – the specter, of course. But yes, I admired that about her. Maybe even loved it, because if I played my cards right and brought her down it would force a toppling of her whole alliance.

"Acceptable effort, mistress mine."

I opened my eyes to see we'd moved. We were deep in the Wittenhame under the canopy of massive trees that always made me feel like a toadstool or a mouse. Their leaves were too high to hear the rustle of the wind, and yet still, I fancied I heard it. Before us, a still lake lay, cloaked lightly in mist and in the moss of the bank facing it, I almost thought I saw the face of the Bramble King before it was suddenly gone, lost in the darkness of the fading night.

I shivered, but it was only half fear that made me shiver, the other half was still anticipation. Three days and three nights and if I played my hand well, I would have my husband in my arms. I swallowed against a dry throat, hands shaking with overexcitement.

A tiny bird chirped in a tree nearby – warbling in a way unfamiliar to me.

Someone had fixed a bill to a nearby tree where it depicted a pair of knights in full joust armor tilting at one another in what might be the most elaborate woodcut I'd seen. I could almost feel the roar of the crowd shown around them. I squinted in the darkness and made out the word "JOUST" decorated with flourishes – some of which looked a little too much like twisted bodies and tortured souls. Beneath the woodcut were the words, "Brave Fools Only. All Comers Unwelcome."

"What an expensive woodcut to make just to tell people not to come," I said grimly. "Where is the house?"

At the word, "house" a pair of doors appeared hovering over the edge of the lake where it met the shore – still as water in a drinking glass. The doors were made of mist, barely discernable in the moonlight, but one thing about them was certain. I'd never seen doors like this before.

The bird's long song trilled out a second time.

"Bellies of Mortals, you're stingy with the information. Are you looking at an invitation to a joust?" Grosbeak said from within his bag.

"It's hardly an invitation. It specifically said not to come."

I examined the doors. They each bore a half-ring pull but the pulls moved and were held in place by a complicated device in the shape of a swooping owl on one side and a leaping salmon on the other. Both hands were required to move the owl, though the piece slid easily like a well-greased geared lock. I moved the bird form with authority and pulled, but though I heard the snick of a latch opening, the other door still held this one in place.

"Well, that settles it," Grosbeak said firmly. "We are going to that joust one way or another."

"You wish to ride in the lists? I suppose you would make a target that was difficult to strike."

I released the owl and moved to the salmon. A ridiculous pair.

An owl should be paired with a mouse or a songbird and an eagle or osprey with the salmon. Behind me, the visiting songbird sang his song as if to emphasize this. These two designs were not of the same kind at all. I placed my hands on the heavy salmon device, but as I shifted it to unlatch this side of the door, the owl shunted back down into a locked position.

A frustrated sound escaped my throat and I moved back to the owl, only to have the salmon slip back to its original spot.

"Ride? You mock me." Grosbeak sniffed. "But the spectacle! The grisly deaths and broken hearts! Perhaps, I will bargain with you, and you'll ride in my place for honor and the token of a lady."

"I care not for the tokens of ladies. I have plenty of my own handkerchiefs, thank you."

I stretched across the spirit door, accidentally slipping into the ankle-deep water as I tried to reach both handles at once. My arms were not wide enough. The arms of a grown man would not be.

A nasty chuckle rang out from my bag. "See? Not so easy, is it? I warned you, but no, for you it's all heart and no head."

"Don't tempt me to drown you in the lake."

"Don't think I wouldn't like it. I have a mermaid waiting for me still."

I ignored him and stepped back. There must be another door somewhere. With a sigh, I resigned myself to hiking around the shore looking for it.

A flutter of wings was my only warning and then soft feathers brushed my cheek as something settled on my unoccupied shoulder. A piece of parchment floated down, and then another brush of wings and as I turned to follow the motion, I saw a bird very much like a small chickadee bobbing through the trees.

I scooped up the missive. It smelled of brine and something like cloves.

That's my last wife watching you with granite

eyes and iron spine. I call her my late

wonder. Her dark suspicions my days lit

and then she was plucked out my arms by fate.

And so, I mourn. My plans hollow with her

Gone, my power lost in her spooled out days.

But love smolders hot in my soul and spurs

Me cling to her and treasure her strange ways.

Forget me not, sharp maiden of ordered

mind. Hold me in your heart as my last breath,

tickles the memory that once bordered

on the divine and shatters me in last rest.

I paused. If these were real and from his hand then it worried me that my husband was spending his last moments sending me these love letters by bird when he ought to be thinking about how he could escape his bonds before he drowned beneath the sea. Wouldn't that be the practical thing to do?

What worried me was that much like Prince, much like my dear mother, my husband was never practical. He may indeed end up drowning beneath the waves while finding a second rhyme for "bordered." I gritted my teeth together. It was up to me to go get him. I was the only one with any sense left to do it.

"What did you mean when you teased me that I'd given my heart to the barrow?" I asked Grosbeak as I made my way along the edge of the lake. I was starting to worry about that phrasing.

"A barrow is a grave," Grosbeak said as if I was a child.

"I know that." As I crept along the shore, the door vanished entirely. Panicked, I backtracked, and it appeared again. Well then. I'd need to be right on top of any alternate entrances for them to show themselves. And I only had a few hours.

"And your husband is a dead man."

A chill shot through me. "I thought you said he still lives."

Could the birds be bringing me messages from beyond the grave? My heart twinged at the thought.

"Well, he did when I saw him. And that was what … days ago in the mortal world? Which could be years here. How long do you think he can live under the sea with his magic gone? You can't live on the echo of it forever. If I was a betting man – and oh, but I am – then I'd bet he is very, very dead and here you are pining for a dead man, risking your entire future on a splinter-thin chance at receiving his corpse back from the sea. Or perhaps only his bones. I'm sure they're lovely and white but hardly worth all this trouble."

My stomach suddenly felt sour. I wished I had not eaten before we left. The scent of pumpkins clung too heavily to us and every waft of it left my nose curling and lips twisting.

"So that's why I tease that you've given your heart to the barrow, for never has such a thing been so apparent. It could inspire a minstrel – if there were any looking for a miserable story about two fools."

"Silence yourself and help me find the door," I muttered. The Wittenhame seemed leached of color now and the sourness of my belly had crept up to my mouth.

"There won't be another door. More fool you are for looking for one with the moon sinking like all your hopes."

His voice rang too full of truth to deny him. Besides, I knew he wouldn't bother lying to me about this. His fate was sewn to mine. Sink me and he sank himself. Irritable, I tromped back around the edge of the lake, my wet foot bothering me. Each footstep was a *squelch* that only reminded me of my failure to open the ghost door. Flowers woke along the path I trod, their drowsy heads rising, opening – as if to look at me – and then tumbling back to slumber. Even they knew better than to get their hopes up about me.

"I can't open the door," I grumbled. "My arms are not wide enough."

"No matter how wide they were, the handles would simply move out of reach," Grosbeak said amiably. "'Tis a friendship door and can only be opened with the help of a friend, of whom you have precious few."

"I rather wonder that Lady Tanglecott is fit to open her own door, then," I said, letting a tinge of bitterness seep into my tone.

Grosbeak snickered. "It seems you're more friendless yet, but don't let me stop your salty chatter. I crave bitterness as the hummingbird craves nectar. I have sorely missed it."

"And here I thought you were already filled to overflowing with the draught. I should point out that despite your insults, you are my friend. Or at least I thought you were."

"If it is friendship you need from me, you have it already,"

Grosbeak grumbled. "If it's hands then I'm afraid you helped bury mine years ago. You'll need someone whose appendages are still unrotted – or at least attached."

Here he gave my gloved hand a pointed look. I flinched. I kept forgetting about it. It was easy to forget with the gloves cloaking my deformity.

"A friend," I said, wary. I glanced up at my shoulder but the specter drew back, hands raised defensively. She was not my friend, clearly.

The forest was of no assistance. No helpful fauns played pipes near this place. No dryads lingered near the water's edge. No strapping young shepherd boys. Less fancifully, none of the Wittenbrand could be seen or heard to be debauching themselves anywhere close or even snoring in the dead of the night.

Friends were in short supply.

I swallowed and looked down.

"I don't suppose you can help me?" I asked the ferret.

Under my questioning gaze, it chittered and disappeared into the bag.

"No, not there! That's my neck, you horrible rat! Izolda, what are my sins that you have judged and condemned me to be eaten a morsel at a time by the lowest of creatures?"

I bit my lip. Think, Izolda, think. What do you have that might work? Perhaps a bit of twine that could hold the latch in place?

"I can see you thinking about wedging the door with a stick or tying it with rope or some other mortal nonsense," Grosbeak said in a muffled voice. "Were it so that life in all her tangles be so simple, but this door is a magic portal, my *friend*," he spat that last word, "and it will only open when its eldritch conditions are met. Find a friend with hands, or risk dying nastily when you fail to enter this house by dawn. I'd say you have an hour, but what do I know?"

So, no mortal items. I still had a ferret and a talking head. The head was, clearly, worthless. I had made my way to the part of the shore where the door was visible. I looked now from the latch to the ferret. Even a highly trained ferret could not possibly manipulate those latches. They took two hands. I'd need a human helper and even a one-handed one would not be enough.

I bit my lip. I would not curse or cry with frustration. I would think. Despite Grosbeak's childish jokes, I always used my head first. Where could I find a friend in the Wittenbrand where I had no people, no home, not even a room to my name.

Wait.

A room.

The words of the poem I'd just read echoed in my head "*That's my last wife watching you.*"

Swallowing, I slipped the key for the Room of Wives from around my neck.

"Going to record your failures in your little book?"

I ignored Grosbeak and turned the key.

The room was *exactly* as I'd last left it seven years ago, bloodstains and all. The women who had once been married to my husband lined the hall, their faces lifeless, their perfect bodies posed like statues, their garb rich and vibrant as they no longer were.

"Your fascination with this place is revolting," Grosbeak muttered as I hurried within. I must be quick. There was no guarantee this crazy idea would work. "You should talk to someone. Perhaps a draught of poppy milk would help. Or the smoke of a cypher tree. Anything but all this lingering in a magic crypt."

"What would you say a friend *is* Grosbeak?" I asked as I ran down the hall to the hourglass full of garnets. There were so many more in the bottom than there had been before. Seven years more. It snatched my breath away like an ill-timed wind.

"Someone who doesn't kill you on sight," Grosbeak said with a grin that rivaled the jack-o-lantern carriage.

"Then all the mortal world is my friend," I said dryly. I snatched up a garnet from the hourglass, trembling at the feel of it in my palm, and gasping at the wall of nausea that hit me when I took the gem. The last time I'd done this, things had gone very poorly. But I had a possible hour – maybe less – to make a friend and very few candidates.

"Someone whose loyalty you can purchase for a sum within your means," he suggested.

"Ah, now we are closer," I agreed, hurrying down the line of Bluebeard's former wives. "Let us both hope I can pay the price."

I paused in front of Tigrane now, Bluebeard's war-like bride, and then reconsidered, circling back to where Princess Margaretta stood in her hourglass perfection.

I scrambled up onto her plinth, awkward with my bag of severed head and ferret and my heavy wolfskin cloak. She was a tiny little thing, delicate as spun glass.

"Take my day and be my friend," I muttered, trying to put the gem into her hand.

"Try the mouth," Grosbeak said unexpectedly. There was a strange tinge of anticipation in his voice as he realized what I was trying to do. "She could hold it there."

It felt wrong to force the gem between her lips, but not as wrong as a messy death and the loss of all hope would be.

I popped the garnet between her full pouting lips and held my breath.

I expected a slow awakening and possibly gratitude.

I did not expect the sudden scream that sent me flying from the plinth and landed me on my back.

CHAPTER TEN

I blinked up at the ceiling, the painted angels and demons on it leering down at me as if they might laugh with the same hoarse wheeze that Grosbeak was laughing.

"She startled you, oh well done, Arrow's wife!" he chortled.

I shook my head like a fighter trying to knock off the blow and forced my shaken body back to its feet. Who knew if she might try again?

Margaretta quivered before me, her deathly pale skin flushed bright rose and her tiny hand raised to cover a wide, open mouth. Shock led her eyebrows to climb higher than I thought possible.

Her voice was tiny as a mouse. "This is not what he promised me! Oh dear."

She sneezed and spat the garnet out and instantly froze in place.

I ran to where it rolled across the floor, picked it up, wiped it on my skirt – ugh, it was still wet – and placed it back between her lips.

This time, I caught her shoulders as she sneezed again.

"Dear me!" her squeak was so like something Princess Chasida might make. Though Chasida hated me, and I had some hope that Margaretta would not.

"Margaretta, Princess of Pensmoore," I said firmly. "I have given you one of my days. Spit it out again and it will not be offered a third time."

Her eyes were wide as a frightened hare as her lips shrank to a rosebud and both delicate hands moved to cover them.

"You can talk," I said, trying to be patient. "Just keep the garnet in your mouth."

"Mine were sapphires," she said, moving the garnet to her cheek in a way that only slightly disguised her speech. "But who are you? Is it time to wake?"

Her eyes danced around the room, little smiles lighting at each wife she saw. "Oh! You're a wife, too!" Everything she said sounded like an exclamation. I watched her, fascinated. "You are breaking the rules and the bargain if you're stealing your own days. You really shouldn't do that," she said shaking her head violently. "You really shouldn't. No."

"Could you pick one with a brain?" Grosbeak said. "Hands might not be enough if she can't think enough to operate them."

"It's for a good purpose," I said slowly as Grosbeak pulled an exaggerated bored face.

Margaretta was like a human butterfly. Utterly exquisite in looks, fluttering with every movement, and bumping up against the glass as if she didn't realize it was there.

"Oh. Well. I suppose you would know. Of what nation are you, Princess?"

"Pensmoore," I answered simply.

She gasped, wringing her hands. "But that's my country. You don't look like one of us! You don't."

"I am Izolda Savataz of Northpeak," I said calmly.

"Savataz? Mercy. Oh no. Mercy." She sat down hard on the ground, fanning her face.

"We really don't have time for hysterics," I said, watching her through the side of my eyes.

Grosbeak snickered so loudly I felt sure Margaretta would be insulted but she just kept fanning herself. "Next time, I pick which wife to wake. I, at least remember some of them."

"My family. My poor family. And all my friends. They must all have perished for so minor a house to have ascended." She looked up, horrified. "I mean no insult, of course."

I could probably tell her that her niece lived, but that might lead to more questions and more hysterics. Especially if she heard that our shared husband had killed Chasida's father. Who would be Margaretta's brother? Nephew? I couldn't remember. Best not to say.

"I require a friend," I said patiently. "Rather urgently."

"A friend." She drew in a long breath as if composing herself. "Yes. Of course."

She stood up, smiling again and curtseying to each wife. "I took such consolation from these dear girls. Each of them is just so precious."

She looked up at me docilely and I found I was without anything to say. What had Bluebeard thought of her? She was so … sweet.

"Were you … married long to the Arrow?" I tried, taking her hand and putting it on my arm as courtly ladies did in Pensmoore. She seemed to relax at the familiarity and allowed me to guide her toward the door.

"Oh, I don't know." She blushed prettily. "He sought neither my counsel nor my bed. I spent most of my time arranging flowers and embroidering. Perhaps you saw my hummingbird pillows?"

"Nevermind. I like this one," Grosbeak said as I walked her toward the door. "I could have danced her all across the Wittenhame and made her bend to my every whim if he'd let me near her. Imagine what she'd look like in a dress made of sewing needles and broken promises? I bet she'd still dance even through the pain. Just to be a nice girl."

"Then let's all be glad he did not," I said in a quelling tone. I needed to get Margaretta out the door and then back here as swiftly as possible. She was more delicate than I'd ever imagined.

"Who is that grim little voice?" Margaretta asked, quailing a bit at Grosbeak's leer through the tear in the bag.

"My pet, I'm afraid," I said.

"Oh dear." She looked at the mouth of the bag where Look and Despair had settled and then back down to the tear where Grosbeak's expression was visible and she bit her lip. "You're an animal lover, then?"

Grosbeak's chortle was disturbing.

"It would appear so," I said dryly.

I opened the top of it so she could see Grosbeak and the ferret. She blanched.

"I don't do well with *creatures*." The last word was so faint I could barely make it out.

"Neither do I," Grosbeak said from the bag. "Not even fine ones with a perfectly turned ankle and a bosom as vast as the plains of Myygddo. Just so you know. They say you killed yourself, you know. Died by your own hand."

"I didn't mean to," Margaretta said, looking guilty. "The glass just broke."

We both looked over at the hourglass and I shuddered. I didn't want to hear more about that.

"Please," I pleaded. "I need your help. I must make haste."

"Yes. Yes, of course. I would love to help and after all," here she gave a very nervous titter. "I am living right now on borrowed time."

"Oh, good one," Grosbeak crowed from in the bag. "Not just a princess of Pensmoore but a princess of puns. Maybe she's the comedic character in this exciting narrative."

"I rather think you are." I leveled a disapproving gaze at him. "Though anyone who laughs at you must have a black, black heart."

"Do we really have to hurry? I'd love to stay and help the others," Margaretta asked, looking over her shoulder as I hustled her to the door.

"I'm doing this to save my brother," I said gravely. "And his wife and children."

Her face brightened. "They live still?"

"Yes," I said, face burning.

She nodded, looking very sober, and then she took my hand in her rose-petal soft ones. "He took that from all of us – family. Love. Devotion. If you still have a chance at it …" She shook her head as her words drifted off. She looked around the room of wives as if memorizing each face. "I will help you. For them. For all of them."

"Thank you," I said, deflating a little in relief. "Can we hurry?"

"It seems we must. But can you ask your pet to be quiet? He worries me."

"I try, but no one listens to me, I'm afraid," I said, giving Grosbeak a pointed look.

"Oh dear," Margaretta said as I led her through the door.

We emerged onto the lakeshore, but we were no longer alone. A host of folk watched us in eerie silence. Antlered men with gaudy doublets and chains of goose-egg-sized jade beads stood beside winged women, pale and slender with hair like dandelions before they blow away, and these, in turn, were surrounded by men with deer legs or women sitting astride bullfrogs the size of carriages.

Every one of them was so still, so silent, that it made me bite my lip. It felt like the calm before the storm.

"Don't tell me your kind grows nervous when placed upon the stage," Grosbeak said with a cruel laugh.

"Stage?" I whispered.

"They've assembled to watch. Someone must have let slip there's a Three Day Bind. Every free soul in the Wittenhame will want a glimpse of it."

"There won't be much to see," I muttered. "Come on,

Margaretta."

She moved to join me at the door, gripping the salmon where I held the owl, and I did not like the sensation that filled me as the silent crowd strained to watch and we disengaged the locks and opened the door together. I felt as though something slinking and slippery had crawled down my mouth and into my throat and lodged there and I did not like it. I did not want it there. I gasped and choked on my own breath as the doors opened and I stepped, unhurried, inside.

I could do this. I could do it for the chance to save the man with bird messengers and obscure verses.

"You don't want to be here," Margaretta said sympathetically as I tried to compose myself. "You feel trapped. Trust me. I know the feeling. It will pass."

"Thank you," I choked out. "Will you go back now to your pedestal?"

"I think you might need me or a bit longer. And we're practically sisters since we're both from Pensmoore."

She nodded gravely as if to impress on me the importance of our faux sisterhood while I tried to compose myself enough to breathe. I hadn't expected compassion. It was surprisingly touching. So much so that I hardly knew what to do with it.

Lady Tanglecott's entranceway was barely larger than a closet and completely dark. A door led further into her house – so close I could have reached out and touched both it and the front door at the same time. A light glowed around the edges of it, inviting me to move on. But I needed to breathe first.

In and out. Come on, Izolda. It wasn't practical to panic when I'd come so far already. It was just that now that I was in her house, I could see all the ways it might go wrong – and if I failed, I didn't just fail for me – I failed for him, too.

"The real entertainment is in here," Grosbeak said. "You saw the crowd wanting to get in. And I have front row seats! Ah, sweet afterlife, you have loved me well."

"Do you take him everywhere with you?" Margaretta asked, staring at my bag.

"He's less trouble when you keep him close."

Margaretta and Grosbeak snorted at the exact same moment.

"I've decided you need a friend very badly," Margaretta said, drawing her narrow shoulders back in a determined fashion. "And I think it will be me."

"I wouldn't get too attached. She'll only be here for a day," Grosbeak warned me and then turned to her. "You shouldn't get attached either. She's very hard on the rest of the cast in this little drama of hers."

I felt the beginning of the kind of smile that creeps up your face slowly like the dawn and I leaned into it, letting my gratitude for Margaretta wash over me, but before it had fully formed, the doors to the rest of the house were yanked open and golden light framed the silhouette of Lady Tanglecott in all her beauty.

She snapped her fingers and Margaretta disappeared.

Before I could even gasp, Lady Tanglecott intoned, "The Lord giveth and the Lady taketh away. I will not tolerate strays within my home. Come now, bound one, and receive your due."

After the silky sweetness of Princess Margaretta, her very presence was like a sharp slap. Like drinking vinegar after apple cider. Like biting into a heat pepper after a strawberry.

"I told you not to get too attached." Grosbeak snickered. He was getting his drama just like he'd hoped.

CHAPTER ELEVEN

"My due?" The words were hardly out of my mouth before she threw something into my face – a powder, I thought. I sneezed and then the world went black.

I woke to the sound of lapping waves and the brightest sun I'd ever seen. It was as if a heavenly body had sprung to consciousness and arranged a personal vendetta against me.

I could not move, but I felt my limbs being kept in an awkward position. I was arranged so that I lay on my left side with my left shoulder and hip pressed against the ground. My right leg was bent so that it was standing on its foot, the knee in the air, my left leg sprawled where it had fallen on the ground. My right hand was turned upward, elbow slightly bent, palm flat, and my head was placed on top of something that pressed it up from the ground so I could see out toward rock and rolling waves and just a little above me up into the sky.

Something soft pressed against my left cheek. It groaned.

And if I could have screamed, I would have. The elongated horror my face was frozen into would have to suffice. Inside, my mind was screaming, "Get it off! Get it off!" My mouth made not a sound.

To my utter revulsion, the squishy thing under my cheek was

Grosbeak. The softness was his tangled mass of drowned hair and the slow decay of his flesh. He'd said the flies were gone, hadn't he? But there were crabs. Had I felt one brush my cheek? Oh, no, no, no.

"Izolda?" he asked, and his voice sounded gritty. "Are you conscious?"

"Oh, she can hear you just fine," Lady Tanglecott drawled, setting a polished sheet of clear glass on my knee and hand. "Hmm, good but still a little bit unsteady."

She drew out Look and Despair from my bag. She was frozen standing completely straight on her hind legs. Tangecott wedged her under the glass to make a third leg. She looked as though a taxidermist had taken his job too figuratively and tried to impress upon the viewer not only the form of his stuffed animal skin, but also the last emotions and thoughts running through its head when it was caught.

I wished I could swallow down the terrible suspicion that I looked the same way.

"We agreed to three days and three nights, Izolda," Tangecott said, with a waspish smile. "We did not agree on how they would be spent. Today, you will serve as my table. You're not pretty enough to wait the table, and your left hand is a terrifying thing – what madness possessed you to strip it of flesh? – but you are perfectly capable of having drinks set upon you. If no one at this council grows so enraged that they smash the furniture, you should suffer through this with nothing but your dignity taken." She paused to laugh – a light tinkling laugh as one might expect from a fairy in a story. "A word of advice – you should close your mouth. Something might crawl into it."

I wanted to scream. I wanted to cry. I wanted to rage. Instead,

I stayed completely frozen as Lady Tanglecott laid out drinks on the table above me.

"How disappointing," Grosbeak said from his place beneath my cheek. I felt his head vibrate as he spoke. "I'd hoped for better than this, Lady Tanglecott. Disabling your competitors is such a boring move."

"It serves more than one purpose today, revenant," she said calmly. "I won't be manipulated into changing it. Not by you not by anyone."

"And yet you let me keep my voice. Perhaps, you couldn't take it. Perhaps, the dead are immune to your charms. Or perhaps you are struck with fear. This is the first game that has seen so many competitors removed from the board along with their pieces. I recall only one player losing his life in the past five games combined and now we have lost two. Are you afraid you might be next?"

Tanglecott crouched down low, still graceful even while her perfect oval face drew level with our ghoulish ones.

"My dear disgraced servant of the Arrow." Her voice was refined as a harp in perfect tune. "You suffer under the misapprehension that I care to hear your commentary. Silence yourself, or you will be returned to the sea. And I shall accommodate you with a swift kick of my pretty slippered foot."

She stood, straightening as easily as a willow freed from a heavy snow, and then lifted her translucent skirt and wiggled a foot set in a perfectly cut and faceted crystal slipper.

"Are you really wearing a glass slipper?" Grosbeak snickered. "Like from a Witenbrand tale told by mortals?"

A quick flick of her ankle and I felt the impact on his head below mine. A spike of fear shot through me at my proximity, helpless and trapped.

"Your point is taken," he said in a slightly muffled voice and then I heard him spit, and on the rock where I'd been placed a tooth bounced and tinkled, leaving a tiny trail of blackened blood.

"Keep it ever in your heart," she said charmingly and glided away.

She left nothing to look at but the glaring sun, the creamy rock, and beyond it a sea so azure, so perfect, so wreathed in rainbows that it hardly felt real at all.

"We still have front row seats," Grosbeak whispered. "That's worth a little indignity."

Front row seats to what? My humiliation and eventual death? I was as stuck as a fly in honey. As trapped as a mouse in a bucket. I wanted to scream.

"Did you know we aren't far from the place your husband stands vigil under the waves? I can almost see it from here."

And just like that, there was fire in my heart again.

CHAPTER TWELVE

I would have thought that by now I was an expert in the briny humors of the sea. I'd watched more than one afternoon move from lazy doldrums to pounding breakers. The Wittenhame surpassed even the greatest transformation. In the space of a long breath, she transformed utterly.

I breathed in and a dozen mermaids leapt from the crystal-clear calm of the azure waves, their hair as tangled as Grosbeak's, their teeth snapping like attacking sharks, and their fish bodies flashing in the bright sun. A song, haunting and sharp all at once, four harmonies interweaving through it, burst out like a clap of thunder as if songs could be war trumpets.

In the time it took to let out that same breath, the siren mermaids had fallen back into the sea without a splash, their song gone, and in its place, the sky turned to a mulish grey, the clouds bubbling up along the horizon, thick and roiling as a pot boiling over. As if to mock the smooth surface I'd witnessed, the sea erupted into powerful waves, tossed one way and then the next as if by changeable childish hands, their roar unsettling in its power.

"A Storm Clock has been declared," Grosbeak said over the sound. He waited but he must have realized I couldn't answer. "That means the participants of the meeting must all arrive before the first rain drop falls or they are barred from attendance, and the meeting will be over the moment the storm clears. It's usually agreed upon beforehand. While the storm is in place, there can be no violence between participants. We, I fear, have no such sanctuary."

Of course.

In the distance, I felt like I could still hear the echo of the siren song calling to me. It seemed, almost, as if my very name was woven into the strands of the song and the beating waves of the sea. Perhaps sirens really could lure people to their deaths just with a song, because that echo seemed to touch every part of me from the inside out.

Light footsteps tapped along the rock and then someone peered down at me. It was Marshyellow. I shivered as I realized he was holding two things in his ancient papery hands. In one, he held a delicate piece of linen, sewn all over with flowers in the exact pattern my mother had taught me, and in the other, he held my flesh and blood hand, severed at the wrist, pinkie lifted as it danced a silver needle through the cloth.

Something like bile rose in my frozen throat. I fought it back, terrified of what vomiting would be like with my mouth frozen and pointing upward. I'd likely choke and die on my own revulsion.

"Lovely sampler, Marshyellow," Grosbeak snickered. "Think you to sell your needlework at fairs? You'd make a fine shop-mistress indeed. You have just the smile for merchantry. I'd watch that hand with care, though. Every part of its owner has drawn only trouble as shavings to a lodestone."

"A talking stump and a stumping talk," Marshyellow said absently before he withdrew. I heard a chair scrape somewhere behind my head and a whiff of ancient man came from that direction.

The words of our bargain came back to me: *Binding to it now all that was bound to you and offering to you its many skills.* He was a fool to have brought my hand with him, for though it showed off my skill with a needle, all I had to do was find a way to snatch it back and I would have all that was bound to him. My fingers itched to do just that. I'd crafted the bargain carefully to be double-edged – even though I'd thought it was about marriage and not about a physical hand. And despite his current mental state, he was a lord of the Wittenhame, and it should have occurred to him to keep it hidden.

I was startled out of my musings by a new voice. Lady Tanglecott's glass slippers tapped on the rock again as she led someone new to the table.

Lord Coppertomb looked down through the glass at my frozen face and if I could have cowered back further from his regular features and angular-cut plum doublet, I would have. He disguised deviousness under simplicity and a tangled mind under a blank face.

"You don't like my trophy wife?" Lady Tanglecott asked in a tinkling voice.

"I don't think you can call someone else's wife you've taken as a trophy a *trophy* wife," Coppertomb said dryly. "It's not an accurate use of idiom."

"Whyever not?" she asked coyly as he seated himself.

"Sooth. Be not insulted. I brought you a gift, Lady of Ilkanmoore." His tone was so dusty it could have made a frog sneeze.

"A gift? Your presence alone is a gift, Prince of Wittenbrand."

He lifted a narrow eyebrow, reached into his doublet, and produced a diamond the size of my ear, strung on three strands of braided black pearls.

"They call it the Heart of the Ocean and you know full well its true nature and provenance," he said, flicking it with a finger so that it spun. At the heart of the gem, a flaw ran down the center that made rainbows dance from its surface when it twisted like that.

"Why such a gift, my lord?" Tanglecott asked and to my surprise, I realized the emotion I saw in her eyes was fear.

"Why not?" he asked, boldly. "When you can best make use of it."

She swallowed and perhaps my angle was the best because I could see where a tiny bead of sweat had formed on her brow and was running down the side of her cheek. It smacked the glass and spread into a flat, wavering droplet. Tanglecott laughed falsely, took the rich gift in her hand, and tucked it into her skirts where a pocket must have been hidden.

"Well, since we are giving gifts, you're welcome to take the trophy wife's pet," she said gesturing.

Coppertomb ducked his head under the table and ran a finger down Look and Despair's chin and chest.

"Delightful though she is, I have rodents of my own already."

"I meant the other one."

"I do not collect heads. Unlike the Arrow, I need none but myself to advise me," he said in a clipped manner, his expression set with vexation.

"Do as you please," Lady Tanglecott said lightly, moving to greet a new guest, but I found the exchange interesting. These two who I had thought were fierce allies were riddled with tension and doubt. I could work with that, if I could just find a way.

"I see you down there, wife of the Arrow," Coppertomb said lightly, smiling out at the gathering storm. There was a yellow tinge to the sky I did not like. It stood out like a bruise against the dark clouds. "Did you enjoy watching your lord and master sink into the heart of the ocean? Does it thrill you to know he's been stolen to be the groom of the sea just as he stole you? Revenge, I have always thought, is a dish both sweet and bitter. Sweet in the tasting, bitter in the aftertaste."

I desperately wanted to ask what that meant. It was the second time it had been suggested that my husband was lover to the sea.

"Did it cheer you to see him offer up his days to another against his will just as you offered yours? Did you savor the vengeance?" He paused as if something had just occurred to him. "Or are you still his plaything even now? His tidy pet to display and direct? Yes, I see that look in your eyes and I know what it means. You're his creature yet. Hmm." He rubbed his chin and looked at me with speculation. "Do not think I am finished with you. Banishment was only the beginning. Your uses are numerous and I will wear you out like a well-worn rag."

A mental shiver rolled through me despite the fact my actual body was frozen.

"Ooooh, big words," Grosbeak crowed. "Challenge her then, Coppertomb! Set her a challenge or a riddle or offer her a bargain. Or maybe ride against her in this Joust. Wouldn't that be a delight to watch? I've heard rumors you're not much of a seat in the lists and upon speculation, I've not seen you ride. Mayhap you'd be only just a match for a mortal woman."

I did not care for Grosbeak cajoling further repercussions from my tormentor, but I could not prevent him. Instead, I focused on every word my enemies spoke. Who knew if there might be a key in one of them that might open my way to save my husband before it was too late?

"I will do none of those things, cadaver. She is a plaything – and a treacherous one, at that. She is such a fool that she bought her own doom with a day. So insidious, she wormed her way into the heart of my enemy and hollowed him as ants hollow a log. If she lives in hell now, she bought every second of it herself. Why would I offer her any relief? I'll give her not one drop of balm, not one ripple of sweet water. If I choose to use her, I will make her feet dance, whether she wills it or no. I need not puzzles, bargains, games, or riddles to make her my pawn. I need only my will and her weak mortal flesh."

The echo of the siren song grew louder as if it were – somehow – trying to dull the pain of his accusations, rising as they rose, rocking me gently in the song like a babe in the cradle.

"I think your fears outstrip your creativity. I could invent better vengeances than you claim to devise," Grosbeak said with a snicker. "But fear not, I'm sure creativity is not required to win your game and you have all the allies you need to conquer the whole of the world and eat it up like a round of rye."

Coppertomb snorted. "I see why they keep you, carrion. You're droll as a fifty-day-mummer. Perhaps I will take you as my party gift, after all. You can amuse the denizens of my dungeons and dull the pain of those trapped in amber beneath my floors."

Grosbeak's mouth shut with a snap.

Coppertomb looked away from us leisurely but then his gaze

snapped back to me. "I see you loaned a hand to a friend, mortal girl. How revealing."

The raindrops were falling harder now, steaming whenever they hit Coppertomb. Someone came with drinks, placing Coppertomb's goblet in such a way that it hid most of his face from me.

My muscles were starting to cramp – never mind that I couldn't move them even if I wanted to. They screamed at me, agonized and painful. I tried to think of something else, anything else, and then – finally – Tanglecott's voice spoke again.

"We asked you here because we find ourselves short a fourth."

"A fourth?" The voice was unfamiliar. Masculine with a hint of nobility and an edge of an accent I did not know. "Were you three scheming with the Sword before he stepped on his own ear so painfully? Or was it the Arrow who chose to die for *love*?"

A note sounded as if someone had plucked the string of an instrument and the specter around my neck slid her dead hand up across my jaw and clamped over my open mouth. I felt far more of it than I ever wanted. My heart pounded with panic. What if she reached down my throat and …?

"Ah!" the newcomer said, and I strained my eyes trying to see, but he was over my shoulder entirely. I could see the edges of Tanglecott and Marshyellow but not a shred of this man. "I see you've sworn yourselves to secrecy and why wouldn't you – and yet even in this you have shown the edge of your slip. Have you not, lady and lords? For is that not the widow of the Arrow beneath the table and is her mouth not bound, too? I see you cannot speak of it, but it worries me that you would ally yourselves to the Arrow and yet allow him to slip beneath the waves to gain yourselves one less competitor. Would you not do the same to me?"

Widow? My heart sped up, my breathing gasping and hitching. He said it as if it were obvious. Was I too late, then? Had the sea made my husband her lover and then torn him apart as she did so many sailors in the mortal world?

"That's Lord Antlerdale, I would swear on it," Grosbeak hissed for my ear only.

"We may not disclose," Lady Tanglecott cut off, and though I could see no specter on her shoulder, one must even now be gagging her. Interesting. Perhaps they could not see my specter, either, unless they were searching for it.

Coppertomb seamlessly picked up from where Tanglecott had left off. "While there may be histories better left untouched, we know who we address. We are not strangers to your ways, Antlerdale."

"He's a serial monogamist," Grosbeak snickered to me – quietly enough that those above us could pretend they hadn't heard. "You'd think the old adage would be true, 'Who could ever learn to love a beast?' but in his case, they line up – still do when he's not occupied with this century's love of his life. Ghastly thing to do to women, keeping them locked up in an eternal library until they die, and you replace them all over again with that 'I'm under a curse, help me!' beast routine, but I suppose some people like thick beards and roaring."

There was so much I wanted to say to that.

Coppertomb's foot kicked out, seeming at random, and Grosbeak *ooffed* in pain.

"Consider," Grosbeak said through what sounded like thicker dead lips, "if anyone knows histories, it's him. He hoards books in that library the way your husband hoards severed heads. It's disgusting. Shelves and shelves of butchered trees shoved right up against each other and," here he gasped, "cataloged. I'll say this for your husband. He doesn't cataloge his trophies. He gives us that small dignity."

"The head has the right of it," Antlerdale said calmly from above. "I've read my share. And that's why you worry me. I hear reports that your people lay siege to Wittentree even as I sit here, Lady Tanglecott. They say her island is selling birds' nests and cat hearts for the price of a good estate, so starved are they. You'll have dragged down another of us before this treaty is whispered so much as signed. What do you need me for?"

The rain was coming down hard now, flowing around me so high that my left boot was full and tugging off and my skirts felt like they weighed a thousand pounds. Grosbeak's voice was muffled by water when he spoke.

"A faithful man, Lord Antlerdale and steady. When a thing works once, he never deviates. He won't join them," my advisor said through the streaming water.

"Won't he?" Tanglecott's voice sounded amused, pitched though it was over the torrent. "You'd be surprised who turns to our cause."

Behind everything, I still heard the siren song, but now the echo was only my name over and over and over forever.

"*Izolda, Izolda, Izolda, Izolda.*"

Perhaps that last crossing directly into the Wittenhame had hollowed my mind as surely as Marshyellow's.

"Tempt me then, lady," Antlerdale said. "And not with your flesh of which I have no need, nor of your goodwill of which there is none to be had."

"Pensmoore," she said softly. "I'll have it as my own by the end of this Three Day Bind. Surely you've heard of the bargain I've struck with the wife of the Arrow."

"Rumors reach even my ears, though they are mostly speculations about this coming joust. You'll be riding in it, of course. How will that influence this comradery?"

Coppertomb seemed unable to help interjecting. "You're as bound as we are, Antlerdale. We can't go where we aren't welcomed, can't steal the mortal nations unless it be by marriage, blood, or pact. You've only the nation you were dealt. What is it? Ptoolemoore? Soaking up the Sword's madness as his people flee in droves to your land. Rumors say you're close to taking Ayyadmoore for yourself. It's a respectable conquest on a map, but in reality, we both know what it means – thousands of hungry mouths. Thousands of fatherless orphans. A hundred thousand headaches. More land, less army, drawn-out, weakened, and ripe for attack." I felt Antlerdale shift uncomfortably. Coppertomb's assessment was accurate. "But if you had Pensmoore – well, that's a well-fortified nation. One that came through years of war with a king and lands and prosperity of a kind. It could anchor your holdings in the north, feed the country south of it, and shore up a lace-woven land for you. What fool would turn his back on that?"

"What fool indeed," Antlerdale sounded sour but thoughtful. "And you will have the lands to offer me in three days."

"Two after this one and three nights. You could have it on the third morning," Lady Tanglecott said smoothly.

"I wouldn't bet on it," Grosbeak said darkly.

"I think *I* will," Antlerdale said steadily. "The price is only my part in this foul alliance?"

"Don't call what is fair foul, Antlerdale," Coppertomb scolded. "Not when together we can endure past the others."

"And then?" Antlerdale asked, a note of anticipation in his voice.

"And then the gloves will fall and each of us may use tooth or claw or a poisoned kiss to bring down the rest."

"Agree and we will bind you as we are bound," Lady Tanglecott said a little too quickly.

Antlerdale laughed. "When the three days are up, Tanglecott. Not before time. I'll make no move until I know your promise is certain."

The rain had slowed now, but the chant went on in my mind.

"*Izolda, Izolda, Izolda.*" In my madness, it had begun to sound like that voice most dear to me.

"Then we four shall meet again, three days hence," Coppertomb said formally.

"Three days porridge hot, three days porridge cold," Marshyellow agreed.

"*Izolda, Izolda, Izolda.*"

"Three days," Antlerdale and Tanglecott agreed in unison, and then as if a candle had been snuffed, the rain stopped, and the sun blazed through the clouds.

I heard the sound of feet as everyone rose, and then Coppertomb's mouth formed a look halfway between a cold sneer and an amused smirk as he looked through the glass table at me. He lifted his goblet and brought it down on the table with a crash and I couldn't even scream when a sliver of glass went into my mouth and another into my open eye as the rest rained down around me in a shattered shower of knife-like shards.

"Tsk, tsk," said Tanglecott. "No need to kill her right away, Coppertomb. We have days and days for that. Come when you're ready, Izolda. If you can."

And then their feet echoed on the stone path, but I was still frozen in place as the voice that had been chanting my name so steadily paused and said, "*Izolda?*"

And in desperation, I asked back, "*Bluebeard?*"

But there was no response except the agonizing emptiness in my chest where once my heart dwelled, matched only by the emptiness in his chest where once there was a rib he gave for me.

CHAPTER THIRTEEN

It was hours before my frozen body finally loosened and collapsed. Hours in which I had been stuck with my open eyes streaming both tears and blood, my open mouth parched to sand, that sliver of glass balanced precariously on my tongue. Hours in which I still heard my name sung intermittently in the most mournful of tones. I clung to it. Mad or not, it was all I had.

I drifted. I dreamed. And in my dream, I heard my Bluebeard saying his vows to me once again, as if we were still on that platform as he confessed them and I swore them with him, each unable to move to the other's side.

"*As long as rivers run and moon shines, as long as the earth has bones and death has claws, as long as the ages pass and fail – that long shall I be husband to you. Flesh of my flesh and bone of my bone you will be. Spirit of my spirit. Heart of my own heart. Fall what may, we shall be one. My body, I dedicate to none other. My days shall be yours and your happiness my own. The bounty of my wealth is yours. If ever it be otherwise, may I waste away with sickness and may famine eat my strength and may my enemies overtake me, and siphon from me the blood of my life.*"

And my heart ached with the memory for he had broken no vows – not a single one. He had been nothing but true to me.

He had given for me his rib and his future. And I was determined that it should end there. I was determined that he should not give his life.

I would lose my own flesh before I agreed to lose his. I felt a hot tear slide from my eye as I thought of my hand. I missed it yet – and still, it was no sacrifice if only I could draw him back from the depth. I would lose my own spirit before I agreed to lose his.

My heart I could not offer. It was already taken, conquered, occupied.

The sea and storm became placid as my mind raged as if it were somehow mollified by my misery.

And through all my revelations and internal passions, Grosbeak complained miserably beneath me.

"If she doesn't release you soon, you're sure to fail your tasks. You can't spend the night in her bed if you can't get to her bed. But she can't make it impossible. That would break the rules of the Three Day Bind. The spectators would revolt."

He went on to tell me of four other times he'd witnessed a Three Day Bind – all quasi-marriage-like, or quasi-kidnap-like depending on how one viewed it. I sympathized with the victims of these forced arrangements, but their stories gave me no hints on how to survive this. Grosbeak seemed much keener on the perpetrators. There was no surprise there. At the heart of him, Grosbeak was a crime waiting to happen.

"Antlerdale tried one before his current arrangement with mortals. It was with one of the Tanglecott folk – a lovely creature, mostly dryad. It's all in his book. They say she chose to root herself to one of his grandfather clocks and hide in the woodgrain there rather than suffer marriage to him." He started to laugh and then stopped. "Poor Antlerdale. He has more remnants of past wives around his house than your Bluebeard does. Love, is not for the Wittenbrand – not if you want to keep it for more than a fortnight. You should remember that, Izolda. Joint purpose, deadly cause, and pacts of murder are far more likely to last."

I had grown so weary of his voice that by the time my body finally collapsed, his sudden silence was relief. I clamped my tongue hard on the glass piece as I fell, and to my relief, I trapped it against the roof of my mouth.

The rest of my body was not spared. My living hand – raised all this time above my head – was lifeless and numb. My right leg was similarly asleep. My eyes had shut involuntarily as I plummeted and the one with the glass sliver in it screamed in pain – along with every muscle of my body and most of the bones. I was a living scream made flesh. Mercifully, I slipped from my balance atop Grosbeak's head and I lay sprawled on shattered glass, a discarded, broken doll.

A small squeak told me the ferret was in the same condition.

"Get up," Grosbeak demanded. "If you have an hour left, I'm a Neverwatch Eve goose."

I neither knew nor cared what that was. Awkwardly and with every bit of strength I still possessed, I rolled onto my back, flopping like a fish drawn from the water and left to suffocate in the emptiness of the sky.

Carefully, I drew my skeletal hand up to my lips and plucked the sliver of glass from my tongue. It is a complicated thing to extract a sliver of smooth glass with two smooth phalanges – more complicated than I had imagined. After the course of several desperate minutes, it was finally out, my tongue only slightly cut. I was left quivering as an agony of pins and needles flooded my right side.

This is good, I tried to remind myself. You need the feeling back.

"Izolda, Izolda, Izolda," the sea half-crooned and half-sobbed.

I looked out toward the horizon as I tried to catch my breath, wondering if I could simply walk beneath the waves and go to him. I could feel him in my heart – so close but so far away. So precious to me and so unattainable.

It was a childish fantasy. I was mortal. I breathed air. I had no business thinking otherwise. I was delirious, my brain looping and drifting when I needed it to focus.

And why was the sea so cloudy?

I lifted my skeletal hand and closed my left eye.

Oh no.

I could not see at all from the right eye – the one with the glass splinter.

Panicked, I scrambled up to sitting.

"Blood of Gods and Men! You're cutting yourself on the glass! Fool of a mortal!"

I crawled out from the glass, stunned as if I'd been knocked flat by a runaway cart, and kept crawling to where the rock overlooked the brackish water.

I peered down with my one good eye and watched my reflection in the calm sea as a drop of red blood rolled from my wounded eye into the water. It struck like ink in a dish of clear water, spreading, muddying. That eye was white already. Didn't it take years for an eye to glass over like that? Even a dead eye? I had not the experience to know.

"Scars and sires, Izolda. Do you see how low the sun has slunk? Like a lover caught with another woman, it creeps away, head hung low."

"Poetic." My voice felt like it belonged to another.

From where the blood had dropped a torrid ripple spread.

As it spread, the chant of my voice faded away. No more song to sing me through.

I sighed and turned. There was no point in panicking about what had already happened.

Look and Despair lay on her back looking miserable but alive. She'd escaped the slivers of glass and as I watched she flipped over very slowly and crept to huddle beside Grosbeak. He looked none the worse for the latest episode. It was hard to get worse than long dead. There was a pearl clipped under a few layers of crusted hair. Had that been there before?

I swallowed, trying to work moisture back into my mouth. In a moment, I would have to stand and face the challenge of finding Lady Tanglecott's bedroom. No time for misery or self-pity. No time to mourn an eye. I gathered myself, preparing to stand, and then a hand slid from behind me and covered my mouth.

The spirit? What had I tried to say that she would censor me?

But no, this hand was cold and clammy. I reached up to fight the grasp and then it spun me, and I was face to face with something that seemed half-woman, half-monster. She smelled heavily of brine as she paused, half in the sea and half out. Her skin gleamed and flashed like a trout's, her eyes were large, round, and protruded too far and her hair hung in tangled skeins, decorated with debris that must have caught in it – a strand of sickly yellow seaweed here, a bit of blush shell there, a generous helping of sand and several skittering crabs so much like Grosbeak's that suspicions dawned.

"Uungantha!" he said, and his voice was worshipful. "Who are we that the most glorious maid of the sea should visit us?"

She didn't even look at him. Her mottled black and silver hand flew up and she put one finger to her lips. I barely had time to note that her fingers were shaped oddly before her other hand darted out and she snatched me, ripping me from the air into the sea. I struggled, thrashing in the brine, sucking in a mouthful of awful brackish water as she pawed at my face with her fishy hand, obscuring what vision I had left. Don't panic or you'll drown, I told myself. Don't panic.

I felt pain in my eye and saw a glimmer of something glittering and red-streaked between her grasping fingers. To my surprised horror, her fish lips brushed mine and then she hauled me from the water as if I weighed no more than today's catch and flung me onto the rocky shore. I crouched there, gasping in breath, as she turned, leapt as a salmon leaps, and re-entered the sea with a nearly silent splash.

I could see. In both eyes, I could see. I was coughing up half the sea, my lungs screaming, my hair dripping around me like weeds and my lovely dress ruined, but I could see.

Who would have imagined?

I swallowed hard, trying to herd my thoughts back like a goatherd with an unruly flock.

"Most glorious," Grosbeak said, longing thick in his voice. "What little sentiment still dwells within me reaches for her. You are honored above mortal women, wife of the Arrow. Honored more than you know."

I pulled myself unsteadily up the rock and to my feet, eyes locked on the ocean. I wanted to follow the violent mermaid to wherever she had gone. I knew a gift when I saw one. And I knew who had to have given it to me.

Even wrapped up in bonds of damning fate, his heart bent to mine. I could not save him from the worst agony and yet he saved me from the least.

I peered into the sea – calm again – but there was nothing there except my own reflection and it stared back at me with two good eyes and a streak of blood running down my right cheek. His sign. His red teardrop.

I gasped, pulled back, and with my flesh hand, I lifted the ferret to my shoulder where she slumped half-dead across it like a lazy stole. The specter peered at me from the other shoulder, misery running cold in her eyes. With my skeletal hand, I gathered up Grosbeak by the weeds he called hair and turned toward land.

"Let us find Lady Tanglecott's bedroom and let us best her at her own tricks, friends," I said.

"If you do either of those things, you'll do better than I expect," Grosbeak said. "But by all means, try not to die today. I'll just be here mourning my one true love."

"I thought you loved only yourself."

"Yes, that's who I'm mourning. You did know I was dead, did you not?"

CHAPTER FOURTEEN

I turned around and around on the rock. There was no obvious way to leave it. On two sides, the waves crashed, spraying everything with brine. To one side a bog lay, thick with reeds and showing no obvious path, to the other side a forest – but this was a tangle of bushes, fallen trees, and driftwood driven high up past the rocks by storm waters and unpredictable tides. It looked like the sort of place a traveler might be lured into that they may be lost for a hundred years. Between the two, a sluggish yellow smoke rose from a tear in the moss cover of the forest floor. I could not see a fire making it.

A raven peered down from one of the trees, seeming almost familiar, though it paid me no mind.

To make matters worse, the occasional face appeared in the clouds or the knot of a tree and then vanished just as quickly. They sent icy spikes down my spine every time I caught sight of one of them.

"Anxiety doesn't suit you, princess of Pensmoore," Grosbeak said after the third time. "You're jumping at the faces of spectators. They come only to watch your drama unfold."

"Perhaps they could offer some suggestions on how to get to Lady Tanglecott's house," I muttered.

"We're in her house already," he said, waggling his eyebrows.

I lifted his head and peered into his face grimly. "Listen to me, Grosbeak, you horrible dead corpse, you repulsive harbinger. If you know how to get out of this place and closer to where I need to be right now, you had best tell me."

I shook him, trying not to mind the small crabs that fell from his tangled locks. One skittered onto my bone hand, slipped, and fell to the ground.

"And spoil the fun?" he said between rattling teeth. "There are bets riding on this. I bet the specter a pair of crabs and a tertiary secret that you'd lose."

"The specter thinks I'll win?"

The specter leaned around so I could see her silent smile. She looked smug.

"I'm gratified I have someone's confidence, at least. But as to you, Grosbeak, I could throw you back into the sea," I said firmly. "No, even better. I could set you down in the swamp and leave you there. I hear there are interesting bugs in swamps. Would it give you joy to have a new infestation?"

He shivered. "Would you lose your guide to the Wittenhame so easily?"

"I would if he didn't guide me. You said you were my friend, but you acquit the post poorly."

He bit his lip. "Fine. Fine. Don't take such a look with me, Izolda. We each have to find our own way and I'm only trying to keep my path smooth, in a manner of speaking."

I poked his cheek with my skeletal finger, and he flinched.

"It's the smoke. I think," he said hurriedly. "Her house is likely sitting in a different dimension only accessed by scent and the smoke will likely take you there. You just inhale. But make sure I do as well, or we'll be in two different dimensions and that will be very, very uncomfortable."

I strode toward the smoke as Grosbeak began to sing the old song that saved me last time I was in the Wittenhame. For such a terrible singer, he certainly loved the sound of his own voice. He let it warble and wander and sang with the gusto of a tavern maid newly hired.

I was grateful for the distraction. An entirely different song kept on echoing through my mind, and it felt like base treachery to turn my back on the man in the sea and walk toward land.

"*Fly with the Arrow,*

Dance With the Sword,

Give your Heart to the Barrow,

Die With your Lord."

"*With* your Lord?" I asked, interrupting Grosbeak. I was inspecting the smoke. It was a black-laced yellow and I didn't like the way it shifted toward my face no matter where I stood or how I leaned. It was giving off the scent of cedar and gingerbread. "Not *for* your Lord? As in during a battle or trying to achieve his aims?"

"It's definitely *with*," Grosbeak said nastily. "And maybe you should get that part right since you've done the rest."

"Are you saying all I have to do now is die?"

"It's inevitable, wouldn't you say? One last piece of a puzzle."

I rather hoped he was wrong. I was not in the mood to die.

"You are mortal. Have you forgotten that? Brushing shoulders with your betters doesn't change your twilight life. It's over almost before it begins. I'll barely be finished introducing you to the Wittenhame and already you'll have withered and died and I'll have to find someone new to protect me from my fate as the Arrow's trinket."

"Are you sure we have to inhale this smoke?" I asked, wondering what might happen to me if I did. I didn't trust the Wittenhame or the tricks of the Wittenbrand. I'd have to if I accepted breathing in this smoke, but I'd rather know more about what awaited me.

"Lily-liver," he accused. "Callow heart."

I shook my head. He was more nuisance than a help.

I stepped into the smoke and inhaled long and hard. On my shoulders, the ferret and the specter both coughed and then the smoke cleared and we were at the foot of a glass staircase. Through the glass steps, the bog and forest could be seen, but if I followed them with my eyes, they opened up to a crystal balcony above and a wall filled with open windows and misty curtains waving in the wind.

"Ah," Grosbeak said, stopping his mockery for a moment to cough horribly as if he were going to die right there. "The mist dimension. You should have expected that with her affection for Mist Lions. Well, carry on, then."

He went back to his song.

"*Sing for your sovereign,*

Bow to your dream

Make haste for the fallen,

Rise in esteem."

The words "make haste for the fallen" skittered up my spine. What if I wasn't fast enough? What if I ruined everything?

"Perhaps we should try entering quietly," I hissed as I crept up the glass stairs. It was a terrible feeling to climb them. I kept feeling like each step would sink right through and I'd fall on the rocks beneath, which in turn was replaced with fear of falling into the trees beneath, and that in turn with the misty clouds beneath. It took all my nerve to mount them as the sun sank lower and lower toward the horizon, bleeding out across the Wittenhame like a fallen foe.

Even worse, I could see all the spectators peering up through the glass stairs, grinning, or leering, or licking their lips hungrily.

Worst of all was that never-ending feeling of betrayal with every step I took that propelled me further from the sea.

"Ignore me all you want," Grosbeak said primly, "But you'll be sorry you did if you forget the words to the song. After all, it helped you once. It might help you again."

"That's all well and good," I said, feeling a little dizzy now that I was so high up with nothing to hold onto but my drowned friend and nothing beneath me but invisible stairs. "But I don't exactly know how to sing for my sovereign or bow to my dream."

"You didn't know how to hold up your fine token and that still worked out," he said smugly.

We reached a door, but this one opened with a single touch, and I found myself in a glass room, with a glass floor over the clouds. Glass walls were barely discernable by their edges, glass decorations by the way the light bent around them. A glass grandfather clock filled the entrance, *tick, tick, tocking* away and glass doors decorated in glass scrollwork led from the hall to other rooms of the house.

"If you're so confident, then why are you betting against me?" I snapped at Grosbeak. All the glass was making my head ache. I couldn't tell where one thing ended and another began. I was going to walk into walls. And then they would shatter and I'd cut myself and fall to my death.

"What's the fun in only playing one side?"

My voice was tight with fear. "You are the worst of knaves and death has not succeeded in reforming you."

"And may it never succeed! I'd drink to that, but drinks are in short supply."

"I'd think that would be a pleasant turn of events after the last seven years of drinking the sea." But my heart was not in my words. I was rattled by this empty glass house.

"I think you'll find that closing your eyes helps," Grosbeak said blandly.

I closed my eyes, drew in a breath, and felt my way to the nearest door. I had no idea where I was going, but the red sun told me I didn't have much time to get there.

"Is the whole place like this?" My voice sounded small even to my own ears.

"Only in this dimension."

"How many dimensions are there?" I was feeling my way down a hall, door after door lined it and my heart was in my throat because I didn't know which one to try.

"How many do you want there to be?"

"One! I want there to be one clear, practical dimension."

"How utterly absurd. If you don't like this one, I'd inhale some more smoke, just be sure it's one where the house stays visible."

"How will I know?" And now I really did feel panicked. This was so far beyond me. Why had I thought I could trap the Wittenbrand when all they did was trap me again and again?

I smelled garlic and oranges and my eyes snapped open. I was standing in orange smoke. I must have blundered my way into another smoke pillar by mistake. Grosbeak was inhaling audibly beside me. I followed suit and reluctantly found myself in what felt like a rabbit warren inhabited by a human. Glowing silver footsteps that looked just like they might belong to glass slippers marked the down the hall, bypassing door after door.

I followed them, running now, until at last, I came to a door at the end of the hall. I opened the door and stepped right through a wave of pale pink smoke and then into a room with glass walls and a glass ceiling but a floor of wooden planks, a huge roaring fire, and a bed so high it should have been higher than any other ceiling could accommodate.

Through the glass walls, the sun had reduced to the merest red echo of light and darkness was swelling to fill the sky. And from the top of the bed, piled in mattresses, eiderdowns, furs, brocades, silks, and satins called a voice.

"Up here, Princess of Pensmoore. Up here on my bed of conquest by the time the last shadow reigns or you've lost your bargain."

I swallowed down a wave of worry and grabbed the side of the mountainous heap, jaw set and determined.

How hard could it be to climb up into a bed? I tied Grosbeak's hair to my belt, shuddering at how utterly disgusting he was. I was a practical girl. I could do what needed to be done. Even if it meant hanging severed heads from my belt.

I stood on tiptoe and reached up. My hand sank into something soft. A feather bed perhaps. I gripped it with my skeleton fingers and pulled, finding footing in the soft mattresses.

On my shoulder, the ferret squeaked weakly.

I pushed up a single step and checked the grip of my skeletal hand. It didn't tell me often enough what I was feeling.

My skeleton fingers were jammed in something soft, alright.

Someone's eye.

A beautiful, pale, pale man's staring white eye, his eyelashes frost white, tinged pink by the dying sun.

I screamed, lost my grip, and fell to the floor, rolling over just in time to projectile vomit across the wood floor and into the fire.

"Thank you," said the fire.

"You," I gasped, and it flared brightly.

"Teeth of the Gods that hurt," Grosbeak moaned. "What happened?"

"An eye," I gasped, wiping my mouth with the back of my living hand. The skeletal hand I held out far from the rest of me as if the simple touch might contaminate the rest of me. Perhaps I should scorch it in the fire to clean it. But would I feel that?

From my shoulder, the ferret chittered something and then climbed to balance on the top of my head. Her little claws dug into my scalp, making my skin crawl.

"I know," I muttered to her, "I don't like it either."

"On one of the dead men?" Grosbeak practically shrieked at me. "*That's* all? You'll need to be made of sterner stuff than that, my girl. Hurry! We're almost out of time!"

He was right. I could barely see the red thread of the sun anymore but the thing that worried me more was the phrase "one of."

I looked up at the bed a second time and this time, I saw what I had failed to see in the mess of drapery and blankets, quilts and coverlets, feather beds and mattresses. Squeezed between the layers lay open-eyed corpses. All male. All lovely, half-dressed, and all very, very, very dead.

Or at least, I hoped they were.

Because if they were not, then they might reach out and grasp me back as I climbed. Perhaps a wrist, or an ankle and then they might gobble me up.

The ferret chittered, claws tightening in my hair as if it had the same thought, and Grosbeak sighed.

"Don't tell me you're scared of a few dead men? A scrappy little thing like you? With the fate of your brother, your nation and that fool you call beloved all tied up in your success and failure?"

It was exactly the right thing to say. Heart in my throat, iron in my spine, I reached for the stack of mattresses again and began to climb. Who would do this? And why were none of the corpses rotting?

"They say these are her lovers," Grosbeak said, and I could hear the grin in his voice even though I couldn't see his face. "I dare say that the rumor is true. That looks very much the image of Cryptalis, and that poor fool mooned for Lady Tanglecott for all of the Moonless Fox Hunt before he went missing. Perhaps this is why. Perhaps she took him to her bed and decided to keep him forever."

"Surely someone would notice if all her lovers went missing," I said between gritted teeth.

"Notice? Of course. Care? I fear you have misjudged us yet again, Izolda. Why do you expect any of us to care about men unable to keep their own souls inside their bodies?"

"I care about you."

"Fool that you are, it seems that you do." His tone was dry as dust. "But don't blame me for that. I've done everything possible to disabuse you of any affection."

"Fool that I am," I agreed darkly. But it was not for him I was doing this but for my husband. It was for him and the possibility of freeing him. Three days. Three nights. And all I had to do was not die.

It had seemed easier before I was climbing past a steady stream of the corpses of those who had failed. Before I was looking into their dead, glassy eyes and taking in their states of dress or undress, now curled happily with face pillowed on a tangle of blanket, now sprawled half hanging from the morass with arms draped down like tree branches, now with only a single perfectly-formed arm sticking out of the mountain of soft covers. I shuddered.

"There's a tale in my land about a princess," I told Grosbeak as I climbed.

I felt something tickle the back of my mind, but I ignored it. I didn't dare lose my nerve now.

"Dead or living?"

"Living, in the tale."

He grunted as I ascended. The corpse nearest me held a golden dagger trimmed with gilt bees. A weapon that had not been enough to spare him. I swallowed back nausea at how much he looked like a perfect version of Svetgin. It could have been my brother tucked away in the last layer if not for me.

"A prince was thinking about marrying her, but he needed proof of her delicacy."

"That's not usually what they want proof of. Usually, mortals want childbearing hips. No scars from pox. Virginity. That sort of thing."

I coughed. "Anyways. He insisted on proof she was royal, so he insists she sleeps on ten mattresses without knowing why and secretly he placed a tooth from his childhood under the bottom mattress."

"That's dangerous magic there. You shouldn't waste childhood teeth on brides."

I kept climbing, face screwed up in concentration. How many layers were there? Did Lady Tanglecott just lay a new mattress over her last dead lover and start again?

"The next morning, she claims not to have been able to sleep all night and when they check she's bruised on her shoulder just from sleeping on the tooth, so he knows she's a true princess."

"Ha! No. She knows he's truly cursed because a single bone from his youth causes a malaise. She should stab him through the eye with a ruby dagger, or through the liver with a sapphire dagger, or if she only has iron, she could use it to pin his liver to a birch tree a one-mile distance from the rest of his body."

I was silent for a long moment, climbing. The man nearest me had a wing. It was broken in half, the bone jutting out in stark ivory and shrunken dried tendons between the black feathers. I retched, closing my eyes for a long moment.

"What would that achieve?" I asked at last.

"It would break the curse and eliminate it from haunting his descendants forever."

"I'm pretty sure that a basic murder would do the same thing."

I forced my eyes open and climbed further. Almost there. Almost. There.

"You never know, and you can't be too sure," Grosbeak said, knowingly. "What's the point of the tale?"

"I've forgotten. I just think that maybe Lady Tanglecott isn't a true princess since she sleeps every night on a lot more than teeth."

A hand reached over the edge and hauled me up to the top of the swaying bed.

"I never claimed to be a princess. I want so much more than that," my hostess said, and behind me, the last light of sunset winked out.

CHAPTER FIFTEEN

"By the time this Three Day Bind is complete, I plan to have doubled the kingdoms under my charge and be ready to crush my enemies, put them under the heel of my boot, and drag their miserable corpses through the slime of defeat." Lady Tanglecott's mouth formed a vicious bow.

"How lovely for you." My tone was dry as week-old bread.

All around us, through the glass walls and roof, the stars bloomed and flared, filling the sky so full they became a spill of froth across it, bright, pale, and unfurling. With them, the moon rose, silver, winking, and half full. I watched that sky warily. That was not the moon I'd left in the mortal world. How much time had passed?

A chilling *tick-tock, tick-tock* seemed to beat where my heart used to be.

"You do well to watch the heavens, Izolda. You must stay in this bed until the dawn breaks the night sky or our bargain is void." Tanglecott lay back against a wealth of pillows, her golden hair spilling around her like an unearned halo.

I took up a spot on the opposite corner of the mattress, legs crossed before me, back straight. I didn't dare sleep and I did not care for the uneven lumps beneath my straight spine.

"You should rest. The days will be eventful," she said, her eyes closing as she lay back.

"I have no certainty that, if I drift off, you will not fling me from this bed and into the fire."

"I hunger," roared the fire from below. A little spill of sparks emphasized his words.

Lady Tanglecott laughed, long and tinkling. "And spoil the fun? I think not. That fire has not visited me in two centuries and now he makes an appearance for your sake. Surely, you can see the delight in this charming pantomime. Besides, you're already destined to die of a broken heart. Why should I speed the process? I will plant my poison dart in your mind tonight and watch as it slowly takes you down. There is a wingless dragon in the southern isles – a miserable, unformed thing, slow as the mud of summer, ugly as your bodiless friend there," she pointed idly at Grosbeak. "But when this dragon bites, its poison lingers, slowing its prey, deadening its response, slowly draining the victim of life. I do so admire such an approach and I think to use it with you. Let us see how long you kick and thrash against the inevitable."

"How will you do that?" I asked, but my teeth were on edge, fear thick in the air around me. I caught the scent of oranges and fresh-washed linen. Had she filled the bed with more of her smoke to cloud my mind? Had she laced the sheets with poison – beyond the obvious poison of seeping corpses?

"With words, mortal girl. Are you not aware that is how we women fight? The jab of the insult aimed perfectly to strike the liver of your faults, the bludgeon of endless politeness barbed with the need to respond in kind, the twist of the compliment that shines false, the turn of the words that tilt your beloved out of your reach." Her smile was angelic. "It's been too long since I employed these well and now, I find myself surveying my arsenal and choosing the exact weapon required."

She tapped her chin.

"Is that what you did to these men in the mattresses?" I asked boldly.

She chuckled, low and sultry. "Ah, those lovely fools. Did you not enjoy observing their exquisite faces and sleek forms?"

"I prefer my men alive," I said pointedly.

She quirked an eyebrow. "As do I, but once I'm through, I hate to share. I'll not allow what's no longer needed to be claimed by another. Not with men. Not with nations. Not with anything."

Her hand hung idly from one wrist, and she plucked a golden curl from her bed, twirling it around her finger.

A chill flooded my senses. What would she do with me when this Three Day Bind was past? I was her plaything. She wouldn't want to share that.

She lounged, smiling like a cat watching a bird in a cage, her eyes bright and large.

"While you sleep here, perhaps you can be of some use to me. You seem good at riddles. See if you can learn the answer to this one. It's the latest from our sovereign, the Bramble King."

"You think I'll answer riddles for you?" I asked in disbelief.

"I think you're a practical girl. Answer this for me and perhaps I'll spare you."

"How can you spare me?" I asked, unable to keep the wryness from my tone.

"I can offer the antidote to the poison I'll give you next." She raised a single brow, shifting to spread her arms and legs wide as if she was enjoying every moment of her time resting in bed. "So, set your mind to this riddle, *From stone to feather, from stillness to motion, from stagnant to shift – the time has come. Sing the song of genuflection, bow ye to your broken dream.*"

"I'll work on that," I said, but it was hard not to betray my excitement. I had the clue that Bluebeard had missed while under the water and he'd need it when I finally rescued him. I could be helpful. All I had to do was remember.

"Don't look too happy, because now comes your barb," she said, winking as she sat up, as if she was doing something playful rather than trying to kill me with words. "You thought that by taking this Three Day Bind you could save your husband from beneath the waves. You thought your bargain with me would give you a safe release back to the mortal world with one other." She held up a hand. "Don't interrupt. I am not going back on the bargain. You can have whoever you want – whoever I can access. You can have that horrible rotting head, or the half-dead weasel draped over your shoulder. Strength of men and beasts, but that thing stinks. You do realize it smells, yes? Your mortal nose is not too dull to smell it? I digress." She waved a hand. "Know ye this – you cannot have your drowned husband. The bargain for him was with the Sea, and to get him back, there can only be a strict exchange – Wittenbrand for Wittenbrand, body for body, soul for soul. In order to get him back, you'd have to trap one of *us* - one of those better, stronger, more magical, more beautiful, and more clever than you. And you would have to give *their* life to the Sea in exchange for your husband. And you have no chance of that, whether you survive my home or not. You can't even cheat and give up your own mayfly life. You aren't Wittenbrand and your life does not count."

And then she was gone, slipping over the side of the bed. From the floor, she called up, "The words of the bargain said you'd spend three nights in my bed. They never said I had to spend them with you or with your repulsive pets."

She left through the door, and though it was glass, she was gone the moment she shut it behind her.

Frustrated, I threw myself back across the blankets, trying with all my will not to think of the corpses layered beneath the mattresses and blankets. Trying not to think about what it might do to a person to spend a night of repose over the dead – even the unrotted dead. Wondering if, perhaps, we all did that as there was only so much earth in the world and so, so many bodies to have buried over the years.

My Bluebeard had wives sealed in a room – carefully preserved and tended, frozen in time and space, like preserved flowers. I'd thought that a horror before. Upon seeing what Tanglecott did to her beloved, I saw it from a new perspective. There was a least some faint sliver of honor and respect in his methods. He had not layered over them to cavort with his next victim over their unfinished remains.

Who would have thought I'd consider as honorable what had once held me in claws of fear? The heart was an odd winding path, dark and tangled even to its mistress.

I sighed.

"She's going to win," Grosbeak said very sincerely.

I ignored him, my eyes stinging with tears of frustration.

"She's going to win because she's right. Her poison will break your heart. Mortals aren't very strong. She must have seen – as I did – how your heart is as a wrecked ship on the teeth of an island's rocks. You have not simply given your heart to the barrow, you have cut it from your breast, butterflied it, and forced it through the barrow's teeth and into its maw."

"Your metaphors disgust me," I muttered, but my heart was not in it. I would not cry. I would not bend.

"And you won't be able to do it. We both know you're no murderess. You nearly killed yourself in Ayyadmoore to keep those lily-white hands clean. To plot, to plan, to execute the extinction of another? You haven't the liver for it."

How in the world could I trap a Wittenbrand? How could I do it while I was trapped here in Lady Tanglecott's bed? I was of no more use than those poor dead fools who shared this bed with me. Despair grasped for me and I barely held it back.

I turned to Grosbeak. "Are there spectators here? Is anyone watching us?"

He snickered. "They can't come into her bedroom. The only ones listening now are the specter and the fire."

"I hunger," said the fire.

I checked carefully under the pillows and the top two layers of blankets. There was nothing dead under them.

"Is it just me, or are these riddles from the Bramble King too easy?" I asked.

"You call that one easy?" He scoffed.

"Clearly he means that it's time to take the arrow from the stone." I poked around on the mattress, investigating any lumps or bumps. I did not want to sleep here, but if I did, I definitely did not want to sleep on something dead. Or at least, I didn't want to sleep too closely on top of something dead.

Grosbeak snickered. "It can't be that. *That's* impossible."

"Nevertheless," I said dryly. "The Bramble King plans to die and pass on this realm to the winner of the game. He wants that one to take the arrow first. It's all very transparent."

"Or you're wrong."

"Or I'm wrong." I massaged my own forehead with my living hand. All these sacrifices. All this striving. I was farther away than I had been before.

"Why would you tell me the answer to the riddle?" Grosbeak asked warily.

"Your my ally, aren't you? My one friend in this deadly game?"

I flopped back on the pillows, confident that the dead were at least a mattress-length from myself.

"What about the song part?" Grosbeak pressed.

"That I must still consider," I replied but my mind drifted back to when I'd touched the arrow only hours ago. Something in it had sung to me. Perhaps it was related.

The fire flared extra bright, making a sound not unlike a belch and then a scrap of flame drifted upward and while I was still too surprised to think beyond the unthinkable thing my eyes were seeing, it transformed into a bird of flame, bearing a flaming parchment in its fiery grip. It flapped twice to me and offered the conflagrant note. I took it in a trembling hand, huffing to blow out the flames before they consumed the entire piece. The bird blew out with the flames, leaving nothing behind him but a puff of smoke that smelled like the intoxicating scent of the smoke of a birch fire.

"Thank you," I said stupidly.

"You are welcome," intoned the fire.

Feeling foolish, I unfolded the note and read what was written on it.

I waste.

I fade.

I am borne below.

She lingers.

Lasts.

Against the foe.

Live now my heart

Live now for me.

I gasp.

I die.

I ache for thee.

I crumpled the letter to my breast, crumpled myself around it, and I thought of how different Bluebeard's bed with the night flowers, and the window to nature, and the disgruntled mirror were to this monstrosity I was trapped in tonight and how the Wittenhame shaped itself to its princes and princesses it was dominated by. And I wondered – not for the first time – why my husband allowed himself to be so misjudged when he had a heart that loved beauty and kept all it could pristine.

And then I couldn't help the silent sobs that shook me like a rag doll in the mouth of a mastiff. Because he was drifting away, and I was still here and I didn't think I could murder someone to bring him back.

"What will you do?" Grosbeak asked me, breaking into my misery.

"I'm going to try to sleep," I said miserably. "It's been a long day."

The ferret crept wretchedly from my shoulder and curled up against me as I settled on my side, my skin crawling at the act of relaxing on *this* bed. My heart heaved up great miseries at every thought that surfaced. I pulled Look and Despair close to my chest. She reeked of musk, but her chest went up and down when she breathed, and her small body was warm. I appreciated the life there. I appreciated that she was still so solidly real in this land of nightmares.

"And what about me?" Grosbeak complained, sounding put out.

"You should sleep, too," I said in a small voice.

His mumbled curses were the last thing I heard as I sank into the pillow – and I would have been shocked if I were still awake, suspicious of magical influence at the very least, for I fell immediately into sleep without dreams.

I woke abruptly, blinking in the darkness. I'd sunk into the thick blankets and soft mattresses of that terrible grave of a bed. So deep was I between soft layers that it felt as if I were being slowly digested by a terrible cloth-layered beast.

I swallowed down bile and clawed myself up. The ferret chittered sleepily, clawing to drag itself up my shoulder and under my braid. I heard a squawk and a squeal as it fought with the specter for pride of place, but I ignored them both.

I peered around the star-lit bed, over the rumpled tangles of blanket and sheets, and to my horror, I could find no sign of

Grosbeak.

"Grosbeak?" I whispered and then a little hoarser, "Grosbeak!"

Had he rolled off the side?

The bed leaned precariously when I tried to look. Carefully, I lowered myself to my belly, so only my head was over the edge as I checked on every side. He was not on the ground. He was not dangling from a hand or foot of a corpse.

"Grosbeak!" I called louder.

The only sound in the darkness was the sound of the fire snoring.

I did not need him here to tell me that I could not climb down and get him. Not with the dawn not yet arrived.

I made my way to the center of the mattress, drew my belt knife, and sat with my arms clasped around my knees, shivering in the cold.

My only friend was gone.

The ferret chittered.

My only friend who *could talk* was gone.

In the back of my mind, the mournful sound of the chant returned.

"Izolda, Izolda, Izolda."

"I love you, Bluebeard," I tried to say. *"I will save you if I can."*

I thought I heard a reply – only a breath of a mental sound. *"I come."*

I gasped, clinging to those two small words as a man clings to the last scrap of bread he has.

But the voice could only be my imagination because no one was coming for me. No one was staying with me. Not among my friends. Not even the dead.

I squeezed my eyes tight and clenched my fists, flinching at the grinding bone-on-bone sound of my skeletal phalanges forming a fist.

"I will not let her poison kill me," I whispered to myself. "I will not let this bring me down. If I need a captive Wittenbrand to feed to the ocean, I will capture one. I will force one beneath the waves. If I need to solve a riddle, I will solve it. I am not helpless, and I am not yet dead."

And those words gave me strength as I thought long and hard about which Wittenbrand I had a chance to trap, how I might trap them, and whether I would ever see my bodiless friend again.

CHAPTER SIXTEEN

When dawn finally lit the sky, creeping in like an embarrassed friend, I gathered Look and Despair into my arms, looked her in her black eyes, and said firmly, "Today, we find a way to get some of our own back, ferret."

Her chitter could have meant anything. I took it as support. With precious few on my side, I had to take what allies I could get.

The way down the side of the bed was worse than the way up. I had to find my footing blindly, unsure if what I stepped on was blanket or corpse until I drew level with it. By the time I reached the bottom, I felt both overwhelmingly nauseated and in need of a priest.

I searched fruitlessly for Grosbeak, but there was no sign of my severed head friend, no trail of crabs or streak of briny rot.

The fire burned so low it was barely a smolder, but I approached it anyway, crouching low beside it to warm my hands.

"I wish I could take you with me," I told it. "You, at least, are a friend."

"Thank you," said the fire – somewhat predictably.

"If Grosbeak were here, he would have some kind of advice for me." My voice sounded lost even to myself. There was no way to bathe in the room – though I badly needed a bath. No way to change my clothing nor any clothing to change into – though I also needed that. My wolf cloak was long gone. My black dress dirty and torn.

I made my way to a small dressing table to one side of the glass room, hoping for a glass comb or a faint mirror to fix myself with. There was nothing on the glass table except for glass bottles – nearly transparent. Something to drink, perhaps? I took one up at random and removed the stopper, sniffing it with my eyes closed. It did not smell potable. It did not smell of liquor. Rather, the scent of moss and musk and something almost like melting snow filled my nostrils and when I opened my eyes again, the house had changed again.

Now, the bottle I held was a rich emerald green, and the others on the oaken table were of various colors and shapes. A mirror rimmed in oak leaves showed me myself – rumpled and worn, my hair out of place. I tidied it hastily before turning around.

The bed remained the same, though the corpses in it looked paler and deader and more … human … than they had before. Everything else had morphed into wood and rich cloth, to carved lintels and mantels and heavy baseboards and wainscotting. Pine boughs hung with red ribbon formed a garland over doors and across the walls. The room smelled of pine.

That it had four tangible walls and a firm floor, decided me. I put the bottle of scent in my pocket. If I breathed something worse, I'd like to return to this reality at will. It was one I was more able to navigate.

Without my bodiless friend, I had no one to provide a dry

monologue as I slipped out of the room and crossed a narrow wooden bridge between steep-peaked wooden buildings. There was no way out of this tiny outdoor space. Wood buildings surrounded it on every side, without gaps between them but lined with clinging ivy. On the other side of the bridge, a door was open and glowing with warm light, so I made my way across the bridge, pausing in the middle to look down in the water.

To my horror, there was something in the calm water – many somethings. They were skeletons, I realized after a moment. I flexed my skeletal hand and swallowed. The skeletons of six – yes, I counted a second time, there were six – moose, their antlers hopelessly tangled, were submerged in the still water of the pool. They had died – or settled, with their heads low on the ground, their front legs kneeling, but their back legs still standing, pelvises at the highest point. It made the horrifying sight look like a six-pointed star. Green algae coated the edges of their bones and even in the faint light of dawn, they seemed a stark white against the black pond water.

I shuddered and hurried the rest of the way across the small bridge. That couldn't be natural. But who would do such a thing to such massive creatures?

The sound of cutlery on dishes and the murmur of voices came from the open door and the scent of bacon and something sweet and cinnamon met my nose. I was drawn forward, hungry despite myself.

The door opened into a grand hall, lined with taxidermy – moose, elk, leaping cats, beavers complete with a fully reconstructed beaver house, so many fish of every kind on every wall that any angler would be put to shame. I stared at one near me, trying to determine the species – some kind of trout, I thought – and then it moved. Just the tiniest flicker of struggle.

I froze. The eye of the moose nearest me rolled in its head.

Revulsion rose.

Between these creatures – frozen in place, but not dead – lay a massive fireplace in which a dancing fire seemed to wink at me, and in the center of the room a long live-edge cedar table had been laid with hot steaming silver pitchers and silver trays stacked with glistening bacon, gleaming rolls generously frosted, candied fruits, bowls of creamy yogurt, and tiny delicacies crafted in star-like perfection.

At one end of the table, Marshyellow drooped over his food, a squirrel eating the same food he did from its place on the crown of his head.

At the other end, Coppertomb drank from a pewter mug while reading a book of which something had taken a large bite. He was as precisely neat as always, but today his cheekbones and eyelids were dusted with gold and his jacket was a rich violet. He did not look up when I entered.

To the side, Tanglecott ate, one hand draped on a sleeping winged snow lion at her side. The other occasionally offering a tidbit to a head on a silver platter beside her. The head of my friend, Grosbeak, who leered at me as I entered – not a captive at all, but an invited guest.

I felt the blood rush from my face.

Something dripped onto the cedar table. I followed the path upward and gasped at the chandelier built from a hundred elk antlers and filled with a thousand lit candles. Below it, spreadeagled, belly down, arms and legs arching up painfully above her from the chains suspending them, was Sparrow. Her entire back was encased with wax drippings. They formed strange runnels where they found paths downward from her long hair.

But her underside was wet with red patches and as I watched both wax and blood dripped to fall on the table and the food with equal disregard for where it landed.

I gasped, choking on my own horror. I felt not unlike the fish mounted live upon the wall, left to breathe forever the air they were not meant for.

"Try a sticky bun," Grosbeak said with a snicker. "They have a little extra something. For flavor." He made a sucking sound as if he were licking a non-existent finger. "I think they call this spice, 'Sparrow.'"

"I see you've had a little extra something, too," I said, touching the side of my face where he had a smear of white frosting. "Though I suspect the flavor is 'treachery.'"

"I did tell you I was betting against you," he said dryly. "It's not my fault you didn't account for it."

"He told you he was going to betray you, and you trusted him?" Sparrow's voice was barely audible, more a raven's croak than the voice of a woman. "And to think the Arrow placed his faith in you. He bet his life on you, worthless rag. For what?"

I swallowed, feeling the blood rush to my face as I looked up and met her eyes. She screwed up her face and spat down at me, but she didn't have the strength to aim it right. It fell instead in a quivering gob on top of a shiny orange.

"Mayhap I'll even ride in the joust," Grosbeak said merrily as if Sparrow were not even there. "Or at least have a front-row seat from the end of a pike. I'll take either at this point."

My mind was racing. There was something significant about Sparrow being alive, wasn't there? Because she had taken that message from the Bramble King in Bluebeard's place. It meant their fates were bound together. And that meant that if she lived, then he was still in the game, didn't it? Which was why Lady Tanglecott was trying to get his lands by other means. Did that mean she was forbidden from killing Sparrow outright just as she was forbidden doing that to the other players? I wished I could ask Grosbeak. Judging by the gleam of satisfaction in his eye, he knew what I wished for.

My head whipped up and met the eyes of the golden-haired beauty who had arranged all of this, my bottom lip quivering with something betwixt horror and rage.

"Felicitations," Lady Tanglecott said with an arched eyebrow. "I see you've figured it out at last. But you can't prevent my conquest. I'll take every shred from him, and every ally, and I'll hang them up and cut them to bits like I have that fool woman decorating my chandelier. Did you see the lovely tanglecott in the pond? A rare piece, that. It's what I'm named for. And it's what I plan to do to all of the Wittenhame."

"A bit presumptuous of you," Coppertomb said mildly, licking his finger and turning a page. "But I do like your stirring attitude."

She smiled tolerantly at him. "No great deed is truly done unless it is observed, Coppertomb. You should be pleased that I chose you as my observer."

"And the head?" he asked, flicking a finger at Grosbeak with tolerant amusement as one might do when a child explains the governing of a state in a fanciful daydream.

"Him, I need. I can't let the girl use him to her ends anymore. Not now that she knows a painful little secret."

I gasped. Did she mean that I could have put Grosbeak into the water as an offering on Bluebeard's stead? He was, after all, another Wittenbrand, dead though he was. I had not thought of that.

"I told you she wouldn't figure it out unless you said it plainly," Grosbeak drawled. "You could have left me in her possession, and she would never have thought to use me as her sacrifice."

"Better fortified than ravaged, I always say." Tanglecott plucked up the orange Sparrow had spat upon, saluted her with it, and tossed it at me.

My skeletal hand flew up and caught it before it smacked me in the face. I bounced the fruit on my bones, the fires in my heart flaring hot and fierce.

They were all terrible people – terrible in power, terrible in kind.

"The sun at dusk," Marshyellow said, lifting his pale eyes to stare at me. "The brilliant orb. In the sky. Lived its time. Time to die."

"I think he wants your orange," Tanglecott said with her mouth curling in disdain.

Carefully, I crossed the room, edged past Marshyellow's stony keepers, and dropped the tainted fruit into his hand.

He laughed, his chuckle starting as barely more than a wheeze and then spiraling upward. What would a realm be like with him as ruler? What would a mortal kingdom be like with him at the helm? I shuddered, unable to help myself.

"A curse on you," Sparrow breathed from just above my head. "As he loved you, may our home hate you. As you have failed to rise up for him, let it rise up against you."

I shivered. I would rise up for him if I could. I would do anything for him.

"Izolda, Izolda, Izolda," the echo said, melting me inside until I was nothing but hot wax in an Izolda shell.

I forced it from my mind and forced myself to study Marshyellow before backing away. He was using my hand to prepare morsels to eat. The sight of it made me ill.

"Do you always eat breakfast together?" I asked Lady Tanglecott mildly.

Her laughter tinkled.

"Only when I have weekend parties. These other Wittenbrand are my guests. Even Sparrow, though she does not know how to show her gratitude."

"You won't live for him," Sparrow grated out, still accusing me. "You won't die for him. You won't kill for him. You only drag him further into the depths. His enemies have become your friends because you have not the heart to stand against them."

Harsh.

"Yes, yeas, Sparrow." Lady Tanglecott flicked a bored hand. "You're bitter. We know. Let us at least enjoy breaking our fast without needing to sweeten it with honey."

My mind was racing. I needed a way to get a Wittenbrand into the sea. And it couldn't be Grosbeak. Because if he really was the key, they wouldn't be waving him in front of my nose like that. It was clear enough that he was meant to be a false lead to draw me away from real possibilities. I also needed a way to get Sparrow free. As soon as I might.

My eyes flicked to Marshyellow. He had taken out my hand

and was letting it cut his sticky bun for him.

"Go dress yourself, mortal woman. You're dressed disgracefully for a party. I told my denizens to put something in my room for you," Lady Tanglecott said and there was an edge to her voice that left shivers up my spine. "Run along now and be quick about it. You have ten minutes. Longer, and I will release the lions to take out my wrath on your Sparrow. I won't have you sneaking around my house like a mouse searching for cracks and crumbs while I win this Three Day Bind. Which I will, of course."

Coppertomb clicked his tongue.

"Don't censure me, Coppertomb," Lady Tanglecott said dramatically. "I have more than one chandelier in this house."

"But not more than one tongue," he enunciated clearly. "Don't tempt me to take it."

I was out of the room before they'd finished their banter. I didn't know when the ten minutes started, and I didn't want to guess wrong or what might happen to Sparrow? Would Tanglecott really allow her to be ripped apart by lions?

I sprinted over the wood bridge, trying so hard not to see the tanglecott in the pond. Avoiding it only made it more apparent and I was green-faced and stumbling by the time I reached her room again.

A dress dummy had been set in front of the bed while I was gone, and on it was a dress that clothed from chin to toe and with sleeves that pointed over the hand to cover as much of it as possible. It was a light dove grey and tailored to hair-breadth fit and precision, pieced in such a way that it seemed more like armor than a gown. Tiny onyx buttons ran right up the front to just under the chin. It was so utterly practical that I was shocked Tanglecott had provided it for me.

But there was no time for shock. The longer I left Sparrow in their hands, the longer they had to torment her. I must dress quickly and return. I owed that Wittenbrand, whether she despised me or not. She belonged to the Arrow, and I was the Arrow's wife which meant she belonged to me and it was my responsibility to rescue her and get her to safety.

I donned my dress armor, tied my hair back, and steeled myself for battle.

CHAPTER SEVENTEEN

This time, when I returned over the bridge, I strode like a woman preparing to enter a battle, each footstep stark and echoing. I held my head high. I wasn't sure yet how I would get Sparrow down from that chandelier, only that I would. I would bargain. I would trick. I would beat them at their own game.

I flexed my skeletal hand, reminding myself that I still had power in this strange Wittenhame world. It was a power that should not be discounted – the power to make sacrifices.

Look and Despair shot down my shoulder and back into the bag, huddling in the bottom of it as if the rough leather could shield her from the nightmares without.

"I miss him, too," I whispered. But that was all the remorse I would spare for Grosbeak. He was an untrustworthy bow, shattering at the very moment the enemy came pouring over the hills, useless before he ever truly was useful at all.

By the time I reached the breakfast room door, my mouth was a grim line and my blood thundered in my ears with each clench of my fists. A tiny qualm swam to the surface of my mind at seeing it closed. It had not been closed before. Gargoyles were carved in relief on its surface, making indecent gestures insulting faces at whoever dared enter.

Smoked glass was inset around them and through it, I could see the orange glow of the room beyond.

"Wish for me that all the turnings of fate land in my favor," I whispered to Look and Despair, and then I wrenched the door open.

Some doors squeal on their hinges. This one seemed to give off an eerie laugh-like screech. With it echoing in my ears, I reentered the breakfast room.

Perhaps, if one has never seen a poorly kept slaughterhouse or the aftermath of a battle then one would not know how to picture what I saw. I had seen both and still, I stumbled, gasping as I took in what was before me.

The Wittenbrand had departed, leaving their half-finished breakfasts still spread across the cedar table. Marshyellow – mad as he was – had even forgotten to take my hand. It lay in the center of a tray of oranges, trying to peel one on its own and sliding miserably over the tough fruit hide.

One chair lay on its back to the side. Another was slung over a moose antler as if a scuffle had broken out.

It was none of these things that made the breath freeze in my throat.

It was, instead, the head in the middle of the table.

In gruesome drama, they had severed Sparrow's head and set it directly in the middle of the table. Her corpse still hung from the chandelier coated in its turtle shell of wax, trailing its lifeblood onto the table below, while the head sat pale and pristine in the center of the breakfast table as if it were a match to Grosbeak – salt to his pepper, oil to his vinegar.

I stumbled, reaching for the nearest thing to gain support.

The nearest thing turned out to be a massive two-handed sword with a bloody blade. I swayed, gripping the pommel to keep myself upright, my vision jittering in and out.

The sword pinned a note to the ground, but I did not have the wherewithal to retrieve it just yet.

Sparrow. Dead. She who was right hand to my husband. His most loyal supporter and the link to his fiefdom here in the Wittenhame. I still did not know him well enough, despite how we two had been bound by vow these past seven years, but this I knew – this act would scour him to the bones and wring the marrow out of them.

Unsteadily, I stumbled forward, my mind numb. I'd need to find a place to bury her. Not the tanglecott or the bed. I shuddered at the thought of those two places. No, somewhere respectful. Perhaps I could place her in the Room of Wives until a proper resting place could be found. I could wrap her body and head. I could …

My mind jumped and skittered and I was surprised to find tears on my cheeks. I was not fond of Sparrow. She had been harsh with me when we two led Bluebeard's troops into battle as if she'd lost patience with my mortal heart. Harsh, when I cried over the travesty of war. And yet, she had been faithful. And of all his band she'd been the most welcoming. She did not deserve this.

I crept forward, hesitant, and yet certain. I owed her this and I would give it – ritual, respect, kindness.

Her eyes shot open and an uncalled-for shriek tore from my lips. I stumbled backward, my feet skidding uncertainly.

She blinked and seemed to stretch the muscles of her face before her baleful eyes turned to me.

"Izolda." She said my name like a curse and no wonder.

My hand flew to my heart, and I fought to get my breathing back under control. No need to panic. It was not as if I hadn't seen this before. I'd carried Grosbeak around with me everywhere and he in a state just like this. It was only that ... how to explain? With Grosbeak it had seemed almost a natural state for him, as if he had been born for the indignity of life without a body, whereas for Sparrow it seemed the worst of travesties. It did not seem real.

"Sparrow," I forced the trembling word through my dry throat. I could be practical about this. She was an animate severed head. This was nothing new. No need to panic. Had I said that already?

I straightened my shoulders consciously and stepped forward. She deserved better than revulsion. That much, at least, I could give.

"This is your fault, mortal wife of my prince."

"Of course it is," I said briskly. "In the end, everything seems to be."

"Don't be flippant with me," she said, raising an eyebrow threateningly. "Again, you bear blood guilt. Again, you have brought disaster upon all of the Arrow's dealings. You are the one fly in his ointment, the one rotten apple in the cart, the one glass bauble in a chest of gems."

"The one weed in his garden of flowers?" I asked. I found, suddenly, that I had no patience for this. "If your only purpose here is to fling insults, I fear I must inform you that I have become inured to their sting. They seem to be all the hospitality anyone has for me anymore."

"Don't pout, it doesn't suit you. You're not the one who just lost her head."

I strode forward, scooped up my living hand from where it fumbled, and struggled with the orange. I held it up in front of her face with the skeletal one.

"We've all lost things that can't be recovered," I said grimly.

The hand still moved. Without my control. Without my request. That fact alone left my stomach crawling. I tried not to vomit as I stuffed it into the bag with Look and Despair. That I'd found it again was a stroke of favor in this game. I – alone, perhaps – knew what a great stroke it was for if Marshyellow had suspected the trap I'd laid in our bargain he would have held onto it better.

"I've lost my life and my body because of you. A hand is nothing in comparison."

"Because of me?" I asked, but I hardly cared what reason she had for saying that. I was guilty in the minds of others for all the ills in this world and the mortal one. Why bother disabusing them of their prejudice? I strode to the note on the floor and tore it from where it was pinned, my back to Sparrow.

"It occurred to Lady Tanglecott that you might decide to trade me for my master, and so she eliminated me promptly."

At that I spun around, searching her face.

"Oh yes," she said bitterly. "It was a possible move, though I can see you did not think of it. I am Wittenbrand. I *was* alive. Had you drowned me in the ocean, you could have traded me for your husband."

I felt the blood draining from my face. That, I would never have done.

"Don't look at me in that lily-livered way," she spat. For a severed head, she was very animated. Perhaps everyone gained a dose of spite and two doses of drama when their head was removed from the body. "You'll have to do it to someone, or had it not occurred to you?"

I swallowed. Because it *had* occurred to me. And yet, despite my many flaws, I had not yet reconciled myself to murder.

She rolled her eyes. "What does your note say?"

I turned my regard to the missive. It was written in Lady Tanglecott's elongated hand. I read it aloud for Sparrow's edification.

"Izolda, Wife of Arrow,

Let us adjoin ourselves to the sea where we can spend a pleasant day in the part of my home that hears the echoes of your husband's wasted life, for what is so thrilling as to taste tears and relive sorrows and what shall bind us together more than that?

Distinguished Above All Others,

Herself, Lady Tanglecott"

Perhaps, murder was not unimaginable.

"You really weren't going to trade me for the Arrow, were you?" Her words were said in a strange way, like she wasn't sure what to make of my responses. She'd never known what to make of me – mortal, but married to her prince in the Wittenbrand way. Mourning for the deaths of innocent mortals, yet willing to sell myself to her kind. I was a mystery to her.

Good.

Perhaps I could be a mystery to all of them.

"Should we … bury your remains?" I asked gently, not bothering to answer her question when the answer was so obvious.

Sparrow barked a bitter laugh. "And what? You'll say words over me and then I'll say words over myself? Spare me your mortal sentimentality."

I nodded calmly. "I plan to attend Lady Tanglecott's invitation. Will you join me?"

"You ask as if you want me to attend a ball with you, rather than a death trap along the shore."

"In the Wittenhame, those things seem very much the same," I said with a sigh and then paused. "Why do you hate me so?"

"Is it not obvious?" she asked bitterly. "Since my prince married you, you have ruined his plans, ruined his dominance in the Wittenhame, led to the death of my two trusted compatriots and now my own death, stolen the hearts of his folk and his fire, and twisted up all his well-laid plans so terribly that I fear they may never unwind again and despite it all, he is so devoted to you that he has given himself again and again for you. I hate you for who you have made him – that he has stooped to condescend to you – a mayfly mortal. And I hate you for what you have made me – lackey to a failed lord, dead before my time."

"Fair enough," I said boldly. And her accusations were very fair. My face flamed hot at the shame of it, but there was no use reveling in shame when there was work to be done. "That was the life and death you lived and it's yours to tell as you please. Now, it seems, you have an afterlife just like Grosbeak and, like him, you have the chance to change and live it new or to fall back into old ways and habits. So, what is your will, Sparrow? Do you will me to take you to Bluebeard's Vault or would you be pleased to come with me to see if we can yet pluck your prince from the surf?"

She snorted. "Had I any choice in companions, I would not choose you."

I forced iron into my words, but it was not too hard. I'd been pushed and pushed and now when all was lost, I would not be pushed any further.

"It's absurd to wish for what cannot be. Deal with what is or revel in your despair. But choose quickly, for time is short."

Her tone was bitter. "Don't you know we Wittenbrand are dreamers? Can't you see it in our homes and clothing, in our delights and vagaries? Asking for us to be practical is like asking the wind to sing or the birds to snow."

"I've seen stranger here," I said coldly. "Choose."

I could appreciate that she was bitter toward me – and perhaps with good reason. I could appreciate that her life had just been stolen, and she must feel quite at odds with her new position. But I was not her priest, and I had no time to counsel her. In the back of my mind, the *tick-tick-tocking* was growing more and more urgent. And though I flinched from my own internal honesty, I could admit something to myself now – I *would* give Sparrow's life to get Bluebeard back. I would give a thousand Sparrows for just one of him. And I would not even regret the choice.

"Take me with you," she spat.

Without waiting for anything else, I seized her by the waxy-coated braid, held her head up like a torch, and commanded, "Show me the way to Tanglecott's ocean, bitter ally. And perhaps together we can turn these tides."

CHAPTER EIGHTEEN

It was not difficult to trace the way back to the ocean, though the *tick-tick-tock* in my head sped faster as we wended our way through the halls of Tanglecott's house. I'd brought the two-handed sword slick with Sparrow's blood, even though I could hardly lift both it and her. I let the tip drag on the ground behind me as I hurried, bumping over stones and occasionally smacking into door frames like a toddler tearing through the house dragging a broom.

"You're breaking the cardinal rule of weaponry," Sparrow said miserably.

"And what is that?" I asked her gravely. I did not care. I would break all the rules. I would burn the Wittenbrand down if I must.

"Never choose a weapon you can't handle."

"I'll let you in on a little secret, Sparrow," I said dryly. "It can be just between you, me, the ferret I acquired, and the specter set on my shoulder without my permission. What do you say?"

She grunted. Afterlife was making her grumpier.

"My entire life is a weapon I cannot handle. I was born to a happy family full of laughter and hard work. I spent my days tending our horses with the ostlers, running the errands the household sent a young occupationless girl on when there weren't enough hands for work, listening to my mother's fanciful stories as I helped her with her stitches and embroidery, and with cleaning up after my brothers and father. I was of noble blood in a far-flung holding where we were more like a big rambling rural family than masters and servants.

"I can cook a little because I've helped Cook when she needed it. I can garden a little because I've helped bring in harvests on rainy autumns when every hand was needed and I've helped tend when brown worm comes out of nowhere or drought is upon us. I can hunt because I've been in the party when they were short hunters.

"My whole life before the Arrow came was family – love and loyalty for them bending all my choices to service and kindness, claiming my weary moments, and lighting up my spare ones. And then this came. Snatched from it all, brought to a world where love and loyalty seem as rare in the Wittenhame as magic in the mortal world, where my death is desired and sought by almost all, where my happiness is constantly thwarted, where it has taken time for me to discover who my new family is, only to see them turn on me later. A girlhood of love and hard work and sober sensibility does not prepare one for the Wittenhame.

"And in the seven years I returned to the mortal world, I tasted only bitterness and ashes. My family gone – long dead. My home passed on. My duties changed. My life shattered like a dropped mirror. And no husband or children to console me. I was just as ill-equipped to be princess as I was to be wife, but I dragged a sword through those halls, too, and I learned to wield it – to use it well enough to forge a path back to this mad world to save the last scraps of family I have.

"I don't care that you think me weak and unskilled. I don't care that you despise me. I will do whatever I must, wield any weapon I can find, and I will not stop until there's not a scrap left of me to keep fighting."

I paused for breath and Sparrow said, "Your brother. You came to save him. Lady Tanglecott told me."

I laughed, bitterly. "My brother was the excuse and yes, I will save him with this act too, if all goes as I hope. But there is no guarantee that any of it will."

"You said you came to save the last scraps of your family. Is that not him?" Now she sounded wary.

We exited a last door and stepped out into bright sunlight and the gleam of dew on leaves and grass, and light mist across the murky sea.

I snorted. "You think my brother is the family who has my loyalty now?"

Sparrow frowned. "Who else could there be?"

I lifted her braid so I could look her in the eye and make myself very clear with my furious scowl. "I am loyal to the last family I have – my husband."

She gasped.

I had expected mockery – as Grosbeak surely would have offered. I had not expected sincerity. Her reaction made me suddenly mortified at having revealed my heart.

I lowered her head immediately and began to walk along the shore. Of Lady Tanglecott, there was no sign but as I walked, patches of mist cleared, revealing another Wittenbrand waist-deep in the surf. I gasped at the sight of Marshyellow bathing in the sea, his two guards standing to either side of him, arms crossed over their chests.

In the back of my mind, I could still hear the tick-tock-tick of time running out. And here he was – ready to be forced into the sea. A life for a life. I had said I would not hesitate or regret – so why did I suddenly feel so heavy?

"Tell me about Marshyellow," I whispered as I crept along the shore through the mist. They had not yet seen me – Wittenbrand though they were – but still, my heart was drumming in my chest. Not because I was afraid of being seen, but because what I planned to do next made every pore of my body break out in sweat. The sword grip slid in my clammy hand and my head felt light at the thoughts buzzing so swiftly inside it.

He was my enemy. He would use me and kill me as he saw fit. And if I did not do the same there would be nothing left for me to bother living for.

"Do you want me to recite his misdeeds?" she hissed. "The widows and orphans he crafted and how he tormented them? The women he debauched, the children he desecrated, the spoils he took from the poor, and the agony he inflicted on the innocent? Would that make it easier for you to kill him?"

"It would, rather."

"Justify your actions? Salve your conscience?" She mocked me in her whispered tones.

"Yes!" I hissed back.

"Then I will tell you none of it. Act. Do it dispassionately. A decision made. A balance in the scales. Make your choice, and don't pretend for even a second that it's not murder because you found some reason to make that murder holy in the eyes of others."

I swallowed. She was right. There was no justifying what I

would do next. It would be murder and I would be as stained and guilty as all of them.

In the back of my mind, I heard the echo again, *Izolda, Izolda, Izolda.* But it did not seem real like before. It seemed to only be an echo of what I wished. Perhaps, the lips that once spoke those words were too far gone now to speak them still. Perhaps, the mind too far down death's path to hold them. I grasped for them, and they slid further away. I was about to commit murder and it may very well be for nothing.

How could hollowness feel heavy? My chest felt like it was both.

I set the sword gently on the sand. I was no fool. It could not help me in this.

"That's right. Put the sword down. The question of whether you'd be morally culpable for murder is moot. You have not the capacity to do it at all." Sparrow seemed miserable at this declaration as if she'd hoped beyond hope that I could surprise her in this.

I didn't have the strength for her hopes. My own were pressing so hard on me that they may very well snap my spine.

I crept down the beach trembling so hard I could barely hold onto Sparrow's waxy braid.

"You *can* kill him, you know," she whispered to me. "You aren't a player in the game. It's not forbidden to you. You're a loophole and no doubt one that Lady Tanglecott planned to use to rid herself of a competitor. Did you know that in the other games almost no one was killed? This one is determined to be different."

"I'm aware," I murmured. I should have asked her why she

hadn't tried this. I should have asked her about how she had been caught and how Bluebeard's people fared. I should have done that rather than ramble to her about my past and life. Selfish. I was so selfish.

I set her head down on a rock, high enough that I failed and the tide came in, she would not be swept away, and then I peeled the ferret from my hair to place her on top of Sparrow.

"Keep her company," I whispered and still the stark trio had not moved, though the eyes of Marshyellow's guards were on me now, tracing my movements.

"Don't leave me here," Sparrow gasped, but I could not take her with me. Not for this. I could barely take myself.

I stepped to the edge of the water holding my stolen hand before me in both my living hand and my skeletal one as if I were making an offering. I kicked off my boots in the sand, flexing my toes as they let the sun-warmed sand cup their form. Courage ebbed and flowed within me, one moment certain, the next flown. I did not dare let its whim determine my actions.

I stepped into the brackish water, boldly. Small creatures fled from my path through the water and the waves lapped up, caressing first my foot and then my ankle and slowly wetting my hem as tears wet a handkerchief.

Murderous intent made me heavy. Heavy in heart, heavy in spirit. Even my tongue was heavy, the words like lead, refusing to be spoken lightly.

"Marshyellow," I said eventually, and even that was like rolling a boulder upstream.

He paused in his bathing and turned to me, his shriveled flesh truly yellow as he bathed in the sea. He looked almost innocent as he cradled a handful of crabs in a mirror to how I held my own living hand. The water was up to his waist, and I could not tell what garments he wore beneath it, only that he wore nothing on the top and I could count every rib between his liver spots.

"I've made another mortal," he burbled happily. "Bargain with me, mortal. Bargain for your life."

"I've already bargained with you," I said, slow and heavy, my whole body tingling. "Do you remember the words?"

His guards looked back and forth between them and one put his hand on the hilt at his side. Wittenbrand weapons must be different from ours if they risked bringing them into the sea.

The water surged up to my knees now – or perhaps I had stepped that far into the waves. The heavy skirt of my dress grew heavier as if it, too, would slow my hand.

"We agreed on these ones: *For the winning of a key, a hazard for the release of my heart's conqueror, I would give this hand of mine in its current form, binding to it now all that was bound to you and offering to you it's many skills. And I will forswear all vengeance on the taker – both now and always.*"

I paused. No one ran screaming. No one lunged with a bare blade.

"I fear a harm has come to you, Lord Marshyellow, for this hand has come back into my possession. Now I, and not you, are the taker and with its return are returned to me the skills of my hand and all that was bound to you. Is that not so?"

He laughed and he seemed actually delighted, but Frost and Yarrow exchanged a look of anxiety and then lunged as one toward me in the water. Frost's sword left the scabbard with a *shing.*

"I suppose it is so," Marshyellow agreed. "But will not my companions simply take the trinket back?"

The looks on their determined faces agreed with his guess as they waded through waist-high water toward me. Frost tilted his head back and forth, stretching his neck. Yarrow's expression had turned dark, his mouth forming a slash-like grin in anticipation of the violence to come.

If I hadn't been sweating before, I was now. My dress clung to my spine, stuck fast to the skin. They were only paces away.

"But were not your companions bound to you before our bargain?" I asked lightly but the words did not feel light. They fell from my lips like heavy marble. "And does that not mean that in my retrieval of this hand, I have taken possession of their bonds?"

Frost and Yarrow froze, horror in their eyes as realization rose in them like the tide rises in the sea. Their eyes met and the sword fell from Frost's fingers and sank into the surf.

A look of keen understanding flashed into Marshyellow's face as he gasped, "No."

"Yes," I said gravely, sorrowfully. "And I bid them – I bid you, Frost and Yarrow – draw Lord Marshyelllow under the sea until the Sea takes him for her lover in place of my dear husband, the Arrow of the Wittenbrand, and looses him to fly to me again."

"No," Marshyellow said, his voice trembling so I could barely grasp it.

His two protectors looked down at their own bodies as they pushed through the water back to their master and the twin looks of horror on their faces told me that even they had missed the barb I'd laid in that bargain. But their bodies did exactly as they had been told, bound by geas and honor.

This was worth a hand. Worth so much more than that. Worth even the terrible sick feeling that seized me as they reached Marshyellow in the foaming surf, took him by either spindly arm, and dragged him between them, deeper and deeper into the sea. Unstopping. Unrelenting. Unable to stop their own hands and feet.

Marshyellow's gaze stayed over his shoulder, never leaving mine as his mouth shaped again and again the word "No" until it filled up with saltwater and only bubbles remained. A moment later, his burning eyes were swallowed up by the very thing that had swallowed my heart and hope. And a moment later that, they all vanished beneath the inexorable waves.

I couldn't move. I couldn't so much as shift my weight. Guilt roared through my ears, drowning out thought, dragging me down so that I wondered if I, too, might sink beneath the waves.

My hands were clean. I'd done no violent act. And yet I was a murderess. An unseen brand had touched my heart.

Worth it? I could not tell. I did not have room in my soul for anything now except the burning knowledge that I was innocent no more. I was tainted by destruction, stained by iniquity. There were still bubbles coming up from the place where my victim was sent. I could bring him back. I could take back the sin I'd done. It was not too late.

But worse than the deed itself was the knowledge that I would not call it back to me. I would not purge my own shame.

I was still trembling when laughter drifted to me from the shore, dancing through the air in tinkling threads as if woven of wedding days and safe births. That was not Sparrow.

I whirled, the sea lapping all around me – the water was nearly to my waist now.

"Do you think that will be enough?" Lady Tanglecott asked from the shore. Her perfect face smiled serenely. She was holding something up, studying it in the light of the sun as if she hadn't just witnessed a murder. "How naïve of you, mortal girl. How delectably tawdry. As if you could defeat such a curse with so small an offering."

CHAPTER NINETEEN

"What are you saying?" I asked, "Are you saying this exchange is not enough?"

I could hear the panic rising in my voice. The bubbles weren't rising anymore. It was too late to take back what I'd done.

I'd killed. I'd murdered. Marshyellow's eyes were seared into mine. I still saw them being dragged inexorably under the water again and again and again in my mind's eye. I shivered – that kind of full-body shiver that left nothing out. And still the clock *tick tick tocked* in the back of my mind as if the great hourglass of my life had been shattered and the garnets were pouring out.

The specter on my shoulder shifted as if my despair was contagious.

Lady Tanglecott's smile blossomed like a snake slowly unfurling from its coil on the rock. "Your husband's life was given to the ocean, and he was borne down to the ocean floor pinned to a pillar by an iron dagger. You saw this just the same as I. You've bought his life back – very cleverly, I might add, if predictably. But he's still pinned there. He needs someone to go beneath the waves and pluck the dagger free. Surely, you must realize this, mortal though you are."

"If that was true, you wouldn't tell me so," I said grimly.

The tide was rising, the water very slowly lapping higher and higher up my skirts, soaking my feet and echoing the cold dread in every bone of my body. I had murdered a man for nothing. I had stained my soul and for what?

No Bluebeard emerged triumphant from the waves. No Arrow soared upward in a roar of waters. Only an empty wind howled around us.

My gaze darted to Sparrow on the shore. She was watching, silent, her expression as worried and confused as my own must be. Beside her, Lady Tanglecott had set Grosbeak's head. His mouth had been sewn closed by three thick stitches of something that looked like twine. If she were lying to me and he knew it and he wanted to tell me about it – and none of those things were certain – then he could not help me now.

"And why would I not?" Lady Tanglecott asked. A ray of sunlight pierced through the mist, lighting her golden locks as tinder lights a set fire. They glowed and burned like burnished gold – like a good faerie from a story, like a godmother who grants wishes, like the heroine the prince rides to save. I was surprised the truth of her essence didn't ooze from her pores like black tar. "It suits me to tell you, Princess of Pensmoore. But don't offer your trust to me if the time is not yet come. Let us wait together and see if your husband delivers himself from the embrace of his lover. Let us wait together. Who knows? Mayhap this one time, I am wrong."

We waited for hours, her smug, me desolate.

The sun crept slowly across the sky, an indolent fool, not hurrying, not working, sauntering as though there was nothing of import hanging in the balance. We did not eat. We did not drink. I moved up the shore as the tide began to come in, collecting the two heads and the ferret and carrying them further up the rocks to keep them from washing away.

Despair swept away my senses so that my vision grew dull, my mouth dry and my thoughts sluggish.

Gone. All my chances gone and not one way to get them back.

Tears flowed from Sparrow's eyes, but she did not speak to me, and though Grosbeak's expression wiggled and he tried to tell me something with his eyes, I would not look or acknowledge him. He had betrayed me to my enemy. None of his japes could change that.

It was when the tide began to recede again and all my hopes with it and a low moan of defeat ripped from my throat against my will, that Lady Tanglecott spoke again. The wind had loosened both our hair and hers swirled around her like golden ribbons, catching the sun and rippling bright.

"It suits me to bargain with you, mortal child, for I have precisely what you need. Even now, your husband languishes, trapped forever even though you bought him back, for to purchase and to collect are two different things entirely. You are seeing this now, I think. You might wait here all your life and never see him emerge. Or – you could go to him. I have the means of this. You saw Lord Coppertomb give it to me himself – the Heart of the Ocean."

My eyes darted to the necklace she'd been toying with all this time. It was the very one Coppertomb had offered her. A flawed diamond the size of my ear strung on three strands of pearls. I remembered it very clearly, just as I remembered that Tanglecott had paled when he'd given it to her. She was not pale now. Her cheeks were bright and rose-tinted, and her eyes were liquid and swirling with mystery.

"Wearing this, a mortal could journey beneath the waves on

a single breath. She could saunter down into the depths and retrieve a wayward husband. Would you like that, daughter of dust? Would you like to rescue your drowned half? To haul him up like a deep-water thing and watch his insides swell from the relief of the sea's grasp as he's drawn again to the land of the living?"

I shuddered at the metaphor. I'd heard of such phenomena but my experience with fishing was relegated to streams and lakeshores. I would not venture on a boat again. Not after the first time. The sick feeling in my belly was not just from the memory of that. I had failed. I had given everything I had and used all my ingenuity and I had failed.

"I have nothing to offer you in return," I said grimly.

And it was true. I'd been stripped down to the bone, the last remaining flesh teased from my soul just as my flesh hand had been stripped from its skeletal remains. I'd been pilfered and paupered and betrayed. To my name, I had left one ferret, the head of a woman whose hatred for me fed her afterlife, one silent spirit stuck guarding my words, and one soaking wet dress. I did not count Grosbeak who was no longer mine.

That I had one blackened conscience, rotting and mangled, would not interest her. That, too, had been wrecked upon the shoals of the Wittenhame. I paused at that thought, for it was not true. I was no victim of chance. I had made a choice. I had broken myself on the shoals of my own volition as surely as if I had held my own spine between my hands and snapped it over my knee.

Tanglecott laughed her tinkling, horrible laugh like sugar added to a wound. "You have your beauty, mortal princess, little of it though there may be. It was enough to trap a prince of the Wittenhame, and I would have it for myself."

"My beauty?" I asked, stunned for who would bargain for a thing I'd been told again and again I did not possess.

Her grin matched the snow lions she favored.

"A thing sometimes is worth the pain its owner will feel at its loss more than its objective worth, don't you think? For while you are not very fair at all, I think you will be ever conscious that you have forfeited what little scrap you once possessed. And with that in your mind, you will sink beneath the sea, set your husband free, and see for yourself the horror in his eyes at what has been stripped away from you. And then you'll be nothing but an ugly little murderess, discarded by a husband she gave everything to possess, and all for the one thing she can no longer claim. What a delicious story. I would so like to see it play out, wouldn't you?"

"Will the necklace truly let me find him under the sea?"

My heart was pounding. It was a terrible bargain. Terrible in every sense. But I did not hear his voice calling my name, not even the echo of it anymore. And it had been hours since his last bird arrived. His last poem had been a dirge. If there was any time left at all, it was nearly gone. I had waited hours and he had not surfaced. I had been patient and tenacious. So, what did it matter if I was fair or foul? What did it matter if I gave the last thing I had, paltry though it may be?

"The Heart of the Ocean will bind you to the ocean, so you may breathe the waves and see beneath their darkness for as long as you wear it. And for as long as that may be, your beauty is mine," Tanglecott said. "But know this – for I would have you make the choice with open eyes," she widened her eyes as she said this – the picture of innocence. "You will not be able to remove the necklace with your own hands. It will be yours forever just as your fairness will be added to mine forever."

"Agreed," I said, almost too quickly – for I had given my innocence and my future, my family and my sanity. What more was the one thing I'd never really had at all? But my agreement sounded like a death knell even in my own ears and from the shore, I heard muffled sounds of protest from behind Grosbeak's sewn lips. Who he was arguing for and what he was protesting? No. I did not care what he thought anymore. I would not spare the traitor a single glance.

"Agreed," Lady Tanglecott said with a smug smile. "Hold out your hands."

I held them out, cupped before me, expecting her to place the jewelry within them.

Instead, she tossed the necklace like a horse wrangler tosses a rope and the heavy loop opened and fell through the air and over my head to land with a thump against my chest. I stumbled under the weight of it as I felt my features shift and change.

To my surprise, Lady Tanglecott shifted before my eyes just as dramatically, like the shifting of a sunset – from one glory to the next, so that by a small degree she was more beautiful than she had been moments before.

In my hands, I held ashes, white and chalky, laced with grey.

I gasped and tried to step forward, but my feet could not leave the water. It was just as we'd agreed. I was the ocean's now, with the means to chase after my husband. It was only occurring to me now that there was much ocean and only one of me.

"Where is the place the platform sank?" I asked, and my voice was small in my ears.

Her only reply was laughter as she took a step back from the waves.

"Where?" I asked even knowing she would not answer, and that Sparrow and Grosbeak could not answer.

"You're like a rabbit in a trap," she said, and the light shifted and suddenly the angles of her face stood out more intensely and the shadows deepened and the viciousness of her was seen in every line. "You're chewing your own leg off and you still think you might get free. Enjoy your journey little rabbit. Enjoy rotting alive beneath the sea. At least the brine won't ravish your fair face, for it has not a scrap of beauty remaining, not even in those bright eyes, which I swear were almost charming once. Oh, and I ought to note that you've doomed your land, too, for how can you spend another night and day in my bed and home when your feet are trapped in the blue?"

I felt the blood begin to drain from my face, and I couldn't breathe. My heart was racing so fast it was all I could hear. I thought that Sparrow might be trying to say something, but I couldn't hear it, couldn't think, couldn't do so much as lift my eyes from the white ashes in my hands – the ashes not just of my beauty but of all my hopes and ambitions, of all the Izolda that ever was. I'd never been enough to save him – not at my brightest, not at my darkest, not as an innocent or a murderess, a princess or a wife. It was all just ashes in my hands, ashes in my mouth, ashes in my heart.

I closed my eyes, certain now that my heart was going to explode and hoping it would happen soon because I wasn't sure I could take one more blow.

The backs of my eyes flared bright red and I opened them to see the clouds parting, the sun blazing bright and full in its last golden hours before it died in scarlet. The ocean shone back brightness to brightness, and then in a spray of droplets, a figure emerged clad in seafoam, water, and rainbows, and garlanded in black seaweed. A flight of white birds shot up with him, made entirely of pale seafoam. They flew in all directions, singing a soaring aria as they spun through the breeze and then burst into foam flecks and fell back to the sea.

And the face that emerged from the rainbow brightness bore a blue beard on his cheek and vengeance in his eyes.

And it was at that moment that my heart chose to burst.

CHAPTER TWENTY

It could not be him. And yet it was.

I drank in the sight of him, tracing every line, watching every flicker of expression as if I could make up for seven years in one long drink of sight.

At the edge of my vision, Lady Tanglecott's mouth opened, and she swiveled as if she meant to flee, panic strong in her eyes. I did not care. Who cared about her with *him* here?

Pawing and snorting like a beast cornered, a frothing wave of the sea rose, its crest and rivulets forming the image of a watery stallion for the barest blink of an eye, and then it raced around Lady Tanglecott, flinging up sprays of water as it ran. The spray wrapped around her – a silver net of water and fury. It drew her until she was standing ankle-deep in the lapping sea.

"What nefarious bargain have I stumbled upon?" Bluebeard asked and his face was cold and terrible, his cat's eyes flashing, and his fists clenched until the knuckles were white. And the sight of him was balm to the soul, was water for the thirsty. "Have I arrived just as it is being sealed?"

Even now that he had drawn up level with us, he was still wreathed in rainbows, they danced and frolicked around him, hard to see if you looked directly at them, but filling the edges of my vision. Black, tangled seaweeds clung to him, barely keeping him decent where his clothing was rotted to almost nothing. The seaweed tangled fecund and grasping where the rainbows were light and ethereal and through them all, I saw the jagged, unhealed tear in his side and the open wounds on each palm, peeking between this garb that painted him caught betwixt the heavens and the pit, half angel and half denizen of the deep.

"You're free," Lady Tanglecott gasped, a horror in her voice that jarred against the swelling joy in my heart. "But her actions could not possibly have —"

She swallowed whatever she was about to say and smiled, trying again. And in that moment, my own horror dawned.

Oh no.

She did not think my actions had anything to do with his release. She had led me here, taken my beauty, and watched me murder her opponent knowing all along that my actions could not free him. My stomach fell out from under me so hard that I could have sworn it hit the sea. Something where it used to be twisted into a tangled knot. Murderess, it told me. Guilty murderess.

The world swayed. And still, he had not looked at me — as if he knew that my hands were stained with blood not my own.

Lady Tanglecott tried a smile. "How pleasant that you return to the Game, Arrow."

"The bargain, Termagant."

"It's no affair of yours, Arrow," Lady Tanglecott said, drawing herself up in radiant dignity, her beauty so powerful it hurt to look at her. "While it warms the heart to see you restored to land, whatever has transpired between me and this mortal bound to you is between us two and no other."

He looked at me and it felt as if lightning had struck me. My heart seized. I could not breathe.

Something lit in his eyes behind his immobile mask – something hot and deep, something that burned and judged while eating me up.

I had the terrible sensation that I was shrinking, fading into the background, melting into the sea, and my emotions inside raged like two rams fighting on the mountains, crashing into one another only to fall together down the slope.

Half my heart sang with his return, the colors grew brighter, the light shone fiercer, the world tilted back to turn on the correct axis again.

But the other half asked, how dare I to even look at him? I, whose beauty was stolen, whose innocence had been offered up for nothing, who stood here now with soiled hands and a conscience seared with shame. I was thief and murderess, sullied, soiled, and ruined and I should flee before he discovered all I had become.

I looked away, miserable with guilt, my stomach tilting and teetering with it. I was going to be ill. I was going to fall into my own sick and drown forever.

Bluebeard made a sound at the back of his throat and the water seemed to part before him as he lunged toward me, seized the Heart of the Ocean, ripped it from my neck, tearing out hair with it in his haste. He flung it out as one tosses a ring neatly over a post and it landed square over the head and onto the shoulders of Lady Tanglecott.

"You traded beauty for ashes, wife, and sealed yourself to the sea?"

he asked me grimly with his mental voice, and still, I could not meet his gaze. *"And this fork-tongued adder led you to it."*

Behind him, I heard Lady Tanglecott wail. The ashes in my hands vanished, leaving only the faintest trace of smudge on my fingers. I gasped and without meaning to and I looked up. She regarded me from over his shoulder, and I barely recognized her. That was not her face.

"I turn the bargain back on the bargainers." Bluebeard's voice held a sting.

Lady Tanglecott had lost not just the beauty she'd stolen from me, but *all* her beauty, and in her cupped hand was a heap of grey. She threw it furiously into the sea, took a wobbling step toward land, and stopped, leg raised halfway to the shore.

"As you tried to bind my wife, so I bind you," Bluebeard said, not even looking at her. His eyes were on me, hot and burning and I caught them only with the edges of mine lest I be burned by their intensity. "The terms of her imprisonment are yours – trapped in the sea until such a time as other hands save you. Your beauty plundered and given to another. Your home and lands forfeit. A fitting judgment, I think."

The sound Lady Tanglecott made was not human. It was something between a howl and a roar, but before she'd even finished making it, a gleaming hand reached out from the waves and drew her under, and I saw the trout-skinned mermaid under a blanket of water for only a flash before they were both gone beneath the waves. Tanglecott's last look to me had been one of utter devastation, as though what waited for her beneath the waves was worse than just water and fish and a drowned Marshyellow held under the waves by those who had once been his faithful guard.

The breath caught in my throat.

"*Look at me, wife.*"

I dared not look. It was enough that he was restored to the world. Even if it was not by my hand. Even if all my paltry efforts had been of no more use than the ashes in my hand. It was enough that he was free. I would return to the mortal world, out of his way, out of his life.

I felt the sudden urge to cover myself and my dripping dress. But wrapping my arms around my waist did nothing to hide my guilt.

"*Look at me,*" he thundered in my mind and this time my gaze snapped up to him. I could no more disobey his voice than I could disobey the ache of my lungs to breathe.

My legs trembled, the knees no longer strong enough to hold me.

His side still bore its wound, open and ragged. His hands bore twin piercings, red with his blood, but it was his gaze I was drawn to as the tide draws the water from the land.

What did he see when he looked into my eyes? I knew what I saw when I looked into his. It made seven years feel like no more than an hour. It made everything I'd given up feel like rags and dust. It made the seams of the world seal themselves together again. I did not have to be worthy to acknowledge it was so, to find deep, searing delight in its certainty. I did not need to be clean to know all was right again with the world – even if it could no longer be right for me.

To my shock, there were tears in his eyes, swimming, unsplit.

He reached out – quick as a cat – and drew me fiercely into his embrace. I gasped at the shock of it, clinging instinctively to him. The warmth of his breath gusted over my hair and the way his bare wet flesh fit against my cheek when he pressed me to his breast pushed aside all other thought. If I only had this one, unworthy moment, I would take it entirely.

I closed my eyes and let all my feeling go to my cheek pressed against him, the feather-light touch of his hands holding me, the gust of his breath, the beat of his heart.

"How could you doubt that I would come to you? Me, who would move heavens and earth for you? Why did you think I required murder at your hands? Foolish bargains made in haste? Excess? Wife, what madness has possessed you? You who has been order to my chaos. You who has aced this world with grim sensibility. From whence came this madness?"

And how could I bear such accusations, steeped as they were in truth?

My lips trembled as I held back seven years of tears. To my astonishment, he caught them in his own, gentle at first, feeling their way, imparting to me the softness at the core of his heart and then blossoming into something fiercer. It was wholeness and fire. It filled me like food did not, and seared me at the same time, pain and desire all tangled into a healer's draught.

I was the one who pulled away with a gasp, long, long before I wanted to.

"I don't dare kiss you," I said, aching. "I don't dare touch you." Even though I was still touching him. "I'm stained with blood. I'm ruined in my soul."

His nod of agreement as I spoke hurt more than the cut of a dagger. I knew. I had felt both.

"I have little strength right now, I fear, but what shreds I have of

it are still yours, fire of my eyes."

I could not bear to look at anything other than him. I kept my eyes fixed on his, as if setting my course to the north star. He took something from my grasp – my hand, I thought, and flung it to shore, not watching it, but watching me. So intent were we on one another that I only heard the sound of wings when they beat around us and lifted us into the air. I did not watch it but kept my eyes fixed steadily on him. But I was not surprised by them, for they were at his command and had done this once before.

"I must spend three days in her home and three nights in her bed or Pensmoore is lost," I gasped, sudden fear bubbling up in my throat. Was it already too late? "And I have only spent one of each."

He blew air from his nose as a bull snorts in irritation and then opened his palm and in it were two garnets. He flung them at her beach.

"Did it not occur to you, wife of mine, that you could have done the same, and rid yourself of that grasping gull in one flick of the wrist?"

It had not occurred to me – fool that I was. Nor had it occurred to me to bear us on the wings of white seabirds to a nearby island off the coast – which is what he did. It took only moments and I spent them with my head cradled against his chest and my body snuggled up against his and I tried not to think about how much of him was exposed to my touch and how little right I had to touch any of it. Or how quickly this moment might fade if he changed his mind and held against me all my sins.

"Is this still her home?" I asked with a trembling voice as we set down upon the rocky shore.

"*It is no one's place but ours,*" he answered as he seized my hand and in that strange almost pounce-like way of his, led me to a place where the rocks of the shore had formed a natural cave and the tide had gone out and left only small pools and soft white sand behind it. Sunlight dappled the darkness, filtering down through holes in the rock above.

He leapt into the mouth of it and with only his touch, he led me to sit on a slab of worn stone and he knelt before me, so we were eye to eye, knee to knee, hand to hand. I dared not speak. I hardly dared to breathe. I could drown in those eyes. How could he look at me like that, when I had traded away my beauty and bartered away my innocent soul?

"*What is this, wife?*" he asked me threading his fingers between my skeletal ones and lifting my hand between us to inspect it.

"I traded my hand to Marshyellow for a key to free you. He gave me the key to your Room of Wives and also Grosbeak."

He nodded.

"*And Grosbeak gave you my message.*"

"He told me not to come to you."

"*Not that. The message.*"

"Message?" my words felt foolish, they seemed to stumble as they fell from my lips. "He gave me no message."

The fire in Bluebeard's eyes deepened. "*He did not bid you wait only a little longer? He did not tell you I would soon be free and come to you?*"

"He did not," I gasped. "But the birds brought your words.

They seemed to me the last words of a dying man."

He watched me gravely, his eyes deep and full of things I could not know and they drew from me a full confession though my voice shook with it.

"I thought I could free you if I were just brave enough to try. I bartered with Marshyellow and I bargained with Tanglecott. I thought I could trade Marshyellow for you and come down and draw you from the waves."

He clicked his tongue in a way that seemed both censure and pity.

"I gave up my hand and I … I killed a man. Not by accident. Not because he attacked me. On purpose."

I looked down miserably, but after a moment I glance back at him still watching me as if waiting for me to say more. So I forced out my next stumbling words.

"And they say you are lover to the ocean now, consort of the sea."

At that, he smirked.

"And I woke Margaretta to help me open Lady Tanglecott's door even though I promised you I wouldn't steal any more of my days."

"*You woke my wives?*" I could not discern why his gaze was suddenly so wary.

"Just one of them."

"*Did you put her back?*"

Back? As if she were a dish I borrowed? My brows furrowed.

"Yes."

But now my tears were spilling out because laying it all out before him made me feel so foolish. It had made complete and total practical sense in the moment. I had done exactly what I'd had to do to save my beloved from the sea. But with him here, restored to me *despite* my actions instead of because of them – with him here in front of me, it felt like my hands were still full of ashes.

"I ruined everything," I whispered.

Silently, he drew me into his embrace. Without a sound, his powerful arms encircled me, and his chin rested upon my head and his chest heaved.

"I can never go back." My voice was small against his chest and my tears spilled over my cheeks and ran down his skin.

Something hot and wet ran down my hair, my face, mingling with my tears and dripping from my chin to slip down my neck. To my surprise, he drew back and gripped the collar of my dress and I saw by the red rims to his eyes that he had been crying, too.

He tore my high-necked dress straight down the front, exposing me to below the collarbone. The small black buttons popped off, flying in every direction. Here it was – what I'd been anticipating all along. The judgment. The rejection. I braced myself for it. Apparently, it would start by taking back my ill-gotten clothing.

His eyes met mine, swimming with sorrow mixed with something that looked so much like devotion that it broke my heart. and he wavered in my vision as my matching tears disguised his form so that I could not tell what he was planning next. My cheeks flared hot with shame.

"*Would you be healed, wife?*"

"Healed? I am not wounded. I am the one who made wounds."

"*Would you be washed of guilt?*"

"Yes," I said, my voice so small it was barely there at all. "But such things cannot be."

"*You say this to me who has bought you with blood? You say to me that you cannot be whole again? I will show you otherwise.*"

I gasped when he drew me in again, shocked that his touch was gentle and loving when I'd expected the opposite. His tears bathed my bare skin and my tears mingled with his, and when my chest heaved with a suppressed sob, I thought that maybe his did, too.

His pierced hands came up and caressed my neck, my shoulders, tracing the curve of flesh and bone and the wounds were still fresh, for trails of pink blood mixed with the saltwater of his tears and mine.

"*With sorrow and blood, I wash you, wife.*" And now his mental voice was a whisper. "*To me, your guilt is washed away. To me, you are clean. Speak to my riddle, fire of my eyes. Who may condemn she I have called clean? Who may accuse she who I have found worthy?*"

"But Marshyellow," I stammered as he shocked me by placing a kiss in the curve of my neck, hot on my naked flesh. I felt my cheeks flare hot.

"*Is no more dead than I was,*" he said against my skin. "*Is no more trapped than I was.*"

He kissed the column of my neck and then just under my ear and then my temple – a trail of soft kisses, slightly roughened by his blue beard. And I shivered at every one of them – for their tenderness, for their fleeting sweetness, for the sharpness of how little I deserved any of them.

He drew back and he was smiling very faintly when he met my eyes.

"Let us see if he has the power to return. Let us see if he can rise from the depths with healing in his palms as I have done. I rather doubt it, but I will not tolerate any more self-flagellation from you, wife. You are washed in my tears and heart's blood. That should be enough for you since it is for me."

I did not wait for him to reach for me. Shyly, I slid one hand around his mostly naked waist, feeling the shreds of ancient cloth crumble at my touch, and the other to clasp the muscles tensed at the back of his neck, and – slowly, still not sure if he might reject me and toss me aside – I found his lips with my own and drew them into the welcome of my mouth.

We were occupied in welcoming each other in that way for enough time that he probably could have done a great act of magic if he had spent that part of my day on something else. But is it not magic to tangle futures and limbs? To soften your heart and your body to shelter another? To open your arms and your generosity to them? It felt like magic to me.

"You will need another dress," he said ruefully when we paused our kisses – for even the most ardent of lovers need air from time to time. He traced the edge of my face with a finger. *"The last I remember of you was the repeating of your vows to me – marrying me in the Wittenbrand way with your heart and your bargains just as I had married you. The days I waited to see you again were long, fire of my eyes."*

"The years for me were far longer," I said wryly.

He smirked. *"I would not place that bet. You may find yourself lighter of whatever you wager."*

I turned to kiss him again, my hands drifting lower than his waist but he arrested the motion with a gentle touch. My heart was in my temples and somewhere lower than my belly as he caught my wrists – one flesh and one bone – and drew my hands up to tangle in his and sit between us.

"Not yet, fire of my eyes."

And I felt hollow and aching at his "not yet."

"For I have made my vows to you, yes, but I have made other vows I must honor first."

"And what vows are those?" I asked and I could not keep the edge from my voice. Disappointment will do that.

"I have vowed celibacy until the day I can free my wives and give them back their days and lives. This I told you."

At that, I sat up tall. He could not have surprised me more if he had flung cold water in my face. "What? I thought you told me you were waiting for your true wife."

"And so I was, but there is more. Why think you that I keep them in that room?" he asked me with furrowed brow. *"Did you think me a gruesome collector to take from them their lives and then set them one after another upon pedestals as trophies to my wickedness?"*

"Yes?" My cheeks were hot, but I didn't know why *I* was blushing.

He laughed wickedly, reminding me he was still Wittenbrand and still delighted in my misunderstanding of his ways.

"I plan to give them their lives back – every single one. But not

until my plans have turned from flower to fruit and their days and place in life can be returned in all their fullness."

"But how can that be possible?"

"I will make it possible. And when that is accomplished, on that day, I may seek my own pleasure and not until."

So, never then.

"Has it not been difficult to be celibate all this time?" I asked. I had spent the last seven years in the king's home, listening to his warriors and ladies bragging about their conquests. The idea that a man would be celibate for hundreds of years would have been more impossible to them than that he would fly across the ocean on the backs of birds.

He tilted his head to one side in contemplation. *"I find it much more difficult to restrain myself from killing every soul that irritates me and collecting their heads. Is there a word for murderous chastity? Murity? Chasterous?"*

"I think not," I said, grimly.

"I was afraid that was so."

I turned to kiss him again and he laughed and took my hand instead, guiding me to my feet.

"Even so, you try me hard, wife. Let us return home where clothing and food awaits and where the delicious tangles of your dark hair and the smoothness of your skin stop tempting me to roam to the edge of my vows."

"Must we?" I pressed and his husky laugh told me he was finding the notion as difficult as I was.

CHAPTER TWENTY-ONE

We stepped from the cave and the sun struck my skin where my ruined dress fell over my naked shoulder. I tried to capture the hanging cloth. Bluebeard took one look at it and tore it off entirely.

"Off the shoulder is always fashionable," he said absently. There was a depth of something in his strange eyes that looked like both joy and deep sorrow swilling together into one draught. *"It looks particularly well on you, wife. Who would have thought a woman could look so hale when one of her hands is nothing but stripped bones."*

I held up my skeletal hand ruefully and he laughed. It was one of those laughs that was heavy and meaningful rather than light.

"We shall find a ring to set it off and remind your enemies you are no stranger to pain or sacrifice. That matters far more than a complete flesh hand does." He paused and bit his lip as his gaze raked up and down me and my cheeks heated hot because I'd never had a man dressed in only the barest amount of clinging seaweed and rotted silk look at me quite like that. *"Yes, I rather think the gauche hand sets off the beauty of the rest. You must keep it, wife."*

"It's not very practical," I protested, but why was I protesting.

There was no way to change it. My hand was my hand.

"Speak to my riddle, wife. What keeps the foe at bay and the fool from trying his luck? What precaution ends a fight before it begins?"

"Intimidation?" I asked and he smiled.

From her perch on my shoulder, my specter hissed and I startled. I had forgotten she was there. Had she been there the whole time we were … I looked back at Bluebeard, my eyes wide and he winked, seemingly unconcerned by her presence as his hand came up to stroke his chin, consideringly, and I was reminded again of the open wounds on his hands and in his side. He acted as if they did not bother him at all.

"Do your wounds hurt?" I asked him.

"They're no matter."

"But do they pain you?" I pressed.

"Wounds to the body are always painful. We bear them. Or would you have me writhe at so small a thing?"

"And will they heal? Eventually? Can you use some kind of magic or prophesy or something to mend them?"

He looked at his palm, flexed his hand so that blood welled in his hand, and then looked me in the eye as his mind spoke to mine. "No."

He took my hand as if defying me to object, and then, to my utter surprise he leapt into the waves with me in tow – no. Not into them. On top of them, striding with the soles of his feet cupped in the wave like they were stepping on the lightest coating of snow, sinking in just enough to shape the water to his foot, only to have it smooth back to perfection when he lifted his foot to step again. And I was right there with him, my feet skimming over the surface as he tugged me along at an impatient lope.

"*No boots*," he explained, "*this requires the touch of flesh.*"

But I'd already lost my boots back on the beach. I glided with him on the buoyant surface of the waves, bobbing very slightly with each step in a way that reminded me a little too precisely of the boats of my past.

"*Think not of the waves,*" he said in a voice so low it let like a caress. "*Think only of your hand in mine. Who makes the waves bend to his will? Who commands the brine of the Sea and forces her submission? Who holds your hand in his?*"

He did, apparently. A mad prince to suit a mad princess.

The ragged edge of his wound tickled my palm and I swallowed, but I believed him. I trusted his power right down to the marrow of my bones.

"All my enemies live beneath these waves," I said. "It's only sensible to be nervous that one might surface and drag me under the water."

"*If they appear, wife of mine, we shall dance hand in hand and cast them back to the depths from which they rise. Have no fear of revenants when I am with you. But we must hurry, wife of mine, I can feel the movements of the Wittenhame calling me toward the fourth move and I know not where it might be announced.*"

"Could it be at a joust?" I asked. "The Wittenhame speaks of nothing else."

"*I jousted often as a younger man. I have a scar somewhere from one particular ride … hmmm.*"

He paused, pulling the waistband of his trousers back and

twisting to look back at himself. I kept my gaze fixed steadily forward, not daring to look with him. He couldn't do that and then talk to me about years of chastity.

"Mayhap you'll show me at a later date," I suggested, gaze held steadily forward and cheeks flaring hot.

"*Mayhap I will.*" There was laughter echoing in his mental voice.

"Perhaps you can explain to me how birds bore your messages when you were beneath the sea," I said, trying desperately to distract myself.

The wind rippled his hair and tore at his meager clothing and we hurried forward again, his eyes drifting constantly to any bird in the sky and then occasionally to me as if I were a bird, also, and just as likely to surprise him as they were.

"*I wrote them for you,*" he said, watching a gull as it shrieked above us. "*After seeing a vision of myself beneath the sea on the first night we met. The fire offered it as a wedding gift to me.*"

"The fire did," I said tonelessly.

"*A noble gift, was it not?*"

"But how did they know to deliver them?" I pressed.

"*Speak to my riddle wife. Who knows the twisting of the mind and every echo of the heart? Who guides the hand and marks the path and speaks the night to naught?*"

"Honestly, I have no idea. But it can't be birds."

That seemed to be all the explanation I was going to get because just then a dark raven fell from the sky and landed on my husband's shoulder and at his keening call, Bluebeard gripped my hand harder and broke into a trot and it took all my speed to keep up.

My whole world, for a time, was brilliant sunlight and flashing waves, dancing rainbows, the tearing and wailing of the wind that drowned out all speech, the warmth of my husband's hands and gaze, and the wickedness of his teasing smile.

"I think we'd better get home at once," I said firmly, pitching my voice over the wind, as we drew near to shore. "Someone might see you like this."

To which he only smirked more, and my face went crimson hot.

"*Fear you that another might steal me from you, fire of my eyes?*"

"I fear, rather, that your dignity will be marred by striding about in mostly in your skin," I said. "Besides which, a wind is picking up and you can hardly expect seaweed to shield you from its bite."

And his smirk turned into a twinkle and his twinkle into a laugh.

"*Indeed, my sober monstrosity. Your words ring with accuracy. Let us hie us home. The time has alighted and it sings to me that it is time to tell you my secret, the terrible cause that I hold so close to my bosom.*"

And even more than his torrid kisses and feverish touches, this promise made my heart race and my breath catch for if there was anything I longed for it was to know what plan had led him on this strange, twisted path and how it could possibly turn certain defeat into some manner of victory.

We paused on the shore to retrieve our friends.

The ferret ran up my arm with relief in her eyes and promptly fell asleep slung over my shoulder and dead to all else but sleep.

Bluebeard crouched to lift Sparrow's head in both his hands and hold her up to meet his eyes, and the look on his face as he lifted her was torn with regret.

"What shall I do for you, loyal Sparrow. Speak the words and I will make them so. Shall I shelter you with my wives until you can be bought back? Shall I set you on my wall with my advisors, or would you ride with me as my wife's pet rides with her?"

"As you please, Arrow," Sparrow said respectfully – a tone I still found surprising seeing as she never granted such a thing to me.

"I please to keep you safe and then to return you to your glory," he said gravely. "Your body is near?"

At her assent, he turned to me.

"Unlock for me the vault of my wives. We shall set my faithful servant within that she may partake in their fate with them."

Grosbeak made a muffled sound from the ground.

"Do not bring the traitor within. He deserves his gnat infestation, the crabs, the stitches, and whatever else has been inflicted upon his unworthy form for he did not deliver my vital message to you, nor did he stay by your side as even the most inadequate pet might do."

I did not argue, because I found I quite agreed.

I twisted my key in the lock and Bluebeard disappeared within. I gathered up my living hand and shoved it – wriggling like a dew worm – into my leather bag.

Bluebeard emerged a moment later without Sparrow's head.

"*Wait here but a moment for me,*" he said and there was an edge to his voice that made me frown, but he was gone before I could ask him why he sounded so torn.

I leaned down and regarded Grosbeak.

"You horrible little monster," I told him and his eyes flashed as if he were speaking back and by the spark in them, I could only assume he was speaking entirely in curses. "You were not my pet. You were my friend. What shall I do with you now? I dare not trust you. Did we not have a bargain, you and me?"

His face turned a terrible puce and the muffled sounds only grew worse.

I could kick him back into the sea. I could leave him here.

I could leave his mouth stitched up, which surely, he would find torturous.

He deserved it all. He was a traitor to his only friend and an accomplice to Sparrow's murder. And if Bluebeard hadn't rescued me, he would have been an accomplice to seeing me trapped forever beneath the sea.

But was I not all those things, too? And had not I been forgiven for them.

I sighed, leaned down, and picked the knot tying his stitches in place. Tanglecott had used a wide thread – almost a butcher's string – and it was easy enough to loosen the knot and then draw the string through the running stitch that held his rotting lips together.

"A curse on you and all your house," was the first thing he said.

I stared balefully at him. A less worthy recipient of my

generosity would be impossible to find.

"If you think this one act of mercy somehow makes you better than me, you can think again," he said, spittle flying as he put all the force of his fury behind his words.

"I think that simply not being you makes me better than you," I said coolly. "Perhaps I should seal you to the same fate to which you sealed me. Would you like to be sent back to the sea? Unless I misremember, there was a mermaid waiting for you."

"Mermaids! A pox on them all! She chose the Lady over me, and she with her beauty lost entirely!"

I thought back to the lashing figure that had dragged Lady Tanglecott beneath the waves and I laughed.

"She did, didn't she? Perhaps she prefers an uncouth face, for she chose both you and the besmirched Tanglecott – though of the two I still find you least fair."

He rolled his eyes dramatically.

"Would you like to explain your treachery?" I asked and I couldn't keep the frost from my voice entirely.

"No."

"Not even if it might earn you a place again at my side?"

"I am unrepentant. Badgering me will not alter what has been wrought within my heart. "

"I thought you no longer possessed one of those."

In the distance, a trail of smoke was rising into the sky. I watched it, worriedly. Was that not the direction of Tanglecott's breakfast room?

I heard the sound of something dragging and turned to find Bluebeard shuffling forward with Sparrow's wax-coated body slung over one shoulder.

My mouth fell open and beside me, Grobeak snickered.

"Are you collecting wives still, Arrow? I thought you had put that childishness away."

Bluebeard ignored him, stepping into the Room of Wives silently, and then returning so quickly that it seemed he hadn't left at all.

"A geas I place on you, corpse," Bluebeard said the moment he returned, taking Grosbeak's head up and shaking it as if to dislodge something from him. The slit-pupils of his eyes had expanded and his face held the mournful look of a man who had seen too many things. "Every curse you seek to set upon my wife will be set on you. Any twisting of your loyalty against her will be felt in pain within you. Any lasting insult to her person will be turned on you as an image is shown in a mirror. The arrow may fly toward her sent by your purpose, but the sting of it will be caught in your own soul. The blow may fall toward her, but the blade will cleave your flesh. I bind you now, revenant. I curse you with the twist of your own evil and corruption of your own cursed mind."

"Indignity! Cruelty beyond the pale!" Grosbeak shrieked.

I lifted him by his tangled hair. I'd lost his bag entirely.

"*You ought to leave him here,*" Bluebeard said idly. "*He's of no use to you and of considerable harm.*"

"I'm afraid I've grown used to him. Have you set Lady Tanglecott's home ablaze?"

"*I told her I was stripping her of her home. If she did not wish it so, she should not have tortured and killed my most loyal lieutenant. A millennium of collected curios is too small a price to pay for what she wrought here."*

I thought of the bed and its layers and shuddered in agreement, but I was still worried. "Won't the fire spread?"

"It will only add brilliant reds to our Wittenbrand dance of purple and gold," he said easily, offering me an arm. "Come to my nest, my paragon. Let us line it with the ashes of our enemies."

I took his arm and to my surprise, he led me from the beach and toward the blaze of Tanglecott's house.

"My master," the fire said, blazing violently, and leaping at our arrival as a dog leaps to greet its master.

"My fire," Bluebeard said, satisfaction in his voice. "Take us home old friend."

We stepped into the fire, and once again I felt the pain of burning while not burning at all and the world whirled around me in smoke and rushing flame, and then we were in the main room of his home, stepping out of the hearth, just as we had all those years ago after the petal ball. My heart leapt with joy.

The ferret on my shoulder screamed, leaping from me as if she had been stung and then shrieking in a way that sounded like curses as she rolled across an intricately tufted rug, leaving a trail of soot behind her. Her coat was patched with frizzled hair and her expression was pure murder. Before I could catch her to see if she needed help, she was racing up the mantle, leaping to the antler-and-bone chandelier, lunging at the cat sleeping there, and then tearing up the chain and into the starry sky above. I lost sight of her somewhere near the north star.

"Oh dear," I said.

Bluebeard strode into the room, letting go of my hand and sweeping up a tumble of parchments that had fallen through a hole in his door, making a neat heap.

"Have you considered not making unwilling creatures your pets?" Grosbeak asked me dryly as I moved to join my husband.

I lifted him to look him dead in the eye and said, "You can go down to my husband's wall, or I could throw you into this fire or out the door. I do not require you at my side. If you wish to leave, it can be arranged. I am so deeply wounded by you that I'd be entirely in my rights to abandon you."

"We made a bargain," he growled. "Is your mortal word so thin you'd wrench it apart over hurt feelings?"

"Our bargain was that I would keep you near and give you revenge on the Sword if you would advise me about the Wittenhame," I reminded him. "The Sword is no more."

"And I have advised you! It is not my fault that you ignored my worthy advice, mortal woman. Must I remind you that I tried to murder you in life? Is it truly a shock that I tried to do so again in death?"

Bluebeard didn't even look up at our squabble, his eyes flashing as he raced through one missive after another, setting them on a cluttered side table as he read. They balanced precariously there on something that looked like a snow lion jawbone.

"I thought we were friends," I told Grosbeak, and this time I couldn't keep the hurt from my tone.

"We're friends *now*," he spat bitterly. "Your husband has seen to that with his cursed geas. There's not a thing I can do to move against you."

"And is that so bitter a thing?"

"It is, rather. I deeply enjoyed making your life miserable and it will be a terrible deprivation to give you nothing but joy. And I know you won't throw me away. You have that strange mortal magic you call practicality. It will bind me to you, for you shall know it is wise to keep my unwilling council near, and so with this sorcery of insight and frugality, you will be bound to maintain me."

I frowned, but he was right. It made sense not to lose him as a resource and Bluebeard had pulled his teeth. He could not bite me, bound as he was.

Bluebeard broke the seal on a larger missive and as he opened it the smell of fresh-cut grass and something like clover poured out. He smiled and turned to me.

"We are not too late to join the fourth move. Set your pet aside, fire of my eyes, and let us array ourselves for what comes next." His eyes glittered with some perception I did not understand. "Night has fallen. I will remind you that you are bound once more not to speak until morning, but there are many preparations we can make mind to mind, and I would seek your counsel, for my other counselors have given up their heads or their loyalties and you are my last confidant."

"*Besides,*" I said with my mind. "*I was promised a rain of kisses.*"

He leapt suddenly to my side, leaning forward so that his lips brushed the shell of my ear and made me shiver as he whispered, "So you were."

Grosbeak snickered. "Serves you right to lose your counselors. That's what you get for being so single-minded. Anyone else would have indulged in a little pleasure now and again. Do you think I would have rebelled if you hadn't married her in the Witenbrand way? Do you think Vireo would have?"

I ignored the head and set him on the ground among the roots of the spreading tree from which hung capes and hats and in his place I took up my husband's wounded hand.

To my surprise, Bluebeard, ignoring Grosbeak entirely, leaned down, scooped me up in his arms, and though for a moment there was sorrow in his eyes, still his grin turned boyish as he burst into a run and took the stairs two at a time, bearing me to our bedchamber.

"*I can walk, you know,*" I said practically with my mental voice as Grosbeak's protests faded behind us.

He said nothing, only held me closer as if he were afraid of losing me. When we reached the door to the room, Bluebeard flung it open and stepped inside.

I sighed, sinking into the feeling of being home again.

The fire leapt in the grate as if to welcome us, the gargoyle over the mirror opened its eyes, and the black flowers around the bed bloomed, opening a little more with every breath we took as if drinking in our presence. The open wall was a snow-coated forest, thick and full and heavy but not at all cold, and I was still staring at it when he set me on the bed, drew down my torn sleeve and gentle as the rain of the spring, set one soft kiss after another from the spot just under my ear, slowly down my neck, across my shoulder and down the arc of my arm.

"Rains of kisses, as promised," he murmured and then straightened, looking at me in the reflection of the gargoyle mirror.

"I recall telling you a story when first you came to my home, wife of mine," he said in a burred voice, thick with some emotion I could not discern. It made my belly do flips, but even as I was sinking into his words, something else caught me. My reflection in the mirror was not right.

I stood up and stumbled forward as he spoke.

"I told you of a fox and raven, doomed to love one another forever but only to be one and the same for the blink of an eye at twilight. Remember you, this?"

I gasped, my hands flying up to trace my features as I looked at myself in the gargoyle mirror.

"I think perhaps that we two are like those ancient lovers – apart for days or years, only to intersect for precious moments before we are ripped apart again. Before we plan, I wish to give you assurances, wife, that these stolen moments are as precious to me as the moments in that tale. I live and breathe for the warmth of your skin against mine and the way your hard face softens when you catch sight of me."

He bit his lip a little awkwardly as if feeling exposed by his confession, rather than by the tattered shreds of clothing barely clinging to him.

Sweet as his words were, and scandalous as his apparel, I could not focus on either. I felt ill. My face – my face was all wrong.

I beheld it in the mirror with rising horror.

Those were still my eyes – still a little too large and slate grey. That, at least, was comforting. But the rest – my too-thin face was slightly more heart-shaped, my overly-high forehead softened, my cheekbones a more pleasing shape, my nose and lips slightly fuller. My hair was still dark and long, but its lustrous thickness fell in perfect waves.

I did not like it. Not even a bit.

"Izolda?" he asked and my name on his lips swelled like music reaching a climax.

I tore my gaze from the mirror.

"Do not weep, wife of mine," he said huskily, raising one hand awkwardly as if to forestall emotion. "One day these will not be stolen moments. Like your flesh hand is to the skeletal one, so will our lives be then to what they are now. We taste only the beginning, only the sparest structure. Then, we shall feast on the fullness." He paused. "Still, you mourn. I bid you tell me why."

I laughed bitterly. "*This is not my face.*"

He shook his head, eyes narrowing confusedly. "Is it not?"

I laughed again, but my laughter was close to a sob. "Obviously, it is not! It's perfect, don't you see?"

His smile was smug, and he drew back to cross his arms over his chest. "I do see, and if this is your attempt to seduce me from my vows, it is a valiant one, but I fear my mind is firmly set."

My eyes widened with horror. "*I … No. I'm not trying to seduce you!*"

He raised a solitary eyebrow, his smile shifting to a smirk.

"*I'm upset because I am not this beautiful.*"

"You seem to be exactly this beautiful."

His eyes raked me and I looked down. To my horror, it was not just my face that had changed. My plain figure had – shifted. My waist had narrowed, my hips widened. I was still slender, but now I was a slender hourglass. I could be full of garnets and it would only make sense.

"*Speak to my riddle, husband.*" If it was possible to wail mentally, I was wailing. "*What steals a woman's form and face, and her husband cannot see it?*"

And he – he choked on a laugh, and it took all my willpower not to strike him in his laughter.

"You heard me turn Lady Tanglecott's curse back on her. She is tied now to the sea, bereft of beauty and you are here with me, full with the same."

"*I want to go back!*"

"You wish to be trapped in the sea?" he looked surprised. "Trust me, wife, it is no pleasant thing. The sea would rend you apart, shredding your lungs with her waves and rotting your flesh beneath her weight."

I opened my mouth and shut it twice and the last time was a clash of frustration. This entire – costume. Yes. That was what it was, a costume disguising me! This entire costume was not *me* and I did not feel like myself in it and he was saying it was who I would be forever? My head swam with the impossibility of it.

"Don't look so dour wife, you've not the face for it anymore. Though the hand gives you an eldritch touch. Your pet will also help with that. There is no one so lovely that carrying a severed head does not mar their beauty somewhat."

I blinked at him, too stunned to reply, trying to shoot arrows with my eyes where my words would not express my frustration.

His features turned melancholy. "You tempt me too sorely, wife. How am I to keep my vows with you so near and looking at me so fiercely?"

"Maybe you should have left me ugly and then it wouldn't be a problem," I said dryly.

He leaned forward, eyes narrowing and hands clenched and I could not tell if it was violence or desire that made his every line so sharp.

"I fear it would not help. Ugly or beautiful, skeletal hand or whole, all I see is you, wife of my heart. II am drawn to you as birds are drawn to the south in autumn, pulled by invisible cords, and then driven back to northern climes come the first blush of spring. Where you are, there must I go and where you go, there, ever, I am."

He paused for a beat and then pounced forward, reminding me yet again of a cat, and with one quick movement he plucked a hasty kiss from my lips, scooped me up, ignoring my gasp, and flung me in the hot spring off to the side of the room. The ferret shrieked, clawing her way out of the pool and running from the room.

"Romance aside, you need a bath," Bluebeard said as I gaped at him from the water. "You smell of long-dead lovers and candle wax."

And before I could object, he dropped into the pool with me.

CHAPTER TWENTY-TWO

If I'd been embarrassed by his frank nudity when the Sword took his rib, I was doubly embarrassed to be bathing in this pool just feet away from him – and not even in my own body but in this altered one. My face was hot as I squirmed out of the remains of my dress and shift while staying submerged. I was so preoccupied with it that I didn't even notice him clean himself and leave the pool until I glanced up to be sure that he couldn't see me and found him standing in front of the gargoyle mirror, dressed in breeches and a light shirt and pulling on a heavily embroidered midnight-blue doublet. The cut of the doublet made his hips look narrower and his shoulders wider and it was covered in stitched birds in every shade of blue imaginable and done so precisely that they seemed almost alive. One of them chirped and I startled.

My husband laughed, his gaze flicking in my direction before returning to his task.

"I'll ask the mirror to give you something just as decorative, wife of mine. And then I'll ask the ravens for repast while you finish in the pool."

"I thought you said you'd grow that beard to your knees," I said with my mind when he scratched at the stubble on his cheek.

"I've not yet had the time, though I cultivate it with full

readiness."

Now I regretted teasing him. I was not a lover of beards. Of any length.

He left with only half his laces tied, swaggering from the room like a victorious general. The moment he was gone, I seized the chance to duck under the water, scrub my face and hair fiercely and then hop out of the pool, streaming water as I hurried to the mirror.

"Do you have a drying cloth?" I asked it and then had to lunge to catch the cloth it spat my way.

I dried off furiously, trying not to tangle my skeletal hand in the cloth or look too closely at the rest of my body. I wasn't even close to done when the mirror spat again, and this time, it sent out a bunch of light underthings and a dress of such a dark blue it looked almost black with a pair of red foxes peeking out from under the skirts, a boned bodice, and a swooping neckline. I dressed in the underthings and struggled into the dress, fighting my wider hips through the skirts, and huffing as I tightened the laces. I wasn't finished with the back before Bluebeard sauntered back in, pausing to bite his lip at me from the door.

"You're a tumble of hair and skirts, wife of mine," he said before setting down the pewter tray and hurrying over to cinch the laces up my back and tie them for me. I was fairly certain I ended up with far more knots than were required. There was something about him and string. He couldn't help putting snarls and tangles into everything.

He ran his hand through my hair and seven years had not been enough time for me to forget how much he loved playing with it. He set the wet strands into a braid, taking far longer than efficiency demanded as he played with the strands, weaving a seven-stranded braid, and then he reached into his pocket – for a ribbon, perhaps? And a songbird flew out, cheeping loudly before settling on the gargoyle mirror. I startled, and his breathy laugh was hot on my neck.

I shivered at the caress of his breath. I was starting to resent his vows. Were they really so sacred?

"Peace, woman, your milky neck could be the spill of stars in the night sky," he murmured and then he dropped the braid over my shoulder where it slid to follow the curve of my very new cleavage.

Before I could blink, he had released me and was busily pulling a pair of tufted chairs from their places to sit beside the spill of snow where the wall opened into the frozen forest. He pounced on a small table next, flipping it into place between the chairs, and then set the food he'd brought on the table. There were hot biscuits and hotter tea, two kinds of cheese, four kinds of pickles, and sliced peaches. The ravens, I remembered, did not do meat or eggs.

My mouth was instantly watering even before he invited me to sit.

"Eat, wife of mine, or Pensmoore is famished – as we both are," he said, pouring the tea as if he sat every day and poured from a delicate pot rather than ripping off the heads of his enemies. The look he gave me when he looked up again put an entirely different spin on the word, 'famished.' He swallowed visibly before continuing, "but we have the Wittenhame to conquer, revenge to be wrought, fortunes to be made, and magic to coax to our side, so we must set aside our better judgment for now and attend to our work."

"*Don't you mean that we must set aside pleasure* because of *our better judgment?"*

"I mean precisely what I said. It would be going with my better judgment to take you as my wife right now and here and in this bed of mine."

Was that me who made the strangled sound? I thought I might have swallowed my own tongue. The look in his eyes when he said *'take you'* made the fire look tame.

"Unfortunately, I must work *against* my better judgment today and take care of these other necessary things instead."

"*Of course,*" I said weakly, while my better judgment screamed to me that he was right and there were things I should be focused on that were most definitely not the bed he'd just mentioned. My better judgment was growing very difficult to hear. All the worse judgments were reminding me that I'd been married to him for seven years and really, why not be married all the way. Perhaps, there were some loopholes in these vows he claimed to have made. And hadn't he made some vows to me, too? It was all I could do to force my thoughts back into line. *"Where should we start?"*

"With the joust," he said enthusiastically – maybe too enthusiastically, as if he, too, were struggling – flinging the invitation I'd seen him reading onto the table so that it sat on the cheese plate. "Tell me, wife, does your iron expression extend to an iron spine and iron skin when it comes to racing toward an opponent armed only with a long silver needle?"

"I fear it does not," I said dryly, lifting up the invitation and examining it.

"A pity."

The invitation said very little – only that a Springtide Joust was planned, Buebeard's magnificence was requested at it, and the time stated – but since I knew not the hour or day in the Wittenhame, it was no help to me.

"*When is the first day of Springtide?*" I asked.

Bluebeard licked a finger and lifted it in the air, his eyes seeming to cross for a moment, and then he smiled. "Tomorrow night."

I drank my tea to avoid looking worried. That did not give us much time.

"*I think that perhaps you should give me a list of the vows and promises you've made, my husband – the ones that must be fulfilled during this game and with my remaining time.*"

He nodded. "A sensible path for your thoughts, wife. I would expect no less from you, young as you are. We who are older know that sensible plans crumble as do our days."

He was so grave, that I couldn't help myself.

"*Have you not noticed that I have aged seven years, husband?*"

He looked me over and then snatched up a small silver fish from the platter and tossed it in the air before catching it in his mouth and gulping it down. "No."

I blinked. "*Perhaps the new beauty I wear disguises it.*"

He waved a hand dismissively. "Are you not sitting there fretting over practical things? Then you are my Izolda. We all wear flesh – well or awkwardly, with dignity or without it – it is the one living under the mantle that sears the heart and whose soul I cling to as to a rock in a storm. What flesh you wear means no more to me than what dress you don. Which reminds me, your foxes hunger."

I looked down and one of them whined plaintively while the other licked his chops. Living dresses were a lot of work. Carefully, I fed them smoked cheese from the platter. He did not notice. I had feared he would tire of me and my aging mortal body and plain mortal mind. I had been a fool. He did not seem to notice, never mind care.

"My vows are many, wife of mine but only a few will affect our cause. First, I have made a vow to my folk – that I will renew their lands and glory. That I will bring to them an age of peace and protection from all their enemies."

I nodded at that, slipping a bite of fruit between my lips.

"That vow is graven on my bones. But there are others. My wives, for instance." At this, I forced my eyes to meet his. I would not be jealous. I would not be. I was, all the same. "I have spent their days wantonly on all I required to get this far, but I fear, fire of my eyes, that in marrying you in the Wittenbrand way, I can marry no others."

"*Such a terrible restriction,*" I said wryly.

"Speak to my riddle, wife of mine. Who must win or see his immortality stripped away? Who has but one chance or fail forever?"

"*You do,*" I said grimly.

"Worse than that, heart's beloved. If I lose, I will not only forfeit my immortality but with it my place as Prince of this land. My holdings will go to another, along with all my possessions and even you, love of mine."

"*Wait. What?*" I froze. "*How could I go to another?*"

"By laws of inheritance."

"You can't inherit a wife."

"We balance on the very teeth of the monster of death."

That was not an answer.

He drank his tea and it felt too common a thing to do after announcing that our fate was so grim and staring us straight in the face.

"So. You have vowed safety and prosperity to your people," I said. *"Which can only be acquired by winning this game."* He nodded. *"And to your wives, you have promised …"*

"The full return of their days. Which is why I bid you leave them on their pedestals and do not take them down to play with them again, or if one is broken, my vow to her will fail."

My eyes narrowed. He sounded as if he were discussing dolls.

"But how could you possibly give them back their days?" I did not have the stomach to eat more, now.

His eyebrows rose. "By winning, of course. Surely, you must have figured out the clues by now. If I win, then I will inherit the title of Bramble King, and nothing will be too difficult for me."

I pinched the bridge of my nose, rubbing it. *"The current Bramble King could return their days to them?"*

He hesitated. "The Bramble King fades."

"Then, he cannot."

"He may, perhaps. But what he is now is as the waning of the moon. Whoever replaces him will be as the waxing of it – swelling in power and potential."

I paused, thinking. *"The Bramble King holds this Wittenhame together, doesn't he? I see his face in the sand, the sky, the trees, the rock."*

"You do."

"If you take his position, will you take that place?"

"I must."

A rush of cold filled me and without realizing what I was doing, I reached across our small table and took his hand in mine. The skin was warm under his firm callouses.

"Will you still be a man?"

He seemed wary as he answered. "That is a riddle I have not solved."

Dread weighed heavy in my belly. *"Will you be as he is?"*

"Yes."

His word was like a heavy nail shutting up a door. Whether he won or lost, I would lose him. If he lost, he would fade away, his vows unfulfilled and his spirit hollowed for the rest of what would be a short mortal life. If he won, he would become something completely other, fulfilling his vows to all but me.

I fought against something that had me in its grip. It shook me and tore at my chest and I couldn't draw in a deep breath. I would not have him as a whole husband whether he won or lost. Just thinking it shattered me, broke me in a way these seven years had not. Then, I had hopes of saving him from death. Now, I could see there would be no saving him. He would die a failure, or give his life a victor, but one way or another he would burn it up on this and me with it.

"There is no third option?" I asked weakly. I smelled smoke but

when I looked up there was no fire, and yet the scent of it made me dizzy.

I was being foolish. Wives gave up husbands to duty every day. They gave them to war. They gave them to work so long and vast that they only saw them in barest snatches before the man collapsed on his bed and a snatch again before he was gone into the dawn to toil again. They gave them to months and years away in merchant trade or conquest. I was not unique in this.

I set my tea down heavily and the cup clattered on the saucer.

"There is no third way. Win or lose are my only options. And where I must go, you cannot follow."

I struggled to fight my breath in place.

What he said made perfect sense. It was absolutely practical – so utterly unlike him. I was only rejecting it because I hated it with all my heart, not because it wasn't the prudent thing to do.

I closed my eyes, breathed out through my nose, and was properly composed when I said in my firmest tone, *"Then I will follow as long as I can."*

"You will fight at my side?" Hope sparked bright in his eyes, mixed with a kind of burning pain. It ached to look at it.

"Until my last breath."

He nodded, grim and beautiful.

"Are you sure you must fulfill all your vows?" I asked, looking longingly at his bed.

His voice was iron, but he took up my hand again as he spoke, and his gentle touch took some of the sting with it. "I will fulfill each one to the letter, heart of my own heart."

I took a great breath and then I said with admirable calm, "*Then let us consider how we might win.*"

CHAPTER TWENTY-THREE

"To win," Bluebeard had explained, "We must chisel away our competitors. We must make them flee before us."

To my surprise, he pulled his playing piece from his pocket and set it on the table. It moved, peering up at us, and to my horror, the former King of Pensmoore was now the new King of Pensmoore – my brother Svetgin. The tiny figurine Svetgin looked old, though. His miniature shoulders slumped under the burden of rule.

The specter peered around my shoulder to get a better look.

"Traditionally, we've made them bleed through their human realms."

"*How marvelous,*" I deadpanned.

"Do you know your mortal histories?" Bluebeard asked, so taken with his explanation that he didn't seem to notice when yet another bird tumbled from one of his pockets. It startled, making a *tee taw, tee tee taw* call before hopping up his sleeve and lodging itself on his shoulder where it stared down critically at us. "Was there any reference to one called Romanovich?"

"*Romanovich the rampager?*" I asked, eyebrows raised.

"Perhaps. He would have been from Elkanmoore?"

I shivered. I'd read the histories. The towns put to the flame, the inhabitants savagely brutalized and killed. Whole nations swallowed up in a single bite. He'd campaigned for fifty years by most accounts, destroying the continent, setting everyone back to the dark ages and seeming no more bothered by the fact that every cloth weaver was gone, or that there was no longer a herd of cattle to be found, than most people would be over waking to discover it had rained in the night.

"*There are none who have not heard that name,*" I acknowledged grimly.

"That was the name Lord Antlerdale went by in a previous game."

He stared out into the snowy woods, eyes lost in thought, his fingers tangled around a loose strand of my hair he was tying into knots. My eyes felt dry they were open so wide.

"And that is how he won the game," Bluebeard said grimly, his hand in my hair tightening to a fist. "He was granted … concessions … as a result."

"*Concessions?*" I did not mind him playing with my hair. I only wished his fingers would creep up the strand and tangle in the rest of it and —

"Mortal slaves who serve him eternally. Serve him however he pleases. If we beat him at this game, they'll go free, too. Any winnings of a previous game revert back to nil if that type of game comes around again and the reigning champion fails to achieve victory."

As if we didn't have enough motivation already.

"*Where does he keep these poor souls?*" Even mentally, my voice trembled.

"In his home. But let us not dwell on such right now." Bluebeard poured more tea and poked at the invitation. "This game is running a different course – a deadlier one."

Maybe for the Wittenbrand. From my view of it, watching a few Wittenbrand them rip each other to shreds was less awful on the whole than the death of tens of thousands and the destructions of civilizations.

"We cripple and wound," he gestured at his side where the blood had soaked through his blue coat once more. "And if a player is so disabled that they fail to attend a move, they are eliminated. Sparrow saved me elimination by standing in my place. If some other Wittenbrand feels such loyalty to Lady Tanglecott in this next move, then she will remain among us. If not, then she will be removed just as the Sword was. The same trap is set for Marshyellow."

"Won't his people stand for him? They seem very loyal."

Bluebeard tapped my skeletal hand. "They are indeed very loyal. Loyal to you, I would think. Is that not how you executed him? By means of the loyalty of his folk?"

I swallowed.

"What will you do with Marshyellow's people and holdings, my practical horror?"

"Should I not set them free?"

He snorted, leaping to his feet and moving to the bookshelf. He grabbed a book, thumbed through the pages, and then set it aside.

It was called, *Negotiation: The Subtle Art of Sticking a Dagger in a Belly.*

I shuddered.

"Speak to my riddle, wife of mine. Does the rope wish to flap in the wind? Does the ship sail with no anchor? Does the horse handler rejoice when there is no stable and the merchant when there is no market?"

I tapped my chin. I had enough to do already without bringing order to the chaos of Marshyellow's people.

"I leave that puzzle to your sensible mind." He drew another book out and flipped through it. The title read, *War: A Romantic's Guide to Conquest.* "We must plan for war on the mortal plane. Too long was I beneath the sea. Our armies will be ragged-edged and slack. We must send you to your brother to give him my orders."

"What makes you think he'll listen to me? I am not of much standing in Pensmoore."

He frowned now, throwing various items from his shelf as if he were not the one who would need to clean them up later. There seemed to be more items than could possibly fit on so few shelves. Titles flashed by, but only one caught my eye, *Keep Your Head: How to Avoid Panic and Beheadings.* Grosbeak should have read that one.

"Pensmoore is yet one more thing that we must not lose, fire of my eyes. I would not see my mortals slaughtered or ravished. But I fear your lands once more need the steering hand of a patron. I feel the feet of her enemies edging over her borders and if we do not guide her hand, they may soon storm her gates. More than that, the moves of the game dwindle and our armies must attend the last battle or watch Pensmoore overrun."

"The last battle?"

"You must have rumors of the Plains of Myygddo even in mortal stories and song." His eyes met mine and narrowed as he said. "It always comes to a battle there in the end – a great assemblage of armies. Fail, and the barbarians crash over the land. Succeed, and you may ride home, broken, battered, missing a limb, a friend, an eye – and your nation lives. There are none who escape war unscathed and the winners suffer with the dead, drinking a double portion of the bitter draught until the end of their days."

"*So we will ride to this last battle?*" I swallowed uncomfortably. So much was at stake in two different realms and war was not a thing I had ever wanted to see again. "*I still don't know why you set my hand to fighting Aayadmoore in the last battle. I was not best pleased to ride as their figurehead and watch the innocent slain with the guilty.*"

His burning blue eyes seemed to bore through me. "You would rather another suffered that pain? Who would you set it on? Name the substitute."

I ran a tired hand through my hair, but it was the bone one and it tangled in the locks. I stopped, frustrated, to try to free it with my other hand.

Bluebeard sighed. "Our armies are not the only ones who drink bitter draughts. We, too, must drink this to the dregs. I would spare you if I could – I will spare you from the rest. But you are a woman full-grown and strong, and you must bear this mortal burden. I will treat once more with Wittentree. She will be your ally."

"*Why choose her so often?*" I asked, surprised by the burst of jealousy in my chest. Hadn't he been fighting alongside her and coming to her land's aid when the Sword dragged me into the sea?

He laughed then, snatching something from a small wooden box and throwing the box to the floor in triumph.

"I treat with those who will treat with me, my wife."

And then, in a single motion, he'd moved to kneel before me, and he took my skeletal hand in his and placed on it a bright ring. It was oval-shaped and long so that it covered half of my third phalange from one knuckle to the next. The face of it was split in two – one half in silver depicted a moon crossed by a soaring bird picked out in sapphire. The other half depicted a leaping fox laid out in rubies on the face of a blazing golden sun.

"I thought it fitting," he said and then he kissed my bone fingers one by one, looked up at me with a boyish half-smile and leapt back to his feet before I could so much as move.

"*Thank you –* " I began, but he was already shaking his head before his words slipped out.

"Maps are below. I must study them now, but you are mortal and must rest."

I looked around at the ruined room and shook my head. "*The planning. The joust –* "

"Will wait. Rest now. Do not fear that I will leave you in ignorance, for you are now my compatriot in all things."

He scooped me up, my foxes snapping at him, and carried me to the bed where he tucked me forcefully into the eiderdown and clamped the foxes yipping mouths shut with his fingers before settling them down around me.

"Darkness, my fire," he ordered, and the fire dimmed. The mess grew less bothersome in the encroaching darkness while the moon in the forest beyond grew more full.

"Slake now your mortal need for sleep, fire of my eyes," Bluebeard whispered and I did not know how he possibly thought I could sleep when he punctuated his words by trailing kisses across my brow, down my jaw, along the column of my neck, and ending only just barely over the rise and fall of my heaving chest. He lingered there for a moment and I thought his resolve might finally fail him but instead, he shook himself, grinned ruefully in the moonlight, and – as if admonishing himself – said, "Sleep."

And then he was gone, the door closing with a *snick* behind him, and I was left there in his bed that smelled so richly of him, trying very, very hard to fall asleep when all of me was suddenly awake, alert, and unsatisfied.

One of the foxes snapped her jaws and I buried my face in my pillow and tried to pretend I was not so desperately in love with my own husband that it was making me feel a little ill.

CHAPTER TWENTY-FOUR

I woke, blinking in the darkness to an arm draped heavily over my waist and another slipped under my hip as if I had been lifted sideways into someone's lap.

Someone, in this case, was my husband. His breath purred in my ear, his lips so close that I could feel them shuddering on my skin.

I knew I should get up. I should see to preparations for the all-out battle we were planning. I should learn to joust, or I should scold Grosbeak, or find the ferret, or change out of this dress with the foxes who were currently yawning dramatically and wiggling their way out of the covers to study the wall which had opened up into a dark desert. It was filled with the looming shapes of dried-out bushes, the uncanny pattern of sand formed only by the wind and never the rain, and the strangely effervescent scent of creosote.

I did none of those things. Instead, I let my breathing match Bluebeard's, and I soaked him up as the thirsty ground soaks up rain after a drought. I had missed him for seven years. I'd pined for his presence, ached for his arms. And I wanted this moment, right now, to go on forever.

I wanted the sweet stillness of him resting safe and well beside me. I wanted him, and only him, forever and ever, and I realized

– only with a little bitterness to mix into all this depth of rich sweetness – that I would take whatever he would give. If his vows allowed only this, then this was enough. I would treasure it. I would keep it close to my heart in the stark days to come. I'd honor his word. I'd honor his sacrifice.

I'd woken like this twice before in this very bed, and the echoes of those times added depth to this moment, like seeing a field from three different sides. I liked this vantage best.

I rolled over slowly, so as not to wake him, reveling in the way his arms trailed over my waist as I moved. His face was peaceful in sleep – unlined, relieved of its usual ambition and intensity, and despite his blue shadow of a beard, he looked younger in sleep, sweeter.

I could not help myself. I caught his lips between my own in a butterfly kiss and just as I started to wonder what he would think if he were awake, I felt them curve. Startled, I pulled back to find him grinning sleepily at me.

His voice was husky with sleep. "Your affection, unearned though it is, wakes the fires within."

He drew me in close and tucked my head under his chin so that my cheek was cradled in the warmth of his breast and his powerful arms formed a basket around me. Just as I was once swept away by grief, I was now consumed with contentment. It stole into my heart so unexpectedly that tears formed, and I gasped at the relief I felt as if a burden had been taken onto other shoulders.

"Not yet, wife of mine. Do not surrender yet. This is but a reprieve in our war, a breath between battles."

He drew back to prop himself up on one elbow, keeping his other hand idly on my hip while he yawned.

"Tonight, we attend the Springtide Joust. I will ride in the lists. You will collect valuable information on our rivals – their holdings, their lands, their weaknesses, their mortal allies."

I nodded my agreement. It had worked before, hadn't it? I'd read the Sword's copy of Antlerdale's book and discovered how his army was equipped.

"When we are done," Bluebeard continued, and he seemed tense. "You will ride to the mortal lands – and this is key, wife of mine – and I stress it now in case I am injured in the lists and cannot remind you of it after. You must take my key and go immediately to your brother's house and there you must have him lead his armies to the Plains of Myygddo. You must send this missive I have addressed to the loyal lords of the Aayadsmoore who will join his armies with their own under his command. They must stand and fight on the plains there in the last battle, and you must see that they do."

"Myygddo is far to the south in hostile lands," I objected.

"Even so," Bluebeard said, reaching to find the letter he'd written the night before. It was sealed and tied with ribbons. I found myself more distracted by how the muscles bunch and lengthened in his arms and bare chest as he moved. I did not like my gaze drifting to the open wounds in his palms and his side – did not dare touch them unless I must – but they were there, too, just as much a part of him as his beauty. "Myygddo is where this battle for the mortal lands must come to a head and so that is where we shall bring it to meet us. If we can manage to disable Antlerdale in the lists, then Ptolemoore will be vulnerable and your brother may march his troops through their lands with only mortal resistance, Moravidmoore and Ilkanmoore being crippled by their loss of patrons."

"Mortal resistance is still resistance," I said wryly, *"and we*

mortals find it daunting."

"Hmm." That sound was the same as before – an acknowledgment of what I'd said while being unmoving on the point. "Time to prove, then, that he is made of royal stuff. He seized a throne. Let him earn it."

I hated how miserable my mental voice sounded when I said, *"I do not wish to be parted from you."*

He squared his shoulders in a way that made me anxious. "Where I go next, you cannot follow. I would save you from tasting my fate, for it is bitter indeed."

"Then is this the last?" I asked, catching his hand despite the wound in it and weaving my fingers through his. *"The last night? The last kisses?"*

He caught my chin in a tender pinch, his thumb grazing my lower lip. "Still, I hope for more. Still, I hope for a triumph that exceeds expectations. Am I a fool to hope for the unhopeable? To look for the unseeable?"

"Don't speak to me in riddles."

"Then I cannot speak at all."

His kiss was as fierce as it was sudden, and it fractured with fear and knit itself back together with the intensity of commitment. We broke apart, gasping.

"With my vows, I bound you to death. With my choice of you as my one true bride, I turned the key in the lock of the crypt and bound you there with me."

"I don't understand."

But it wasn't entirely true, was it. I did understand. He was planning to be heir to the Bramble King, to be there and not there, sleeping, drifting, no longer a man. Was that not a death? And even the cords of our love could not take me there with him. I was bound just as he, but I would be bound to a dead man.

The look in his eyes made my heart ache. "Forgive me, if you dare. Forgive me for the doom I've brought on you. You fell in love with the bird, little fox, and now we have only this tiny splinter of time to love a lifetime in. Better, when it is through, that you fight at the head of your people and watch your innocents plucked from the arms of death and saved – better that, than that you stand beside your husband and watch him dragged down into hell."

I trembling cry escaped my list, but he had already leapt from the bed with his usual energy, tugging his high boots on and strapping a sword to his waist as if he hadn't just told me he was going to send me away again so he could pass on to another kind of life without me.

"I think, perhaps, it's time to show you Riverbarrow, wife, and what I first set out to defend. It will do both our hearts good. And then we'll choose a mount for the joust. What say you?"

I smiled tremulously, keeping my emotions in check by will alone, but his answering smile warmed my heart as I rose, and tidied myself. If I had only this day, I must not waste it in tears or misery.

The mirror offered me a crown that I refused and a back-less fur-lined jacket that I accepted. It would sit over a practical dark blue dress – Bluebeard had declared the foxes unwelcome in Riverbarrow – and warm my neck with a collar so high that the fur fringe caressed my chin, while still showing off the scars on my back. They had not left when I donned my new, unwanted beauty. The dress was worked with weeping figures sewn onto the cloth in onyx and ivory beads, their heads cradled in their hands and shoulders hunched with sorrow. How fitting.

To Bluebeard, it offered a short cape in a dazzling blue and a blue-worked black doublet. He looked as dashing as ever. He'd even made the red slit on his cheek that was his mark.

"Can you change me back?" I asked him as I braided my hair before the mirror. My too-beautiful face looked back miserably at me, and he paused in his preparations to look over my shoulder and study my face in the mirror.

"I think not," he said, a calculating look in his eye. "Keep it as a bargaining chip but be clever in how you word your vows when you trade it away."

My eyebrows rose with his words, and he shrugged mischievously. "I would say all things have a price, fire of my eyes. I would say all things can be bartered. Except that I have won you and I would never gamble you away. Meet me below."

He was gone before I'd thought to tell him that I loved him, too.

I finished the braid and drew in a steadying breath, following him down to the hall below, and feeling nostalgic as the nightingale stairs sang my descent. Everything about this place echoed of birds and wings and distant flight.

I found Bluebeard attaching Grosbeak to a new lantern pole.

"Would that I might leave him behind, but I fear you would miss him," my husband said dryly. And I couldn't help the relief I felt at that, for betrayal or no betrayal, Grosbeak was my friend and I had missed him those long years that he lay beneath the sea.

And perhaps, I would at least get to keep him when I lost my husband to his victory.

"He fears there will be no wit to guide either of you unless you bring the brains of this adventure," Grosbeak said scornfully.

"And that's you?" I asked him dryly, but I was fighting a smile.

"It's certainly not her." He scowled as the ferret ran up the pole, down the chain, and settled in a curled-up heap on his head like the worst possible fashion in fur hats. "Tell her I would appreciate it if she did not nest in my hair. I will never get the smell out."

"I prefer your more recent pet," Bluebeard said, running a finger over the ferret's head. She preened to his caress. "She very sensibly has not tried to kill either of us yet. Besides, the fire likes her, and he likes so few people."

"Thank you," said the fire.

"This may remain here," Bluebeard said, holding up my living hand before placing it on the hearth about his fire. "It is less likely to betray us than the corpse is."

"I take deep offense at that comment, Arrow," Grosbeak said with a terrible sneer.

"As you should, damned one." Bluebeard finished his work, passed me the pole, and set a hand lightly on my shoulder. "Dawn waxes, I fear, wife of mine, so with these words, I grow silent, but in my silence, find my duty a delight for it flows ever to your sea." He paused, and in his pause, I felt all the words we wanted to say and couldn't find. "Come, let me show you my lands and holdings in all their aching glory."

"This is what I had to put up with for *seven years,*" Grosbeak complained.

"I thought you said it was only days for you," I said, meeting my husband's eyes and his very gaze was a caress. Something in me melted in its warmth.

"I remember it as centuries," Grosbeak moaned.

And then Bluebeard seized my hand, grinned, and suddenly the room around us grew monstrously large and I jumped as mouse squeaked beside us as it skittered away, its bare tail as long as a cedar tree.

I clung to Bluebeard's hand, small as a bug for the second time in my life. I just managed to throttle back a scream, when I was knocked off my feet only to find myself bobbing and weaving through the air erratically.

"Don't drop me! That grip is not firm enough!" Grosbeak wailed.

Bluebeard's grip on my hand guided me to a proper seat behind him, as I realized – to my utter surprise – that we were mounted on a dragonfly. I clutched his waist with my free hand and found a better grip on Grosbeak's pole with the other.

"You are going to have to do exercises to get a stronger grip. I mean it. I absolutely refuse to be dropped in these mad adventures."

My eyes were wide as they could go. I looked out to my side to see the zipping rainbow wings spread out to one side and then, quickly, I looked out to the other side to watch the matching set scissoring on the other side. Under us, the carapace of the insect was bright as a gem, blue as the sky, and iridescent.

Dragonflies were beautiful when caught in glimpses on the side of a sulky river, darting between tall reeds. They were more glorious yet when they were large as a pair of team horses and vibrating under your seat.

I was so involved in admiring him that when I finally looked up again, I had to cut off a yelp as the dragonfly sped right toward the wall.

"I hate this part," Grosbeak muttered. "Only the Arrow would hide his land in so diminished a manner."

We were aimed directly at the dramatic painting of a riverbank at dawn. The reeds and weeping willow on the bank were so carefully depicted they almost looked real. I could nearly smell the scent of fecund earth and flowering grasses as we plunged toward the painting, my heart in my throat, my lungs caught in that moment of breathless terror, and then I realized we were no longer in Bluebeard's home for when I looked over my shoulder, I saw only the river and the reeds and the sway of the wind and the bright baby gold of the rising sun.

Riverbarrow, it seemed, lay within a painting on my husband's wall.

CHAPTER TWENTY-FIVE

That my husband loved this land was apparent in his every aspect as we skimmed over and through the heart of Riverbarrow. It was just as apparent in the land herself and I felt an ache of almost-jealousy as it reached out to him, every blade of grass and wisp of breeze trying to caress him, to embrace him, to entangle him forever and love him to the end of time.

Mine, I thought viciously at them all, and had to shake myself because I was sounding a bit too much like Grosbeak for my liking.

I had not realized how far and fast a dragonfly might speed and when I finally grew as used to such movement as one could grow – for I was still sitting on the hard, slick, jointed back of a beautiful insect and it was no comfortable ride, nor did I feel secure as we hovered and leapt, sped and dodged – the landscape seemed to rise up and meet us.

Birds dashed in every direction in flights of one or two or two hundred. White and grey, blue and palest pink, black and white flecked or barn-owl brown and eagle gold, they were everywhere, and far from flying away from us, they often flew toward, welcoming their miniature prince on the back of their insect kin.

We dipped down through a flight of birds and while we were still dodging waving grasses too tall and deep that my eye could not find both the dark stalks where they met the roots and the waving tassels high in the sky, we were already rising up above the field again, impossibly fast.

My palms were sweaty, and I clung to Bluebeard's back a little too tightly in my fright. I had never flown. I was not one of his beloved birds darting and swooping along the breeze to be near him, and I did not enjoy the experience of flight even though the practical part of my mind was reminding me that this was a very economical, quick, and effective way to travel and if it had been possible to reproduce in Pensmoore, the trade and political advantages would be numerous.

We skimmed up through oak leaves, their massive proportions sheltering us in dappled shade for moments before we burst back into the golden heaviness of the morning, rising so we could see the next four bends of the river and the reeds on either side. A small family was huddled on the riverbank. At first, I thought them beavers, but as we drew closer, I realized they were some kind of living rock with heavy carved faces and limbs and the parent stones were gently showing the smaller stone children how to cross the still water.

There was no wind this morning, and a peachy haze hung gentle over the calm silver river, its mottled surface intermittently broken by fallen logs or clumps of rock or spreading river flowers.

Drowsy, over-large blooms nodded gently on the banks and then perked up when we passed and opened their tumbled burrows for figures that seemed half-human and yet woven of willow and furze to stumble out and lift a hand of greeting to us.

Small insects buzzed over the surface of the river while below fish broke the surface, their questing mouths braving the dangers of air to lip at the bugs.

A clump of gnarled men in clothing too big for them fished along the bank, smoking cob pipes, eyes closed, as they soaked in the sun's warmth. As I watched, one snapped his fingers, and a trout as large as he was leapt from the water to land with a tumbling flop right in the basket set on the bank. The man closed his eyes again, drowsing as his supper smothered to death in the open air.

One of the smaller of the speckled birds darting around us swept down upon the remaining insects in twin beauty and violence – so very like the husband whose waist I was gripping as if that grip were my life.

And he *was* my life. He was my whole life in a way that felt terribly sacrilegious – blasphemous, as if I may very well be struck down for the temerity to have hitched all my hopes to just one mortal man. And yet he was not mortal. Perhaps, one part of my heart suggested, small and timorous – perhaps, he *can* bear so deep a loyalty, so devastating a love. And yet he'd told me himself that he was passing from this world of birds and pastoral scenes and on to some place where I could not join him.

Pensmoore, his wives, and this Riverbarrow had given the futures of all their thousands to him. Their lives and livelihoods rested entirely on his moves in this game. I dare not step between him and then.

My breath hitched in my throat, and I pressed my cheek against his shoulder, letting myself hold on for this one lone day.

We flew higher as the trees multiplied below, and the river became but the barest ribbon beneath, and his wild folk faded from view. Up we flew, up, up, to where I saw the faint purple peaks of mountains to the east and the periwinkle haze of sea far to the west. The only sound up here was the whooshing of the wing pairs on either side of me as their gossamer thinness was all that was between us and plunging to our deaths.

Small hamlets speckled the landscapes and a bare few towers thrust upward, but no dusty roads or open-pit mines were to be seen.

"What of this is Riverbarrow?" I whispered to my husband over the buzz of the wings of the dragonfly.

"It's all Riverbarrow," Grosbeak said from where he hung on the pole, saving Bluebeard from exercising magic to speak to me in the day. "As far as your eye sees and beyond. There are small villages and the tangled homes of those who live below and above, but it's mostly a wild, untamed place. Nothing like the crypt city of Coppertomb, or the stag hills of Antlerdale, or the populated fortresses of Towerrock. Your husband's people are a plain, peaceful folk – un-regarded, unwanted, non-useful in any conflict. There are no orcs, minotaurs, or tridents here. Not even unicorns as the Sword bred for hundreds of horsey generations. I'll miss that braggart. He was always good for a laugh." My memories of my would-be 'husband' were not so fond. "Oh, there are halls and fortresses of a kind and the food they make here is the best of the Wittenhame," Grosbeak continued. "There are some wise practitioners of this or that, and bold noble souls in strange old-folk bodies, but look not to them for an army."

But it was not an army I wanted to see here. That was not why I'd come. I'd come to see his heart and despite the tranquility of this day, I saw it here in the tangled way the forest grew – inviting and yet terribly wild and fierce. I saw it in the warm smoke curls from villages built on chicken legs that roamed between the trees while beneath them long creatures with longer jaws bit and snapped. I felt it in the way the wind wasn't howling right now but seemed to be suggesting that it might begin to at any moment, and in the way every rock was jagged, every pool held dark shadows, and every tree was the keeper of secrets so aged and ripe that no outsider would be granted them. I saw hints in the smiles of the leaf children we passed, tumbling together in a game – but I saw them just as well in a clump of trees we shot past that held a dangling ghost on the end of a noose from every branch and twig of it. This place was lovely, but not safe; warm, but not tame; sweet as the sweetest nectar, but with a stain of bitterness. It was him, all him in every echo of every strain.

My husband turned his face so he could press his rough stubble cheek to mine, and I felt the muscles in it tighten with a smile. An army was not what he was looking for either, for I saw what he saw. I saw a folk vulnerable and beautiful and ancient in a land wilder than anyone knew, and I knew why he loved them, why he kept them safe with every beat of his heart, and why he'd had to see them one last time before the end.

"They've diminished," Grosbeak said dismissively. "You should have seen this place in its glory – absolutely stunning. The dragons alone were worth the price of admission. I thought back then that he had a point in trying to preserve it. It drains his magic, you know. He sustains this whole place with his power. That's why he has to use your days for extras. He's all tapped out just keeping this rustic haven untouched by the world beyond."

I felt my eyes grow wide at Grosbeak's words. I was looking at a place larger than Pensmoore in size and scope. Seeing this – all of this – added a depth to all that had gone before. I could imagine these folks as they must have slowly gathered to arrive at his home with their plea. I could imagine them stealing away to slip me the note when I was kidnapped. Those things had felt commonplace. I'd scarce known the sacrifice and toil to accomplish them. What other things was my husband gathering together and tying fast in his efforts to fulfill all vows and recompense all people?

We sped toward a waterfall, dipping down from our height to draw toward it.

Someone had built a tall, spiked tower at the peak of the falls. It rose like a singular mountain, but the stonemasonry was nothing I'd seen before in the courts of Pensmoore or Aayadmoore. It was carved as if by inhuman hands – and likely it was – carved almost as if it had been grown of earth. It was intricate in its every delicate detail, woven rather than chiseled from stone.

A pavilion of stone extended from the roots of the tower to look out over the bright falls, and even this pavilion was woven of twisting strands of stone rather than carved from a block. It curled up as tree roots might and the platform it produced seemed almost more by accident than design.

It was to that pavilion that the dragonfly shot.

I clutched my husband tightly as we descended.

"He guards the entrances to this place as a miser hoards his wealth," Grosbeak said. "It makes for an insular society. I do not envy him his wealth in it."

"Don't you?" I asked, annoyed by his scorn. "You who have no body do not envy a man with a whole realm?"

Grosbeak snickered. "I who have no responsibilities nor ambitions, do not envy him who is eaten moment by moment with his. I do envy you, Izolda. Would that Tanglecott's spell had reversed and made me the beautiful one."

"We could bargain for my beauty," I suggested, eager to be rid of it. "Have you anything to offer?"

Bluebeard squeezed my hand in rebuke.

"Undying bitterness and a penchant for evil. Tempting, isn't it?"

I snorted. "Hardly."

"You've grown dull, Izolda. Women in love are always dull because what they want is so predictable. I much prefer women in hate."

"A predictable penchant, as you inspire the emotion so effortlessly."

He snorted, and to my surprise, Bluebeard chuckled with him as he set us down on the massive platform and then gripped my hand. The platform shrunk and the world around us wobbled for a moment and then we were normal-sized again.

I did not see what happened to the dragonfly. I was too distracted when Bluebeard took me in his arms and kissed me long and deep and lingering.

"*Welcome to my lands, fire of my eyes. They know you now as mine.*"

"Oh, ewww. Save it for the bedroom. Some of us don't have legs to walk away."

I could almost have believed that Bluebeard lengthened our kiss just to annoy my friend further. His mental voice was a caress in my mind.

"*With so few prospects left to us, let us seize every one we may.*"

And then he kissed me a second time and pulled back only long enough to bury his face in my hair for a moment before stepping away.

"*If you don't want your revenant eaten we might need to leave*

him here. I must settle a thing or two now that Sparrow is in the
Realm of Patience. I owe her that at the very last for all she's done in
my name. Wait for me?"

"Of course," I replied and to my surprise, he leapt off the platform in a swan dive and slid into the river without making a splash. I would never get used to that man.

"If this is a romance story, the pair of you should stay together more," Grosbeak said. "One of you is always running off to save the world and it makes it hard for your story to progress."

"When I mean to betray my friends and wreak general evil upon the world, I shall consult you. In matters of the heart, I fear you will only lead me astray."

"I told you before that you ought to follow your head and not your heart," he scolded. "If you had listened, you'd be ruling Pensmoore as a new patron saint right now rather than shackled to the Arrow."

"I'd be drowned beneath the sea," I said dryly.

"Perhaps. Or perhaps not. I don't know why you insist on seeing me as your betrayer when what I did just moved the story along. Someone has to do the heavy lifting so you can swan around in fox dresses kissing pretty men."

Bluebeard surfaced a little way up the river and to my shock, a creature rose from the silver water with him, a creature black but dappled just as the river was dappled, not entirely solid, and yet not entirely spirit. It seemed more made of water than made of flesh, its lines and curves made fluid by the water of its equine form. The edges of it flashed in the sun, growing opaque with bubbles around nose and mouth as it pawed ripples into the water.

"That's what I do," I said distractedly. "Swan around."

The horse towered over Bluebeard, three times his height. Its neck curved nobly down so that its wet nose could touch his head, and when it drew back rivulets of water ran down my husband's forehead and dripped through his beard as if he'd been baptized by a roan priest into a church of flowing water and living stone.

"What," I asked, awe in my voice, "is that?"

"The river?" Grosbeak asked, sounding bored.

"The horse!"

"That's the river. Or the kelpie, I suppose, but it's the same thing. The spirit of the river, more real than the water that people name 'river.' He serves as the steward to Lord Riverbarrow when he is absent and a more sober and bromidic a being I have never met, yourself perhaps being the exception."

They were deep in conversation, my husband and the river, their heads close together.

"Your insults warm my heart," I said, but I wasn't paying attention, every part of me was leaning over the edge of the pavilion, trying to see as much of the kelpie as I could. His crystal edged flanks flexed as he stomped and a wave splashed back and forth behind him in a long tail. Now *that* was a mount. Would Bluebeard ride such in the lists?

"Don't even think about it," Grosbeak said, snickering. I forced myself to look at him, but I only wanted to look at the kelpie. What would it be like to run my hands over his sleek coat? "He'd never take his river from the land. It would be robbery and the good Arrow is far too great a Wittenbrand prince for that. Fool that he is. No, if you're thinking about how he'll ride in the jousts, its more likely to be a mist lion as his mount or perhaps another dragonfly, but this one made large instead of him being made small."

"I was thinking a toad, perhaps," Bluebeard replied, and I spun to see him smiling there behind me, drenched in water, leaning forward in that way he had that suggested he might pounce at any moment. My face went hot as I saw how the cloth clung to his shape and I looked at the river abruptly trying to both drag my eyes from his cunning form and to catch a glimpse of the kelpie as he left.

"I would have liked to meet him," I said wistfully.

Bluebeard ran a hand through his wet hair awkwardly.

Grosbeak laughed. "The kelpie *is* the Arrow. And he is the kelpie. And he is the river, and the river and the land together are him. It's all a terribly crisscrossed tangle."

"I don't understand," I said as Bluebeard blushed under his beard. My eyes were only for him, not my tutoring head.

"No one does, but that's how it works for the princes of the Wittenhame. Their lands and holdings *are* them and so is the converse. You won't be fighting the Sword anymore, since he lost the Game, but you might see his heir strutting around learning roughly how to embody Towerrock, and if these folk of the Arrow's were not fools and cravens and we went to war with their folk, then if he came and put this land to the fire, your husband would burn alive from the inside out. When he is weak, his land produces no food and his river sinks into the ground, when he is happy it dances and flowers. And when – as appears to be the case today – he is utterly at peace the place takes on a story-book cast that seems almost impossible to believe. I swear, I've never seen it so."

"I think you've waxed poetic enough, you craven monster," Bluebeard said, flicking Grosbeak's cheek. "Let us hie us to the pastures to find a mount for the lists."

And with my mouth still open, I followed the man who was also a river, who was also a land and a horse and a bird and the most intriguing, heart-stopping, pulse throbbing being in all of the many worlds I'd tasted.

CHAPTER TWENTY-SIX

"Another dragonfly, perhaps. What say you, Grosbeak," Bluebeard had said as we slipped along a path only as wide as we were. The branches reached in to snatch at us from trees that towered far above and Look and Despair snarled and snapped when they threatened to dislodge her from her place on Grosbeak's head.

"Not a stalking cat?" Grosbeak asked. "Not a unicorn? That's what the Sword would have used."

"And likely what his heir will ride."

"Won't you only have to joust against the current competitors?" I asked, worriedly, shivering in the shadows of the narrow way. Bluebeard reached a hand back to take mine in his, warming it.

Bluebeard's eyes were tight, but they softened when his gaze met mine.

"Oh no," Grosbeak said, and I could tell he was coming back into his own by the sound of vicious glee in his voice. "The joust is for any who might wish to test their mettle. There will be prizes for various categories and there will be other bouts of fighting, but the competitors in the Game who ride in the lists and do not fall will have advantages in the Game and that is why they will ride. Additionally, either the players or their representatives *must* ride or forfeit their seats in the Game."

"What types of advantages?" I asked, nervously. This path was bringing back memories from my childhood – stories of children losing themselves in tangled paths in the woods.

"Luck, mostly. Turns of fate. Maybe your mortal land's food stores don't rot and last longer than they ought. Maybe they lose fewer of their people to stillbirth or have cleaner water or an artisan who crafts for them better weapons."

I inhaled sharply. Their game had such power over our lives? It didn't seem right.

"*Who knows if perhaps your very grandparents might have had stronger foal seasons on a year I won, or if your family might have taken the crown sooner had not some other player lost?*"

I swallowed. Sometimes it was easy to forget that there had been many games just like this in past ages and that this man I was married to had played in them – gambling with the fates of people just like me. But Bluebeard hadn't needed to win those like he did now – both because he'd married me in the Wittenbrand way and now could not take another wife to try again, and because the stakes were so high with the inheritance of the title of Bramble King.

"Then we must not fail," I'd agreed as we slipped into the sun-dappled pastures. We came out on a hill from which we could see trampled fields dotted with low stone walls and the occasional spreading oak standing alone as shelter from the weather. "Perhaps you should ride a grand horse, my husband. Something like that which you rode in the races."

"Nonsense," Grosbeak laughed. "There are points awarded for the difficulty of the mount."

"A dragon, then," I said. He shouldn't choose something as delicate as an insect if he was going to win this – and we needed to win. "Something fierce and large. Something like those long-mouthed things snapping at the houses on chicken's feet."

"Admire you those, fire of my eyes? I shall offer a dozen to you as pets."

"More pets would not be practical," I said. "Some sense of what I should watch for at the event would be more useful."

I couldn't help my tight tone. Now that we were getting closer I couldn't help but think about how if he won I'd lose as much as if he lost.

Below us, the pastures showed a streak of antelope running far in the distance, deer and horses closer by but wary of one another. Something huge and shambling like a draft horse made of vines occupied a place under the nearest tree. A winged bear – a terrifying sight – pawed at an anthill halfway across the rippled fields. And was that a leopard with four heads? I shuddered at the sight. There would be a mount here for him somewhere. And then he would ride in the lists and I would lose him forever.

"If you want to watch, then watch for treachery," Grosbeak suggested. "Tanglecott isn't the only one who might want me to turn on you."

I shot him a suspicious look.

"And would you turn again? Even after all this?" I asked him.

"For the right price, I would."

I gritted my teeth angrily.

"Or, you could bribe me."

"Stop trying to deal for my wife's excess beauty you gnarled corpse," Bluebeard growled. "She must save it to deal with others. It would be entirely wasted on you."

"I don't see why." Grosbeak sounded truculent.

"'Twould be a waste as I've already set a geas on you, splinter in my heel. You can no more turn on her than you can dance a jig."

"I dance well from the end of this chain."

"Then, by all means, do dance and do not let me inhibit you." Bluebeard sneered, but his eyes were wandering over the field at the various animals and birds that wandered through it.

"I would think you would take a bird," I suggested but I did not care. I only wanted him to look at me again so I could see the thoughts deep in his eyes. "It would suit your temperament and inclinations."

"*So it would,*" he said, brushing a lock of hair behind my ear as he bit his lip. "*But sometimes one must bring a surprise to gain an advantage.*"

"The four-headed jaguar, then?" I asked and his smile told me it would not be that creature. I did not care. I could lose myself in the depths layered upon layer beneath the surface of his gaze. "The winged bear? He looks to be a terror."

"*Ah. I spot my quarry close by. Wait for me, fire of my eyes.*"

"I have waited these seven years. What is one more moment?"

He kissed my forehead reverentially. "*Jar up that feeling. You will need it often as you grow into being my wife.*"

I gave him a wry look – after all, patience went both ways,

didn't it? – but it was hard to hide the satisfied smile that kept wanting to break through. I liked it when he kissed me. I liked it when he suggested that we'd be together long enough that I would need stores of patience. Even if we both feared it was not true.

"Round and round and round it goes," Grosbeak muttered to himself. "And where it stops, nobody knows." He pivoted on his chain in a way that gave me the creeps. "That's life in the Wittenhame, mortal woman. It was you who thirsted so mightily to return. You can't say now that you don't like it, complain when your husband abandons you for his fun, or object when the head you thought was your pet turns around and bites you."

"It's not your bites that sting, Grosbeak," I said firmly, watching the grass rustle where Bluebeard slipped through it. "Your teeth are half moldered away. It's that I can no longer trust you."

"You never could. Now you know it. You ought to be thanking me for opening your eyes. And all kisses and sweet murmurs aside, you ought not to trust that husband of yours either. Sparrow trusted him and what happened to her?"

"You betrayed her."

"And he didn't stop me. Vireo trusted him for a long time and then he watched you rise while he descended. I trusted him for most of my life and then he married you the Wittenbrand way and sealed our doom. He made you the last chance we had and a grim, miserable one at that. Do you like his folk? Are you fond of this land of his? Care you for his home and fire? Then it should pain you as much as it pains me to know you'll undo it all. If you were one of us, you'd jump ship, too. It's only your mortal frailty that leaves you without options."

"Why would I want an option I'd never take?" I asked coldly.

Bluebeard stalked something in the tall reeds near a pond. I thought I'd seen a tiger with six legs walk into the reeds there and that seemed a likely prospect for a mount for this joust where they rode everything but horses.

"If you wouldn't take it then you're three times the fool," Grosbeak said scornfully. His head was vibrating on the end of his chain. "Love will only bear you while it lasts – which for you will be short. He's loved you for a pair of weeks in our time. And for the Wittenhame even that is an aged love, so close to death that one might as well measure it for a shelf in the crypt. If he loves you the rest of the week out, you shall indeed be a lucky mortal."

"He's vowed to love me forever," I said, and I was proud that my voice did not tremble.

"And how miserable will he be when he's bound by vow while his heart strays and tarries with every passing Wittenbrand lady."

"He wouldn't," I said and this time I sounded just slightly less sure because time really was different to the Wittenbrand.

Grosbeak snickered nastily. "Or, perhaps he wouldn't. Perhaps he'll merely wither and fade from loving something so beneath him as a mere mortal. Don't think your unnatural beauty will bridge that gap – it can't. You are rotting as fast as I am, but I'll still outlive your mayfly span, even now that I'm dead. Or perhaps he'll spend himself for love of you – fast and hot as a candle burns, and he'll die knowing he lost everything for a mere slip of a woman with only forty more blinks of an eye left to her span of years. It matters not how you make his vow chafe – only that it will, as sure as the tide turns and the moon wanes."

I didn't expect to feel so heavy. I'd thought he'd lost the ability to wound me.

I couldn't even seem to shake the melancholy that descended when Look and Despair rose on her hind legs and Bluebeard landed suddenly beside us on the back of a knobbly cane toad larger than even the winged bear had been.

I gasped as he reached down for my hand from his seat.

"Speak to my riddle, wife? What rides the wings of surprise? What sends shivers of shock down the spine and tingles of anticipation along the fingers?"

"You do," I said wryly, and he seemed pleased.

I found my seat behind him. It's surprisingly easy to steady oneself on the back of a toad because of the knobs that hold one in place, but a toad this large made my legs spread so wide to straddle him that the muscles were aching before I'd even arranged my skirts and I did not like how his juices dampened my skirts.

"A truly terrible choice," Grosbeak opined. "No one has ever won a joust on the back of a cane toad."

"Then I shall be the first," Bluebeard said idly, but when his eyes caught mine, he switched to his mental voice. *"As you are my first, fire of my eyes. First that I've loved. First who I've given such vows. First I think of in the morning. First in my heart forever."*

And just as my heart swelled and my cheeks flamed the toad leapt and a shriek tore from my lips amongst the howls of my pets.

CHAPTER TWENTY-SEVEN

"Have you any fears surrounding this joust? Will there be trickery?" I asked as we made our final preparations. We ate a small feast of foods – once again, courtesy of the ravens – and changed our clothing. Bluebeard, into light-weight garb that could slip under plate mail for the jousting, his tabard worn over it all, though he'd put that over the plate mail later. It bore his sigil – a black arrow with a red streak of blood behind it and a black bird above on a field of blue.

He wore a matching red streak down his cheek where he'd nicked it – as he'd nicked mine immediately afterward – to make his mark.

The spirit on my shoulder eyed the sigil suspiciously as if she thought I might spill the secret I was bound with now that I saw the glory of his standard.

He shot a glance over at me in his too-quick way that always reminded me he was more than human. *"Would it smirch my script to admit I paw the earth at the mention of a joust? That my lance arm tenses and my knuckles go white in the hunger of anticipation? That already I see my opponents behind the lids of my eyes, and they fall one by one? That the wind in my face and my shoulder – aching from bracing against the blow of toppling them, ignites in me a thirst for more? Trickery is the road I ride and treachery is ever waiting for me in the shadows."*

"So, you're excited?"

His bright eyes lit, and he paused to dart over and place his forehead against mine. *"Only you thrill me more than the expectancy of battle. And it is a near thing."*

He stalked away, cat-like, and began to pull the plate mail from an innocent cupboard. His readiness was dulling his attempt at moving and behaving more like a human, and the edges of his inhuman speed and inhumanly bright eyes were peeping through in every movement and glance. He was more than a man right now. He was a force of something greater and he reared in the thrill of the battle. I wondered if that swiftness and brightness were the river part of him, swelling with spring melt and glittering in the sun.

Grosbeak sneered.

"Not much of a knight if you keep your armor in the cupboard. It shows a lack of fighting readiness."

"Or perhaps it shows I'm so ready I will not stand for laborious lacings and bucklings when I could leap across the room and carve my claws through my opponent's throat."

"Why are you called the Arrow?" I asked, admiring his inherent speed and precision.

I was adjusting my own matching tabard between bites and offering tiny tidbits to Look and Despair who had planted herself back onto my other shoulder.

Bluebeard – to my surprise – and his conspiring mirror, had dressed me for the event. My jerkin, unlike his loose one, fell halfway to my knees in imitation of a tidy skirt and was cut to arrange itself around my borrowed curves. He'd provided an overcoat for warmth. It was plain dark blue and pleated and starched to hold a stiff shape that gave me a very martial feeling but even with a long jerkin and overcoat – fitted as they were to my female form, I still felt too naked in only tight hose and high boots to cover my legs. The one thing that cheered me was that the severe tailoring of the clothing and the long tabard carved away the curves of my overly pretty body making me look more like my old self.

"I've seen you use bow and arrow to great effect," I continued, "but I've seen the same with throwing knives and with the sword. You're capable in all weapons so why are you named for just this one?

"He's so dubbed for his role in the court of the Bramble King," Grosbeak said. "Did I not tell you this before? He's meant to fly true to the heart of what the King would seek. Just as his fellow, the Sword was meant to strike as the Bramble King desired."

"Then the Sword failed that most incredibly."

Grosbeak laughed a terrible, half-gurgling laugh. "Do you think so, fool of a mortal? Think you that he failed simply because he pitted himself against you? What if I told you they both served their purpose and served it well? What if I opened your mind to the fact that the purposes of the Bramble King are not your purposes, and his ways are so beyond mortals as to be incomprehensible to you. His left hand deals a strike and his right hand tends a wound and who are you to say otherwise? Who are you to step in the way of that?"

"Who are *you*?" I shot back. "You are the one who lost his head. It must mean something that we have not yet lost ours."

"Not *yet*," Grosbeak agreed. "Throwing that against me in endless mockery is growing stale. You need fresh insults if you wish to sting me. But rest assured, this game is always satisfying and I'm certain there are twists and turns yet to come. You should know by now that I will cheer your husband's demise as hard and as merrily as I cheered the Sword's."

Bluebeard walked by, idly flicking his hand out to cuff Grosbeak and set him swinging on his chain.

"That hurts, you know!"

My husband didn't deign to respond. He was fumbling through a cluttered cupboard, tossing everything onto the ground until he found a tangle of leather and knife sheaths. He strapped one to his thigh and another on his forearm, checking the knives within for sharpness by shaving the hair on the back of his hand and making small noises of satisfaction when he found them sharp enough.

Those little noises made my blood tingle and I swallowed, trying to concentrate on my moldering head friend.

"You bring all this on yourself, Grosbeak," I told him. "I offered you friendship and you discounted it. If we're truly in a grand dance before the Bramble King then you should pick a side, or you might find yourself abandoned far from the action while others are showing their mettle."

He sputtered at that making incoherent noises and then calmed, his eyes far away as if he were really considering my words.

Bluebeard strode to me and gestured for me to sit and to my surprise, he knelt before me and paused on one knee looking up into my eyes with a gaze of such devotion that my knees felt weak. He could look at me like that forever and that would be enough. He could melt me for an eternity just with those eyes.

I swallowed hard.

He cocked his head to the side as if in question and my answer came out a little breathless.

"Whatever you are asking, the answer is most certainly yes."

I swallowed down a lump of nervousness and then his knuckles grazed my thigh as he felt his way gently upward and I bit my lip before I realized his purpose. He gently fitted the leather of the knife strap in just the right place and cinched it tight around my thigh, over the snug hose, tight – but not too tight.

But his touch when he handled me – his every movement around me – was so fluid and gentle, so utterly different than his violent purpose with everything else, that my heart tumbled further toward him. I was hopelessly devoted. I did not think there was anything he could do now to shake my allegiance.

"*I fear we lost your swords – Angstbite and Dreadtang – during our battle with the Sword. I will need to replace them. May this dagger serve for now. I still have possession of Edgeworthy – the token you gave me, but I will keep it within my home, I think, and not risk it today.*"

I barely had time to catch my breath before he was pulling me to my feet and guiding me from the breakfast table.

He passed me Grosbeak's pole, speaking to his former friend as he did so, "Come, rat of a Wittenbrand and watch the joust you so crave. Revel in the drama and hatred, the small cruelties and massive shifts in fortune, for you shall find them all, and with them the intoxication of senses they call the Springtide Joust."

"That's what I'm asking for! Is it really so much?"

And then we were away, leaving the warm familiarity of his home and heading out into the gloaming on the stinking back of the biggest toad I'd never wanted to discover.

As darkness fell, I reminded myself grimly that I must not speak to Bluebeard and I pressed my lips tight together to remind me.

I did not know if the house on grouse feet had borne us closer to the event while we were traveling in Riverbarrow or if the toad was simply covering so much ground with every stride that it felt close, but in two great leaps, the lights appeared and in three more we were sailing between poles strung with bunting made – once again, because who doesn't love to terrify the spectators? – with the howling spirits of the departed, tied up on a string of glowing spirit, and jeering those who arrived between their despairing wails.

I swallowed, feeling small at the sight of them, but Bluebeard seemed to worry not at all.

The Springtide Joust seemed to be equally joust and fair. The entrance had been laid out for grand effect and as we entered the grounds, everything we might indulge in was spread before us. At the lowest point, where it could be seen from every surrounding hillside, was a long flat field separated by a meridian of wooden rail along the center. Someone had taken their time with the rail, carving a series of severed heads pulling terrible grimaces all down its length that I later realized would move to turn their eyes so they could watch the competitors.

Everything was well-lit though it was night, poles lined the sides of the joust field and were spaced all through the hillsides, and at their crests fire danced, lighting everything with the flicker of flames and shadows. Huge bonfires had been lit at the entrance, down by the stands where spectators watched the festivities, and throughout the grounds.

Pavilions had been set in clusters at either end of the field and they glowed from within though they were no mortal pavilions. They were decorated with banners of old man's beard and rosettes of twisting ribbons as if the decorator cared not at all whether he used made or found materials to fit them. And the actual shelters were not of fabric made but woven of leafless vines that appeared dead and yet flowered with bowing, bell-shaped, white flowers.

On the other side of the field was a stand of boxes woven and decorated in the same manner – for the more formal spectators, I thought, and in their center, almost obscured by dead vines, was the sleeping Bramble King.

And all of it was washed in the flickering there-and-not-there light of dancing flames and cast shadows that made even mortal things appear haunted and brought a fresh shiver and twist to those things of the Wittenhame.

We wove our way through the gathered spectators on the surrounding hills who were attending the booths set up all around. There were fair games that at first, I thought I recognized until I realized that nearly every one contained a violent twist to an old favorite and I learned to quickly look away after a shooting contest that awarded points for how many live foxes weren't alive anymore when the shooter was done and another one where competitors faced each other and drank poison until one succumbed to paralysis and the other was declared victor. A heap of staring-eyed losers was shoved off to one side and when one of them twitched madly, I almost lost the quick dinner I'd eaten at our home.

The Wittenbrand celebrating were always terrifying to me. A group of Wittenbrand in elaborate matching costumes that made them look like birds of prey decorated with golden coins over their eyes and long beak-like masks, formed what I first took to be a terrifying group of torturers, but were in fact a musical group. They beat long lines of varied skulls as drums, and played upon flutes made of bones.

As Bluebeard hustled us around him, we nearly tipped over a knee-high table surrounded by rabbits with antlers who had been enjoying a mug of something green and frothy. They squeaked their protests, baring pointed teeth before we passed them, too.

The hillsides were alive with tableaus like this.

People gathered to sit and drink their choice of bubbling, foaming, melting, or fermented drinks, or to eat pastries and delicacies of an odd variety. One woman wearing a dress entirely made of living squirrels, who churned and tussled over her so thickly they served as a cloak, was eating something that looked like an upside-down silverfish full of pastry cream. A man with the horns of a bull ate a large pastry horn and with every bite he tore from it a cloud of bees whirled into the air. I turned my gaze away promptly.

Those who weren't eating fought, or gamed, or kissed with abandon and everywhere I looked there were bodies and more bodies behind those bodies as if we'd been set into a stew of life at a roiling boil.

I clung to the toad, and to Grosbeak's pole, as Bluebeard's lance and plate armor bumped against me. I was glad to not to be on the ground. Glad to be well out of this madness even if the toad had slowed to short, delicate hops so as not to squash anyone under his stout body.

We were just around a corner between two booths taking a quick breath before plunging into the fray again, when a white elk rode into the same tight spot and I gasped as the rider pulled down her hood to show the face of Lady Wittentree, patron saint of Rouranmoore. Her single yellow eye glittered and she leaned out over her majestic elk's back to whisper lower her voice enough for us to hear.

"Arrow." She said it as if she were giving a command.

"Wittentree," he responded idly, as if her sudden presence were of no matter.

"I'm glad I caught you in an eddy from the storm."

"I see only blue skies," Bluebeard said which was certainly a metaphor as the night sky was black as ever and pierced through with starlight.

"I wanted to tell you face to face. Always, you have treated me with honor. Now, I do the same." She drew a blue feather from her pocket and promptly broke it, tossing him the pieces. "Thus, I break our alliance."

"So soon?" Bluebeard asked.

"Too late, perhaps."

"You're a losing prospect, Arrow. You were battered and overwhelmed by the Sword and then nearly lost all to that clever play by Tanglecott."

"Sometimes you must appear to lose in order that you may win," Bluebeard said, but his muscles against mine were stiff.

"With you, it is more than appearance." She gave me a significant look that I could read quite well. I was a liability, in her eyes, as in the eyes of all others, and he was the fool who chose me instead of victory. And what did they expect him to do about it now? He could not un-marry me after marrying me in the Wittenbrand way. There was no going back, only forward.

"And then what? Will you fight Coppertomb yourself, head to head, when he's beaten the rest?"

"Yes," she said, her mouth thinning firmly. "When he's weak from his battles and my hopes are less grim. He has what it will take to vanquish you, Arrow – newcomer though he may be – and I do not. If I aid you to the end, and then we turn on each other, I will surely lose."

"And when do you begin to aid him?" Bluebeard asked, raising an eyebrow.

There was a chill in the air that had nothing to do with night.

A tick beside her grim mouth made the chill worse and then she shook her head and began to ride past us with the words, "I already have."

Bluebeard cursed viciously and I was forced to cling to him as he spurred the toad, uncaring now, as we leapt out into the fray. We came down on something – someone – who screamed, and I clutched at him, barely remembering not to speak to him now that it was night.

"*You're going to kill someone!*" I protested.

"Do I look like I care?" he snarled, glancing at me over his shoulder and his eyes were bright and vicious. He did not look like he had even a hair of compassion. I felt my own eyes going very wide as we leapt forward again, and my belly lurched and churned.

We flew through the air, Grosbeak shrieking like a ghoul as he bounced madly on his chain with every landing.

I did not look down. I did not want to know who was being trampled by the toad. At one point, I heard a horrifying *pop* that could not be good, and the frog's leap seemed to slide slightly as if he were launching from a wet surface.

Don't think about it, Izolda, I told myself sternly. That can only lead to trouble.

And then we were all breathing hard – even the toad – and Grosbeak was cursing so loudly that I thought he might turn the air blue.

"Silence your creature, wife," Bluebeard said, and his voice was so cold that I felt ice shoot all the way through me. Could this still be the man who played with my tresses and dressed me to his tastes?

"Be quiet, Grosbeak," I managed breathlessly.

We'd landed directly beside Coppertomb. He sat upon a proud jaguar whose inky pelt contrasted perfectly with his citrine eyes and the white teeth revealed when he curled back his lips.

The Bramble King was before us, his eyes half-lidded as he looked out from the mass of dead vines speckled in spring drop flowers at the heart of the stands of watchers. He blinked slowly at us, unconcerned by our sudden arrival.

Behind us, I heard the drum of hooves as if someone was bearing down on us, but when I shifted to look, I saw that I had misjudged. The joust field was directly behind us, and even as I twisted to look, a pair of hooved creatures thudded by – one a stag with tattered white skin barely clinging to it as its rider – a wild-eyed Wittenbrand with bone wings jutting from its back – angled his lance toward the other rider, a figure so swathed in plate mail that I could discern nothing about them except that they rode on an over-sized warthog.

I yanked my gaze away. This was not the main concern. At that moment, the competitors crashed behind me and the crowd roared.

Coppertomb's gold-lashed eyes caught mine for a brief moment, glanced down to catch on the ring decorating my bone finger, and then his eyes tightened into something that looked very much like cruelty before they dragged past me.

"Ah, Arrow," he said silkily. He was perfectly groomed, his cheeks highlighted again with gold and his plum coat embroidered with crowns. "What excellent timing. You can listen to the Bramble King rule on my case. I've requested the armies of Aayadmoore to be given to me. As well as Ilkanmoore and Moravidmoore. Fitting, don't you think?

CHAPTER TWENTY-EIGHT

"After all," Coppertomb said, with a secretive smile, "it was I who pitted you against the Sword, causing his downfall."

I couldn't breathe. My spirit was covering my mouth with both her hands, wailing as if someone she loved had died, but it was not me giving his secret away and it should not be me suffering for it.

I fought her with all my strength.

"Is this so?" Bluebeard said with dangerous frost in his tone.

"Of course," Coppertomb said with an arrogant tilt to his chin – how he'd changed from that first move when he'd tossed the tokens so officiously for the others. He was wearing the crown the Sword had made – the one that held my husband's rib within it – now bleached white. The sight of it made all the blood drain from my head until I saw spots of black dancing in my vision.

And I realized his spirit was gone from his shoulder and no one was gagging him even as I was being choked to death for his words. I needed air. I needed it now.

The hands released and I gasped in relief, my throat agonized and raw. On my shoulder, I heard a chitter and felt a scuffle and my relief turned to gratitude. Look and Despair had driven the spirit from its attempt at murdering me.

Behind us, there were shouts and the sound of something heavy being dragged away. I risked a glance, nervous as a new-broke stallion. It was the plate mail figure who had ridden the warthog – or what was left of him. Four people were dragging him away ... in three pieces.

Heavens above! That was not normal for jousts. Or at least, not in the mortal world. A scream caught my ear and now my gaze darted to see the crowd desperately trying to catch the reins of the warthog as it trampled through the edge of the spectators, its head tossing to catch them on its cutters. That was also not normal for human jousts.

I gasped and returned my gaze to Coppertomb who was speaking again. Neither he nor my Arrow, nor the Bramble King seemed to care about what had happened behind us. Even Grosbeak, lover of drama that he was, seemed to lean forward as if this exchange before the King was more riveting than the death – or deaths – of the jousters and crowd.

Bluebeard leaned forward, a grim expression on his face. "Speak to my – "

"No." Coppertomb cut him off. "No riddles. Just facts. It was I who gave Tanglecott the Heart of the Sea." His delivery was grand as any speaking minister before the court, "Which she so foolishly used to her own downfall. And it was I who pushed Marshyellow to deal with your hideous wife, Arrow. Each tiny win you think you've managed has been a gift from my hand – well, not a gift. A gift implies that you get to keep it. Call it a temporary reprieve. And now, I come to receive my due. To lift the reprieve. To once more ride forth in the great Game of Crowns."

There was a shifting sound as all the dead vines seemed to move like crawling snakes, white drop-like flowers trembling, their petals falling like snow.

"Stand before me as men alone," the Bramble King intoned.

Bluebeard stiffened and Coppertomb clenched his jaw. Neither man spoke, but they gave each other a hard look before turning. Coppertomb set his jaguar into a loping run toward the end of the field where the warthog had rampaged, just as the toad leapt in the opposite direction and I had to grab at its knobbed back to catch my seat.

"Wait in this pavilion for me," Bluebeard ordered breathlessly, as we reached one of the glowing vine-covered pavilions.

He coaxed the toad within and turned him around so that he faced the entrance. The large amphibian took up most of the space within. Anyone wishing to don plate in here would be very cramped.

Bluebeard dropped the plate armor on the ground, but shoved the long black lance into my free hand so that I was stuck holding the lance in one hand and Grosbeak's pole in the other.

"Stay calm! Stay calm." He kept saying it as he worked – loudly, as if he were scolding me.

"*I* am *calm,*" I said with my mind after the third time, and he glanced up at me with a peculiar blend of perplexed fury. The words were not for me.

"Stay calm," he said through gritted teeth, closing his eyes and balling his fists for a moment before he spun to me with sharp orders on his lips. "Stay here with the toad. Don't leave the tent. Don't drop the lance."

I'd never seen him so shaken. Not when the sea was taking him. Not when I betrayed him with that stolen gem.

And then he was gone, his muttered "stay calm's" trailing him as he loped down the field. My belly felt like that fish full of cream.

If Coppertomb found the favor of the Bramble King, we'd lose all our gains up to this point – all the armies of the defeated players we'd brought down together would be his and not ours or even off the playing field. Without an ally left, what would we do? All our many sacrifices made for nothing. Seven years of misery for nothing. My skeletal hand, for nothing.

I bit my lip until I tasted blood and shifted to move the lance across the toad so he could bear some of the weight. My arms were tired.

"Don't even think about dropping me," Grosbeak growled. "You're in enough trouble as it is, don't you think?"

"Yes," I agreed, my face pale and drawn. Maybe I should chant "stay calm" at myself, too.

The toad rocked back and forth under me.

"You'd better stay calm, too, toad," I muttered.

"You realize you're ruined, don't you? Both of you are," Grosbeak said delightedly. "Both of you are. The Arrow thought he was so clever, but Coppertomb has out-plotted him, out-maneuvered him, out-done him. And I get to be here to watch it all. Do you think I'll get to watch him rip out the Arrow's heart?"

"Why would he do that?" I asked, but my voice was trembling.

"Well, your precious Bluebeard bid his immortality. If he loses, that's what they'll do to him. Rip it out while he's still alive – though he won't be that for long."

I leaned to the side. If I vomited, I shouldn't do it on the toad. My head was swimming. I couldn't hear what they were saying in front of the Bramble King, but I could hear Grosbeak's wheezing laugh going on and on.

"Serves you right for being fool enough to fall in love with a prince of the Wittenbrand. I thought your strength was in your common sense. Wasn't that your bid for relevance? And you threw it all away on a man." He snickered a nasty, rattling snicker. "I love it! It's a perfect star-crossed-lovers tragedy, better than the theatre because it's all real and I get to taste your every ache of despair."

"I tire of you, Grosbeak," I murmured, but I was seeing stars. I felt like I needed to be sick.

"But you won't leave me. I've learned that now. I can say anything and do anything and there's no real threat because you won't leave me. You need me to tell you what's what even if I turn the screws when I do it. And I adore your torture. I thrive in your pain. I love to ache, watching your doomed romance flower and fall. It's the absolute most delicious drama and I get to be here for all of it. I must have pleased some far-flung god in my last life to be treated so well in the hereafter."

He sighed and in the distance, a horn sounded and then Grosbeak made a strange hiccupping bleat.

The toad under us leapt forward in a leap so massive that my head crashed into the dead vines over me. I bit my tongue, tasting blood as the vines ripped away, and we were flying through the air as I clung desperately to the lance and the pole Grosbeak was hanging from and hoped that my legs could grip hard enough as they sank into the toad's wide, soft sides.

The lance rattled against Grosbeak's chain as he screamed,

"Stop it! Stop! Oh, teeth of gods and men, I'm going to die! I'm going to die!"

I felt small feet running back and forth across my shoulders and neck as the ferret panicked with him.

We'd reached the top of the toad's leap and now, as he leaned forward and I frantically shifted my seat to stay on his back, the scene before me spread out.

"Stay calm," I wanted to say to myself, but it only came out as a muffled moan. Everything unfolded slowly, but slow as it was, I could no more stop it than I could stop an avalanche.

Everything was below me – the crowd amidst the leaping bonfires and horrifying bone music unfurling on every side, the sleepy gaze of the Bramble King regarding me from in front of the twin looks of horror and glee on Bluebeard's and Coppertomb's faces to the right, the meridian and a charging grey lizard to the left.

The rider of the lizard had his lance trained toward where the toad was about to drop.

I did not scream. I got that much right.

But I definitely fumbled as Grosbeak's head chain tangled on my lance, driving it from the resting place I'd had it in and pushing it forward. I dropped his pole, clutched the lance with both hands, and braced myself with gritted teeth.

We dropped and I couldn't tell if the rider was past me, or under me, but the lance was pointing down and I was afraid it would rip my arms off if we all hit at once. I tried to bring it up and at first, it moved and then it hit something hard as rock and was torn from my hands. The frog turned sharply to the left, his rear skidding to the right. I grabbed him under the front legs with both hands, my face pressed against his knobby back.

I sucked in a desperate inhale and then sat up.

There were no lances in me though I was trembling from head to toe. I looked over the head of my toad just as he opened his mouth and a tongue that was far – far too long to all fit inside this huge toad flicked out, unfurled, and grabbed the fallen rider *and* his mount from over the other side of the meridian and lifted them into the air.

I had just enough time to see my lance skewered through both of them before the whole lot were drawn into the mouth of my mount and with a terrible shudder that I felt right up through my pelvis and into my spine, he swallowed them whole.

The seat under me shifted, bulged, shifted again, and was now at a different angle.

I couldn't move. It had all happened in seconds. Just seconds and I'd accidentally … oh, sweet heavens … I'd jousted. I'd killed a man. Or a woman. Or a something. And some kind of grey beast.

I couldn't quite draw in my shuddering breath. It kept escaping me.

Something moaned nearby.

"Is that how you treat a friend?" Grosbeak moaned. "I thought better of you mortals."

The tongue shot out a second time and I reached out, mouth open in a protest that would not come, as the toad snatched up the pole with my dangling friend hanging from it.

"No! Down, frog! Down toad! I taste as terrible as I look!" Grosbeak pled.

But to both of our surprise, the toad reached his tongue back and let me pry the sticky bar from the curl of it before he tucked the appendage away again.

"Well," I said, with nothing else to say.

"Beautifully played, Lady Arrow," a voice pierced the silence. "Who knew you were so keen to enter the lists."

I turned to see a smug Coppertomb adjusting his rib crown.

"I haven't entered the lists," I said in a small voice.

Beside Coppertomb, Bluebeard's face was completely ashen as if he'd seen – well, not a ghost – those are everywhere here. As if he'd seen his own ghost. Or mine.

"A man is dead. A Komodo dragon eaten. It seems like you've entered to me," Coppertomb said silkily. "And you're doing so well. I congratulate you, Arrow," he clapped Bluebeard on the back in a way that would seem jovial, were he not wearing one of my husband's ribs on his brow. As if on cue, the damp patch in Bluebeard's shirt widened. "You've picked a fine substitute for this game. I'd never considered running a mortal in such a deadly joust, but then again, I've not your gift for stratagem."

The last was said with such venom that I flinched, and then as if he'd been there all along, Bluebeard was at the toad's head, leaping onto the mount in front of me. He made a sound in the back of his throat that sounded an awful lot like the one Grosbeak had made in the pavilion, and then the toad leapt, and we were in the air, sailing toward the vine tent while my husband muttered as if he were praying, "Stay calm. Stay calm."

CHAPTER TWENTY-NINE

The moment we were in the tent, he spun the toad around, leapt from its back, grabbed Grosbeak's pole from my hand, and hurled him across the room.

"A pox on you!" Grosbeak yelled as he smacked a clump of vines and tumbled to the ground, bouncing off Bluebeard's plate armor before rolling to a stop on the floor, his eyes seeming to roll in two different directions at once and the pallor of his skin looking deader than ever.

"Don't speak, revenant, lest I strike you in my anger and you never speak again"

There was cheering outside and the sound of metal hitting metal. There must be another joust taking place.

"Stay calm. Stay calm," Bluebeard chanted, running a hand over his face before looking up at me, his expression agonized. "What have you done? What were you thinking? Why would you do that?"

His hands shook, his normal tight control flapping in the wind like a torn flag.

"I wasn't thinking anything. The frog just leapt!" I pled with my mind.

It had only been seconds. There had been nothing I could have done to stop it.

"Your lance was pointing at the opponent! If you'd dropped it, then it wouldn't have counted as a run!" his voice was growing louder but he sounded like he was pleading with the past to change. He pressed his palm to his side, and it came away scarlet but he didn't seem to notice. He ran the hand over his face, streaking blood through his short beard.

I couldn't stop the trembling of my hands. I slid down from the toad.

"*I didn't know! You said not to drop the lance.*"

"Because I didn't want the point chipped! Not because I wanted you to joust in my place!" He sounded frantic.

I didn't know what to say. I was starting to worry that this was worse than killing the person I'd ridden against – and the horror of that still hadn't hit me.

"*It was an accident,*" was the best I could do.

I fumbled with my clothing and found a handkerchief too small to be much use. I tried to use it anyway, reaching to pad his wound. He shrugged my hands away.

"You've ruined it all. All of it. It's gone. It's just gone, Izolda."

He reached for me, and I froze, not sure what he was going to do. He tugged off my belt with a single movement and threw it aside. I gasped, as he yanked the tabard over my head to the angry chittering of the ferret and the wagging finger of my haunting specter. He threw it over the back of the toad, and I didn't know what he was doing or why he was undressing me but I didn't like it. Not here. Not like this. I stumbled back a step, my hands rising to hold him off.

"Would you calm down?" he asked, not sounding calm at all. "I'm just trying to put the plate mail on you before you have to ride again."

"*Again? I'm never doing that again!*" My thoughts came out with a very physical snort of disbelief.

He took two steps away from me, hands clenched into fists. "Stay calm. Stay calm."

He snatched the plate armor from the ground violently and I didn't think he needed to kick Grosbeak's head away like he did.

"Ooof. Would you do me the courtesy of *not* kicking me?"

"You didn't warn her, bodiless refuse," he snarled. Whatever trick he was using to stay calm with me wasn't keeping his frustration with Grosbaeak at bay. "It's your only job. The only one."

"This makes a better story," Grosbeak said thickly. His face was pressed into the mud too much to speak clearly from the place he'd landed. "You're such an accomplished jouster that none could be expected to give you pause. Her, on the other hand, she's inexperienced, frail, mortal. The true underdog. I didn't make her do it, but I'm delighted that she did."

"*I don't understand,*" I said, barely holding back tears as Bluebeard fitted his breastplate roughly around me and cinched the straps. It was too large by half. "*It was all just a terrible accident. It happened so quickly.*"

"Stay calm," Bluebeard told himself and I was starting to hate hearing him say that. He turned to me, and I'd never heard this kind of despair in his voice. "You're going to die. You're going to be killed and there's nothing I can do to stop it.."

"*I didn't mean to!*" I said again. Could he not hear my mental voice? *"It was not a conscious choice. It all happened by accident, even the lance in my enemy."* And now I was crying despite all my work to hold tears back. *"There has to be some way to fix it. There has to be."*

He cinched armor onto me with rough movements and at such an alarming rate that I couldn't quite catch my breath. One hand was jammed into a gauntlet. He didn't bother with the skeletal one – wise, since I could barely keep the metal on with my flesh hand. It slipped if I didn't curl my fingers.

"That you rode, weapon in hand," he said grimly, "means you rode in my stead. That you won, confirms it, and makes you my substitute. You must ride thrice more. If you die, all is lost, and I will become mortal and any hope for Riverbarrow, or Pensmoore, or my former wives, or Sparrow, or any of those I have made promises to is gone with us. If you refuse to ride again, the same. If I try to flee with you, the same."

"And if I lose?" My mental voice sounded small and hollow. I *felt* small and hollow.

"A loss is permissible. But if you die or show coward, there is no quarter given."

"I don't have a lance." My teeth were chattering. I didn't mean for them to do that.

He picked up Grosbeak's pole and shoved it into my hand so roughly that my skeletal bones hurt as he jammed it against them.

"Try not to lose this one."

"I am not a weapon!" Grosbeak protested.

"No, you're a schemer and you stepped tidily around that geas I set on you since you did nothing directly against my wife, so consider this your fit punishment."

"They'll break me like a melon!" he protested.

"Good riddance, then."

Bluebeard knelt, buckling the greaves over my legs.

"I'm sorry," I said. *"I'm so sorry."*

"So am I." But he didn't sound sorry. He sounded furious.

"Do I have to win?"

"You have to not die. It's harder than it sounds."

"Any tips?"

He lifted me, armor, Grosbeak, and all, onto the back of the toad. It burped loudly – which only proved it was a Wittenbrand creature and nothing like the toads of the mortal world.

"Couldn't you have picked a horse? Or a dragon? Or anything classier than a toad?" Grosbeak complained.

"No," Bluebeard said, but then he leaned in close to me, his gaze so heavy it could have sunk a ship. And without warning, he took my face gently between his hands and kissed me, long and slow, as if he were kissing me for the last time and he tasted of bitterness and honey and the salt of my tears and his sticky blood all rolled together.

"Enough tears now," he said when he pulled back. "Aim the lance low and then bring it up to the center mass of your opponent as you leap. Cling tightly to the toad and try to let the opponent's lance skim off the plate mail rather than skewering you."

Well, that didn't sound so bad.

"And when you die and you go to the next life, you'd do well to forget me and move on into the glory of that place alone."

"As a failure who ruined everything?" I asked bitterly.

"As a beloved wife, loved no less for falling, but free now of her deadly vows to me." And then he jammed the jousting helm over my head and my world shrank to what could be seen through the narrow window.

"I'm pretty sure the rivers will still be running and the moon rising even when I'm dead. I won't be free o my vows to you. And what if I don't want to be free?" I asked him, my heart feeling like it was ripping inside me.

Grosbeak interrupted, "Stop with the sweet talk, we're up!"

"What if I waited seven years for this and I'm owed at least a little time with you?" I pressed.

The frog shuffled forward, peeking its head outside the pavilion.

"A three-headed grizzly bear!" Grosbeak hooted. "At least I'll be crushed in a glorious tilt for the ages!"

"Then live," Bluebeard said, his voice harsh with emotion. He slapped the toad on the rump, it leapt, and he fell behind me with everything else.

CHAPTER THIRTY

Last time, we'd just leapt into the fray. Not so, this time. We leapt only a little way and then paused and on the other end of the field, I saw that Grosbeak was wrong. The three-headed bear that had stood there was being led away and another mount was being led up in his place. It was a grey stallion with a swirling horn jutting from the center of his skull and with only the faintest look at him, my breath caught in my chest.

Someone's voice rang out over the field, and I spared the narrowest glance to look at him. He was a man with goat feet and goat horns, holding a horn in his hand that looked very much like the one on the unicorn's head, but when he spoke into it all the crowd could hear his voice.

"Qualifications are completed! The first round will now commence, the competitors are …" he paused and glanced us over to check who we were, but my eyes were back to the unicorn, my heart frozen in my chest.

The unicorn was white, white, white with only the faintest taffy hints at tail and mane and the man sitting astride him was helmless, his light golden hair picked up in the wind, brighter than hair should be, the collar of his red coat edged in gold peeked up from his plate armor and the tabard he wore matched it, crested with crossed swords and a wicked-bladed knife crosswise below them.

The Sword.

I couldn't breathe. I couldn't tear my eyes from him.

"Ferna din Brayen, now named the Sword, Lord Towerock!"

The crowd cheered and over them, I could hear Grosbeak whistling his appreciation. "Ferna is a fine figure of a Wittenbrand. You're honored to be jousting him."

I was going to die.

"And his opponent, standing for Lord Riverbarrow, a mortal woman of no consequence!"

There were confused murmurs and when I glanced over at the announcer, Coppertomb was leaning over him, a calculating look in his eye.

He lifted the horn again. "I apologize. Riding for the Arrow, Lord Riverbarrow is Lady Arrow!"

For no reason I could discern, the crowd cheered for me, too. Maybe they were all Grosbeaks. Maybe they were just here to watch someone die in an interesting way and it mattered not to them which of us it were.

I swallowed, made sure of my seat and then a burst of red and gold sparks went off in the center of the field and my mount must have known them for he immediately leapt.

The world sank behind me and all that existed now were my mount, my grip on Grosbeak's short pole, and my tattered courage. I held to them all with the strength I had.

On my shoulder, Look and Despair shrieked her ferret battlecry.

Just like we had before, the toad crested his leap and then turned to plummet forward. We were still descending as the unicorn bore down on us, forehead thrust forward as if that were the only lance he needed, feet churning the mud of the course.

My eyes narrowed on the new Sword's lance as it began to rise toward me. I was no warrior. I knew not when to dodge, but to my surprise, the toad dipped at just the right moment, belly to the ground and I fell as the lance struck over my shoulder and past it, the wind of its passing grazing my cheek. Something seemed to tear as it passed, but I had no time to look to see if cloth or skin or even mail had been scored. The unicorn had closed the rest of the distance, and now we rose just in time for me to flail at it with Grosbeak's pole.

I missed the horse entirely, though the roll of its eye would haunt my dreams forever, but Grosbeak struck the new Sword hard in the head and to my utter surprise his teeth bit down on the man's ear and he bore him off his horse and to the ground, ripping the pole from my grasp.

The new Sword screamed as he fell and his unicorn spun, front hooves churning the air before him for only a moment before slamming down on his rider. I gasped as the horse reared again, slamming a second time and a third, narrowly missing Grosbeak who rolled to the end of his chain and was stuck there screaming a combination of the vilest curses and terrible derision as you'd expect to hear from a damned soul.

"Try again, equine maladroit!"

Before I could do more than rip off my helm with my skeletal hand, the new bearer of the name that had haunted me for so long was nothing but pummeled flesh and a rag that had once been a gold and crimson tabard.

I was still on the toad. I clung to him as I vomited over the side, clutching the helm to my chest.

"A draw!" the announcer declared.

Confused, I looked from him to my dead opponent. Had losing my lance lost me the match?

But then I saw it. The Sword's lance had killed, too. Just not me.

Stunned, I stumbled from the toad's back and across the field to where the specter who had sat so faithfully upon my shoulder these seven years was pinned to the ground by the Sword's lance. I fell to my knees beside her. The plate mail – awkward and overlarge – was not inhibition enough to keep me from ripping the lance from her poor tattered spirit body. She smiled – the first time I'd seen a real smile from her – and then she was gone.

To my surprise, I felt as if I'd been kicked in the belly. She had not been my friend but my warden – and yet, she'd bet on my side when Grosbeak took wagers. She'd seen all I'd seen these seven years. I would miss her always there, always reminding me of what had happened that terrible day she was affixed to me.

"I didn't know you could kill spirits," I said sadly.

"You can kill anything you want if you just know how," Grosbeak said miserably.

I turned to see the toad bearing him to me, pole in his mouth. Around us, the crowd cheered, and I was starting to suspect they'd cheer anything at this point.

"You need to make your bow to the Bramble King so that the next set may ride," he advised me.

Miserably, I donned the helm again. Gathered up both

Grosbeak and the lance – the new Sword wouldn't need it now – and found my seat on the toad again.

"They'll need to find a new Sword. Three in almost as many days." Grosbeak chortled with apparent amusement. "I wonder if they'd consider a severed head."

"By all means ask," I said bitterly. "Then when the Lord and Lady Riverbarrow must dispatch yet another Sword we'll know the best way to do it."

The toad – a truly well-trained mount – hopped in front of the Bramble King for long enough for me to bow and tip my lance. From the corner of my eye, I watched Coppertomb staying right beside him and watching me with that slitted gaze.

"Oh, and how would you kill me?" Grosbeak asked me as we leapt back to the pavilion.

"I'd drown you in a chamber pot. It's the only fitting end to one such as you."

He was still laughing when we entered the tent again. Still laughing when, to my utter shock, Bluebeard ripped the helm from my head, caught me in his arms, lifted me from the toad and dipped me backward to kiss me like a prince from a fairytale.

Well, then. Perhaps he wasn't furious after all.

CHAPTER THIRTY-ONE

After that kiss, I'd expected an apology of some kind – but I had forgotten that Bluebeard didn't apologize. The kiss was, perhaps, the closest I would get.

"I commend you for taking the lance, fire of my eyes," he told me with a wink, taking it from my hand and examining it. "It will serve you for the next round."

"Does that mean I may see a reprieve for the next round?" Grosbeak asked, sounding almost too hopeful. "It draws near."

"How soon?" I gasped.

"There are sixteen qualified competitors of which one has now departed this living realm," Bluebeard said, stripping the armor from me as quickly as he'd put it on originally. "We have the time of the other fourteen clashes to check you over for hidden wounds, check the integrity of your armor, check your mount and spear, and talk about your strategy, though truth be told, accident has served you well so far."

"*What happened to the Sword?*" I asked, still reeling from his death.

"One shouldn't ride a unicorn if one is not ready for the risks," Bluebeard growled, checking each piece of plate as he stripped it from me. "They will trample any unhorsed rider – foe, or in this case, friend, indiscriminately. You think I chose the toad at random? His reliability in the fray is unparalleled. Not the proud stallion too arrogant to serve, not the vicious cat, or the violent buck who put their lives before the rider, no give me the stability and hunger of the mighty toad."

"You're going to inspect me, too, right?" Grosbeak asked. "This right eye definitely feels wrong, and I think I've lost all my crabs."

Bluebeard ignored him, moving to inspect my mount as I drank water from the beaded pitcher at the side of the pavilion. While I was gone, someone had brought refreshment and while my belly could not take food, I was parched from the effort so far.

"*How did the Bramble King rule?*" I asked carefully, worried at how Bluebeard might react to the question after his outburst from my accident.

Bluebeard froze in his work and looked up at me with his mouth set in a grim line.

"Against. He ruled against. Coppertomb is to have the mortal kingdoms of all those we have felled."

"*All?*" I couldn't believe it.

Grosbeak hooted and this time, I did the honors. I lifted him by his pole and set him outside the pavilion.

"Wait! I won't be able to hear from out here!" he complained.

"Or laugh."

"You'd rob me of the succor of lightheartedness?"

I ignored him and went back in to see Bluebeard cleaning his hands in a basin before he turned to me.

"Now you. You were hit?"

"Only my specter."

He examined my shoulder, running his hands through my hair and over my neck and shoulders.

"Is there pain anywhere?" he asked, his hands continuing in their search as they carefully felt down my back and arms, his fingers swift but kind. He seemed to be looking for lumps or wounds or breaks.

"*No pain.*"

"This ruling makes our plans more urgent," he said as he skimmed my waist and ribs, still searching me for injury. "If you live twice more, then the moment you are victorious we will send you through to your brother. He must gather those he can and proceed immediately to the Plains of Myygddo."

"But without allies," I said, horrified. "*Without our help, he'll be marching Pensmoore to their deaths.*"

"He's a king. He can handle this."

"He must cross other nations – territories who have no good will for him. Why must he go at all?"

Bluebeard was finished examining me. He stood, his eyes boring into mine.

"Any who survive this fifth move must gather their mortal armies to the Plains for the last battle. Fail to do so, and their nation falters and they have lost. I had thought to bring him there with two or even three more armies under his belt through the lands of Aayadmoore. Such hopes are dashed now."

My mouth was dry. Svetgin could lose his whole force just

trying to drive through to the Plains. We could all be ruined.

"*And if he doesn't?*" I asked in a weak mental voice.

"Then the horrors we have discussed will befall Pensmoore and all the mortal realms."

I swallowed. Years of starvation and grinding poverty after Pensmoore was ravaged by an unanticipated force. Darkness sweeping across the world, knowledge lost, cultures eaten as by vermin.

"He must attend with his armies or see another age come and pass as that one did. And you will tell him so, if you survive this."

I was nodding.

"*Surely we must have some allies, though,*" I suggested. "*Surely someone must have freed you from the iron knife that pinned you to the pillar. You never did say who.*"

He lifted my chin with a finger so he could look me directly in the eye as he said, "Recall that I told you that time is different in the Wittenhame?"

I nodded.

"Then know, too, that there are ripples and wells in this realm that change the experience of it. You say you waited seven years for me in the mortal world."

"*I did. Though Grosbeak says it was only two days for him.*"

"It was three days for me. And also three centuries and three eternities and in time, the rock pillar broke apart and released me and I scraped the dagger from the wound and freed myself."

I gasped. That sounded like torture.

"I suffered every moment of it in the firm knowledge that it was for the good. And we will suffer what comes next in the same spirit. Come, let us arm you again."

"Shouldn't we see to your wound?" I asked pointing to his bleeding side.

"That wound will not fade until all my work is accomplished. We shall not waste our efforts upon it. You are fit. The mount is fit. Let us armor you once more and then to the battle."

"You'd better hurry!" I heard Grosbeak call from outside. "They're going through the lists awfully quickly! It would be a shame to forfeit, don't you think?"

"I may yet take more than his life," Bluebeard muttered but he was hurrying now, dressing me as swiftly the second time as the first. He cinched the straps a little more gently, though, and when he was down just the helmet left, he surprised me by leaning his forehead against mine. "I would shelter you from this if I could, but you do me proud. I have not before – nor am I likely to again – put the gamble of my plans on the shoulders of another. I am better suited to take heads and destroy all those who stand against me than I am to bind myself to the sidelines while another rides out for me. And yet, I have married you in the Wittenbrand way and you are heart of my heart, and bones of my bones, so now you will be the hands of my hands. Strike hard, and true, and without remorse, and know you have my heart."

And then, so sudden that he surprised me, he thrust the helm over my head and lifted me – armor and all – onto the toad, pushing the black lance into my hands.

"You shouldn't be lifting me when you're wounded. You're going to tear something," I scolded.

"I shall lift all the world," he said fiercely. "And I shall smash it in the hearth flames like a crystal glass brought in tribute to a king and drunk to his health."

"Well, if that's the way it is, don't expect such tribute from me," I teased, trying to distract from my fear.

Bluebeard led the toad to edge out of the pavilion.

"Finally!" Grosbeak croaked from the side. "You've been missing everything! It's glorious! Tanglecott's heir won her ride from the back of a golden gryphon. She'll suit as heir, oh yes! Almost made me miss the original Tanglecott. Oh, the glory! And Bluffroll slew an upstart from his own ranks who dared to ride against him. He does not have your macabre habit of taking heads, but I did see him snatch a tooth. What a joy to see."

His voice drew closer and then to my surprise, Bluebeard set the severed head in front of me, removed from its hook on the end of the chain but positioned so that Grosbeak could ride just ahead of me, facing outward. Balance, it seemed, was not a concern for him.

"This time, you'll suffer her fate, betrayer," Bluebeard said lightly.

Behind us, the crowd had burst into their favorite chorus once again.

"Fly with the Arrow,

Dance with the Sword,

Give your heart to the barrow,

Die with your Lord.

The lights flared as their voices came together in a sound both merry and haunting, otherworldly and slightly vicious.

"And if ever you be broken

And gasp on the ground,

Hold up your fine token

And join with the sound,

I shivered at those words. I'd already felt their truth. I dreaded where else this song my lead.

"Sing for your sovereign,

Bow to your Dream,

Make haste for the fallen,

Rise in esteem,

There were definitely going to be fallen again. I watched as a Wittenbrand clad in nothing but a loincloth, his own antlers, and his wild, thistle-strewn beard settle his mount at one end of the field. He rode a creature with curling rich brown hair and a pair of curved horns. Its head and shoulders were heavy and its beady eye glittered as it watched the crowd.

"And if ever you be broken,

And gasp on the ground,

The word may be spoken

And salvation found."

On the other end, a woman with silky moonbeam hair sat astride a white tiger and both she and the tiger were strung with silver bells.

"Close your eyes," Bluebeard whispered to me as the song faded out and the competitors were announced.

"Riding for himself, Lord Antlerdale!"

The cheers chilled me. I opened my eyes for a moment to scan the crowd and what I saw there chilled me more. Their eyes were alight, fists raised, faces twisted into uncanny hunger. They loved this. Loved the death and violence. Loved pitting their own against one another and watching them fall and die.

"Riding as an independent, Lady Moonshine!"

I snapped my eyelids shut. What future had I in such a place? None, perhaps. Perhaps these were my last days, lived with my wild husband in his wild world and trying alongside him to shift the tides of fate and time. Even tasting the edges of my own death, I knew I wanted no other end.

"Keep them closed," Bluebeard whispered.

"No, keep them open," Grosbeak said, naked bloodlust in his tone. "Watch a life end before you. It's more powerful than any other thing you can witness. It changes the world, plucking a soul away forever."

"What about birth?" I protested. "Is that not just as powerful?"

He snickered. "Your naivety is sweet to the palate. Never lose it, Izolda."

"Keep them closed," Bluebeard murmured and then the sound of the feet of large animals moving and the sound of a thousand pairs of lungs gasping in a breath ending in a piercing, high pitched scream that went on and on and my imagination was too much for me. I couldn't take the suspense.

I opened my eyes and immediately wished I had not. Lord Antlerdale rode right past us on his fierce, snorting beast. Dangling from his lance – and how could something as slender as a lance hold such weight? – was the crumpled corpse of the moonlight lady, her silver bells still tinkling even after her spirit fled. She waved raggedly from where she was pierced through like a bedraggled banner. I felt ill.

"Why do you Wittenbrand bathe in death when you could live as immortals in peace and security?"

The question ripped from me almost unwittingly.

"Peace wears thin beside power," Grosbeak scorned.

"It is for this that I have entered the fray," Bluebeard said in a low voice. "It is to upend what has been and forge it new, to wash all in seas of my own blood and paint it back in the colors of peace. You see as I do, wife. But peace is never bought by inactivity and the plant does not thrive from neglect. You see now why the path is fraught and painful – for nothing short of pain and death will save us now."

I didn't entirely understand him. I did know I didn't like the idea of washing everything in seas of his blood. That couldn't be right.

"You're up," Grosbeak said. "Ready to die on the end of a spear."

I swallowed. "I fear I am not ready, Grosbeak. How fortunate that I have you as my vanguard."

Bluebeard caught my shoulder in a last firm grip. I found it oddly steadying. My name was being announced again – this time with less derision and a bigger cheer from the crowd.

"Do not die. A thousand centuries would not be enough to ease the pain I'd feel at your passing."

Still not an apology. But I would take it.

He slapped the toad's rump and it leapt to the starting place, my stomach lurching up at even this small hop.

Look and Despair chittered into my ear, joining me in the helmet. The stink of her musk filled my nose and mouth, and I would have protested, but in a way I was grateful. It was hard to be properly afraid when you were gagging on a gross smell.

The announcer was declaring my opponent.

"Riding for his own glory and the fifth move of the game, Lord Bluffroll!"

My heart was in my throat as he burst forward, mounted on some terrible creature twice the size of my frog. It had five legs – no – four legs and one was its nose. It curled upward, trumpeting from the strange feature, as ears the size of ship sails waved in the breeze. Clumps of thick hair hung from its sides and back and formed a thick curtain over whatever eyes it might have. The hair billowed behind it like witch's hair moss hanging from the branches of trees in a wind storm.

Bluffroll sat the back of the enormous shaggy creature, lance held in a hand and braced over the shoulder so it pointed downward where his foe must be. His wide grin and the green skin of his face made my belly roll wildly.

I just had to live. I just had to live.

"Any advice?" I asked Grosbeak.

"Try to die in an interesting way."

"I loathe how you plot against me," I told him. "I'd give you all this beauty of mine if you'd but return to my side as friend."

He snorted. "That's exactly what your husband didn't want."

The sparks shot and my toad leapt forward. I gripped the lance in both hands, but even as we reached the peak of our leap, we still weren't as tall as the massive creature. Bluffroll, confident in his height, wore no helm and his grin was yellow and wide.

"No beauty necessary," Grosbeak wailed. "Throw me over the side and I'll be your man for life."

"Promise?" I gritted out.

"I do! I promise!"

I let go of my lance with one hand, dashed Grosbeak over the side, and then returned my grip to the lance, aiming it up as my frog leapt a second time.

At the peak of our leap, I brought my lance as hard as I could, and to my surprise, the toad veered hard to the meridian, smashing into the massive creature and crushing my leg between the bodies of both mounts. I had no time to register more than pain as musk filled my nostrils, my vision was obscured, and then a dark shape shot down my lance as my weapon found its target while at the same time that something slammed into my shoulder.

I caught a last glimpse of my ferret leaping from where my lance had struck to the face of my opponent and then I was flying from the road, through the air, and falling in a burst of pain to the ground.

A roar rose from the crowd and behind the roar, a scream pierced the air, but my head was spinning, everything numb. I thought I found my way to all fours, my head ringing. I pulled my single gauntlet off and removed my helmet, but the world was whirling far too quickly.

I vomited again, my whole body heaving and curling on itself.

"Seriously? I only just promised to be your creature and already you are splashing your filth near me? Can you not survive a single tilt without showing your mortal underbelly?"

Grosbeak. I knew that voice.

I scrambled forward – or tried to. I couldn't tell which way was up, couldn't tell which way was down. Something in my right side hurt so much and I couldn't feel enough of my arm to know what was injured.

And then I stumbled and fell face-first into the mud.

My last thought was that so many different creatures sure let a variety of terrible manure smells. And then everything went black.

CHAPTER THIRTY-TWO

I woke to something cold on my face and a pair of cat's eyes close to mine. Curses turned the air bluer than my husband's blue eyes and blue beard.

"Well, now you've gone and woken her," Grosbeak complained. "You shouldn't have done that. She'll have to ride again."

"And who would you have put in her place, revenant? You? You can't hold a lance. Besides, both our fates are tied to her now."

"Both?" Grosbeak sounded disbelieving.

"My magic sustains your life, you fraction of a man," Bluebeard said. "If I die, you wink out with me and what's left of you will rot where it sits or feed the birds."

"Ugh. You can't be in earnest."

"Believe as you wish, it changes nothing. If she does not ride, I do not live, and you do not get to keep watching the world like a favorite drama."

"Then you'd better work fast," Grosbeak said, and I realized that – true to his word – he was on my side again. "They've decided she's at a draw for that one since her ferret chewed

Bluffroll's face half off. A pity the stinking creature didn't survive its encounter. It was finally making itself useful. There are only two more jousts before her name is called again."

Poor Look and Despair. She was no more made for this Wittenbrand world than I was but she'd fought as hard and intently as any ferret ever could – tenacious to the end.

"Don't look at me like that," Grosbeak said. "It's not my fault you're madly in love with her."

"I am not."

"There's no point bluffing me. I've been here the whole time."

"'Madly in love' is too weak an expression. It is mild as a sun shower to my howling winter storm."

I could hear Grosbeak's eye roll in his voice. "Oh, forgive me then for underestimating your madness."

"I forgive the trespass."

A wave of pain washed over me, and I moaned.

"Fire of my eyes? Can you hear me?"

I nodded, struggling to try to sit. A sharp pain flared in my shoulder and collarbone and I fell back gasping in agony. I wouldn't be sitting up yet.

"I have to strip this armor from you and heal you. Will you take a day?" he asked, briskly. "You have refused them before – to your credit – but heal you we must or you will not ride again, and we'll have lost all your days in a moment."

I nodded again, feeling too thick-headed to speak with my mind.

He bent over me, and I realized he was loosening the straps on my breastplate. He pulled at something, and I couldn't hold back the scream that tore from my lips.

"Hold fast," he said, gripping my flesh hand as if to comfort me and then trying again.

I would like to be someone who screamed less, but today was not the day to begin that.

There was a rustle from behind us as I fell back against the cloak spread on the ground, gasping wetly.

Bluebeard cursed, running a hand over his face. It left trails of blood and dirt on his nose and cheek that were more dramatic than even the tiny decorative cut he gave himself. They mingled with the anxious sweat on his face to make him look as if he'd just left a battlefield.

"Whoever has entered this pavilion," he growled, "Will be made to eat their own toes one at a time unless they give me a good reason for their presence here."

"It's stuck on bone," a crystal voice replied. "Dented in so deep that the broken edges can't come loose."

"I'm well aware," he snarled. "Why have you crawled into my fold, serpent? Once you've bit me, will you bite again while I am occupied?"

He turned to address her, and I saw a flash of Lady Wittentree's scarred face. She peered past him.

"That I'm tied by hands clasped and words spoken to your enemy does not make me a threat to your wife, Arrow. I came to lend you a pair of hands. Your only other helpers," here she shot a look at Grosbeak and the toad, "seem bereft of them, and it's impossible to heal her while she's still full of the earth's ore. Tell me you don't require the aid and I shall leave."

Bluebeard said nothing, but the lines of his face were tight. He moved slightly to the side so she could join him in watching me struggle to breathe.

"Where's the javelin?" Wittentree asked, her slender fingers tracing something on my chest as her single eye roved over the mess of armor and Izolda.

"I don't know," he snapped.

"Tip is likely still in the wound."

"I thank you for the observation," he growled.

Their words washed over me through waves of pain and I was too occupied with riding the swells and ebbs of it to do more than listen.

"Don't act the wolf with the sore paw, Arrow," Wittentree said firmly. "It is not I who bid you risk your immortality on this venture. It's not my responsibility to guarantee you win over me when I set a wager, too."

"A light one, if I recall. A winter palace," Bluebeard growled.

"I am very fond of that palace. The fishing in the nearby lake is beyond compare. Some of us do not hold our immortality so lightly."

"I have aims of which you know nothing."

"Hold her down and I will wrest the armor from her," Wittentree said in a clipped voice. "And do not think I don't guess your aims, Arrow. You think you can set all right by taking the Bramble King's place. Don't look at me like that. I can parse riddles, too. But there is no reason that the Bramble King couldn't be the Bramble Queen. Why should I roll over and offer the seat to you simply because you have so many wrongs to atone for and I have only a missing eye and a few missing fingers on the tally?"

I felt pressure on my shoulders and then my scream ripped through the air again as Wittentree pulled. It felt as though I was being torn in half while still alive. I could feel all the bones of my chest flexing and levering apart in ways they shouldn't. I couldn't breathe – as if someone had banded my chest in iron like a barrel newly hooped – and my scream choked off to wet gurgles. I collapsed against the ground – but still, my breath wouldn't come. My heart stuttered. My vision was whirling.

Their voices had faded over me to nothing but scraps. My mind could not hold them. I fell in and out of a blurry consciousness.

I woke to something soft on my lips and I opened them wider, trying to suck in a breath.

"Kissing her like that is going to make it harder for her to breathe," Wittentree commented.

My eyes flew open and met the blue cat's eyes so close that I found them only after his nose grazed mine as he pulled away from the light kiss.

His face was clean or at least somewhat clean, as if someone had swiped a wet cloth over it as an afterthought. There was still grit and dried blood between the hairs of his beard.

I blinked back sudden tears, not able to form clear thoughts to define the soaring relief shuddering through me.

I could breathe.

I sucked in a clear, trembling breath, letting it fill me enough to sit up.

Wittentree smirked when she met my eyes.

"Truly you've found devotion and undying faithfulness," she said ironically. "How tragic that it is with a man so other than you, that he cannot enter your world or you his."

Nothing in my body hurt anymore and the release of that gave me boldness that perhaps I should have inhibited. I lifted my skeletal hand and held it up to her palm forward. Her eyes caught on the ring Bluebeard had placed on it and they narrowed in consideration.

She thought I could not enter his world? I had paid a hand for the privilege.

She snorted. "Oh, I see your entry fee well enough, but now look to your left."

To my left was my husband looking like a rag rung out. His side had bled so much that his entire front was soaked in blood. His doublet and shirt were crumpled, his hair mussed, and face smeared with dirt and blood.

"There's your real price and if you love the man, you'll stop paying it and go stay in whatever crypt or closet he's stashed the other mortal wives he took," she said grimly.

"Your words on this are not welcome," Bluebeard said grimly. He was trembling head to toe, but I could read his expression enough to see he was torn between fury and gratitude.

"I thought the Wittenbrand did not give gifts," I said hoarsely, sitting up. Gingerly, I felt my chest and shoulder. I was whole. I took in a deep breath and let it out. My body felt completely well – in utter contrast to my heart. Ready, I supposed, to go and possibly die one more time.

"I'm most generous," Lady Wittentree said, collecting herself to her feet.

"It was not a gift," Bluebeard objected. "You owed me a debt."

"Consider it paid," Lady Wittentree said. "And think again about this mad plan of yours. You can only lose and lose badly. Why not accept your fate? You have lost. You are not the prince you thought you were. So be it. Go live what mortal life you may with your mortal wife. They say that mortals enjoy marriage sometimes. They raise children, and I know not what else – horses, perhaps, or goats. Tame mortal creatures so solid and substantial that they are always themselves. And the mortals who raise them grow old and see some manner of dignity in it. Go, and do that, and trouble us no more with grand schemes meant to upend the world."

She took my skeletal hand in both of hers, ignoring the ring most pointedly, and said, "You, at least, ought to hear the wisdom of my words, Lady Arrow. Return to Pensmoore and haunt our lands no more."

And then she dropped my hand and was gone, and I did not know why I hid it, but I stashed the tiny object she'd pressed into my grasp in a pocket for something about her furtive gift felt … different. It felt like dull colors and food without taste. It felt mortal and it sang to my mortal bones.

"One more, then?" Grosbeak called cheerily. "One more ride for the win?"

"Or the draw," I said grimly, pulling myself to my feet to face my demons one more time.

CHAPTER THIRTY-THREE

My clothing, it turned out, was ruined. So ruined, that my simple shirt and doublet would not be able to hold themselves up. To my surprise, my husband stripped his own off and offered them to me, soaked down the front with his own blood.

I wasn't excited to wear bloody clothes. My own were ruined with the same but it was *my* blood and that made it somewhat less revolting. The hopeful look in his eyes and the fact that one side of my shirt almost fell off entirely, exposing my shift underneath was what eventually swayed me and I changed quickly, glad that at least my flimsy shift was still mostly intact. His doublet was far too large, and his shirt so bulky and wet that I didn't want to tuck it.

Even without his proper raiment, he looked all the prince as he helped me onto the toad. There would be no helm or breastplate this time. Both had been ruined past any saving. One greave had been bent clean in half – suggesting that Bluebeard must have fixed a break in my leg when he was healing me from my other wounds. I wore the remaining gauntlet on my flesh hand. My too-big clothing with my hair all tumbled around me untidily made me look more like a wild Wittenbrand than ever before.

I'd lost my lance. Bluebeard was rigging my lantern pole to

stand in its stead one more time.

"Usually there are more weapons available, but you can only ride with what you carried in the qualifiers, or you take from your enemies. Don't think for a second that you can sacrifice me as you did your other companions," Grosbeak lectured. He seemed happier now that we were at peace once more. "I'll not go quietly into anyone's dread night."

Bluebeard set him on my lap.

"We're at a clear disadvantage," Grosbeak said, slightly muffled until I set him straight. Bluebeard had not been gentle. "We haven't been watching the others. We don't know who you'll be riding against, and we don't know how he's behaved in the past."

"It will hardly matter," I said grimly. "I've only made it this far through chance and pure nerve."

"Skill would be better," Grosbeak said, sagely.

I didn't bother to answer such an unnecessary remark. Instead, I leaned down, not waiting for him to initiate, and kissed Bluebeard gently.

"You've done what you can for me." I made sure to keep any tremble from my voice. I must be brave now. *"Do not mourn if I die here. Make what you can of your mortal life. Find an understanding wife and make babies with blue cat eyes and an undying thirst for adventure – just like you."*

I forced myself to smile my goodbye. I'd been lucky three times. There could not possibly be a fourth.

"If you're saying goodbye, you'd better hurry," Grosbeak warned. "The crowd grows boisterous. This must be the last tilt of the main tournament."

"I'll do none of those things, wife of mine," Bluebeard growled, leaning in so he was close enough that his lips brushed the shell of my ear, and his scruff tickled the sensitive skin along my jaw. "I planned all this to be done alone – a solitaire knight errant set to right all wrongs, but you have bent me and made me half a double. I can no more conquer without you than I can breathe if you do not breathe, too."

And then he stepped back, and without giving me a chance to say anything he swatted my toad on the rump, and we leapt from the pavilion and into the field of gore and offal beyond.

The faces along the meridian mocked me and the crowd looked no more civilized than the carved horrors as they offered insouciant leers and wild hoots of excitement.

I did not do this for them. I did not care if they so much as noticed.

Grosbeak did. He hooted loudly, trumpeting his excitement to the excited waves of anyone who caught his eye. One winged woman winked and a girl with double pairs of swan wings made a moue with her mouth at him

In the stands, the announcer lifted his horn.

"The final tilt of the day will be watched and judged by our good lord, the Bramble King!" The crowd went wild at that, and the Bramble King's eyes opened enough that he almost looked interested. "Make your bows to him, competitors!"

"You need to hop up there!" Grosbeak instructed and I quickly whirled my toad to obey. "When you get there, bow."

I was aware of a figure swathed head to toe in a black velvet cape, the hood of which hung low over the face, but I did not focus on who I was fighting. I made my obeisance focused instead on what I was fighting *for* or rather who, my eyes drifting to where the Arrow stood with his arms crossed over his bare chest, the gaping wound in his ribs exposed for all to see.

I couldn't tear my eyes from him, not when we were told to rise, not when we made our way back to our opposite sides of the run, not when the announcer gave my name. I managed it, though, when he gave my competitor's name and my eyes went wide as the black cloak fell, revealing the man I feared most, the man who had slowly conspired against me and everything I did from the moment I met him.

Coppertomb.

He saluted.

I tried to imitate his motion.

But all I felt was boiling fury.

Of course, it was him. Of course, he was here to force me to fall. He'd take back those few things I had left. And he'd love doing it. He was rot in solid oak, mold in the crust of good bread, stink in a cut of meat. And here he was, prepared to take my life, to spill out all my hopes and future over the mud.

He'd been planning it all along from the day he bid me steal my own garnet and give it to him and I'd played into his hand again and again. If you want to change an outcome, you have to change one of the decisions that brought you to the result – right? Was there anything left that I could change? Anything he hadn't thought of first?

"A wager," I called out to Coppertomb, my voice stuttering slightly with nerves. "A wager to you on this tilt!"

The crowd cheered. Added drama was always their favorite thing.

Coppertomb paled under his gold highlights.

He was wearing the crown with my husband's rib in it like a badge of violence, but if he was wearing armor I could not see it. Perhaps he was being a sportsman since I'd lost mine – though that didn't sound like him. Perhaps he'd lost his own in the earlier tilts. Or perhaps, this was his arrogance, his strong assurance that no mortal could touch him.

"You've nothing to offer me, mortal woman," he called back to the hushed boos of the crowd. They seemed as disappointed as I was.

"It's bad form not to take a wager when offered," Grosbeak grumped. "Bad luck, too. It could doom him."

Coppertomb must have felt the same. "Why take a wager for dust? Why judge as precious what is worthless?"

"Why run from a child with a sling?" Bluebeard asked and suddenly he was at my side, shoulders bent forward as he slung his verbal insults. I was surprised to see him there. I'd have thought he'd be upset that I'd offered anything to my opponent – especially when anything I might wager was his. "Why flee in terror at the dawn?"

"Hear, hear!" someone from the crowd yelled back and there was jeering laughter amidst the cheers.

"If you think her so like to win, Arrow," Coppertomb called, "then you should make the wager with me. Wager something I want and cannot get with the sheer expediency of removing her head from her body."

He shook his hand and the lance in it – while short – shivered up and down with bluish-white light.

"The Lightning lance," Grosbeak hissed. "I hadn't realized he'd brought that. With that, he could blow you into the next world, Izolda. If I could pee myself, I'd be doing it right now. Just a suggestion."

"And what good would that do?" I hissed.

"Maybe he'd let you wear your skin to the grave if he thought it too much trouble to take from you?"

I shivered at the terrible thought he'd put in my mind and then squared my shoulders. There'd be no signs of terror from me. I could do that much. And I would.

"Is it real lightning?" I asked calmly, my question hidden by the mad jeers of the crowd.

"It will turn living human flesh to marble on touch," Grosbeak replied, his tone bordering on awe.

I shuddered.

"A venture then, Coppertomb – all the mortal kingdoms you possess shall be mine if you fall in this joust – those you've won, those you've negotiated for, and that whose token you carry."

The crowd fell quiet, ears perking up and with them the corners of their lascivious mouths. There was nothing the Wittenhame liked more than a wager. But my heart was heavy. I could not deliver. My husband would never get what he bargained for.

"A hazard it is," Coppertomb said, and his careful expression cracked into an unstoppable grin. A smile on his face looked as wrong as a dead talking head. "I will take your bet and match it – if your substitute falls to me, she will give me her heart."

Fear sweat slicked my brow and trickled down my spine.

"I carry that," Bluebeard said easily. "And it is from me you would have to collect it."

"Then make it so," Coppertomb said.

"It is agreed," Bluebeard confirmed.

And before I could even think of what that wager could possibly mean – was it literal? Was it metaphorical? Was it something somehow worse? – the sparks burst in the center of the field and like it or not, my toad leapt to the line.

CHAPTER THIRTY-FOUR

Coppertomb had chosen to make his passes on a horse made entirely of bone. Wisps of glowing purple mist held it together as it raced toward me.

"This is bad," Grosbeak whispered fervently – as if I didn't know. "This is terribly bad."

My heart was in my throat. I clutched my lantern pole in both hands, knowing it could never possibly be enough.

"Do not fail, fire of my eyes. Use all that good sense you so embody and carve me a path so I may ride over him and grind his bones to dust." He sounded so certain, like he knew I could save all this when there was just no way that I could.

My toad leapt into the air once again, and my belly lurched. I fought the nausea of the lurch, so preoccupied with it that I didn't realize until too late that my pole had jammed into the meridian as we leapt. It ripped from my grip, tearing away.

No weapon. What would I do now? How could I possibly pit myself against a weapon that froze living flesh if I had none of my own? Not even a lantern pole?

"Lost!" Grosbeak wailed from in front of me. "Lost, lost, lost!"

My heart hammered in my ears. I opened my mouth in a gasp

at the same moment the crowd roared, and we reached the apex of the leap.

I looked down at what could easily have been the last thing I ever saw. Wild-eyed and bloodthirsty, the crowd pushed in, eyes bright, mouths snarling, or open to shout their support. Coppertomb's lance was aimed perfectly to catch me in the un-armored torso. His clever eyes narrowed in concentration.

The lance gleamed a bright copper in the moonlight as if it were a living thing, craving my blood, longing to turn the softness of my living flesh to stone. Perhaps it really was as alive as I was.

As alive as … I … was.

I flexed the bones of my skeletal hand in thought. A simple problem required a simple solution.

I saw it all in the space of a heartbeat. I forgot my fear, forgot my nausea, and angled sharply to my right and forward, twisting so that as we landed, I could reach out and grab the lightning lance with my skeletal hand. Coppertomb had braced it against a pocket of leather in his belt – wise, if you were planning to use the full force of your charge to plow your opponent off their mount. Unwise if their hands were free and they could grab it. I used it against him, leaping from the frog's back, ignoring Grosbeak's scream as I shoved all my strength into forcing that lance back and to the left.

Grosbeak's cry faded and cut off in a stream of curses, but I didn't dare look at where he might have tumbled. I was off the back of the toad and hanging – for one impossible second – in the air, as the full force of my downward, leftward trajectory combined with the force of Coppertomb's forward trajectory angling the opposite direction. The combined force spun us both, toppling him from the saddle as we flew out from the lance pinned between us.

For one terrible heartbeat, we both hung in the air, and I knew from the shock on his face that his lance should have frozen my flesh and stopped any movement. But he hadn't bet on my skeletal hand. He hadn't bet that I had a way to touch this terrifying weapon without being burned by it, for I thought that perhaps metal gauntlets would be just as affected as human flesh, drawing that heat into their metal surface and searing a person right through.

My triumph lasted barely a flash of thought, and then I fell heavily – belly-first – on the stone meridian and the air was knocked from my body. I pitched over it, head-first, and fell in a crumpled heap.

The crowd gasped.

I blinked hard against pain and the black and white flashes popping across my vision. Perhaps my head had been injured.

I heard nothing.

I shoved a hand under me and forced myself up from the mud. Something in my ribs screamed. It would have to go on screaming. I could do nothing for it now.

"*Heart of my heart, your victory will be sung in the Halls of Riverbarrow for a generation hence.*" Bluebeard sounded shockingly proud.

I was barely up to all fours when a roar – like a fire when the door of a furnace opens – rolled over me, leaving me lightheaded and disoriented.

Up, my mind urged me. Get up.

Or maybe it was the voice in my head that was pleading with me, *"Get up."*

I found my feet and the cry redoubled. In the fog of my surroundings, I made out the wide-mouthed faces of the crowd as they bayed their approval.

And then Bluebeard was beside me, landing lightly on his feet, head thrown back and arms wide, the ultimate showman.

"My surrogate has unhorsed her opponent. I claim this victory for Riverbarrow."

With another roar, the crowd closed in further – too close – their faces alight with frenetic enthusiasm. Between them and us, a dazed Coppertomb found his feet. He seemed uninjured, though he favored his right leg. His cloak and lance were gone – sunk in the mud somewhere. And his expression was one of absolute fury.

I didn't see why. We'd both lost. Or we'd both won. Surely, there could be no forfeits from wagers that no one had won.

"The mortal woman was unhorsed just as I," he bellowed. "And just as I have been laid flat before you, so has she been. There is no victory here."

"No victory?" Bluebeard asked, dramatically, physically recoiling. "Can such a thing be so?"

He was clearly playing to his audience. His eyes were still spread wide and then he snapped his fingers, and something belched behind me. I spun to see the toad, squatting happily before the spectators surrounding the Bramble King in the boxes. He opened his mouth and his ridiculously long tongue flicked out, caught something from the ground, and flicked it toward us.

I dodged on principal and shooting pain froze my chest in

place as well as any lance could do. I couldn't breathe. I couldn't
… I leaned on the meridian for support, losing my chance to
watch Bluebeard catch the missile. I didn't miss what happened
next. He held the head of Grosbeak high, considering it with a
thumb and forefinger to his chin – for all the world a Master of
Ceremonies playing to the crowd.

"What say you, Traitor Grosbeak? Surely a fine connoisseur of
drama and intrigue such as yourself might have an opinion. Is it
victory to snatch an opponent's lance from his hand? To leap like
the pouncing puma and tear out his throat? Or is that defeat?"

"Oh, a fine victory," Grosbeak intoned, laughing cruelly.
"For to add insult to injury, the green Lord Coppertomb found
himself bested by a mortal with no battle training. As like to
see a knight unhorsed by a white rose as to see the Lord of all
Coppertomb unhorsed by so dainty a blossom. And her riding a
toad of the mud, while he barreled forth on fine horseflesh!"

"What say you, Wittenhame?" Bluebeard asked, looking out at
the crowd as if in need of advice.

The response was half cheer and half laughter, but
Coppertomb's growl of annoyance was met only by snickers. He
swallowed, brushed himself off, and tried another tack.

"I appeal to the Sovereign," he said coolly, turning his back on
them and toward his lord.

"Speak to my riddle, Grosbeak," Bluebeard said, but his voice
was pitched to carry. "What cries as a seagull when there are
entrails to eat but hides as a sand crab when challenged?"

"Is it a yellow-streaked coward, m'lord?" Grosbeak asked
and then paused and melodramatically squinted. "Or is it this
so-called prince of our malevolent Wittenhame, begging for
adjudication when all who watch know him whipped like a cur?"

"Silence your pet, Arrow, or I shall silence both him and you," Coppertomb hissed and this was *not* for the crowd though they hung on his words, eyes fastened to every movement, however small it be.

"DRAW," the Bramble King's voice boomed out.

"Then shall we ride again, Lord Coppertomb?" Bluebeard asked with a mild smile. "But I find myself so inflamed by the desire to sport against you, that I must ride for myself this time."

"I think not." Coppertomb's words were clipped. "I think rather that the joust is done, the players secure. And you and I must collect our bets."

Was I the only one who saw my husband pale? His eyes flicked directly to mine and then to the Bramble King. He drew his arm close and whispered something into Grosbeak's ear. My friend snickered.

"PRESENT YOURSELVES TO ME," the Bramble King said, his rumbling voice shaking the field and jarring my painful ribs against one another. "AND THE TERMS OF SURRENDER OF PROPERTY WILL BE DICTATED."

I caught the look of triumph in Coppertomb's eyes and the slight smile as he looked at me and then Bluebeard eclipsed him, jamming Grosbeak's head into my skeletal hand and twisting the silver key from around his neck to hang around my neck.

"We've no time to waste, fire of my eyes," he said, tucking his head down close to mine so it looked as if he were wooing me rather than desperately spilling all I needed to know into my ear. "Coppertomb has made a pretty bargain and I must pay it full. But you, sweet fire of my heart, bright light of my eyes – I gift to you Pensmoore – yours already and tied to your blood – and with it, I gift you the kingdoms I have won in my wager today. Take

Aayadmoore, Ilkanmoore, Moravidmoore, and Salamoore, and march them fast as you dare to the Plains of Myygddo. Dare they flinch at your command, you need only spill your own blood and seal your orders with it and they will be bound to obey. Go, now, while still I live, for the Last Battle comes and your five nations must hold off the other three or see themselves sunk, their land ravaged, and their people destitute. Do not return to this place having failed. Promise me."

"*I promise,*" I agreed. But I was afraid. What did it mean that Coppertomb had won my beating heart? "*Tell me they aren't going to kill you.*"

He pulled back enough to look in my eyes and tangle his hand in my long hair and the look on his face was agony and then he shook his head as if dislodging a thought and whispered.

"I know this, I nothing else. You must flee this place. You must save your mortal world. We dare not fail in that. And if any breath of me remains when all this has passed, know it breathes only and always for you."

My heart stuttered and my breath hitched then.

"*I wanted a life with you as wife,*" I admitted as his fingers tangled so tight in my hair that it stung. "*I wanted all your tomorrows, to touch you with tenderness, and care for your heart as if it were a precious gem, a field of good crops, a stallion of perfect bloodlines.*"

"I would wish all that and more," he said, his voice a harsh pain. "But it was always running this course, always galloping to this cliff, from the moment I saw your grey eyes and determined ferocity and knew I must not sacrifice you as I had all those before but must take you to wife by blood and vow. Promise me this, fire of my heart. Promise me you will think of me at the last."

"Who else would I think of? Who else has my heart?"

He looked wistful for a moment, and then his fingers untangled from my hair, and he wrapped my fingers around the silver key, pressed his lips on mine, and turned the key.

I was ripped from his arms and into the instant hell of the passing from the mortal world to the Wittenbrand and as my spirit screamed, I howled with it.

I was not ready to go.

I needed to stay to help him, to save him, but I could no more save him from this, than I could save him from the sea and as I was dragged through a living hell, every imagined horror I feared for him was played out before my eyes, until I was left a sobbing, howling mad woman, screaming into the blackest night in a world robbed of color and warmth.

"I always hate that passage," Grosbeak said glibly. "They really ought to build a less traumatic way back and forth."

His words grated on my bare soul until I opened my eyes.

"Done sulking?" he asked brutally. "Because I thought you had some work to do and since I promised to stay with you, I suppose I'm along for the ride. You'd better make it worth my while."

CHAPTER THIRTY-FIVE

Luckily for me – I returned to Pensmoore exactly where I'd left it – the battlements of the palace. Unluckily for me, it seemed some time had passed since I'd been there last.

"She says she's who?" the Captain of the Guard asked the pair escorting me as if I wasn't right there to ask in the flesh. A nervous wen appeared between his eyebrows.

"The mad princess!" the first guard said. "Our lord the king's sister, Izolda Savataz."

The captain peered at me and then at Grosbeak, gagged a little, held down his dinner manfully, and then looked at me again. He looked green. Green and slightly terrified. The lantern he held up flickered as everyone shifted uncomfortably. That I didn't recognize any of them was worrisome.

"Can't be," the captain said grimly, white around the mouth. "She must be a witch."

"I am no witch," I said calmly and with as much authority as I could muster. "And I request an audience with my lord the king."

"If you were really his sister," the captain said gravely, "you would know he lies even now on the verge between death and life."

"All the more reason to permit me an audience. But if he is in no state to receive a sister, then I will speak to General Volkov."

The captain snorted. "Shall I raise him from his drunken grave to receive you?"

Volkov dead. My brother ill. I shook my head in wonder as Grosbeak cleared his throat, reminding them that even a corpse was not past being bothered by me.

"Emelina, then. Your queen," I replied, not put off by his derision. "Tell her that her 'sister' has returned and comes to collect on her debt." I paused. All they saw was a defenseless woman. What could I say to shift that balance? "Remind her of what grave threat she avoided when I offered to take my brother's place with the Wittenbrand."

The captain of the guard snorted, but the white spots and green wash were gone, and his color was coming back.

"Keep her here until I return," he said before leaving us in the small guard room adjacent to the battlement. I hadn't made it very far from where I'd been found.

"Do any of you play cards?" Grosbeak asked brightly.

"We don't play with familiars," the first guard spat.

"What would you even bet?" the second countered.

I took a seat and set Grosbeak on the small table. This tower had been fitted as a place for the guards on the battlement to warm up, complete with a fire, a small table, three chairs, and a light repast laid out – cheese and bread and water, simple food for simple men.

I ate, not caring at the annoyed looks they sent my way. I hadn't eaten in a full day and in that time, I'd been battered pretty badly. My ribs still twinged with pain when I sat down or stood up or moved at all.

"How about ears?" Grosbeak suggested. "We each have two of them. Well, I have one and a solid half, but the whole one is twice the size of yours, so I say it evens out. 'Twould make for a lively challenge!"

"You're seriously asking us to bet our ears?" one of the guards asked, his eyes goggling. "You can't be serious."

"I am very serious, and also in earnest," Grosbeak said. "Whist, perhaps? Or do you play Nine Men's Knuckles? Merels? Copper flutes?"

The guards looked at each other and then back at him in horror. "We need our ears. We aren't deformed corpses set alive by the black incantations of a witch."

"Neither am I," Grosbeak said darkly, "And why do you maintain she is a witch when she has denied it? There's not the slightest whiff of magic on her person."

I ignored them, trying to think of what I would say if Emelina denied me access. I didn't like being here any longer than absolutely necessary. What might be happening to Bluebeard even now? Were they sentencing him to some terrible torture? Killing him? Was he imprisoned or thrown once more into the depths? My stomach knotted around the bread and cheese at the thought, wishing I had not eaten at all.

"She is too beautiful to be a normal woman, mad princess or otherwise," the guard said knowingly. "Surely such charms are only the result of the blackest of magic."

"Surely," Grosbeak said wryly. "I never see a beautiful woman without thinking, 'Now, that's some black magic right there!'"

I shifted my position to take the pressure off my screaming ribs and something poked me in the leg. Irritably, I reached into my pocket and pulled out the token Lady Wittentree had offered me – a carved mermaid set on a round base, made entirely of jade. It looked like a piece in a game of strategy. I played with it between my fingers.

"And you," the guards were telling Grosbeak, "must be her familiar, the source of great power."

"I tell women that all the time and they never believe me," Grosbeak said sadly.

I was surprised by how quickly the Captain of the Guard returned. Grosbeak and the others were still wrangling the details of their possible game of chance when he entered the room, another man hot on his heels.

He spoke, but it was to the younger man that held my attention. He was maybe twenty and one. Blond. Well dressed. Average in height. He had my brother Svetgin's exact eyes and the bearing he once had when he was a younger man.

"Queen Emelina will not see you," the Captain of the Guard said to me, "and she has made it clear that the mad princess died fifteen years ago and will never again grace us with her presence."

"Not her, then?" I said grimly. "And not Volkov and not my brother. Do any of his counselors from his early reign yet live?"

"I told you already that Volkov was dead of drink these six years and more," the captain said grimly. "And any other counselors from that time are only memories now."

I sighed. "That's the problem with mortals. They all die almost as soon as you get to know them."

"What then," the young man asked, taking one of the seats

across from me with a flourish, "are you, if you are not a mortal?"

"Your aunt, if I'm not mistaken, Rolgrin," I replied, meeting his eyes, "and as mortal as the next woman. You're named for the brother who was born between myself and your father."

He swallowed, his eyes drifting to my hands, seeming to widen at the sight of the mermaid I was playing with even more than at the skeletal hand.

"I told you she was a witch," the captain of the guard muttered.

"Who gave you that?" Rolgrin asked hoarsely.

"Does it matter?" I let my eyes narrow. Better to make him think I knew more than I did.

"It does. To me."

"Hmm." I tapped it against the table. "Tell me, then, Rolgrin," I said. "Do you know a lady with one eye and eight fingers?"

He flinched. "That sounds like a riddle. Are you really in a position to be telling riddles?"

"You want a riddle?" I asked, my eyes narrowing and my skeletal hand reaching to set itself on top of Grosbeak's disgusting mass of tangled hair. Predictably, he snickered right on cue. "I can oblige. What has a crown waiting for him and a lady love in Rouranmoore?"

This time his flinch included a swift look at the Captain of the Guard who cleared his throat noisily.

"I think the prince has this in hand," he said loudly to the room. "Best we get back to patrolling."

As if the Captain of the Guard did any patrolling. I didn't

watch them leave. I didn't care. All mortals were as wildflowers
– here for a day or a week and then blown away on the winds of
time. And I knew that I was one of them, of no more value or
significance than they. Despite that, I held the means to prevent
deprivation and death for my people.

I didn't want to be here. I wanted to be with my husband,
standing by his side as he faced – whatever it was that he had lost
in that bet. But this was his will for me, and it was my will to
save as many as I could from the fires to come.

When they left, my nephew's eyes met mine. He was young
and he looked younger with that pleading in his eyes and the
scant beard covering the trembling in his jaw.

"What do you know of the Lady Hazinth?" he asked as if his
words weren't confirming what I'd guessed.

I placed the mermaid deliberately on the table between us.

"I know she has powerful friends. I know they threaten her
future."

The second part could be said about any living mortal, but he
didn't seem to notice that.

"And?" he pushed.

"And if you do exactly what I tell you to, we can save her, and
your sister and brother, and all of Pensmoore."

The combination of bitter and desperate in his eyes was far too
familiar to me these days.

"Nothing can be saved. Even now, my father lies prostrate
on his death bed. Soon the crown will fall to me, and I will
have to marry for peace. Aayadsmoore, perhaps, which has
overcome its chaos to amass on our border, or Salamoore which

has been raiding the border since my grandfather's time and now congregates armies in the determination to take us once and or all. Rouranmoore has turned away our diplomats, but that's a new bitterness and we have no call for a state marriage there."

I looked at the green mermaid and I thought of Wittentree giving it to me. She must have known about this secret romance.

"How long have you been in love?" I asked him quietly.

He snorted a laugh, looking at the fire but not seeing it.

"When I was a child, Lindra would come and visit the former princess, Lady Chasida. They are cousins by marriage. I've known her all my life. We started to write when she was twelve, nigh on seven years ago now. I do not think I've disguised my interest as well as I would like, but it is not well known. Who gave you her token? It would not have been her. I gave her that chessa set and she has treasured it since the day she received it direct from my hands. We play by mail."

"Rouranmoore's patron saint gave it me," I said, watching him closely.

"The Lady?" he gasped, eyes wide.

"I am married to Pensmoore's corresponding saint, as you might have been told."

"I thought your husband was dead. I thought that was why you went mad. That's what father always said."

"We were merely … parted," I said carefully. "And now I have returned on his behalf. And I would see my brother before I carry out the tasks I must do for Pensmoore."

"What tasks are those?" he looked almost excited.

I steeled my jaw. Despite my promises, I had hoped to deliver my messages and then hurry back to my husband, but here I was faced with an un-bearded youth and a kingdom on the cusp of change. My stomach rolled at what I must say.

"I shall lead the armies of Pensmoore along with Salamoore, Ilkanmoore, Ayyadmoore, and Moravidmoore to the Plains of Myygddo for the Last Battle."

He laughed long, hard, and disbelieving. Until Grosbeak began to laugh with him. My bodiless friend's dry laughter sounded like snapping sticks and harrowing calls in the night. Rolgrin paled, straightened, and regarded my bodiless friend with revolted horror.

"Is that thing really alive?" Now he was the one who looked green.

"Yes," I said crisply.

"I'm alive enough to know a chalk-faced rat-eater when I encounter one," Grosbeak complained.

"And the hand?" my nephew pressed, turning his ill expression to me.

I lifted my skeletal hand, wiggling the metacarpals so he could see them move. Bluebeard's ring rattled against them.

"Also alive."

His throat bobbed. "This is why they call you the Mad Princess. Though your portrait doesn't do you justice, and neither does my memory. Were you always so beautiful?"

"No."

"Then how did it happen that you grew lovelier?"

"In the same way that I lost the hand." Had young people always been so exhausting? I grew tired of his prodding.

"Then I should take you to your brother," he said, at last, his eyes brightening shyly. "Do you really think I could marry Lindra?"

"I think there will be trouble if you don't," I said grimly, able to read a hint when one was shoved into my hand.

I found Svetgin exactly as my nephew had suggested I would. Unconscious. Hot with fever. Wasted away. I felt – to my surprise – a twinge of nostalgia for when we two had been children together, a quick memory of my mother running her hand over our hair and whispering sweet words as she tucked us into blankets on a pallet beside the fire during a fierce winter storm.

He was the last of my direct family still living and he would not be living for long. His room smelled of illness and death, the bed curtains heavy, the fire built up hot, the curtains closed over the narrow windows. I left as quickly as was polite.

I did not speak to my sister-in-law. If she had no time for me, then I had none for her. Some debts, it seemed, were easily forgotten. Her debt to me was weighed by the worth of her life. Perhaps, her indication that she owed me nothing was a confirmation of her worth.

Duty done, I begged parchment from Rolgrin, and to my surprise, he brought me to my brother's secret room – the hole – and offered me the desk there and as I wrote missives to the rulers of distant lands, sealed them with my own blood to ensure obedience, and bid him send them by messenger. His advisors came and went with excited glances at me, hopeful whispers, and at last, when I was done, one brave man dared to speak.

"You're truly the M- the Princess Izolda?" he asked.

"I am," I said firmly.

"Our Lord the King had a statue of you made in the Grand Hall and a feast is celebrated in your honor every year to mark a time you took – as he told us – death in his place. Is it true that you did?"

"I am very much alive," I said, skirting the question.

"But did you take a desperate penalty for his sake?"

"Yes," I agreed, finally turning to look the man in the eyes. He was older than I expected. Old enough to be my father.

"I remember that day in court that you spoke and came under the Law of Greeting," he said – which meant the Captain of the Guard had lied and this man could have been called to confirm my identity. There was wonder in his eyes and pain in mine for while I would not give up my husband for anything in all the world, that day had stolen much for me – much that ought to have been here in Pensmoore when I returned to it. "I remember the day you returned with your brother, dressed in black. Our Lord the King managed his holdings very well while you were his secretary. If a princess may be called such."

I lifted a brow.

Interesting.

He knew, then, that I had been the brains behind Svetgin's early rule.

"And you've come now to help Prince Rolgrin as he gains the throne?" he asked hopefully.

"It would seem so," I agreed.

And whatever it was that he heard must have pleased him,

for after that, there were no doors barred to me, and I moved through the days with willful purpose and found every branch bending to my breeze, every trail twisting to my inclination, and every road made straight for my feet.

It was less than a week before we rode out to the border of Pensmoore but even such a precipitous departure was not brisk enough for me. I did not sleep – or did not sleep well. Food was as dust in my mouth and wine of no comfort. When Svetgin the Bountiful died on the third day and was laid in state for the court to view, my dour spirits were attributed to grief and seen with strong approval. It was a sharp lie.

Every moment, my nerves jangled like bells. The need to be moving filled my every limb. Who knew how much time would pass in the Wittenhame? Who knew what measure of torture Coppertomb might set to my husband? And all that time I was here, sleeping in a royal bed, eating royal food, and being griped at by a royal annoyance.

"It does no one any good to watch you play-act the widow with your husband not even dead," Grosbeak complained.

Another time he said, "All that beauty is wasted on a frown."

But we were both happier when – at long last – Rolgrin was crowned, and we rode out to the south, fully anticipating the armies of Salamoore and Aayadmoore to join us in peace.

It seemed a fool thing to expect when they had long been enemies, but I could feel their lands as I felt Pensmoore. I could feel deep in my bones that they had been given to my husband exactly as was his right and that they were now connected to me. They must have been able to feel it, too.

Each message was returned with a rider from that land, and I felt the pull of their earth from each of them. They seemed as tied to me as strands of web around a spider. The wager had been honored. They were my people now.

Rolgrin's only regret was that he could not wed before he launched this campaign.

My regret was that we had to ride forward blind, not truly certain of our allies or enemies.

We met the first of our new compatriots at the southern border. The men of Aayadsmoore wore a mismatch of ancient armaments and refurbished uniforms, their soldiers all too old or too young – those of fighting age cut down during the long wars. I watched them with a heavy heart full of memories of slicing through their country alongside Sparrow as she led Pensmoore to victory after victory like pearls on a string.

The men of Salamoore – whose land we must march through to reach the Plains of Myyggdo at the northern portion of the Ilkanmoore desert, reflected their patron in a precise manner, aping his simple dress and economical speech. Allies or not, I felt ill at ease with them – with all of them, really, until we stepped over the border into Salamoore, and to my shock, the land rose and reached for me, greeting me like hounds to the hunter. Blossoms and green grass swirled out from my feet and swept across the ground, consuming the dead weeds of spring and musty bogs of old-melted snow.

After that, I was regarded in such awe that none dared speak to me except in low respectful murmurs.

"You've snuffed out all the fun," Grossbeak complained three days past the Salamoore border. "There's no amusement in riding to everyone's deaths if we don't get to take part in the last revelries."

And revelries there were. One would think we were the largest band of traveling mummers ever to be seen and not a group of diverse armies.

I did nothing to stop the armies at their sport, though I left Rolgrin with strict instructions that the locals were to be paid and unmolested, and camp followers were to be strictly prohibited. All the thrown axes and darts, all the feats of acrobatics and strength, and all the drink they wanted to consume bothered me not at all. I kept my own counsel and tended my own worries, which grew until they echoed from moment to moment in my hollow heart.

What if I returned and they'd taken his heart? He'd said he held mine, but mine was clearly fine. And hadn't he said something once about how they'd take the living heart from his body? They had meant to take something. Clearly, we had his bet in hand or the land of Salamoore would not welcome me. What, then, could be assumed in the other direction?

The birds did not help my worries.

Everywhere I went, songbirds appeared, singing to greet me, alighting on head or shoulder or outstretched arms. My horse – not Prince who was long gone, but one of his line, which had grown a reputation as fierce and were known as Mad Princes in our honor – grew weary of shaking his head to dislodge them, and instead bore them on his long neck with dour stillness. But not a one of them bore a letter to me. Not a line of poetry, not a scrap of parchment.

One morning, I woke to find a nest woven into Grosbeak's hair and three speckled eggs laid within it. I refused to remove it or its occupants, simply carrying them with him as I went.

"It's a disgrace, Izolda. An embarrassment!" he protested to my deaf ears.

What the armies thought of him, I did not know. I heard the words "witch," and "saint," and "revenant," and "power of the dead" as I drifted through the camps, but I did not quell them. It bound them together, these three great enemies.

And then, at last, we reached the Plains of Myygddo, and the echoes in my mind turned to the roar of a fast-approaching storm the moment my horse's hooves hit the hard-packed white sand.

"*And lo, the armies gathered and at their head was death and despair traveled alongside,*" Grosbeak quoted as we stood and looked out over it.

"I suppose that makes you 'despair' then," I said, taking comfort in his grim snicker.

I'd done it. I'd done exactly as I was bid.

Why, then, did I feel so hollow?

CHAPTER THIRTY-SIX

"What are we waiting for?" Rolgrin asked me once we had our camp set up and our defenses dug in.

"*You*," I said with emphasis, "are waiting for the arrival of our allies and enemies to fight what some will call the Last Battle. *You* are waiting to be either the greatest hero-king Pensmoore has ever known or very, very dead."

He straightened at that, back and chin stiff with the starch of resolution.

"The two aren't mutually exclusive," Grosbeak interjected. "I've been dead now for quite some time – decades, by your standards, and yet I find I am more heroic than ever."

"A multiple of zero is still zero," I said dryly.

"How did you die?" Rolgrin asked him. I snorted. Rolgrin was so grave and dignified that he seemed too noble to even be told the answer. "Was it in the execution of an act both brave and true?"

We were seated in his kingly pavilion and the servants he'd brought had made the place light and almost cheerful. His armor was polished and hung over a stand in one corner. A pallet was hidden in another corner behind a curtain, and we sat in the main area where a brazier burned lazily to scare away the late spring chill and folding three-legged leather seats had been placed around a low table.

"I was trying to kill *her*," Grosbeak said, sneering in my direction. I had not yet removed the bird's nest from his hair, and the bird was nestled down in it, sitting on her eggs. "And her husband took my head for my insult."

Rolgrin's eyes widened but he said nothing. He was surprisingly practical for a mortal, much more than his father had been. Instead, he turned his gaze to me.

"And what are you waiting for? Have you reconsidered leading our armies into battle, Aunt? I would not resist your hold over us. But I think you are eager to be off."

I offered a grim half-smile. "You see clearly. I have other troubles that must be met. I wait only to treat with your allies when they arrive. As Salamoore and Ayyadmoore were persuaded to see that your causes are one, so it must be with the other nations that join us."

He nodded. We'd been over this.

"And then?"

"And then I must go to the Wittenhame," I said grimly. "And face whatever awaits me."

"Must you?" he asked easily. At the rise of my eyebrow, he shrugged. "You aren't saying it but if you are here carrying your husband's authority and in his stead, then something terrible must have happened to him. Some grim fate you fear to share. There, your life may be forfeit. Here, you are a valuable advisor to our court. We would even endure the black magic of your companion."

"It's not black magic. It's called living the life you're given not the one you asked for," Grosbeak complained.

We both ignored him.

"You could stay," Rolgrin offered. "You could have your own lonely tower to live in like a proper widowed aunt." He smiled, teasing me. "Or, if you prefer, a suite of rooms in the palace. Another husband perhaps." He must have seen the hardening of my face. "Or not. You would be under no obligations except the ties of family and the vows of loyalty to Pensmoore."

"It is ties and vows that bid me leave you," I said. "Ties to the man who has become closer than blood to me. Vows to him."

Rolgrin tapped his fingers on the table. He was playing with the jade mermaid in his other hand as he often did when he thought no one knew he was pining for his lady love.

"You love him, then, your kidnapper?"

"He's not that anymore. Maybe he never was."

"He stole you away. You missed the lives and deaths of your family. I'm named for the brother you barely knew." His words were bald and cold.

I swallowed. "I did lose that."

"They said he'd been here before – that you were not his first bride. How many more were there?"

When I did not answer Grosbeak answered for me. "Fifteen and all of them dead as doornails. He keeps their hollow shells lined up in a hidden room."

"It's not like that," I said carefully.

"It's not like what?" Rolgrin said with the kind of calm that spoke of violence.

"He has been working for centuries toward one goal – to change all the violence and trickery into a place that is safe for his folk and that shields and guards Pensmoore. He plans to give the lives of his other wives back to them someday."

"You can't draw back death," Rolgrin said grimly. His lower lip shook slightly as he said it. He'd been manful about his father's death, but still, it stung him. "And it sounds as if your husband demands much and gives little."

"He went under the sea for me," I said. "To save my life. He drowned under the tide for seven of our years."

"It was only a few days," Grosbeak said scornfully.

"He gave a rib for me when I was kidnapped from his arms," I continue, not mentioning that it was Rolgrin's father who had stolen me away. "His wound doesn't heal. Even now he lives with the bleeding wound in his side and two matching holes in his hands – all wounds he took for me."

"Mmm," Rolgrin said, but he was not convinced. "And what is so valuable that he spends you and fifteen others and the life of this horrifying creature." Here he flicked Grosbeak's ear, ignoring his *Ow!* "And all his resources to pursue it?"

"He would be king of it all," I said grimly. "Sovereign to the Wittenhame. The one who sets the rules and makes the land flourish. The one who ends these predations on mortals."

"Would he now?" Grosbeak hooted. "And no one told me?"

"I thought it obvious," I said tightly.

"And this king he would replace," Rolgrin asked "What is he like?"

"Remote," I said. "We barely see him and yet he is everywhere speaking cryptic words, watching from afar, never getting his hands dirty in the affairs before him."

"You say that with censure. Perhaps, though, it is the only way to rule such a land. What if your husband succeeds? What if you find that in replacing the sovereign, this husband of yours becomes identical to him – far away, other-worldly, hardly a man at all?"

I swallowed hard on my first response, silent as something twisted inside me.

"What happens to you then?" Rolgrin asked. "Are you set aside like a ceremonial garment, used for a short time and no longer needed?"

"He loves me," I said in a small voice.

"Can immortals love as we do? Can they grasp tightly to every moment knowing it may be their last? Can they multiply, and delight deeply, and throw all their passion into a few short decades when for them that is but a breath?"

"Yes." My voice was too small.

"No." Grosbeak's voice was much firmer. "And it's a lie to say otherwise. We live as immortals do – tasting every flavor, sweet or bitter, with equal passion. Having no attachments for those who fade and fall."

"The death head's words ring true," Rolgrin said grimly. "Think on it, Aunt. Stay with us mortals. Live out the rest of your life in peace and away from the menace of the unfathomable. I will not use you as my father did. I will not demand marriages. I will not give you in sacrifice. I will give you a home and work if you want it. I will tolerate your hideous pet, and I will leave you to live your life in what peace you might find for yourself.

Abandon this immortal world you keep reaching for. It eats up your humanity as the flame eats the grass."

I looked away. I did not like how he saw my life and choices. From his view, they were not noble sacrifices at all, but the desperate grasping of a foolish girl. A tear fell and I dashed it aside.

"Think on it," he repeated and then stood up and left his own tent and his shaken aunt behind.

I sat there a long time, ignoring Grosbeak's occasional comments.

"Mortals," he sneered. "No better than dirt. Always wrapped up in morals and ideals. Nearly as bad as the Arrow. You'd think dwelling beneath the sea with a love-lorn captive would be the worst that could happen, but oh no, it's twice as awful to watch his heart-sick wife not even able to shepherd mortal armies without having some sort of crisis of conscience."

His grumbling went on and on. My thoughts were elsewhere.

Eventually, I left the tent and stepped out to join my nephew, lifting my skirts daintily. I was dressed again in embroidered wool with a modest headpiece as befitted my station in Pensmoore. It made me feel small as a wood mouse and just as plain.

Rolgrin stood looking out over his resting camp, a goblet in one hand and the other at his hip just over his sword belt.

"All men are as grass and their glory fades," I told him as I joined him. He didn't look at me and I joined him in gazing out over the thousands settling in before us. "Those of this separate race of Wittenbrand, this seemingly immortal kin not held by time or aging – they may seem as if they've slipped the noose of all that binds our days. But their glory is just as fading, just as passing, their years merely measured differently."

"All things pass," my nephew agreed.

"All but love and loyalty," I said grimly. "That echoes on and on past life. Still, I feel my mother's smile on my shoulders. Still, I feel the kindness in my father's gaze. And if our priests and wise men tell true, and we find ourselves in a life beyond this one when all else passes, I think it will be the love we wove here that greets us in that beyond."

He said nothing, but he took the mermaid out from his pocket and turned it over and over in his hand.

"Maybe you'll fall here in the battle. Maybe I will fall returning to my husband's side," I said gently. "But I can no more shirk my place beside him than you can shirk your place as king of Pensmoore. And his sacrifices, while twisted in your eyes, have cost him everything and all for the love of a wife his peers judge valueless. Can any love be purer than a love that gains nothing from the beloved except a return of affection?"

"I suppose not," he said, and now his eyes strayed to his mermaid again.

"Hold fast," I told him, and I left him there and went to retrieve Grosbeak.

I had planned to stay to bring Moravidmoore and Ilkanmoore tightly into our alliance, to exert on them whatever pull bound Salamoore and Ayyadmoore to me. But our conversation had swayed me. I must leave Rolgrin to fulfill his vows and stand firm in his role.

And I must leave to fulfill my own.

I took out my key.

"Not now!" Grosbeak squeaked. "Your timing is horrid. The battle is going to start in the next few days, and we'll miss all the good bits! The brave charges! The terrible defeats. Bodies stacked toward the heavens like monuments raised to catch the eye of the gods!"

Gently, I took the bird's nest from his hair and set it in a dry desert bush. Hopefully, the bird would adapt. She would have to.

"And now you rob me even of my souvenirs!"

I turned the key in the air and gritted my teeth as the madness swept me away.

CHAPTER THIRTY-SEVEN

Madness is not something one grows used to. Perhaps, the truly insane forget they are insane and drift into it as a rock is buried beneath drifts and blankets of snow. Perhaps, they take comfort in the strange simplicity that finds itself on the other side of sanity. I was not so deep into it. I was only insane enough to know sanity had slipped away, and that all my fears and horrors were being realized.

When, teeth chattering and hands flexing and clawing like talons, I finally came to awareness of myself again, Grosbeak was moaning beside me and a small bird – such a bright yellow that I would have thought his coloring impossible – was plucking at my braid as if trying to drag me after it.

I coughed, choked, finally caught a breath, and pawed blindly for Grosbeak's head. He screamed, startling me for a moment, as his scream echoed and reverberated back to us. I blinked hollowly before I realized it wasn't an echo at all. Someone not far off was also screaming. Perhaps they, too, had just made the passage. Or perhaps not.

A second bird joined the first – this one a brilliant sky blue – knocking my Pensmoore headdress away and tugging insistently at my ear.

I found my feet, swaying, skeletal fingers tangling in

Grosbeak's hair.

I needed to get my wits back.

A scarlet red bird descended on us like a falling stone and this one grabbed Grosbeak's hair and pulled.

"I'm coming," I said.

Already a second yellow bird had arrived, joined by a whole flock of his kind.

I stumbled along behind them, my ears full of faraway screams and the insistent chatter of an army of songbirds. They plucked at me, drawing me through the trees until we came, at last, to a twisting path.

White light – too white for daylight, too pure – burned through the trees, making the shadows stand out blacker than black.

I swallowed, for it seemed inevitable that this path would lead me to the place Bluebeard had spoken of when he said:

"One day, blood will be spilled on the Wittenbrand, the brand will turn gold, and on that day a great hero will arise, and he will pluck that arrow from the stone and he will be marked with white and chosen by the Wittenbrand to lead the people to an age of glory."

I shivered and it was not just for the haunting laughter coming from between the trees, it was with a sense that this prophecy, so long in the coming, was now about to be fulfilled before my eyes. I could feel it in the same way that I could feel Grosbeak's hair despite having no flesh on my fingers and in the same way that I could sense my husband was somewhere ahead and that these resolute songbirds were drawing me to him.

The path turned suddenly and I forced my reluctant feet

down it, emerging to where a surprisingly reverent crowd of folk – each one bearing a blossom in their hands – walked up a stairway made of granite steps and edged with dark openings. Each opening bore a symbol and name over it and I realized with a stabbing sense of horror that I was walking up to a great tor burial mound.

At the top of the mound, the heather grew and the graves turned from tombs to marker stones and on the tallest of them, I saw the familiar arrow burning with the white heat of the Wittenhame. To one side of it, the Bramble King's face formed a faint outline in a stand of three ancient oak trees. His face reconfigured itself when they shivered in the wind, his eyes closing and lips moving as if in strangled speech though no sound emerged.

Before him, to one side of the arrow stuck in the stone, the remaining players were arranged, looking ill at ease – Bluffroll, Antlerdale, and Wittentree.

To the other side, someone had erected a standing pole – like a grave marker of its own – and carved into its full length the images of birds and beasts, angels and demons, one atop the other. I thought – perhaps – that I saw Marshyellow's face in the spire and guilt bit hard into the flesh of my heart.

It was not the pole that froze me in my tracks, however, but he who stood lashed to it, the wound in his side gaping open. At his feet, blossoms heaped in a fragrant pile that crowned as high as his waist. My husband, the Arrow of the Wittenhame.

Beside him, Coppertomb lounged, wearing the Rib Crown he'd taken from the Sword, arms crossed over his stark white doublet. He watched the crowd as if they were his servants, performing a task to his specifications.

To my horror, I realized that as each person passed, they dropped their posey and spoke funeral words over Bluebeard. They were half dressed in mud and blood-caked clothing and half dressed as if going to a grand gala as if they'd been called to it so quickly that no one had time to dress properly and had just thrown on whatever they had that was best atop or around what they'd worn to the joust.

One woman had thick leather boots and mud-caked hose but over it, she'd put a coat made of living snakes, sewn together lengthwise but still hissing and rippling as they tried to move. Her hair was pulled half up into a similar gold net and half falling down in a tangled mess as if she had been too hurried to dress it. Likewise, a gentleman nearby was shirtless but had found for himself a small cape and baldric of black velvet speckled with diamonds which he'd jammed over leather breeches and hooved feet. Their state of dress or undress bothered them not at all as they paraded past.

"He once turned an apple silver and gave it me at the faire," a mousy woman with the tail of a rat said as she passed, dropping a dandelion on the pile.

I mounted the first step, losing sight now of the top of the hill as I pushed in and through the procession.

"He was quick in his movements as a fisher cat," another intoned, and I could not see what she laid down in tribute.

I rushed up the steps, using elbows and Grosbeak in equal measure to clear a path, meeting cries of pain and husky laughter both.

When I crested the top of the burial tor, I caught sight of him again.

I bit my lip hard, tasting blood. My husband's gaze was on

the arrow in the flame, but as my feet touched the hilltop, his head whipped to mine and his gaze met my own from under a floppy crown of flowers someone had woven and placed on his head. The flowers were speckled with blood as if they had bit the weaver, thorns their swords, and spines their daggers.

There must be some way to get him away from here, but how did you steal the grand spectacle from an event where every eye was on him?

His voice as it dipped into my mind was honey and incense, cedar and cinnamon.

"Are your armies in place, wife of mine?"

"Yes," I gasped, my mental voice stuttering in horror.

He smiled and my heart lurched. *"You've done well, then."*

His eyes closed as if in satisfaction.

"Is this your funeral?" I asked, creeping forward.

"Of course," he sounded somewhat amused. *"They send me off in style. I told you once that they would pluck from me my still-beating heart. I did not lie."*

He could not mean that.

I bit my lip, glancing quickly around the crowd to see if my suspicions were correct. Coppertomb was dressed exactly as he'd been when I left except for that bright white doublet. Wittentree too, I thought. The players I recognized were styled in dust and sweat with the occasional splash of blood. There had been no time or them to hastily don finery, not even scraps of it. So, it had been … what? An hour or two since I left them? If that? Certainly, it was early the next morning. No later than that.

"Ah, what a great honor," Grosbeak sighed happily. "To be present at your own funeral. To hear all that others would say about you before you are gone." He raised his voice. "You were violent, Arrow, and purposeful. You took my head fairly from my shoulders and planted in me a seed of hatred I have nurtured every day since. Without you, I would have a working body and a future, half my load of bitterness, and a way to plant a posey on your grave."

"That sounded more like an accusation," I said between clenched teeth as I made my way slowly through the crowd, not shy about using a quick kick to the back of a knee to force the crowd to part.

There were a few ragged cheers for Grosbeak's loud pronouncement.

"Me? Accuse a man unfairly here at the Great Barrow? I think not!" Grosbeak protested.

"Great Barrow?" I murmured, sliding past a woman whose collar was a snake as thick as my thigh wrapped around her waist and then up her back, so its head draped over her shoulder. It smelled exactly as I expected it would.

"The silver arrow is buried here within the Wittenbrand – the White Flame. I told you this."

"I don't think you did."

"It changes the form of the landscape around it. You've seen it thrice before."

"I would have remembered this."

"Well, you crashed a pumpkin beside it. It's not my fault if you don't remember that. The poets call it the Great Barrow. And certainly, there are many whose ashes were spread here, or bodies secreted into the surrounding earth or buried under turned soil or in caverns dug for the purpose. As your husband's will be. Will you remarry? It might be convenient for you to take me as husband since we spend so much time at each other's sides."

"A woeful necessity," I muttered. "Not a thing I'd wish on myself perpetually."

"You say that, and yet here we are, together as always."

We had been making our way through the crowd, forcing a place between one knot of Wittenbrand and the next around the grisly marker poles that seemed to depict the faces of the dead and those they killed while alive.

In fairness to Grosbeak, he'd done his part, biting anyone foolish enough to get near his teeth. But now, we were nearly through, and I saw my husband's eyes open to watch me as Coppertomb moved to stand in front of the marker bearing the arrow and the white flames. He leaned on a copper cane. The long grey beards of moss hanging from the oak trees swayed woefully behind him.

He'd prepared for this. The way he stood told me it had been his plan all along.

My heart stuttered wildly at the thought. How many steps ahead of me was he?

"With a bold heart, I welcome you, folk of the Wittenhame!" Coppertomb said, his voice echoing across the field and cutting through every other conversation.

The Wittenbrand woman eulogizing my husband dropped her pansy and skipped back and around me all the remaining flowers drifted to the ground as the Wittenbrand reconfigured themselves to listen.

"And here, just in time, comes the mortal wife of our friend the Arrow. Welcome to our Gathering, mortal woman. Welcome to our Feast of Hearts, our Spring Crowning, our Opening of the Barrow."

CHAPTER THIRTY-EIGHT

"All those things at once?" I asked, surprised by the boldness in my voice. "You do know how to satisfy a social schedule."

Grosbeak snickered from his place dangling from my skeletal digits and a few others joined in. There was no one like the Wittenbrand for enjoying a bit of mockery at someone else's expense.

Coppertomb's lip curled. "I also know how to satisfy prophecy. A talent your fool husband thought he was singular in."

"*What holds you here?*" I asked Bluebeard in my mind. "*Can it be broken?*"

"*I am held by my own vow.*" His eyes met mine. Resolute. Determined. "*And as such, that bond cannot be broken.*"

I shivered, feeling the weight of his words here on this burial tor with the long green moss waving a farewell and his people offering a last tribute. Fate marched toward me, uncaring, inevitable. I gritted my teeth in the face of it. What was not yet final could still be undone.

"Does our song not say," Coppertomb asked, and his voice took on an orator's quality, arresting the crowd so there was not a murmur as all fell quiet to listen. "'Fly with the arrow, Dance with the sword, Give your heart to the barrow, Die for your Lord'? Perhaps, like the Arrow here, you thought he could confidently say it spoke of him. And did I not sweat, as I watched him fulfill it step by step. Perhaps you noted it, denizens of Wittenhame?"

There was a murmur of appreciation and a few nasty snickers, but I could tell even those who derided him hung on his words.

"Lord Riverbarrow flies as like an arrow, indeed. And he brings with him this mortal wife to whom – or so my spies in Ayyadgaard tell me – he gave the gift of flight that she might escape his rival's attentions."

He held up a single finger as if making a list and the eyes around me lit with appreciation. *Tell us,* they seemed to say. *Tell us a story.*

"He danced long and hard, back and forth, in his scheming and posturing against the Sword. You saw that yourselves at the Petal Ball and later when he sank to his temporary death in the arms of the Sea."

A second finger flicked up and the crowd sighed. I edged closer to my husband, but it was harder to move between all these still, watching people.

"And perhaps," Coppertomb said, lifting a third finger, "Perhaps, giving one's heart to a mortal – who is as much dead as alive so short are their lives – may indeed constitute giving your heart to the barrow. What say you, noble Wittenbrand?"

There was a cheer. But it was not wild celebration rather it was subdued as everybody leaned forward, hanging on his words. They could tell this was all building to something. And it was certainly not building to the glory of the man tied to a stake to witness his own memorial.

I glanced around me and saw the same knowledge in every eye. And the crowd had grown, the edges thickening and filling as more Wittenbrand hurried to join what might be the spectacle of the season.

"Draw back now from this prince of the Wittenhame," Coppertomb said, and his voice was low with the threat. "Draw back now or share his fate."

Around me, the crowd receded like a tide.

I did not recede.

And perhaps I was my impractical mother's daughter after all. For as they drew back, I marched forward until I stood at the side of my captive husband.

"What do I do?" I asked him.

"*Walk with me into the darkness?"* His gaze was intense, but there was something else behind it. Some grim anticipation I did not know, and it chilled me to my core.

Something had changed in those eyes. When they had sought to guard me, they had been firm and impenetrable. Now, a softness filled them, a surrender that shook me to the marrow. When he had sunk beneath the sea for me, he had been so full of words. He'd recited vow on vow. His silence now was eerie.

"*Where you go, I will go,"* I told him firmly.

"Listen now to another story," Coppertomb said, and as he leaned forward, I saw his allies whispering to one another. Wittentree looked pale and Bluffroll as ill as a man with already green skin can look. "Listen to how I flew with the Arrow, racing beside him as he shot out, snatching his certainty with a word in his wife's ear and bending his flight back toward the mortal world. I set him on his course as surely as if I drew the string."

A single finger was held up again, but this time higher, like a proclamation.

"Watch as I bargained with the Sword, dancing him to his death at the hands of another. Watch as I sank both these competitors beneath the clawing waves."

A second finger snapped up and it was met with silence. Not the owlish silence of disbelief, but the tingling silence of anticipation.

"And think now of how I have won, by barter, the Arrow's heart – the heart he gave his love and which I won in the tilts. Watch how in just moments, I will offer his heart to the barrow." He spread his hands wide to illustrate where we stood. "Two can play at games of prophecy. Two can fulfill them." He raised three fingers high over his head. "Who is anyone to say whose story is the right one?"

He waited a beat as all were silent.

"Who?" he said again, echoing himself rhetorically.

But I know drama when I see it. I'd been friends with Grosbeak long enough. And I know the best way to ruin someone's grand speech is to reply.

"The Bramble King," I said, just loud enough that it echoed across the field and was whispered to those who did not hear from the lips of those who did.

All eyes turned to the shifting face in the oak trees and to our collective horror, it flickered, formed a face of screaming agony, flickered again and then faded until there was nothing left but the waving branches of the trees and a sick feeling deep in my core.

"The Bramble King," Coppertomb repeated in a low, menacing voice, and now he laughed and laughed in his carefully clipped, sophisticated way. "He and his grim riddles. 'Their glory fades,' he said. And then '*From stone to feather, from stillness to motion, from stagnant to shift – the time has come. Sing the song of genuflection, bow ye to your broken dream.*' All his riddles bent in the same direction. Did you earnestly believe, mortal fool, that you comprehended what we did not? This is and has always been about succession. And when I finish here today, I will take the place of the Bramble King and reign Sovereign over the Wittenhame. And will not all the Wittenhame honor me then?"

He looked out over the crowd, and they answered with a loud cheer, but still, it did not break into giddy majesty. Still, it was held on a leash. There was not one here who did not know drama inside and out. Not one who did not love the theatre of life and death, and all their instincts told them the best was yet to come.

"The game is not yet won," Bluebeard said, his first words since this began. "Nor is it likely you will win with your pieces forfeited."

And this time, Coppertomb's smile widened so far that I thought it might split his face.

"Ah. Your point is taken, Arrow. But while you – ancient even in this world – thought only of the game given us, I winkled out a different game and set it in motion. I care not what happens to the mortals. This will be over long before they set steel to steel."

Behind him, his allies shuffled uncomfortably.

"But even when that battle arrives, I have laid plans that have sown the dandelions into the fields of my friends. Their armies will be gripped in blood lust and shall wash over your showing – larger though it might be – with heedless abandon."

"That wasn't the plan," Wittentree said testily.

Coppertomb turned to sneer gently at her. "Plans change."

She flinched, but I saw her take hold of herself and stiffen. Surely, she could see, just as I could, that Coppertomb had command of the people right now.

"I don't need to win the Game of Crowns and Houses," Coppertomb said. "Not when I can negotiate a better victory. I see you are not shaken by my declarations, Arrow. And that is because you know a secret, do you not? A secret you planned to keep to yourself to the very end?"

And for the first time ever, I saw my husband's face go blank and pale.

"The secret of the Wittenbrand – the White Flame. How many of us have spilled our blood hoping to collect the Arrow? How many of us have done so in vain? But do you know what I have just discovered? When I use the knowledge we two have, I will claim the Arrow, and it will make me Bramble King beyond all dispute."

"What is this knowledge you claim to have?" Antlerdale asked without inflection. He must be as furious as Wittentree and just as controlled.

"Ah," Coppertomb said. "You are upset you were not told. But why would I tell you? Why would I open the door for another to take it first? You still have your life, and your pieces in the game you care so much about. What do you care if I take this? Do you really want to rule these lands?"

Antlerdale said nothing, his face an immovable mask.

"I didn't think you would."

I didn't care about their interplay. I was thinking – perhaps too hard – about Rolgrin waiting to do battle against the three armies coming to him on the Plains of Myygddo. Was it a drug Coppertomb had given his opponents? Or some kind of magic? I'd sent my nephew to that battle. I'd sent them all.

"What is this secret, then?" Wittentree asked, her tone bored. She wasn't fooling me.

"That sacrifice is powerful," Coppertomb said. "I wouldn't have realized this on my own, not being one to so foolishly give another what is manifestly mine. But my opponent winkled it out and by the process of deduction, I found what he was hiding. He was planning all along to carve out his own heart and place it here on the root of the ancient arrow, were you not, Lord Riverbarrow? And with that sacrifice, he planned to buy for his people a future. For as Bramble King – made so by winning the game – the worth of his life's blood given freely would be enough to work any wonder he chose."

"Is this so?" I asked, horrified.

"Speak to my riddle wife, how do you mend the unmendable and fix the unfixable? How do you roll back time and give back days? How do you unravel wickedness to the very root and burn the place where it dwelled?"

"Surely, the answer does not need to be your death." My mental voice sounded small.

"Answer this riddle another way, if you can, for I cannot."

I felt as if I'd been hit in the head with a branch. Or shot between the eyes with a stone. All this time when he said he had a plan, his plan was to die. My knees felt like water.

"Will you still walk with me, wife?"

The question hung in the air as Coppertomb, smiling smugly at his own cleverness, continued. "Since the heart was offered, the heart I will take, and it will win for me the arrow, the crown, and my right as Sovereign. And we shall all savor how it kills my rival – a delight I shall enjoy both now and in cherished memory all my days."

My heart stuttered, hardly believing this was real.

"*I will walk with you,*" I told Bluebeard while I still had the chance. It was a vow and a choice all in one. A firm commitment despite my bubbling fear. "*I will walk with you wherever you go.*"

But I could not keep the tears from my eyes as they tumbled hot down my face. I was not ready to die yet. There were so many things I'd hoped for with him. So many things I would never do with him or see with him or share with him now – we'd share only death instead – and the taste of disappointment was bitter on my tongue.

"*No tears now, fire of my eyes,*" Bluebeard said grimly. "*No tears.*"

"*I want to save you,*" I told him, because this couldn't possibly be the answer. Not from a man who commanded birds and freed himself from the sea. Not from the man who led troops into battle and took the heads of his enemies as trophies. This man did not submit to death without a qualm … did he? "*What can I do?*"

"*Only stay with me. Do not let go of me. No matter what happens, don't let go.*"

"*Or you die?*" I asked, still desperate for someone to tell me that this wasn't really going to happen.

"*No. Or* you *do,*" he said and before I could ask what he meant, Coppertomb raised his hands wide, and I saw a knife the length of my palm flash in the morning sun. Such a small thing for what he was threatening, but I'd seen deer gutted with knives no longer than my forefinger and I knew that small does not mean ineffective.

"What say you, Wittenbrand?" Coppertomb roared. "Shall we see if I am to be your King?"

And this time, the roar was deafening.

CHAPTER THIRTY-NINE

"This could not possibly be your plan," Grosbeak hissed, furious. I'd almost forgotten I was carrying him. Quickly, I tied his long hair to my belt, trying not to gag as I worked. I needed both hands free for whatever came next. "You kept saying it was all in service of a grand plan – my death, Vireo's death, Sparrow's death – and your plan was to *die*? Don't talk to me of betrayal when you've betrayed us all."

His whisper was becoming a whine.

"My plan, revenant, was to free the world and preserve my bride. And my plan *will* go forward," Bluebeard said through clenched teeth.

"*Now, fire of my eyes, I plead with you.*" His eyes met mine and I shivered at the contact. "*Keep your hands on me. Let me feel the warmth of your touch. For you are one with your mortal land and one with those given to me. I have bound you together, but I must draw now on that tie.*"

I put my flesh hand on him, and he shivered, his eyes rolling in pain or relief – I knew not which.

Coppertomb had been busy laying the rib crown on the marker before the silver arrow in a formal manner with elaborate gestures and ceremonial words that meant nothing to me but terror.

"*I meant to spare you this,*" Bluebeard gasped in my mind, "*but it seems that you must walk this path with me.*" His words felt the same way a door does when one pokes one's head without and feels the howl of the wind rushing by. They echoed as if they came from a long way off – or a long way down – as if he were already buried beneath our feet with those who came before him. "*So let us walk this path side by side, then, for I cannot shelter you and yet I am loathe to give you up, here at the end.*"

I shuddered at his words in my mind my teeth chattering harshly together.

Last time we faced our deaths together it had been with triumphant vows – a blossoming of a love we had not yet realized.

This time, we spoke with terse simplicity, as if words could not hold all the meaning we must wring from them. This time, we faced the tempering, the beating on the anvil of suffering that would shape this love for which we'd dared to hope. He must know this more than I did, for his trepidation seemed even greater than my own.

I looked out across the crowd for any hint of an ally and saw only a thirst for what came next. The Wittenhame was united in one purpose – to taste the drama Coppertomb had offered to serve up. Their anticipation was palpable, their delight building up like water behind a beaver's dam, just waiting for the moment that a log was torn loose, and it could spill over into revelry.

I clung to my husband's side, heart in my throat. Perhaps, I could take the knife from Coppertomb. Perhaps, I could fight them off. Maybe it if I took the key from around my neck and opened up the Room of Wives or took us to the mortal world.

"*Wife.*"

I met his eyes – his strange, slash-pupiled, cats' eyes so pale a blue that they were almost white. Within their unnatural form I saw only familiar affection and devotion.

"*Flee if you must. Go where you will. I will not hold you with me unless you choose it. But do not think to fight off my accuser or steal me away from this place. I am bound by vow and word to see this through.*"

"*I won't.*" My mental voice was too small. I wished it could roar like a lion.

"*To be married to me is to be wed to death. I can offer you only this – I will not abandon you, nay, though death drag me deeper than the sea did dare.*"

I swallowed and let go of the keys at the same moment that Coppertomb finished his intoned words and stepped across the stone toward my husband.

Behind him, the three remaining competitors watched, still silent, still stone-faced. Were they as bound as the Arrow was? Were they, too, surprised by how this newcomer to their ranks had twisted the game around and was seizing the keys to their kingdom?

If they were, they showed me nothing in their expressions. Their eyes would not meet mine. There would be no help coming from them.

Coppertomb strode forward and a hush fell again on the crowd as he called out to them.

"With full right and before you all, I claim the heart that was promised to me."

He leapt, his arms striking out toward my husband.

I clung to Bluebeard, feeling my mortal feebleness in the face of this strike, hoping not to let go, as my husband's body heaved and jerked under my hands. Bluebeard gave a strangled cry – but I could see nothing. The force of the action had thrust me backward, stumbling, and the only way to keep my hold on him was to fall slightly behind him. I kept my hands on his side as a terrible wet sound met my ears and then Bluebeard slumped suddenly forward, and the crowd roared.

His mental voice was faint. *"Walk with me, wife, through these gates of death."*

And if this was his last request then he would have it.

I shifted my grip on him so that I could lay his slumped head upon my shoulder and hold him up with my insufficient mortal arms, tucking him into the feeble warmth of my mortal embrace. The wound in his side gaped wide – twice as wide as it had been and ragged around the edges, as blood flowed from it. I shuddered, barely keeping down my gorge.

All he asked was the last shreds of my broken heart and they were his, all his.

Many wives watch their beloveds die, I told myself firmly. Your father watched your mother die, though you were not there to see it. Just be glad you get to be here for his last breath. Just hold onto that.

But my wisdom was hollow, breaking between my fingers like poor-fired clay. And I could not help the way I flinched as the crowd roared behind me like surf breaking over a rock – and if I were a rock then I was limestone, wearing away. No, if I were a rock, then I was a heap of sand piled by children, decimated by each wave until I was nothing more than a memory.

I risked a glance over my shoulder to see Coppertomb holding something up to them. Something dark and wet. The sight of it both revolted me and drew me as if a thread ran from it to me.

I was too stunned to cry. Too stunned to think.

It felt as though this terrible thing had happened to someone else. It could not be happening to me. Not after everything. All the pain, all the patience, all the sacrifice, and this was what I'd earned? Hollowness? Brokeness? An ending that fizzled to nothing but the same death everyone had in the end. My mouth smarted at the bitter taste within. Would that I could spit it away. I could not sweeten it with hope. There was no hope now.

I must be sensible. I forced my traitor thoughts aside.

Bluebeard should be cut down.

With his head still on my shoulder, and my arm wrapped around his waist, I pulled his shattered body to me. I reached into my belt and produced a small knife, reached up, and severed the cords that held him. He fell heavily onto me, driving me to my knees with a gasp. We slumped into the heap of flowers, their sickly sweetness drifting up and mixing with the smell of blood and bile. By sheer force of will, I kept him upright, still leaning against my strength as I hugged him to myself.

And even if I hadn't promised to stay with him, I would have. I could not possibly have let him go now. Not even when his body as it pressed against mine had not a single beat of his missing heart. Not when this may be the last real embrace of my life, the last time my heart was ever full and ripe with love. The last time.

"I love you," I whispered. "I love you. I love you."

He trembled beneath me, but was that him trembling, or only

the heaving of my chest as I clutched him to me?

The Wittenhame had paled when I looked up, washed of color, shaded in tones of copper and gold.

As Coppertomb laid my husband's heart at the base of the silver arrow, the flames flared a rich gold and then went dull. And as he drew the Arrow from the flame – just as he said he would – he seemed flimsier in my vision, frailer, as if he were the one turned mortal and I the immortal.

The white flame which was now gold – the Wittenbrand they were all named for – shot up to three times the height, the wet heart disappeared in a burst of flame, and its vanishing quenched the fire so that all that was left was an afterimage against my lids.

Coppertomb lifted his chin arrogantly as he held the arrow aloft in the view of the crowd and blasphemous cheers swelled around us. He retrieved the Rib Crown and placed it once more upon his head, this time it was printed by his fingers with blood, a permanent reminder of what had been done.

In the oak trees, the Bramble King's face formed, deformed, and then ripped to shreds, disappearing like clouds when the wind shifts. I needed no one to tell me he would not be back.

"And thus, I defeat all competitors," Coppertomb intoned, barely masking his overwhelming emotions at this final triumph. Tears and joy swelled equally in his voice. "And I crown myself the Bramble King, Conqueror of the Wittenhame."

And the roar of the crowd should have drowned out all else. It should have drowned out my very thoughts. But instead, I heard an echo on the cusp of hearing, whispering in my mind.

"Hold me in your heart as my last breath,

tickles the memory that once bordered

on the divine and shatters me in last rest."

I clung to the writer of that poem as my hot tears finally released into sobs, heaving like the sea, under the crash of cheers and applause. Sorrow clung like the tide, rising ever higher. And it seemed that the Sea and I had two things in common – neither of us would willingly give up my beloved and both of us wanted revenge.

CHAPTER FORTY

I stroked his hair and his sweet face, pressed my cheek against the top of his head, let my tears flow down his neck, and let the last echoes of his life wash over me. My future flapping free like a flag torn in the storm, loose, and then carried aloft never to be seen again.

"I waste. I fade. I am borne below." His mind rambled to mine. I recognized one of his poems to me.

And I hoped he wasn't in pain.

And I hoped he wasn't longing for release even as I could not loosen my hold, would not lessen it by so much as a twitch. He was mine. These last moments of his were mine, and I would not give up the last of my treasure. Not to anyone.

Around us, the ghoulish celebration had started. Lines formed as the folk of the Wittenhame lined up to kiss the hand of their new sovereign. He exulted in their praise, head thrown back, arms raised high, glory sweeping across his features as happiness or sorrow might do and cloaking him in gold.

My stomach soured at the very sight of him.

"She lingers. Lasts. Against the foe." My Arrow's voice had lost it's surety, drifting now as the voice a dreamy child.

How long could a person hold on while his life drained away? Even an immortal Wittenbrand? It couldn't be long. No wonder he'd asked me not to let him go. No wonder he'd asked me to walk through the dark with him. No wonder he'd been so quiet. He'd known.

And what was there to say when all had been said already?

Someone was making a pitiful sound, miserable as a newborn kitten. Me. I was making that sound. The last sound he'd ever hear.

I cut it abruptly, sucking in a shuddering breath and forcing myself back under control. It would not be the last. He deserved better. He did. Even if his plan had failed, was it not valiant to have tried or so much? A holy ambition. A righteous hope.

I could not fault him for reaching for more than he could grasp.

"Live now my heart, Live now for me." His mental voice *sputtered and broke and then gasped out the last, "I gasp. I die. I ache for thee."*

My vision was blurry from too many tears and something in my chest ached in raw pain as if I were the one who had felt her living heart torn away. I clutched him to my breast as tight as I could and let his last thoughts flow through my mind like molten gold. They seared into me, leaving indelible marks – scars, some might say – but these scars would be my last remnants of him. I wanted every slash and sear.

His fingers tightened on me and then fell away, and then tightened again as if finding one last spurt of strength.

"I love you," I whispered one last time my voice trembling badly, stretched thin with sorrow. "How can you die when I love you?"

His touch fell away.

The absence roared like pain through nerve of my physical body and tightened round and round my heart until I thought it could not possibly manage a beat.

They were singing that awful song again. The one I'd thought would be my salvation. The one that never could be.

"Sing for your sovereign,

Bow to your Dream,

Make haste for the fallen,

Rise in esteem,

And if ever you be broken,

And gasp on the ground,

The word may be spoken

And salvation found."

There would be no salvation for me. Not from a song. Not from anywhere else.

And yet I couldn't help myself.

"Mercy," I whispered through my chattering teeth, and I did not know who I whispered it to, but for a moment, I thought I saw something. It was probably the haze of my tears making me see ghosts, but for the blink of an eye, I thought I saw the Bramble King's face in the strewn flowers heaped around us and I thought I saw him wink.

I blinked hard, and when I opened my eyes there was a face

there, level with mine. I bit back a yelp.

Wittentree leaned back on her heels, squatting in front of me, Bluebeard between us. Her one good eye bored into mine.

"I'll give you mercy if that's what you want," she said grimly, holding up a curved knife the length of my forearm and making a subtle slicing motion with it to emphasize her point. "But I don't think you do. I think what you want is to keep suffering. I'll give that to you, too, if you bargain for it. But it will cost you."

"I won't give him up," I said raggedly, my voice torn by tears, the hands holding his warm body trembling so hard that he shook.

Someone laughed close by, merry and bright in contrast to all my black shadows. Murder filled my heart.

She snorted a laugh. "I don't want him. And I wouldn't be Saint Wittentree, Boon to Lovers – which is what they're calling me in the mortal world, by the way – if I kept taking one half of the couple as my own. No. I want what Tanglecott gave you. Not all of it. I'm not as cruel as my looks suggest. I just want the extra – what wasn't yours to begin with."

"You want my beauty?" I asked, shocked that the price was so small. I would give anything – everything – what was so fool a thing as looks right now?

"Don't sound so aghast." Her eyebrows rose. "You think the price too steep? He gave his heart and all his plans to protect you – the one fly in the ointment of his perfect scheme – and you won't give up a heart-breaking face?"

"What will you give me in return?" I asked, not willing to waste time disabusing her.

"What do you want?"

"I want him to live." My voice broke on the last word.

"He stays alive while you are touching him," she said.

Dancing had begun behind us, and someone called for a roasted pig. I'd kill them all. Rain fire from the sky. Carve out their … oh sweet mercy.

"That seems a poor bargain." I managed with trembling lips. But I'd take it. I'd take it and be glad.

She barked a laugh. "That's not the bargain. That's already a fact. Or it might be. These things are dangerously slippery to work out. Didn't you know it? Isn't that why you cling to him as you do? As long as your flesh is in contact, he can siphon your days to keep him alive. Maybe. It's a shock to his body that his heart is gone, but he lives still until you abandon him, or until you run out of time. So, that's not the bargain. I couldn't bring back the dead, anyway. That's not where my talents lie."

"Can you keep us bound, flesh on flesh so that I do not lose touch with him unless I wish it?" I asked. "You said that might keep him alive."

She looked at us pityingly. "Think you that he'd want that? A ghost half-life stuck forever with you? Lingering in agony on the edge of sweet relief?"

"I think he wouldn't want to die until he'd won," I said fiercely, practically spitting the words as I blinked back hot tears. Would they not stop?

She shook her head. "There's not much chance of that now, not even if you meet all the requirements."

There was certainty in my voice. "I'll do whatever I must do. I'll walk this darkness with him to the very end. I'll die if I must."

"Then tell me, what do you want?"

I must stick to the practical. I knew nothing else.

"Can you make it possible that if he falls, as he has fallen now, that I may have the strength to carry him? Will you bind us that I may not fail him by losing my grip."

She looked at me long and hard.

"So, it's to be suffering then. Long, hard suffering. What strange creatures you mortals prove to be. So close to death that you seem almost to call to it, as if the great leap is no more than the hop over a mud puddle."

Some kind of dark longing swam in her single eye.

I jutted out my chin. "Once you make it possible, I will be no concern of yours."

She laughed at that, and I thought I saw approval in her eyes. "Fair enough, mortal girl. Consider this our bargain then, your excess beauty, above what you had before you met Tanglecott, will be transferred to me and in exchange I will bind to you the strength to carry your husband when he falls, and I will bind your flesh with his so that you will not lose that touch unless you ask it. And if you ask it, you must say these words, 'I beg release from this binding and I beg it sincerely.' Are we agreed?"

"Agreed," I said.

I felt the narrowing of my hips and bust, felt my dress hang looser, and my center of balance shift slightly while at the same time, I watched Wittentree's scars vanish, her hollow cheeks fill, her thin lips grow plump, and her hardened eyes brighten.

"Enjoy your suffering," she said.

"Wait," I said, and she turned halfway back toward me as if reluctant to say more. Around her the carousing was intensifying. Colored sparks flew into the air above her head. I forced the plea from my lips. "What do I do now? How can I save him?"

She snickered, proving she was Wittenbrand after all.

"I don't know if it will be more fun to watch you flounder at this or to watch Coppertomb squirm, so I'll tell you for a price."

"What price?" I gasped.

"That living hand of yours will do. I have heard interesting things about it from those who call themselves my allies." She raised an eyebrow.

"I don't know where it is," I said, truthfully. We'd left it on Bluebeard's mantle, but where might it have gone since?

"No matter." She snapped her fingers and my living hand appeared in her palm. She cocked a lovely eyebrow at me and then ripped off her eyepatch to reveal the other eye perfectly beautiful, though white as a pearl.

"The hand is yours," I agreed, unnerved by her eye of fog.

Her smile was smug. "You should have bargained, mortal girl. Never make deals when you are desperate. It blinds the eye and dazzles the mind. But here you have it: a riddle to guide, a path for the mind. Attend me." She paused, took a deep breath, and then spoke her riddle as I clutched my beloved to me like a lost doll newly found. "What once stood in a line, but now is missing a brother? What was taken for wealth and refined by another? What holds death or life in the gap left behind? What holds endless damnation in similar kind?"

And then she was gone, disappearing into the mass of dancing, drinking, hooting bodies.

And I was left in a heap on the ground, holding my slumped beloved.

Carefully, hoping I'd not been tricked, I stood, dragging him up with me. I angled my arm under his knees, the other still clutching his back, and I lifted him. He was no heavier to me than a small child.

From somewhere at my side, there was a spitting sound.

"Drown me in flowers, why don't you? What a terrible way to be buried. In gold? Of course! Under stone? Acceptable. Beneath the waves? If I must. But in rotting plants? The indignity!"

Grosbeak, it seemed, was still with us – unwanted though he may be. I should have traded him away and been double the winner.

I turned, my husband in my arms, to see the Wittenhame celebrating on the barrow of their dead.

Not a single eye glanced toward us.

Not a single hand turned to help.

Long tables had been brought and heaped with food. Casks of ale flowed. A band of musicians played instruments made entirely of bone for a crowd that danced with the fervor of slaves freed. Coppertomb sat in their midst on a throne made of heaped bones, his stolen arrow in one hand like a scepter, and his crown sitting very precisely on his grave brow. Courtiers were still trailing up to kiss his ring as I took a step backward, and he set a benevolent hand on the head of each one.

But to my eye, every Wittenbrand here was dull and grim, a parody of people, and all the Wittenhame had lost its taste and color. It was dead and faded and lost to me.

Dust in my hand.

Sand in my mouth.

And I wanted not a mote of it to stay with me.

I turned on my heels and fled as fast as my feet would take me, clutching my beloved to me as I ran madcap and trembling down the back of the tor and out into the deadly Wittenhame with a riddle in my mind, a sob in my throat, and the love of my life and death cradled to my chest, the ashes of all my wished-for future fluttering behind me.

***

Read the end of Izolda's Story in DIE FOR YOUR LORD.

BEHIND THE SCENES:

USA Today bestselling author, Sarah K. L. Wilson loves happy endings, stories that push things just a little further than you expect, heroes who actually act heroic, selfless acts of bravery, and second chances. She writes young adult fantasy because fantasy is her home and apparently her internal monologue is stuck in the late teens

Sarah would like to thank **Melissa Wright & Eugenia Kollia** for their incredible work in beta reading and proofreading this book. Without their big hearts and passion for stories, this book would not be the same.

Sarah has the deepest regard for the talent of her phenomenal artist Luciano Fleitas who created the gorgeous cover art that accompanies this book. Without his work, it would be so much harder to show off this story the way it deserves!

Thanks also to the Noble Order of Female Fantasy Authors who keep me sane – sort of. And for my beloved husband, Cale and sons Neville and Leif who are endlessly patient as I talk to them about bookish passions.

And a HUGE THANK YOU to my patrons, **Mike Burgess, Jennifer Wood,** and **Carly Salsbury** for their support. I couldn't do this without readers like you!

Visit Sarah's website for more information:

www.sarahklwilson.com

Printed in Great Britain
by Amazon

56783622R00225

THE STARLIT CITY

THE SHIFTING FAE: BOOK TWO

BY

ELIZA TILTON

THE STARLIT CITY

Cover art by Eliza Tilton

www.elizatilton.com

Give feedback on the book at:
elizatilton@gmail.com
Twitter: @elizatilton

First Edition

Printed in the U.S.A

"We do not merely destroy our enemies; we change them"

-George Orwell

Author's Note

If these characters seem a tad familiar, it's because this series was originally released under a pen name a few years ago. The stories were novellas and while I loved the world I'd created, it wasn't working. These characters needed more depth and for their tales to be told in the right way.

I made the decision to take down the series and it's been re-written and re-imagined into a full-length epic Fantasy Romance series with a fleshed-out world, plenty of action, and swoon worthy romance.

For those of you who have met our heroine and hero before, I hope that you love their new adventure and stay along for the ride.

Eliza

ONE

KELIA

The magi prison was located on one of the isolated islands off the southern coast; cold, wet, rocky, and ominous. A strange whirring sound filled the air outside the stone enclosure. Magic, deep, and dark. Only the most dangerous of creatures and villains landed in this isolated place, and I had come to release one of them.

I waited outside by the carriage for the guards to bring out the mage.

Callum Deathstrike. Though, from my research, that wasn't his true last name. I wondered how a dark fae who had been locked away for decades would be of any use to us, regardless of his power.

But I had my orders.

The driver opened an umbrella to hold above

me as rain fell from the darkened sky. Oscar was taller than any other man I'd met, but anyone who worked for the magi was always more than what they seemed, including me. His lanky arm held the protective covering high above my head, keeping most of my dress dry.

A grinding emanated from the black iron gates as they opened outward. Four guards escorted the fae out. Two held poles connected to a collar around his neck. A magical dampener to keep his power at bay. The other two stood behind the prisoner, staves pointed at his back.

The rain fell harder, making it difficult to see.

I walked forward; the driver quickly followed.

Mud sloshed against my boots and dirtied the hem of my once white dress. Callum had his head down, staring at the ground. When I drew closer, the stench of his prison sentence nearly made me gag.

"Why is he not cleaned?" I demanded, holding a hand to my nose.

One of the guards glared at me. "Not our job to bathe the beast."

With a flick of my hand, I sent my magic forth to wrap around the guard's throat like a noose. "Do not get clever with me."

The guard dropped the pole and clawed at the magical lasso as I tightened it around his pitiful neck.

A smirk appeared on Callum's face. The rest

of his features were covered by shaggy magenta hair that fell past his pointed ears. Dark fae were known to have silver hair or varying shades of white not a bright color that stood out against the surrounding rock.

"Do you have bathing amenities here?" I directed my question to the guard holding the other pole.

He nodded.

"Then take us to them. I will not travel with this man reeking of defecation." I released my hold on the guard and grabbed my skirt in both hands. "Bring fresh towels and a set of clean clothes, on order of the Magi Council."

The guards turned and led the fae back inside. He shuffled as he walked, a chain between his ankles. The stained gray uniform he wore had ripped in odd places as if he'd worn it for his entire imprisonment. The magi were not known for their empathy, but even prisoners deserved basic amenities.

Past the gate, we entered through an enormous set of steel doors. Oscar waited outside, knowing full well I could handle this on my own. There was a reason the magi sent me, one of their best. Even after the unfortunate events at Farrow's Gate, I'd proven over the years that very few could match my power, and those that came close had died, including Demious, even if it wasn't by my hand. Lord Demious had always been a powerful ally, but the magi did not know the extents the magistrate had gone to empower himself. If they had kept their spy network intact, the magistrate would still be alive and neutralized.

We headed into a tunnel that seemed to be a separate area from where the prisoners were kept. Because of the prison's location, the guards had to live on site, and I assumed we were headed to the guardhouse where the area didn't smell of death, decay, and years of unwashed captives.

The common room we entered held a library, an eating area, and off to the side, a wooden door with a picture of a toilet carved into the front. The guards pressed Callum forward. His expression never shifted to anger. Instead, he peered at me beneath dark lashes as if he had no idea why I would be here.

"There's no exit," one of them said to me. "We'll take him in, and you can wait here."

"No."

While one guard walked off, the other three stared at each other in confusion.

"He is my charge. I will make sure he cleans and dresses. He's too valuable to be left in your incapable hands." With that, I grabbed the pole and tugged on it. "Come, fae."

Callum kept his head down, not saying much. The other guard followed behind me, carrying two white towels and a folded set of guard clothes. Black shirt and trousers, with the blue symbol of the magi on the front pocket.

I pushed Callum forward into the baths.

The showers were an open, large room with steel heads on the left wall, and benches on the right where clothes and other items could be left. I unhooked the pole connected to the collar on Callum's neck—I'd need the guards to give me the key for his magical dampener. I pushed open the door and called for the guard to remove the chains around Callum's hands and ankles. Once completed, the guard left the set of clothes and quickly exited the area.

"Go and wash. We need to be off the island before dark," I said to Callum, leaning against the wall and folding my arms.

Callum unbuttoned his shirt, then dropped his pants, his head bowed.

The natural light from the glass ceiling danced across his shadowy plum skin highlighting the rosy accents that matched the light tones in his hair. Muscles rippled down his back, something I didn't expect from a fae mage, and one who had been locked away for decades. Naked and unabashed, he moved to a showerhead and turned the metal knob.

He sighed as hot water pelted his skin.

With his back to me, I could see how his corded muscles moved when he washed his magenta hair. How each piece of flesh was honed and strong. His thighs showed years of work, and his backside was something to be admired, even from a woman who had no interest in that sort of thing. There was no time for relationships or anything similar when war raged and darkness covered the west northern lands. One day when the past was only a fleeting thought would I even consider fraternizing with males.

For all his mystery, I'd yet to see his face, at least not all of it.

Curious, I asked, "How long has it been since you bathed?"

He glided his through his hair then his cheeks. "Years."

His husky voice rumbled in my ears, a dangerous sound that made my heart constrict. It reminded me of thunder and lightning when the two sounds collided and created something wholly unique and utterly terrifying.

A bar of soap hung on a nearby rope, and Callum took it in his hands. Some might think it rude to watch, and I decided it would be prudent of me to turn away and give the fae his privacy. He wouldn't be escaping anywhere without the use of his magic, and thanks to the collar around his neck, his abilities were under control.

Growing up with the magi, I had spent years with old men and women who cared for nothing but lectures and research. The tedious repetitiveness of my days had prepared me for this mission. While I had recently been on many, this was my first alone. There were always guards with me, but I'd proven repeatedly that the only weapon I needed was myself.

Over the years, I'd met many races, but the fae always seemed like a mystery to me, and the dark fae culture was well guarded and hidden below the surface of Saol. Would this male be like the one I had encountered back in Farrow's Gate? And if yes, I would need to guard myself well.

After a while, Callum shut the water off and took a towel off the bench and lifted his head.

Our gazes met and I wasn't sure what transpired, but my stomach clenched oddly. His almond-shaped silver eyes sparkled with mischief. Water droplets ran down his high cheekbones and slender nose. I followed the rivulets as they traveled down his chiseled chest, quickly averting my gaze before seeing anything more. A fae's aura seemed to sizzle with magic more than any human gifted with power, making them interesting, but dark fae were something else, like a refined piece of ore that had been transformed into a precious alloy that flecked with every metal known.

He grabbed the clothes, and I heard the shuffle of fabric as he slipped into them. "What's your name, little sparrow?"

He rubbed the towel against his wet hair. Light from the skylights in the room highlighted the luminous tones in his plum skin and made the lightness of his eyes haunting.

"Kelia," I replied, ignoring the nickname that jabbed at both my height and title. "We need to move. There's a storm brewing and we need to make port before it starts."

With a flourish of his hand, he motioned for me to move ahead. The collar dampened his magic, though I wondered if unleashed whose power would be greater. Stories surrounding Callum had been riddled with exploits and unbridled power, all which seemed plausible standing next to him now. Even with the collar on, I sensed a rich rumbling of magic rolling under his skin, like a roaring river waiting for the dam to break.

The guards stood to attention as we exited the baths.

"I require his collar key." I held out my hand.

The guard nearest me unhooked a silver key from a massive ring on his belt. "I'd keep that on if I were you."

"It's a good thing you're not me." Taking the key, I sighed, and hurried outside, eager to leave the dank and acrid smell of the prison.

Callum strolled beside me squinting at the hazy sky. His mouth slightly parted, slowly drawing a breath in. Was he excited to be out? How long had it been since the sun touched his face?

Oscar waited outside the carriage. Seeing our arrival, he opened the door and allowed us in. I seated myself, Callum across from me. He stretched out his arms and legs, nearly taking up the whole space with his body. The guard clothes hugged his frame revealing he hadn't spent his prison sentences sitting idly by.

"Are you going to tell me what I'm doing here?" he asked in a drawled-out breath as he leaned his head back against the seat.

"No one's told you?"

His full lips curved into a smile. "Not a thing, darling."

"My name is Kelia, and I'd prefer if you used it."

"I'd prefer not to."

He smiled again, and I found him to be a curious thing. "The magi need your assistance acquiring a fae light bearer from the Starlit City."

Callum's gaze darkened. "You're human. Humans aren't allowed in the city."

Before he could interrupt with his disdain, I continued. "In exchange for your cooperation, the magi will release you from your imprisonment."

"You jest."

"Why would I joke about this?"

His eyes widened, and he moved so quickly to grab my hands, the movement shocked me. "You would release me?"

I snatched my hands away from him. "As soon as the child is retrieved, and we return to the magi. Yes."

He quieted for a moment, sliding back into his

seat, tapping a slender finger against his chin. "Why me? There are other fae who aren't in prison that could go."

"Queen Merelda made the exchange. We don't know much, but she said we'd only be able to reach the city with your aid."

"That doesn't make any sense."

"There have been rumors the city is at war. There's been little communication from the Underground. It started a few months ago."

Callum rubbed his chin. "I see."

"If you know something, tell me."

He shook his head, and his shoulders sagged. "I've been away a long time. I'm not sure of anything."

His piercing gaze met mine. There was something ancient and wild in his eyes, and I was curious to find out what.

TWO

CALLUM

The painfully beautiful woman sitting across from me wasn't ready to venture into the depths of the Underground to the Starlit City. The Underground was hostile to the surface dwellers during times of peace. If what she said was true, she would be killed outright, from both fae and beast. Then again, even with her innocuous and youthful appearance, there was a cold calculating intelligence brimming in her large cobalt blue eyes. If the magi sent her alone, then her power would be sufficient for the task. After all, she was charged with my retrieval and my escort to the city. I could probably snap her neck with relative ease, even without my magic. Yet there was something about the way she carried herself.

Closing my eyes, I reached out with my primal instincts. I sensed the magic within her. The current filled the air, and my skin prickled with excitement. It had been many years since I'd been in the company of such power. This was no prey animal before me. I could feel the energy emanating within her, a raging torrent of magical aptitude. The fact she was holding her poise with no hint of the inferno raging within was delectable. It might prove an exploit to use in my escape, and I would love to see that fire unleashed.

"You're young for a mission like this," I said, watching how she neither smiled nor frowned when I spoke.

She conjured a blue ball of fire into her palms. "Age is not a requirement. Power is."

There was no emotion in her voice. I found her entire persona intriguing. Dressed in a white bodice that covered a voluptuous chest, and golden silky hair that flowed around her shoulders. She appeared to be a delicate mannered thing, but something lacked in her voice and eyes.

"You must be very powerful if they allowed you to come alone."

She dismissed my question, not bothering to respond. The blue ball diminished, and she sat back in the seat, looking out the window. "We'll take a ship off the island tonight, then head toward the Crusted Mountains in the morning."

The Crusted Mountains, certainly the quickest route to the city, but not the easiest path. "Am I to venture into this peril unarmed? Or are you fearful that I would be too much to handle if given even footing?"

With a blank stare she tilted her head at me. "I am the weapon, and you wouldn't last more than a few seconds if you tested your thesis."

We stared at one another with spite in our glare, neither blinking for many minutes. I couldn't tell if it was a sneer or the hint of a smile forming around her lips and nostrils. Perhaps it was a mixture of both, and just like that her interest in our little stare off waned as she turned her gaze back to the rocky terrain outside her window. Was this how our journey would be? When there could be so much more offered? Certainly, a young woman of her power and beauty required certain appeasements.

"How long have you been with the magi?" I asked, curious about her history with the old order. She was young to hold such an important position.

"Since I was a child."

I arched a brow, thinking there was a story behind that statement. It wasn't uncommon for the magi to take in children. They preferred to groom their weapons from an early age, but it was uncommon for the magi to trust a younger mage with such a dangerous quest.

The carriage rolled along the uneven road that wound around the rocky and somewhat desolate island. Kelia looked out the window with an empty stare. I found it intriguing she was not frightened or intimidated by me.

The prison sat on an island far from the mainland. The rocky cliffs and dangerous seas made escape impossible. Only one ship transported goods and guards back and forth. When the magi had imprisoned me, I knew it was indefinite. I wasn't worth anything to anyone, especially the queen of my people. Why was she calling on me now? My last conversation with Merelda did not go well, and if I was to be honest with myself, she was the reason I was imprisoned, even if my actions had been just.

With the sun high, and my gut aching for food and water, I thought about how I could manipulate this pretty thing in front of me to release my dampener. Surely, she had enough magic to challenge me if she needed no guards. I didn't enjoy being out in the open without access to my power.

The road dipped over the hill and down toward the only port. One rickety looking ship docked at the pier, and a bunch of prison guards sat around a wooden table playing a game of dice. Life on the island was anything but exciting.

We stopped, and instead of waiting for the driver to open her door, Kelia flung it open and jumped out. Mud splattered the bottom of her white dress, but she didn't seem to mind.

"Come," she said, glancing over her shoulder at me.

I followed her out and down the pier. Her driver carried only a single black bag. How would we travel through the mountains with no gear? "We'll need more than a single handbag if you want to venture through the Crusted Mountains."

My stomach growled, loudly enough for the pretty human to turn and acknowledge it.

"When was the last time you ate?" Kelia asked, as she waved her driver over.

"What day is it?"

Kelia took the black bag from her driver. "Oscar, let the captain know we've arrived. I want to leave as soon as the ship is ready."

Oscar nodded and walked to the ship. I followed Kelia over to a bench where we sat. The guards playing dice eyed me warily. While I may have dressed as one of them, the steel collar around my neck gave away my true identity, and dark fae were not a common sight on the surface.

"Ignore them. Eat." Kelia shoved a roll and salted beef into my hand. She unscrewed the top of a canteen, drank, then handed it to me.

I wiped the rim before drinking, earning an insulted glare from my pretty captor. "I don't know you that well, *yet*, little sparrow."

Chugging the rest of the contents, I wiped my

mouth with the back of my hand and handed it back to her. She shook the canteen then frowned. "I see you've lost your manners while in there."

"Darling, I didn't have them to begin with."

"Just eat," she sighed, shoving the canteen into her bag. "The ship will take us over to the mainland and we should arrive just before dawn."

A piece of the roll crumbled off and hit the dirt. I had to hold myself back from snatching it off the ground and eating it. I didn't want her to see how hungry I truly was. My best defense was to seem unphased, I could tell she was sizing me up, gaging a way to apply leverage.

Oscar returned, eyeing me a bit as he approached. Perhaps the old fellow didn't care for how close I sat to his pretty charge. "The captain has allowed us to board."

"Good." Kelia stood and grabbed her dress in her hands. "Let's be on our way. I'm tired and wish to rest."

Rest? It's the afternoon and we've barely traveled. If this human couldn't manage a few hours on a rocky road what about when we hiked through the mountains? Shaking my head, I followed her down the pier and to the ramp that led onto the old ship. A breeze passed through, and I inhaled the salty air.

It felt good to be outside, unchained.

And as soon as the opportunity presented itself, I would be free.

The back of Kelia's dress dragged across the sodden planks. Water had soaked up a few inches into the cotton. If this was her adventuring gear, she was not prepared for the trek ahead. The mountains would be an opportune place to renegotiate our arrangement.

An older man with a black hat that flopped sideways motioned for us to head to the lower level. The ships that sailed in and out of this port transported both goods and people. If we were lucky, we'd have a room not reeking of sweat and sailor piss.

"Your room, milady." The older man swung open a small cabin. "We'll keep the fae in the barracks—"

"He stays with me," Kelia said.

"What?" The old man and I said at the same time.

The expression on Kelia's face held no emotion at all. "He's my prisoner and will stay where I can watch him."

"I assure you, milady, our barracks are secure."

I expected Oscar to add his own thoughts, but he simply waited as if he expected this from her.

"I'm sure they are, but until his task is done, he stays with me."

The old man cleared his throat and lowered his voice. "It's not proper for a young lady to share a cabin with a male, especially one like him."

"That'll be all, good sir." Kelia took the black

bag from Oscar and nudged my arm. "Inside."

"Gentlemen." I nodded with a smirk and cocked eyebrow at the two surly humans before following Kelia into the room.

The cabin held a single bed and not much else. A chamber pot sat in the corner near a desk with a lantern on it. I closed the door behind me, wondering how I'd be able to spend a night in such tight quarters with this woman.

It had been too long since I had been this close to a female. Her floral scent permeated the tight quarters, her presence saturating my senses.

Kelia sat on the bed and began untying the laces on her brown boots. She sighed and kicked them off onto the floor. She laid back on the bed, wiggling her toes. I sat with my back against the door, directly across from her.

"Are we to stay in here all day and night?" I asked.

"Yes. I've been traveling since yesterday to come here and need to rest." She whispered something inaudible, and I felt a shimmer of magic tingle my skin.

"What did you do?"

"Barrier spell. You can't leave this room, and no one can enter."

"So you are no different than my previous masters. I am to lie on the floor like some animal, some kind of pet perhaps?"

She swung her legs around off the bed. Her feet

barely touched the floor. "You are my charge."

"That doesn't mean we need to spend our time down here when the weather has cleared, especially when it's been years since I've had the breeze in my hair, inhaled the fresh air, or felt the warmth of the sun on my face." I met her wide-eyed stare, trying to figure out what secrets she held in those big blue eyes.

The silence stretched between us until she finally stood, gathering the front of her skirt. My heart raced as she moved closer and I held my breath, wondering what her little mind was thinking.

She squatted in the corner over the chamber pot.

If she hadn't still been holding my gaze, I might've been a little less uncomfortable. "This isn't a vacation for either of us."

"If you want privacy, I can leave." I shifted my gaze from her unusual antics. She wasn't shy, or ladylike. Everything she did was unexpected. There had to be an angle.

"No need. You and I are bound to each other on this trip, and I'm not letting you out of my sight."

With that, I gave her a smirk. "Are we to be bathing partners then?"

No change in her demeanor, not even the slightest flush in her cheeks. Instead, she narrowed her gaze. "This mission is a top priority. If we need to bathe, then you will do so in front of me. You are not leaving my sight."

She finished with the chamber pot and stood. "If you're uncomfortable, you may close your eyes."

I laughed at that. "Don't flatter yourself, darling. I have seen my share of naked females. There is no mystery to uncover."

Kelia folded her arms, her face as hard as the floor I sat on. "Then it is settled."

I shook my head. "Are you sure you're up for this mission?"

Her eyes glowed an eerie blue and the surrounding air tingled. I waited for a reply, but she just sat there glaring at me until I was the uncomfortable one. She had eyes that were so bright and wide they were hypnotizing me into a state of stupor. That or I had been in prison much too long.

"Sleep." She climbed into the bed and tugged the blanket over her shoulder.

Kelia may have been young, but anyone who could fall asleep with an unchained prisoner in a room was either out of their mind or extremely dangerous.

I'd yet to figure out which side she tilted toward.

Three

Kelia

Even with my eyes closed, I felt the fae's gaze on my back. He unnerved me in an odd way. He didn't react to my provoking, and by now I had pushed him enough to elicit a response to better gage him. During my years at the Magi Academy, I'd been exposed to plenty of men of many races, except a dark fae. They kept to themselves, and those that traveled the surface lands were mercenaries, hunters, or emissaries. One or two may have passed through the High City, but they were old and withered.

I glanced over at my charge.

He leaned against the side of the building while we waited for Oscar to bring us the horses. Callum's magenta hair reminded me of wild magic, and I wondered what his silver eyes would look like when he cast. From what I had read, he controlled two out of the thirteen elements, though the scrolls didn't say which ones. It seemed he had altered his magic making it difficult to know what he used other than fire, and no one had any record of which elements he controlled.

There were thirteen identified elements of power: earth, water, wind, fire, lightning, ice, force, time, flower, shadow, light, moon, and aura. Mages were born with their gift. It was not something that could be learned, though certain stones and crystals impacted the elements giving them altered effects. In some cases, users could twist the way their power worked and then there were others like me who had a mutation. My blue flame had been found by the magi to contain the elements of light and force. No other caster had my mutation, and it was another reason the magi considered me for most missions.

My skin itched to test Callum's abilities against mine. Could I control a mage of his level? What capabilities did he possess? Wouldn't it be better to find out now? The council wouldn't be pleased if I removed Callum's dampener, and they'd be more furious if I didn't retrieve the prodigal child from the Starlit City, but after . . .

Oscar arrived with the two horses. "Are you sure you don't want me to accompany you?"

"I'll be fine. Return to the council and let them know I'll make contact when we reach the city."

"Very well." Oscar bowed and handed me the reins. "If you ride all day, you can reach the first peak before sunset."

"Thank you."

I waited for Callum to mount his horse. He glanced at me once he was ready and nodded. With a slap of the reins, we left the port and rode out onto the highway. The enormous mountains filled the skyline. Peaks topped with snow disappeared behind the puffy white clouds that circled them. I'd memorized the maps and trails and knew exactly where we needed to go to reach the first underground caverns. It wasn't the easiest or safest route, but the quickest from the port. I was lucky that the magi prison island was so close to our destination.

Riding under the sun, I thought of my caretaker, Mr. Assan. He had the duty of raising me in the order, mainly because his power complimented mine well and he could handle my outbursts . . . if he were still alive, he wouldn't be happy about me being out here all alone with a male, a wild one at that.

Mr. Assan reminded me day after day that people like us had to focus on controlling our powers and emptying our mind in order to hold the magic at bay. Relations of any kind were forbidden.

And I had never desired anything but to protect and serve.

The dark fae gave me an odd feeling, one I didn't quite understand, but it had me questioning many things. He was smug and had an answer for everything. He was my captive, yet at every command, he challenged my authority, and questioned my abilities. Was he capable of magic with the collar on? Was he a moon element capable of charming and enchanting?

Whatever it was, I didn't like it.

We made our first checkpoint an hour or so before sunset. A farm sat at the base of the mountain. Behind the long farmhouse, the path wound into the rocky cliffs, disappearing behind the bend.

"Are we staying here tonight?" Callum asked as we slowed the horses.

"No, we'll leave the horses here and go on foot. The farmer expects us."

"Do you plan to hike the cliffs at night?"

I jumped off the horse and grabbed the reins. "Only until we can't see."

Callum's brow furrowed, but he said nothing else.

A man in blue overalls and a wide straw hat waved at us. "Hello!"

We walked the horses over to the barn where he patted mine before taking the mare's reins from my hands. "You're early."

"We're in a hurry. Do you have our stuff ready?" I asked.

He nodded. "George is ready to go. I got his saddlebags packed with what you asked for."

"Thank you." I followed the farmer around the back of the barn to where George waited, nibbling on the grass.

"We're taking that?" Callum pointed to the mountain goat, whose large curled horns seemed more menacing than the charge beside me.

"Yes. He'll carry our supplies and knows his way across the mountains."

Before Oscar and I went to the prison we came here to make sure Callum and I would have everything we needed for the road. Time was critical and why we had to keep moving.

"He can't come with us underground," Callum grumbled.

"Of course not. He'll return here on his own. George knows this land very well." I patted the goat who chewed on a long piece of grass. "Lead on, George."

The farmer waved as we left, Callum sputtering under his breath. "These mountains are not friendly to travelers, and we aren't exactly dressed for the colder climate."

I paused and turned to Callum, annoyed. "Are you going to complain the whole way? I'd like to get to a safe vantage point before nightfall."

Callum glared, a wicked smile on his lips. "Safe

you say? On what scale do you weigh this metric? Is it the same one you used when agreeing to free a dangerous dark fae who little is known about, to trek off to one of the more dangerous mountain ranges known, on a quest into an underground civilization that would love to peel the flesh from your pretty face, accompanied by a goat navigator who would serve us better as a meal? Is that the type of haven we will find up ahead?"

The fae could whine all he wanted. I didn't have time for it. None of us did.

Every day the Rift in the Never grew, allowing more of the demons into our world. Soon the Rift would be too large to control and our lands would be filled with nightmares. The spell the magi prepared would be our last hope. In order to ensure the spell's success, the council needed every light bearer ever born. "You aren't here for council or conversation. I, unlike you, am not afraid of the path ahead. If you are scared stand behind me when the danger presents itself, and I shall show you that I am the most dangerous threat in these peaks."

"You've told me where we're headed, but not the why." Callum walked beside me. "What's happened that would send you on such a suicidal mission? Even if you do possess the abilities you boast of, once we are among my people you will find that your powers are not some unique characteristic of prestige, but a mundane quality in all around you. Why would someone of such stature be risked on such a perilous quest?"

He'd been imprisoned for decades, not centuries, and would know about the dangers our world faced. "The magi have a plan to seal the Rift."

"Really. That's refreshing, and here I thought it was something more dire."

"Nothing is more dangerous than the Rift." I stormed ahead, following the goat along the rocky path leading up the mountain.

"The Rift has and will always be our curse." His voice lowered, almost as if he blamed himself for the Rift, though most of his kind held a similar shame since it was a dark fae who created the hole to the Shadow Realm.

"No. We can end it."

Callum sighed. "You are but a baby, my little sparrow. There will always be doomsayers and men who think they are more than an insignificant speck of dirt who reside on a less significant speck of dirt. The Rift has outlasted many generations. When you have lived as long as I have, you'll understand."

"And how long is that?"

His lips curled in a grin. "Three hundred and five years."

"You don't look three hundred."

"It's something I doubt you'll get to enjoy considering your proclivity toward a fool's errand."

He was testing my response, gaging me as I was him. "And yet here we are."

The goat bleated and stopped. From here the path split, our trail leading west and through a dense wood. I patted George on the head, and he continued on. Though we were still near the bottom of the mountain, the incline in this particular area became steep.

Deep green moss covered the rocks and crept up the trees, covering the landscape in a rainbow of earthy tones. The dewy air reminded me of home or what my home used to be. The cottage I grew up in wasn't massive or awe-inspiring, but it was warm and inviting surrounded by lush greenery and an abundance of sunflowers.

My foot slipped, and I threw my arms forward, expecting to crash face-first into the dirt.

"Steady, there." Callum grabbed my waist, holding me upright. His tight grip stayed until I straightened out. "It must've rained recently; the moss is slippery."

He said the last part in a whisper closer to my ear. My stomach clenched, and I pulled out of his grip. His gaze darkened, the silver in his eyes swirling into a blue-gray. I didn't understand the odd look he gave me.

"What is it?" I asked, frowning, wondering why he seemed so tense when he was finally outside after being caged so long.

"Nothing." He stepped aside creating distance

between us. "Why are they risking both our lives, and what do they possibly think I can do to assist someone who obviously needs no help in her course? What is the magi's grand plan?"

"I don't know."

"What do you mean you don't know?"

It bothered me the magi didn't explain more, but that was how they worked. "Only the inner circle knows the exact spell and components. The magi are afraid someone will interrupt, though I don't know why. We all suffer from the Rift."

"Not all." There was a coldness in Callum's voice. "There are necromancers, and I'm sure some of the twisted folk would enjoy the darkthings being loose, including their Lich King. There are many that thrive in chaos."

The darkthings served no one. Eventually our world would be gone. That didn't do anyone good, and what was happening to the younglings being born even near the Borderlands was a fate no one wished, regardless of race. Those soulless children were a warning to us all that if we didn't stop this blight that was our future.

"I suppose," Callum said, sliding his hands into his pockets. "If the magi succeeded it would be cause for one epic celebration."

"They will."

The conversation ended and we walked the rest of the day in silence with George giving us a bleat here and there. I checked the map to see how close we were to our first checkpoint.

"We should reach a walkway ahead. From there we can camp for the night." Rolling the scroll back up, I scanned the trees. "There should be a ravine somewhere."

George bleated and walked ahead. Soon, the sound of rushing water met our ears, and I ran forward through the thick foliage curious to see what lay ahead.

The land split, a ravine with a rushing river pulsed through the gorge hundreds of feet beneath us. A weathered wooden walkway swayed, connected to the other side of the wide chasm. George stood at the front, almost waiting for us.

"Here's where we cross." I turned and noticed that Callum's eyes were wide with fear.

"Callum?"

"That's a big drop."

"Yes, but the bridge will hold. Let's move." I patted George's side. "Go on."

The goat stepped onto the plank bridge. It barely moved with him on it. Once George was halfway across, I placed a foot on the wood, testing its strength.

"Wait!" Callum reached forward, grabbing my arm. "How can you be sure it's safe?" Sweat beaded his brow, and by the way he gripped my arm, I could tell he was terrified. "Maybe there's another way."

"Here." I took his hand and held it tight. "Close your eyes and I'll guide you."

His eyes almost seemed to go as round as the full moon.

I squeezed his hand in reassurance. "Don't be afraid. I won't let you fall."

"Can you fly?" His hand trembled in mine.

"No, but if you fall, I go with you, and we'll be safe. My magic can protect us and soften the fall into the water. It may hurt, but we'll live. Trust me."

"That is not helpful." He shook his head and let out a shaky breath.

"You're my charge, and I'm not going to fail my mission by allowing you to die here."

A single bead of sweat slid down his cheek and he nodded. "Go."

With slow, steady steps, I led us across the swaying bridge. I wasn't afraid of heights. If I ever fell, my shield protected me just like it had on that fateful day when it manifested for the first time, but that was a memory for another time.

I peeked at the ravine below us. Anyone who did fall would certainly be broken to pieces. Callum bumped behind me and gripped the back of my bodice, his fingers digging into the fabric until they touched skin. His fear was so palatable, I could taste it on the air.

"Be careful," I hissed as the bridge swayed.

He cowered against me, refusing to release me

from his vicious grip. "This is not worth freedom."

"It is. We're halfway there. Why don't you tell me about the Starlit City? What's your favorite thing about it?" Taking one of his hands, I tugged him forward. He immediately gripped the rope on the bridge with his other and shuffled behind me, breathing down my back.

"The cave butterflies."

"Butterflies?"

"Yes, luminescent and the most beautiful creatures. Their wing spans are longer than my hands, and they leave a trail of glittering light."

"They sound beautiful."

Callum's voice calmed, though the hand I clenched became clammy. "I've never seen their equal, and I've seen much."

"I would like to see one when we are there."

"Of course."

We reached the end of the bridge, and I pulled Callum forward. He lifted his head, looking around, a bit surprised. "We're across?"

George nibbled on a nearby fern.

"We are, and it's almost sunset. We should settle in for the night."

Callum blew out a long breath. "I hate those bridges." Leaning over his knees, he seemed a bit disheveled.

"I would think a mage of your power wouldn't be frightened by such things."

"Everyone is afraid of something."

"Not me."

He straightened and crossed his arms, not believing my statement. "You are. You just won't admit it."

"You can't be afraid if you don't feel."

Puzzled by my answer, he shook his head. "Everyone feels. Those who think otherwise are fooling themselves."

FOUR

CALLUM

Kelia tilted her head but said nothing. I shouldn't have acted like such a fool, but I had never enjoyed heights, and being locked in a prison for so long . . . I had yet to adjust to the openness around me. My body reacted on its own and I was helpless. Thankfully, my captor didn't seem bothered by heights or anything for that matter.

"There's an old shack not too far from here. We can reach it by nightfall. Can you hunt?"

"If I had a weapon, but you've left me unarmed." I held my palms out. "Feel free to remedy that."

"You haven't earned a weapon yet. I'll grab something on the way."

She patted the goat and pushed him forward. I walked behind her, watching the way her hips swayed. Even in my moment of panic, I could feel the curves of her as I foolishly hung onto her like a newborn babe. What did she look like under all that lace? A tiny waist for sure, thick thighs, and a plump backside that I could curl into . . .

I shook the dangerous image out of my mind. My emotions were all over the place. Before my imprisonment, I had been popular with females, no matter the race. Never once did I need to coerce or pay for a woman's touch. If this was any other situation, I'd find out what Kelia hid underneath that frilly garment, but I wasn't with a normal woman, and this female held my freedom in her delicate hands.

Ignoring the storm brewing in my thoughts, I focused on what Kelia had said about the possibility of war in Starlit City. My homeland had enemies both above land and below. Fighting wasn't something new, and there were plenty of powerful mages and warriors in the city. The queen had no need for me. Something wasn't right. Things had to be pretty terrible for her to call me back, especially after she exiled me. Either the magi lied about the real reason of our journey, or my homeland was in danger. Both explanations bothered me.

Kelia stopped short, causing me to bump into her.

"Quiet," she whispered, holding a hand out for me to stay still.

My chest pressed against her back. Her long blonde hair held the faint scent of oatmeal and not the kind they served in prison. No, it was a scent that reminded me of lazy mornings and warm blankets. This close, I could feel the thickness of her hips against my hands. If Kelia was bothered by my closeness, she didn't show it. I had to fist my hands to keep from touching her, the urge to be with a female, taking over any good sense.

Did Kelia not understand I had been locked away? Did she know nothing about the hunger of a male? Taking a deep breath, I contained myself. I couldn't give her the advantage of knowing I was attracted to her, no matter how long it had been since I had been with a female. Kelia was cunning and already knew of my fear of heights. If she knew I wanted her how much more could she manipulate me?

I waited, squinting at the waning sunlight pouring in between the greenery. The leaves shook and instinctively, I shifted to move Kelia behind me. I may not have had access to my magic, but I could still fight, and do it well.

Kelia grabbed my forearm and shook her head.

"What?" I mouthed.

She turned toward the forest and slowly headed in the noise's direction. I didn't see anything out of the ordinary, but I sensed something there.

Blue light shot out from Kelia's fingertips like a whip. I jumped back, giving her distance, not wanting that magical lasso of hers to touch me. She flicked her hand at the bush. Leaves shook, and a massive rabbit came tumbling out of the brush with a blue magical rope tugged around his neck.

Glancing at Kelia, I noticed she had no emotion, not a smile, no regret for needing to kill something so gentle. She rolled her hand in an arc and with a *crack* the rabbit stopped moving. The blue light disappeared and Kelia bent down to inspect her kill.

"Carry it with us. We'll cook it at the shack."

Normally, I'd complain about being ordered around, but her magical display was reminder enough that she wasn't lying when she said she was the weapon. A fact I didn't want to further test. I grabbed the rabbit, wincing at the soft fur, and feeling guilty this poor creature would be our dinner, and tossed it across my shoulders. Rabbits were native to the surface, and I found them quite enjoyable little creatures.

"How much farther?" I asked.

"We're not far."

The path we walked led to an old wooden shack. A firepit and long log sat outside off to the side near a well with a few missing bricks around the top. I dropped the rabbit on the ground as Kelia checked the front door. She turned the knob and the door swung open with a creak. I was surprised about the size of this shack. From the outside, it seemed little larger than a room in an inn, but the back of the structure extended out creating a massive room holding enough space with a kitchen and sitting area, mostly covered in a film of dust.

"At least we'll be safe from the elements tonight." I breathed in the air, relishing in how it didn't have any putrid odor. "Smells like rain."

Kelia shut the door. "Then we better cook fast."

I glanced over at the rabbit. "If you can start a fire, I'll take care of turning that beast into a delicious meal. We'll need a knife to skin it." I held out my hand.

With a glare, she leaned over. "Nice try."

Blue light left her fingertips and reached out like spindly fingers to the critter in my hands then in a disgusting, yet impressive display of power the magic seeped into the fur and *ripped* it out. The mass of speckled gray landed on the grass with a *thump.*

"Go wash it off with the water," she said.

A little shocked, and a bit intrigued, I grabbed the hind legs and brought the rabbit over to the wall. Placing the creature on the grass, I tugged on the rope to bring up the bucket then rinsed off the blood from Kelia's violent skinning procedure. I really hoped she didn't plan on using that trick on me.

She moved to the firepit which held a spit across two iron, perfect for roasting. Kneeling, she arranged the kindling into a pile then reached into that black bag of hers to pull out a piece of flint.

I grabbed the sharp spit and shoved it through the rabbit. "I see the magi at least trained you to survive in the wilderness."

Kelia narrowed her gaze at the kindling and began striking the metal to spark a fire. "Mr. Assan taught me every important skill."

"Is he your teacher?"

The kindling lit and she blew on the small fire, coaxing it into a bigger flame. "Was."

She abruptly stood, causing me to quickly step back. "I need to relieve myself. Stay put."

This time she went behind a tree instead of right in front of me.

With the fire now roaring, I sat on the log and stretched out my legs. George chewed on the nearby ferns, seeming completely at ease in the woods. It wouldn't take us long to reach the River of Night. An ominous path I didn't want to take, but clearly the quickest route, though I wasn't sure how she planned on getting us to the underground river.

Kelia sat next to me on the log, bumping her leg against mine. The movement sent a wave of need through me, and I gripped the wood with my fingers. Too many long cold nights in an empty cell had made every nerve supercharged.

Careful . . . remember who she is and what she can offer.

But why does she insist on sitting so close? This woman is not making it easy.

Needing to break the intensity, I decided having a civil conversation was in order. "Tell me, little sparrow, why you?"

I waited for her to scowl or frown, but again her stoic expression showed me nothing of her feelings. "I possess the power to control and protect you."

"Surely, there are more experienced and older candidates."

At that, she turned on the log to face me. Her blue eyes held a luminous glow. "Would you like to see what I can do?"

Holding my tongue, I kept my true thoughts to myself. "It's an honest question. If you know of me, you know I am very capable even without my powers."

Suddenly, she shoved me off the log and landed on top of me, straddling my waist and glaring. The normally blank expression shifted to something much darker. And yet, having her astride me in such a position did not invoke fear, but something else. She leaned forward, a blue flame in her palm. "So am I."

She gripped my neck with that blue hand, sending a shock through my body. Realizing my error and the real threat behind her movements, I grabbed her neck in return with both hands.

"Do you think your magic can kill me before I

snap this pretty neck?" The sentence came out a bit strangled.

She tilted her head, a curious look in her eye. I didn't squeeze, but I applied the slightest amount of pressure. My arms rested against her breasts which were much larger than I originally thought. My eyes flicked to them, and I couldn't stop the longing in my gaze.

In that moment of weakness, my grip loosened, and my arms were thrown over my head with that magical lasso of hers.

Damn it. "My mistake," I said with a smile. "You are clearly more qualified than I expected."

Her gaze narrowed and she lowered closer to my face. The proximity and position of her body sent my resolve of repressing my desire for her into the roaring fire behind us. I turned my head, attempting to escape her beauty.

"You are not scared of me, but you shy away." She pressed against me, examining me like a cat would a mouse before dinner. "You're bothered by mc. Explain."

How could I explain her legs wrapped around me instilled a vision of lust in my mind? Clearly, the magi did not have the sex talk with her. "You're heavier than you look, and I'm not bothered by you, I'm your captive, and just like that rabbit you killed, my life and what I want, means nothing to you."

The magic holding me at bay, tightened, and

I gritted my teeth. "If you are done making your point, may we return to sitting quietly waiting for our food."

"If you wish to have your freedom, remember that I'm in charge. You do what I say without question and when I say it, or I will tell the magi you didn't fulfill your end of the deal then personally return you to that cozy cell you seem to be fondly missing."

"Understood."

When she was off and had released me from that treacherous lasso, I laid on the dirt taking a few deep breaths. I would have to be careful with Kelia. At the end of this journey stood my freedom, and once it was mine we could revisit this discussion without my collar on.

We spent the rest of the evening in silence, enjoying our meal and the warm fire. When the first drops of rain fell, we gathered our supplies from George and headed into the shack. With a full belly, fuller than it had been in decades, I laid out my bedroll and relaxed. Things could be worse, and the magi did send an interesting companion. Yes, Kelia was odd, crazy, and mysterious, but she was also incredibly strong. I admired that.

She sat on her bedroll playing with a strange glowing ball. The more time I spent with her, the more fascinated, and a bit terrified, I became. Unlike most humans, she spoke her mind and didn't seem afraid of anything, not even me.

I wondered if her immense power made her act the way she did, or the magi kept her so isolated she didn't learn the proper social skills. There were many questions I had about this human, and chances are she would answer none of them.

Even though we weren't under the stars, the fresh breeze coming in through the window eased the tension in my shoulders. I had spent so many years in that prison, I missed sleeping in a place that didn't smell of piss and mildew.

Closing my eyes, I grinned at my luck. I'd play along with Kelia and this quest, until she removed my dampeners. I'd gain her trust, and once we were in the Underground, she'd have no choice but to let me loose. Monsters in the Underground were far more dangerous than the beasts on the mainland, but thanks to my little secret, nothing was more powerful than me, and once the collar was off, perhaps a renegotiation of terms would be in order, especially about her returning me to a cell.

Something pressed on my legs.

I opened my eyes. Kelia sat on my thighs, head tilted, staring at me with a curious look . . . or crazed, they were hard to tell the difference.

"Go to bed," I said and laid my head back down.

She slid on top of me as she straddled my waist. The action instantly woke me.

"What are you doing?" I asked and moved to

get up before we entered dangerous territory. I didn't have the willpower to say no to such a gorgeous creature.

With a flick of her wrist, my arms went above my head and that damned magical lasso held them in place in some bizarre attempt of control.

"Kelia, I am not some pet you leash," I growled. The human was pushing my sanity.

"I find you interesting." She leaned over, gazing at me with a weird intensity, somewhere between curiosity and hunger. "There's something different about you."

"Surely, you've seen fae before?" My voice lowered as my heart rate increased.

"Yes, but I can sense your power even with the dampener on." Leaning closer, she tousled the top of my hair. "Dark fae don't normally have reddish hair like this. It's usually a shade of white or silver."

The buttoned-up bodice covered everything which made my desire to see what she kept hidden intensify. "I'm not a specimen to be prodded and poked, little sparrow." I tried to warn her away with my tone, but once again she seemed unbothered.

She pulled back and pressed her hands on my waist. "You keep calling me that. Do you mean in age or height?"

"Both."

"I'm not little anything. That's what you call

children."

"Isn't that what you are?"

Her light eyes darkened. "No, I finished schooling years ago. Why do you refer to me as little?"

It was too late, and I was too tired to explain sarcasm to her. Closing my eyes, I put my head back down. "It's just a nickname."

She poked me in the chest.

"What?" I groaned.

"Are you feeling well?" She put a hand on my forehead. "You feel warm and you're very fidgety. We cannot afford you to be sick."

How could I explain that my fidgetiness was her? "Well, you are sitting on my stomach and I'm pretty full. It's been years since I've eaten that much."

With that, she slid off, moving to sit next to me. "Is that better?"

"Yes." I didn't need to open my eyes to know she was watching me. With a resigned sigh, I sat up and decided a nice conversation about proper prisoner etiquette was in order.

"Kelia," I said, and propped an arm over my knee, keeping a barrier between us. "If you think I'm acting odd, it's because I haven't been around a female in decades, and I haven't seen the sky in just as long. Remember where you took me from. I was beaten and mistreated by the guards. I'd go days without food and at times would have to drink from the dirty water buckets I cleaned the bathrooms with. I was humiliated and degraded. Now I'm some captive on a crusade to find a solution to a problem that cannot be solved, and here you are intrigued by my roguish demeanor because I'm unlike anyone you've ever met? How many fae have you ever spoken to? I'm an outcast even amongst my own people. What a marvelous spectacle to examine."

"Do I bother you?"

"No, no, not like that."

Had the magi kept her hidden her entire life? Even with my leg keeping a slight distance between us, the tension grew until sweat slid down the back of my neck. "You are the first human who has shown me any decency in the past few decades. I had forgotten how fresh air feels in my lungs, or how big the sky truly is, I was robbed of the setting sun's beauty, sitting alone in the darkness of my cell trying to remember the moon in a starlit sky, and right now, none of it compares to the way you are looking at me."

"You think I'm beautiful?"

I reached up and brushed her cheek with my thumb. "I do."

Her face flushed red and then I was thrown on my back.

"Kelia!"

She leaned over me with that magical lasso of hers, holding my hands above my head, pinning me to the floor.

"What are you doing?" I yanked on the restraints, glaring at my captor. "Release me."

"No." Slowly, she came closer to my face, her nose almost grazing mine. "Do you think I'm a fool? That your clever words could trick me? Do you think you can flatter me to win your freedom?"

The closeness, and my current position, made my body heat. If she touched me anymore, I would make a fool out of myself. "No, it was a compliment."

A rose hue tainted her pale cheeks, and I couldn't decide if she was angry or excited, either way I was about to lose control. I bit my lip to stop myself from doing anything embarrassing, causing it to bleed. What Kelia and the magi didn't know was that I wasn't just a dark fae, I was something else, and if this female kept prodding, she'd awaken the beast within.

"You're bleeding." She wiped my mouth with her finger, making me tremble under her touch. "What is the matter with you?"

"Please," I begged. "Let me out of these magical handcuffs and let me go to sleep. Don't we need to leave early?"

At this point I would say just about anything to get her away from me. The desire coursing through my body was unlike any I'd encountered before, more than just a needed release from being locked up for so long. I wanted her in an animalistic way. Her scent, her touch, all of it drove me mad with need.

The pressure on my hands released and she moved away.

"You can't leave this shack," she said, standing and dusting off her dress. "If you need to relieve yourself, wake me, and I'll release the barrier for you. We leave at dawn."

With a nod, I rolled onto my side, watching her walk to her bedroll and thanking the All Father that nothing else transpired here tonight.

Kelia was an insane woman, and her madness was beginning to engulf me whole.

FIVE

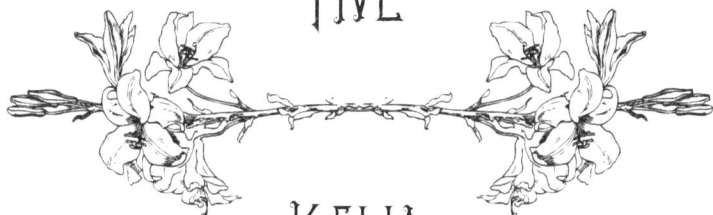

KELIA

The fae slept soundly, a faint snore escaping his full lips.

Since I'd woken, I'd replayed last night in my head trying to understand my actions. He was a prisoner, and yet I found him interesting, and not just in looks. Almost everyone I had met held back their opinions when speaking to me. Callum couldn't bridle his tongue if the All Father himself fastened one on.

Conjuring a flame in my palm, I let the magic dance across my fingertips.

Since I'd met Callum, I sensed something different about him. Whenever he touched me, my body reacted with a warm pulse, similar to how my magic felt. Were we connecting on a deeper, psychological level? We were both high level mages, that I knew for sure. Mr. Assan never let me have any relations with any boys, and my friends consisted of teachers and the servants who tended to me at the hall. My power was too dangerous, and any emotions could cause the magic to spiral out of control.

For my entire life, I trained the emotion out of me, not giving in to fear, anger, or love. It kept me safe on my missions and made it easier when the magi ordered someone's death.

Callum's candor had been a slight reprieve from my other interactions with non-humans, and part of me wondered about his magic and if the power he held inside was as great as mine. Not many things excited me, but being able to test my strength against another? That was the one thing I cared about. It wasn't about being the best or the strongest. I needed to sharpen my skills at every opportunity so that what happened to my family would never happen to me.

I shook my head, removing the thoughts from my mind and refocusing on the mission. Today would be our longest and most dangerous part of the journey, and a dress would not suffice for the climbing we would have to do. Reaching into my bag, I dug out a pair of brown tights with a thick fur lining and a form fitting black sweater that would keep me warm. I'd packed a similar outfit for the fae, though it would be a bit snugger than I originally thought. Oscar had done well by packing boots and gloves, but we wouldn't need any of that until we got closer to the ridge.

Dressed, I grabbed the clothes for Callum and moved to his bedroll. He rolled onto his back, still sleeping, arms spread out. Curious, I stood over him and then slowly settled beside him. His pointed ears poked out from beneath those locks, and I reached over to touch the very tip.

"Kelia?" He sat up startled, and the movement caused me to fall back. "What are you doing?"

I paused for a moment, unsure of what to say about my actions. Why had I done that? "It's time for us to be going."

His chest heaved up and down and he went very still. "You should be careful around a fae's ears."

"I was waking you up."

He narrowed his gaze, giving me a smirk. "Okay, then what's the plan for today? Going to risk my life on another high bridge so I can cower before you again?

"No, but we need to get moving and get to the Underground as quickly as possible."

"Ahh, yes, this prodigal child." He ran a hand through his hair. "How old is this child?"

I shrugged. "We don't know. Only that the child is a powerful light bearer."

"Will you use that lasso of yours if they don't

comply?"

His frivolous tone irritated me, and a blue flame sparked in my hand.

"You don't have to tie me up every time I say something that irritates you. I'd be bonded to you for life if we continued in this manner. You could always just try and talk to me," he pleaded with a slight grin.

"Fine. What do you want to talk about?"

"I'd like to ask you some personal questions."

"Why?"

He shook his head and ran a hand across his face in a moan. "*Please*, Kelia. You can't lasso anyone who doesn't do what you want."

"I can and I have." Feeling more annoyed, I went to my supply bag and searched for the dried honey cakes Oscar had packed. We needed to eat before leaving. There wouldn't be a lot of time to stop.

Letting out a long breath, he continued. "Your social skills need serious work."

Handing Callum a cake, I sat across from him on the ground, eating. "I've been taught by the very best teachers in Saol about proper etiquette."

He scrunched his nose, looking puzzled before he took a bite. "The Underground is a dangerous place, and once we are around my people, the way you conduct yourself is going to get us both killed. Would it be so terrible to be more compassionate and friendly?"

"I'm not here to be your friend or anything else."

His eyes sparkled. "Oh? And what would that something else be?"

"I'm not unwise to the guiles of males like you. You seduce gullible women to your bed and do as you please."

With a cough, he laughed, and punched his chest. "Darling, I wasn't the one straddling someone and tying their hands over their head last night. You seem to have your kinks in order. If I wanted to kiss you, I would have."

Why was he prodding me? He may have been three hundred years old, but I was not a child. I was a woman. A powerful one with his future in my palm.

With a flick of my wrist, my magic wrapped around his arms.

"What are you doing?" The playful expression faded from his face.

My chest heaved with fury and something else. Turning my hands, I yanked him across the ground until he was right in front of me. "I am not a game, or someone you should take lightly."

Without flinching, he leaned over, close enough that his face was an inch from mine. "Who in their right mind would want to mingle in your waters when they are infested with man eating sharks? You think I want to be intimate with a psycho who can't even take a compliment the right way? What do you know of intimacy that makes you think you could spot the difference between it and guile?"

"Intimacy?"

The question jarred me, but he didn't stop. "You speak like one with experiences, yet I don't believe you've had any. I'd bet my freedom you've never even been kissed."

Heat flared in my cheeks.

"Hmm, well, my little sparrow, let me explain about where we're going." He tilted his head, keeping his gaze firmly on my mouth. "Your special abilities are common, not only are the denizens of the outer regions monstrous and deadly, but the city and its civilians are just as dangerous. Your council must see you as expendable because you're not long for this world. The only chance we have is me. The dark fae use guile and sly words to get what they want. If you want to survive our political battlefield of deception, you need to think like one of us."

"One of you?"

Bringing his bound hands up to my face, he grasped the bottom of my chin. "We are intimate creatures full of passion and rage. You have much to learn to be one of us."

"Why? Our deal is already sealed."

He licked his lips, smirking. "My queen is fickle and intelligent. She bargained something in return for something, and that price was not me."

"Yes, it was. Our deal—"

"Is irrelevant once we breach her city. If you fail to please Queen Merelda, you'll never see the surface again. That is if she doesn't let her pets pull you limb from limb for the sheer entertainment of watching something beautiful die just like you flayed that rabbit."

Callum could be lying, but I had done my due diligence in researching Queen Merelda and her infamous Starlit City. She was not known for kindness, and humans were forbidden from entering the dark fae kingdom. "What do you get out of this?"

He dropped his hands and held up his palms. "You are in charge of my freedom. You succeed, I get to disappear. No questions asked."

"The magi expect us to both return with the child. Only after, will you be released."

He sighed and held up his still tied hands. "We both need to complete this mission, and I don't see the downside to a little schooling on the dark fae social skills."

I folded my arms. "I still don't see the point of this."

"I do," his voice softened. "You've been sheltered for too long, and my kind will eat you alive. If we're going to survive this mission, we need to trust one another. You'll need to blend in because if you can't you'll wake up with a dagger in your back."

Passion, rage, intimacy? These were all

emotions I buried, and some I had never experienced. I didn't quite understand what he meant by intimacy unless he talked about certain relations which I was not going to do.

"What is it?" He sighed. "You look like you're contemplating something."

George bleated outside, bringing me back to the present. We'd already wasted too much time. With a snap of my fingers the bonds broke off Callum's arms. He rubbed his hands together.

"Thank you." He stood. "Shall we be on our way? The road ahead is quite long."

I pushed away from him as a wild panic beat against my chest. "I'll wait outside. Get dressed."

"I follow your lead." Callum gave a wave of his hand, letting me by, and I didn't miss the smirk of his lips.

Heading out the door, I didn't close it and stood in the doorway, but I turned giving him privacy. Summoning my magic, I created a barrier around myself in case he tried anything while my back was to him. "Grab the bags when you're done."

"Done," he said softly behind me, and I jumped at the sudden closeness.

A grin etched his face and he looked down at me, being exactly one head taller. The clothes hugged his frame, highlighting the muscles. He must've spent all his time exercising in the prison, as if there was anything else to do. "Where do you want these?"

"On the goat. He'll carry what we need. If we make good time, we can make the next checkpoint by nightfall." After Callum secured our belongings to the goat, I patted George on the head, urging him forward. "Take us to the ridge."

"I don't like the sound of that," Callum grumbled behind me.

"Afraid of heights?"

"Depends on how high and if it's instant death or not. I'd be less afraid if I had my magic." He pointed at the collar around his neck.

"I'll keep you safe. I promise nothing will happen to you."

With a resigned sigh and shaking of his head, he fell in step beside me.

The path continued up through the dense foliage, closer toward the mountain top where the vegetation would thin, replaced by evergreens and the cold chill of ice and snow. In order to make it to the River of Night we had to pass through the ridge. A jagged area of the mountain that had been carved with steps to traverse around the side and head toward the other end. I had never been to this region, but from the few people I'd spoken to, everyone would rather take the long way. Besides the dangerous ledges and walkways there were mountain cats that roamed the area, fast deadly creatures that blended into the surroundings until it was too late.

If the cats were able to cause even a drop of

blood, the ridge vultures would come out in droves and start pecking away at your skin before you were even close to being dead. The magi had offered to send guards with me, but I refused. After what happened at Farrow's Gate, I needed them to regain their confidence with me. Lord Demious had come close to seriously injuring me with that shadow magic of his. The last person to inflict any wounds on me had been Master Assan.

This mission was a test, and one I would pass.

Callum kept quiet as we walked, his hands in the pockets of his pants. As we moved higher the trees thinned and spaced out, revealing the open expanse. All around us large mountain tops could be seen to our left. Stone replaced dirt the farther we walked north toward the rocky incline that would lead us around the mountain. The sun peeked, making me sweat under the fur lined clothing, but that would end soon.

George trotted along in front of us, his steps never out of place, his footing steady over the uneven ground. Gray sleet rock formed jagged outcroppings, blocking out the sky. The path we walked on narrowed through a rocky valley, the walls reaching toward the clouds. The fae beside me walked in silence, his expression pensive and at times awed. Had he ever traveled to the mountains before or was it being out under the sky for the first time in decades?

Majestic eagles flew high around the stone,

reminding me of the utter beauty of the place. I may have controlled the emotion out of me but that didn't mean I couldn't recognize beauty when I saw it.

I glanced over at my prisoner, seeing how under the bright light his silver eyes sparkled with an iridescent hue. If I was closer, I'd be able to pick out the little flecks of color, but the distance needed to be maintained. The sharp angles of his cheekbones and piercing gaze gave him this deadly, almost animalistic quality. Mr. Assan had taught me about the fae, all the many variations, and in almost all of their kind, one theme rang true.

They could not be trusted.

For as fickle as they were their love was more dangerous. It was a dark fae who created the Rift and all because his own kind had slaughtered the human he loved. In a desperate attempt to bring her soul back from the Never, he created a tear between the two realms . . . one that had been growing ever since.

Another lesson in love.

It was better not to have it.

George bleated, making a sudden stop.

Callum stepped next to me, his eyes wide with wonder.

"Have you ever been to the mountains?" I asked.

"No. I've been to the surface many times, but never here. It's . . . I don't have words to explain it."

Following his gaze, I looked over at the expanse and how from here we could see the life tree in all its wonderous beauty.

"Is that . . . ?" his voice dropped, and he stepped forward.

"It is. The life tree."

From our position we could see the massive tree that sprouted from the ground and rose high past the clouds. The center of our world hummed with energy and shapes floated around the branches, flocks of birds so big from here you could see their shadows. Ancient dryads protected the tree from harm, and anyone who had attempted to cut the precious bark had been struck down with lightning and killed instantly. The life tree was the heart of our world, and something that could truly be appreciated from this view.

"That's not all you can see." Touching his shoulder, I pointed to the northwest where the sky darkened and shadows covered everything.

"The Rift."

"Yes, and why we need to keep moving."

His brow furrowed as if seeing the darkness made it all real. With a nod, he moved aside so that I could follow George up the incline. Up and around we went, our path rocky and difficult. To our right, the edge dropped and sloped down and to our left the mountains blocked out everything else.

When we reached the top expanse near the rest area where we would stay for the night, both of us were sweating. The land flattened out, the one place in the ridge that had fresh water and a cabin. Water fell from the mountain into a serene lake with tall evergreens and the bluest water I'd ever seen.

"Please tell me that's fresh water," Callum said, practically bouncing on his heels.

"It is."

He took off running, pulling off his shirt as he reached the bank.

"Callum!"

He yelped with excitement, kicking off his boots then his pants next.

"What are you doing? It's freezing here," I chased after him, grumbling about his absurd behavior.

With a wide smile, he jumped in, splashing and howling before diving under the surface. He popped up with a shout. "Oh, that's colder than I thought!"

Averting my eyes, the fae ran back out, and shook off the water, splashing me.

"That was incredibly foolish. We're in the mountains and I don't need you dying of frostbite."

"I'm sorry," he said, grabbing his clothes. "I haven't swam in years. It was a bit too cold, but definitely worth it."

Keeping my back to him, I dug into one of the bags on George's back and pulled out a blanket. "Dry off and get dressed. I've already seen you naked more than I care for."

He laughed, a deep, rumbling noise. "Oh, darling, I doubt that."

Ignoring him, I grabbed our two canteens and walked to the edge to refill them, making sure not to look at him, though I did find it curious he didn't care that I saw him naked. I was not one to be shy when it came to my body. Everyone had the same parts, but I only changed around people when necessary and in my position, I didn't always have privacy, but even during those times, I never felt odd or uncomfortable.

This fae unsettled me.

He was no different than a human male, but I had never seen one with muscles so defined or one with a chest and shoulders that showed years of intense training. It wasn't wrong to admire someone with peak physical health which I found odd since he had been a prisoner for so long. I'd expected to find an emaciated fae, broken and weak. What happened in that prison? Did he get special treatment?

Boots crunched on the ground as my companion moved closer, hopefully fully dressed. I leaned toward the water, dipping the canteen in.

Callum squatted behind me, his body too close to mine. He hovered by my ear, his wet hair tickling my cheek. "We're being watched."

Looking up, I searched the area. There were no animals in sight and definitely not any travelers.

We'd passed no one on our way here. "Where?"

"By the trees." He took the canteen out of my hand and drank from it before continuing to speak.

"How many?" Slowly, I stood, watching the tall evergreens surrounding the lake.

"I can't tell yet. What's the plan?"

"See that cabin, farther down with the fishing pier? That's where we're staying. We'll bring George inside."

With a hand to my back, Callum moved beside me, keeping his voice low. "Walk slowly. Whatever is following us will attack if we run and if there's more than one, we'll be in trouble."

Putting the canteens back on George we ushered the goat forward and walked slow and silent. The cabin wasn't too far and if we were careful there'd be no incidents, not that I was worried. A few mountain cats wouldn't be an issue. I'd handled much worse.

My mind replayed the fight with Lord Demious and how close he'd come to overtaking me. If my guards hadn't dragged me away, I don't know what would've happened. His magic went *inside* me. The feeling unnatural and vile that even now it gave me a chill. How had he become so powerful and so quickly? Though, it didn't matter anymore. The magistrate was dead.

"We have a problem." Callum's shoulder brushed up against me and I glanced to where he looked.

Across the lake a group of mountain cats walked. Big, snowy white creatures with fangs that fell past their maw. I counted five which meant we had a pack on our trail. We were still too far from the cabin, and our goat guide would be slaughtered in the fray.

"Take George and run to the cabin. I'll watch your back."

"No." The fae stepped in front of me, his gaze darting to the animals then to me. "That's a terrible plan and one that will get us killed. Take off my collar and those beasts will be dead."

"That is not an option." Walking past him, I nudged George to keep moving.

"Don't be a fool," Callum hissed. "What do you think I'm going to do? If anything happens to you or George, I'll be living out my freedom on a mountain top and that's not the future I want."

He grabbed my arm and I ripped it out of his grip. "Do as I say. You do not give the orders."

His jaw twitched and he glared at me. "Very well, *master*. I'll be a good little prisoner and do as I'm told. Let's hope you don't get yourself killed."

With that, he shoved past me, grabbing George's saddle, and ran.

The moment he took off the cats moved, running around the lake. The cabin was on our side, but that meant Callum had to run faster and maybe he could if he didn't have a bleating goat by his side.

I ran, my focus on the creatures heading our way. I'd need to be closer for my magic to reach them, but once it did, they would all be dead. Callum didn't need a weapon.

He had me.

Sprinting, I caught up to the dark fae, moving as fast as I could. I needed to get ahead of him, quickly. Calling my magic to my hands, I let the blue flame cover my arms and build up, keeping the energy concentrated until I was close enough to attack.

The cabin was fifty feet away.

Now!

Casting out my magic, shaping the light into a spear, I reached the first cat, slamming into its chest with the polearms sharpened tip. It howled, sending the rest of the pack into a frenzy. Still running, I shot a hand out toward the two beasts flanking my left. Manipulating the elemental fields of force, I willed a hammer the size of a bull into existence. Its broad malleted face smashed into one of the beast's sides crushing its flank. The two-hundred-and-fifty-pound projectile collided with the feline next to it as both cats were flung into the icy water.

From a large snow-covered bush to my right, I caught a glimpse of commotion. From its depths a spray of misty snow mixed with claws and fangs emerged. I rolled to my left, but the dodge wasn't quick enough. Swiftly, the cat pounced onto my chest, pinning my back to the snow-covered terrain. My innate command of force enveloped my body in an energy cocoon, the cougar's claws raking its adamant shell. I grabbed its neck with my magic tendrils, squeezing it as its jaws clamped on my shield. The transparent blue barrier, between me and a suffocating death, began to crack under its crushing bite.

A dark shadow hovered over me and suddenly the cat went flying with a whimper.

"Get up!" Callum reached out and yanked me off the ground. In his other hand, a crude tree limb freshly soaked in blood. "To your right."

Swiveling on my heel, I swung my arm in a back handed strike. A large arc of energy slicing from my fingertips swept through the leaping mountain lion's gut. The heightened sense of danger had amplified my magic's fury, and the deadly pendulum cut through the cat's torso, connecting with the next beast behind it. The blade transformed into a lasso, which acted like a leash around the lion's throat. With a snap, its neck twisted wildly as the powerful whip swung its lifeless body into a massive tree.

A powerful arm wrapped around my waist, twisting me around where another beast launched at us. With a yell, I thrust my hands out to intercept the aggressive charge. A beam of blue light rammed into the cat's chest, flipping it backward as it rolled out and broke for cover.

Two more cats approached from my back. Callum was already in motion. With a wicked grin, he dashed forward then flipped over the beasts before they fully stopped. Confused, the cats turned their heads, right into a vicious cleave that shattered the wooden limb. The first cat dropped instantly, but the second was still on attack. It lashed out trying to bite the fae's neck. Callum caught the beast's paws, wrestling with it while trying to keep its fangs from his throat.

Reactively, I conjured a blue sphere in the lion's open maw, it could no longer bite down as the wedge prevented its jaws from doing so. Callum twisted and threw the animal off him, the beast shaking its head wildly as it ran off trying to rid itself of the magical muzzle.

The cat Callum had smashed with the club whimpered; its deformed face devastated by the powerful blow. It rose from the ground with bewilderment in its large eyes and limped off. The remaining members of the pride had already retreated to the edge of the thicker brush.

I fell to my knees, catching my breath.

Callum slapped a hand to my shoulder. "That was fun. I haven't felt that alive in years. Great plan."

Out of breath and a bit exhausted from all the hiking and the energy I just spent, I grabbed his arm and pulled myself back up. "Let's get inside before they come back. Is George okay?"

The goat bleated and walked toward a trough near the cabin.

"He's fine." Callum kept a hand on my waist, keeping me steady. "And what about our little sparrow? You okay?"

There was no snark in his question, and his expression softened as if he actually cared. "Yes. I just need to rest."

His lips curled into a grin. "Then let's get you inside. I know just what you need."

"I doubt that," I replied with a grumble.

He laughed, that deep thundering noise that had an odd effect on me.

Why did hearing him laugh make me want to smile?

I was beginning to question my decision to be alone with him. If I had known this dark fae would make me feel anything, I would've left him back in that prison.

SIX

CALLUM

Oh, I was going to have fun with this human. Not only was that magical display outside impressive but fighting alongside her had awakened a long lost urge. One I hadn't felt in years. Her magic was extraordinary, and without access to my own powers, I had to be obedient or appear that I was a good little prisoner. If I was going to survive and get my freedom, I had to make Kelia need me in a far more pleasurable way. The magi clearly kept the pretty human caged for too long. While I jested about calling her little, she had all the curves of a woman, one who would soon be tied to me in more ways than one.

I didn't lie when I had told her about life in the Underground. Her way of conversing would end with a dagger in her back. I'd prepare her, and once this odd journey was over, I'd disappear back on the surface and far away from anyone I ever knew.

George bleated, pulling me from my dangerous thoughts. He bumped into my leg as I shoved his fat body into the cabin. This log home was surprisingly well stocked for such a remote area. In front of the fireplace sat two old, yet comfortable looking armchairs. The material had been worn in some areas, but the cushioning was soft. A white fur rug lay next to the hearth and I wondered if it belonged to one of those cats outside.

Kelia tugged George into the kitchen area where a half wall with a door separated it from the living space. I spotted two rooms with plain beds with the linens folded on top. Between the two rooms another smaller room, and I was surprised to see the washroom held a toilet and tub.

For a place so remote someone's been taking care of it.

"Are you hungry?" Kelia called out from the kitchen.

"I am." I walked over to the counter and sat on one of the stools opposite her.

She rummaged through a cabinet pulling out ceramic plates. As she reached for one of the higher doors, her sweater lifted a bit, revealing creamy skin.

Needing to distract myself, I looked over at our

tour guide. "Is he staying in here all night?"

"Yes." She placed a rectangle shaped tin on the table then went into one of the bags to pull out a knife. "There's a wet room behind the kitchen he can stay in."

"Does that fireplace work?"

"It does. Will you start it?"

With a nod, I moved to get this place warm. Whoever kept the cabins stocked, managed to leave firewood. Shoving the planks inside, and making sure the flume was open, I took the tinderbox and started lighting the kindling. With slow breaths, I fanned the fire alive until the flames were a decent size.

"That feels nice." Kelia stood behind me holding two plates with a dark brown rectangular substance that looked worse than the three-day old oatmeal served in prison. She handed one to me then took a seat in one of the armchairs.

Outside the sky darkened, and if this had been any other situation, I'd say it was a bit romantic. Taking my plate, I sat in the opposite seat, examining the object I was supposed to eat. I picked up the slightly sticky substance and sniffed it.

"Sorry, it's not more, but I don't think fishing is wise with the cats out there. The pemmican tastes better than it looks, especially if it's cooked right," she said, and she sounded tired, and who wouldn't be after the day we had. "If we leave early, we'll make the town by sunset."

"And from there?" I took a bite, pleasantly surprised the jerky didn't taste like rotten fruit. In fact, it had a sweet-tarty flavor of a cranberry.

"To the River of Night." She leaned back against the chair, closing her eyes. "Thank you for your assistance out there."

"Of course. I couldn't let my little sparrow be bested by a bunch of furry kittens."

She opened one eye to look at me. "I would've been fine."

"No doubt," I replied with a grin. "Is there anything to drink in this place? Or are the magi as boring as one would expect?"

"Try one of the cabinets. This cabin is stocked regularly."

After checking multiple cabinets, I found a glass bottle of brown liquid underneath the sink. Screwing off the top I took a sniff. *Mmmm. Whiskey.* Bringing the alcohol to my mouth, I savored every drop as it slid down my throat.

"Did you find any?"

"I did." I brought the bottle over and held it out. "Want some?"

She took the bottle and chugged three long sips. A little bit of the whiskey slipped down the side of her mouth and kept sliding until it reached her neck. Handing the drink back to me, she glanced up and wiped her mouth with her thumb, and oh, did that set my senses on fire.

"Not bad," she said, her voice hoarse.

Standing over her, I took another swig, watching her watch me. Yeah, this would be easy. Whether she realized it or not, I sensed the attraction, could feel the tug, and I would use that to my advantage. Kelia was the key to my freedom, and I needed to unlock her secrets before we reached the Starlit City.

Going back to my seat, I kept my gaze on the human, eyeing her and how she stared back. Her big blue eyes were curious, but her expression showed nothing else. I'd need to be careful in how I played this game with her.

Curling up into the chair, she rested against the back of it, closing her eyes.

Was she really going to sleep with me right here? Even if I didn't have my magic, she saw how I handled those mountain cats. I was still a threat. Wasn't I?

Taking another drink, I thought about her abilities and what they could do. I'd never encountered anyone with magic like hers. It was both protective and offensive, almost as if that blue light was an extension of her, and maybe it was.

The alcohol warmed my belly and for the first time in years, I actually relaxed. Watching the flames, I yearned to feel my own fire. I hated having this dampener on. There was nothing worse than having as much power as I did and not be able to use any of it.

During our hike, I thought about the queen and what Kelia had told me about the dark fae's predicament. The magi were fools to trust my queen. Not only was Queen Merelda tricky and capricious, but everything she did had a purpose and it was always to protect the Underground. Calling me out of prison meant things were bad, and a desperate queen is not what I wanted to deal with.

Soft snores poured out of Kelia, the human passed out from exhaustion. I went and took the plate from her hands before it crashed on the floor. Her hands were cold and she curled more into herself, making her seem fragile when she was anything but that.

Putting the plate on the counter, I searched the bedrooms for a blanket. Taking a soft wool one, I placed it around Kelia, draping it across her body.

If I wanted to, I could kill her, and part of me argued that this might be the only opportunity to do so.

A horrible thought, but a possibility. My hands would be around her neck and before she could lasso me to death, I could break her and be free, though I wouldn't get far with this collar, and I had no idea where she had put the key. And of course, there was the fact that we were up in a remote area and I had no idea how to escape and the entire Magi Council would be after me if I killed one of their own.

She moaned and her brow furrowed as she tugged the blanket around herself, her hand brushing up against mine. Tingling warmth spread up my arm and I groaned, moving away from the sleeping human.

It didn't matter what I thought or wanted. I'd never kill someone while they slept, a coward move, no matter if that meant my freedom.

Tonight, I would let her sleep.

Tomorrow, the games would begin.

***

Kelia had us on the road before sunrise and when that beautiful orange orb crested the horizon, she coincidentally called for a quick water break. If she stopped for my benefit, I had no complaints. Resting against the slate gray rock, I gazed out over the lands below us. Slowly, the world woke with a warm glow that sent a calming through my body. Squinting at the fire like tones spreading across the grass and mountains, I smiled into that warm gaze, letting the light lift the heaviness that had been on my shoulders since the day I had been imprisoned. No matter what happened next, this moment was worth it.

The next time we stopped, it was at a fork in the path, one winding down the mountain on the other side. Kelia looked at the scroll before rolling it back up. "If we hurry, we can reach the settlement near the river by nightfall."

"Then let's hurry."

And so, we did, quiet, distant, me thinking about last night. Did I miss my chance of freedom? No, I couldn't do anything that stupid.

Kelia hiked in front of me, following George down the rocky and steep trail. A few times we were close to the edge and my heart raced in fear of her slipping. I didn't think the magi would be happy if one of their prime prospects died in a gorge. While we walked, I thought more on this prodigal child. Our queen wasn't one to make bargains with the surface races often, and never at the expense of one of our own. Darkthings didn't venture into the Underground. No one knew why, but we assumed the life tree's roots, where life crystals sprouted, which ran across the long cavern walls, kept the darkthings away. The crystals being one of the few elements in the world able to combat the shadow magic. Something must have changed in my time away, but what? What would be so dire that our queen would call for me? I couldn't stop thinking about it.

By the time the sun had set, we made it down the side of the mountain to the settlement. Lantern light flickered from the windows of the thatched huts clustered together. If we we're lucky, we'd be able to find some type of inn, but it didn't seem like a large enough establishment for that.

"What's our plan?" I asked.

"This is where we let George go back home. We

should be able to find shelter tonight and then leave for the river in the morning."

Kelia grabbed her bag and bedroll from George, I did the same.

"Thank you, George, you may return home." She patted the goat on the head before giving him a little smack on the butt. "Go."

With a bleat, our guide trotted away.

"Will he be all right?" The goat seemed a good enough beast. I didn't want the poor thing getting eaten on his way home. I'd grown rather fond of our traveling companion.

"Yes. This is his job." Kelia watched George for a few more moments before turning toward the settlement.

I wondered how often this secluded community received guests, and if they were hospitable. Not that I worried about our safety, Kelia could handle a few farmers, and I would thoroughly enjoy watching her do so.

We passed a long building with an image of a beer stein etched into the door. No matter who Kelia was, I was a dark fae. My presence would make anyone uncomfortable. "Do you think it's wise to stay here?"

"Anyone who denies the magi risk the wrath of them." With her head held high, she pushed open the door to an empty room. "We need food and drink."

"Where is everyone?" I asked putting my hand

on my belt only to realize no weapon hung there. "You really need to give me a knife."

"Shh." She moved deeper into the quiet room. Lanterns flickered on the empty bar.

A cigar lay in an ashtray on the bar, still lit.

My senses tingled and I turned to see a crossbow aimed at us. I grabbed Kelia by the waist and dodged out of the way as a bolt thudded into the table behind us. "Get down!"

I laid on top of her, using my body to shield hers.

Blue magic shot out of her fingertips. The blast threw our assailant against the wall and the crossbow slipped from his hands. Kelia and I quickly got to our feet.

"How dare you," she snarled.

The man's gaze narrowed at me. "His kind are not welcomed here."

"Whatever grievance you have with the dark fae," I said, stepping behind Kelia who held her hands out. "It is not with me."

The man grunted. "What do you want?"

"We need shelter for the night and food," Kelia said.

"That's all?"

"That's all. Will you behave?" Kelia let the blue fire dance on her fingers.

"Yes." The man grunted, and she released her hold.

"Good. I'm hungry." She dropped her bags on

the floor. "Get us something to eat."

The man grumbled and scurried behind the bar through a door.

I leaned near Kelia's ears. "That was fun to watch."

"These people don't realize the danger we're all in. It might change their attitude if they knew who they were assisting." She found a table and sat. "I'm thirsty."

"I'll see if I can assist our innkeeper to find us some ale."

The innkeeper mumbled to himself, and I heard pots banging against something. Not wanting to bother the man, I grabbed two steins and poured ale from a barrel behind the bar. The amber liquid sloshed in the mugs as I walked back.

"Here we go." I placed them down and Kelia snatched one.

She guzzled the ale, the liquid splashing her chin and sliding down the corners of her mouth. I was beginning to think my little magi had a drinking problem, that or she held her liquor very well. She certainly didn't act like a drunk.

"Steady, little sparrow."

She slammed the stein on the table and burped, loudly. "Don't call me that."

I tipped my drink at her. "Very well, *Kelia*."

The innkeeper approached our table carrying two bowls. "Some nettle soup and bread."

"Thank you," I said while Kelia ripped into

the bread like a savage. She really did not care what anyone thought, and I liked it. Who knew being raised by a bunch of old men could make a woman so likeable?

"I don't have any rooms here, but there's a barn out back that you can stay in."

Kelia eyed the innkeeper and his face flushed before he stumbled back and out of our sight.

"Odd fellow," I said before taking a sip from my drink.

"Eat so we can sleep," Kelia mumbled with food in her mouth.

I eyed my companion. Sleep. I wish I could sleep. Since I had been around this human in such close quarters rest was impossible. Her scent alone made my mouth water. Half the night was deliberating on how I could create a scenario that would give me a chance to touch those plush lips with my own, the other half was convincing myself not to just strangle her in her sleep and be done with this farce of good little slave boy. I wondered if she could sense how bloodstained my soul was. Did she know of the monster she was truly traveling with?

We ate in silence and though I normally wanted to chat with my odd companion, I thought on tonight. If we ventured into the Underground tomorrow then tonight would be my last opportunity to break free. Sure, I could lose Kelia in the tunnels, but then I would have to face the queen if she didn't have her spies already waiting to ambush us.

Killing Kelia left me with two choices: run from the magi or deal with Queen Merelda. Neither of those options sounded enjoyable. If I had learned anything useful about Kelia it was that she followed her orders. If the magi offered freedom for my assistance then I would make sure this little sparrow wouldn't get us killed before that.

Finishing the soup and ale, the tavern keep led us out to a small stable with an empty stall filled with fresh hay. He quickly bid us goodnight and scuttled off.

"What are the chances of our host slitting our throats while we sleep?" I said, stepping into the cramped stall, I closed the latch on the door behind us and dropped the bags we carried.

"My shield will protect us while we sleep." She stretched out, her arm nearly bumping into my chest. "Do you need to relieve yourself at all before I put up the barrier?"

"No."

With a nod, she sat on the hay, spreading out the bedrolls. The ten-by-ten space was more than enough room for us, but with the temperature dropping it would get colder. Lying down, facing the opening above the stall door, I threaded my hands behind my head and gazed out at the night sky.

Kelia lay on her side, the thin blanket wrapped

around herself. "Have you ever seen the surface sky at night?"

"Yes," I said, admiring the tiny pinpricks of light that created images in the sky that told stories of their own. "And it never gets less beautiful."

Turning my head toward her, my breath caught at how close she was . . . too close. Needing to keep my wits about me I asked, "Do you know how the Starlit City got its name?"

She shook her head, the moonlight touching the button tip of her nose, making her look more innocent than she had the right to be.

"Centuries ago, there was a quake that ruined many tunnels and areas of the Underground. When that happened, it also caused one of the life tree's roots to shatter and fill the caverns with crystal shards. One area had been so impacted by the shards it created a starlit ceiling with a light source the Underground has only seen in the lower oasis, miles below the surface."

Kelia's eyelids fluttered as she listened, sleep slowly taking over. She flicked her palm and a tingle washed over me, most likely her barrier spell—I wondered if it also shielded her. "That is where your people made their home?"

"Some, yes. Others, like the deep fae shunned from all the light and stayed in other areas that were free from light crystals."

She shivered and hugged herself.

"Cold?" I asked, turning to lay on my side and

face her.

"I'm fine."

Curling more into herself, I could see she wasn't. "Here, turn around."

"Why?"

"Body heat. It'll keep us warm."

She scoffed. "I have survived worse."

"No need to boast about your conquests, little sparrow." Her gaze narrowed at the nickname, and I continued. "We need our rest, and our dear host has neglected to give us better shelter."

"Fine," she said, rolling to her other side so her back faced me. "But if you try anything, our agreement is over."

"Relax. I've no interest in anything other than sleep." Wrapping an arm around her waist, I tugged her into my chest.

Her petite frame melded into me as if the All Father himself had created her to fit perfectly in my arms. Though my arm stayed directly curled around her stomach, her head snugged right under my chin. Warmth spread through my chest and the tense human relaxed in my arms, even adjusting herself to be completely flush against me.

She was delicate, yet muscular, trained to not just fight with her magic but with her fists. The tempo of my heartbeat sped up and I slowed my breathing, ignoring the desire that followed whenever Kelia moved. Keeping my breaths even, I cleared my mind, focusing on the mission, not how conflicted this human made me feel.

The sensible part of my brain screamed, kill her.

The rest of me wanted nothing more than to sleep and keep her warm.

With another few steadying breaths, I stilled my warring thoughts and decided that tonight, I would let her live.

SEVEN

KELIA

The man with the barn ushered us out early, probably eager to see me go and I was happy to be on my way. Not only did Callum hold me while we slept, but at some point during the night, we had tangled around each other, legs entwined, me resting on his chest. I had never slept next to anyone other than my sisters when I was a child and that was nothing compared to the entanglement I awoke to.

"Thirsty?" He handed me his canteen, a quirk to his lips. He hadn't mentioned last night, but I didn't miss the smirk on his face when I woke up.

"Thanks." I took the drink and greedily chugged the cool liquid. We had walked all morning to reach the mouth of the river.

"Out of curiosity," Callum mused. "How are we going to travel down the river without a boat."

"We're not." I searched my bag for my true-seeing eyeglass. Somewhere hidden around this bush was a re-enforced rowboat that would get us through the rapids before dipping into the Mouth of Omens and taking us into the Underground.

Holding the mystical tool up, I slowly turned and scanned the area. In front of a trio of maple trees, the air shimmered, revealing a black boat with two sets of oars, and glowing purple runes on the sides.

"There." Knowing where the illusion hid, I walked over and grabbed the side of the boat. The moment my hand touched the wood, the illusion shattered.

"Clever," Callum said and helped me drag the boat to the shore. "This will do. Climb in and I'll push us out."

I grabbed our stuff and tossed it into the boat then jumped in. I sat on one of the benches and tied our bags to the ropes secured at the bottom against the sides of the planks.

Callum shoved us across the pebbled ground. The sunlight made his hair a wild color and it covered part of his face. He was handsome, and I bet he knew it too. As if his ears prickled from my thoughts, he looked up and smirked as he jumped into the boat.

Grabbing the oars, he guided us out. "I can row

for now. We'll trade off when one of us gets too tired."

"Okay." I sat back on the bench, admiring the serene view around us. "Have you traveled this river before?"

"Once or twice." Callum pushed and pulled the oars in and out of the water in slow strokes. "It's not a pleasant journey."

"What do you mean?"

"We'll need to go under a waterfall without losing ourselves or the boat."

Holding a hand to shield my eyes from the sun, I surveyed the river ahead. My power would protect us from capsizing. "That won't be a problem."

He arched a brow. "If you say so."

The river wound through the woods, picking up speed. Birds flew across the water, singing, and playing with one another. Beautiful birch trees dotted the banks and the sunlight hit the water in a sprinkling of rainbows. My home had a river like this, one I had played on many times. Years after the attack, I could still hear my mother's voice calling for my sister and me to come home when we were playing in the woods, but not anymore. No matter how hard I tried, I couldn't remember what my mother sounded like.

A slow painful ache bloomed in my chest. I fisted my hands and shoved the emotion back down in the dark where it belonged.

Feelings were dangerous.

"What are you thinking about?" Callum asked, his voice lifting me out of the darkness of my thoughts.

"Nothing important."

"You seemed far away."

"How long before we reach the cave?"

"Here," he said, stopping the oars and pulling them in. "Why don't you row for a bit." He pulled his shirt over his head, showing off a muscular chest. "It's hot today."

I gripped the handles and began rowing. "It's summer."

Callum chuckled and threaded his fingers behind his head, leaning back against the boat. "Tell me something about yourself."

"Like what?"

"Anything. Favorite hobby, a funny story. We've been traveling for three days and I don't know anything about you outside of that little blue light you throw around."

"There's nothing to tell." I kept my voice even, hiding the flutters in my stomach.

Why was he smirking at me like that? Was I doing something funny?

"All right, I'll go first," he said, tilting his head toward the cloudless sky. "I have a fondness for fluffy animals."

"What?" I thought I misheard. I tried to picture Callum snuggling a white floppy eared bunny and the image seemed ridiculous.

"It's true. If I cross paths with a silky cat, I must stop to pet it."

He met my gaze and the wistful look in his eyes made me laugh. Callum smiled, hesitant at first, but then laughed with me.

"You're lying," I said. "I don't believe it."

"Is it so difficult to imagine me with a furry friend?" That sly smile crossed his face and his eyes darkened. "You should smile more."

I straightened, realizing my slip. When was the last time I had laughed? It seemed so long ago.

Callum slid forward, placing his elbows on his knees. "How about our first lesson? I did promise to teach you about our ways and you should learn before we meet the queen."

"Now? I'm rowing."

"Exactly. It'll help to pass the time." He paused. "Unless you've changed your mind?"

I'd play along for as long as I needed to, any advantage with the dark fae would be necessary. "Go ahead then."

The front of his hair fell over his right eye. He pushed the strands back, the muscle in his arm flexed. "I'm sure those wonderful magi taught you about the basics of males and females, but not about passion. There are many types of intimacy, one being a simple touch. Give me one of your arms."

"I'm rowing," I said, stating the obvious, again.

"You can pause for a moment. The current is moving us in the right direction."

Questioning where this lesson was going, I settled the oars into their holders, and held out my right arm.

He traced a finger along my skin, up and down, slowly. His touch grazed me, only applying a light pressure. "Tell me how this feels."

"Soothing."

"One touch builds upon another, each one directing the moment." Callum moved his finger along my skin then placed his free hand on the top of my knee. "Tell me how you feel now."

"Warm, eager."

With a heady gaze, Callum dragged his fingers to my hand where he gently squeezed me. "And now?"

"My heart's racing. It's . . . I don't know how to explain it." Or didn't want to. I'd always been able to speak my mind, but Callum made my head spin weirdly and the unfamiliar warmth spreading through me made me uneasy. I could handle anything, and partly because I refused to allow any emotion to control my needs.

"The gentlest of touches can incite a myriad of feelings," Callum's voice deepened as the tip of his fingers danced across mine. "It's not just about the physical interaction. True intimacy is connecting with someone on an emotional level."

He wrapped his fingers around mine, holding

my hand. The touch sent a wave of warmth through my body, and a bit of sadness. Had it been that long since someone had held my hand? I raked my mind trying to think, and the only memories belonged to my family, and I hated replaying those in my mind. The loss was too painful.

"Hey," he said softly. "What is it?"

I snatched my hand out of his. "I get your point."

"Very well. A lesson for another day. I'm taking a nap." He stretched and leaned back against the side of the boat. "Wake me when it's my turn to row."

How was it so easy for him to relax? Was it one sided? Is this how intimacy worked? If only my mother had lived long enough to teach me. My life would be very different if my family hadn't been slaughtered like cattle.

Callum couldn't understand me, no one ever did.

Sweat slid down my neck and I rowed harder.

I was a high-level magi, the youngest to be inducted. I shouldn't be playing with the dark fae, even if it would help in his world. The flutters he inflicted were not welcomed, and I could not afford to be distracted by anything.

Sunlight glistened along his sculpted body, every hard muscle in perfect shape. What was his goal? I was the only one who could give him his freedom. Was he placating me like a child? No, it wasn't quite like that.

He's playing a game, but to what end? If he does as I say, he'll have his freedom. Why do I suspect his intentions are not for my benefit?

The current got stronger tugging the boat, making my arms burn from the strain. "Callum."

He blinked his eyes open. "My turn?" With a yawn he stretched and sat up.

"No, the current's changed. We're moving too fast."

The sleepiness left his eyes. He grabbed his shirt and threw it on. "We're close. Let me take over."

I turned around to see where the river headed. The water churned, splashing against the rocks. I held on, watching the calm river turn into rapids. "Callum."

"Hold on and get ready to use your magic. I hope you're as good as you say, otherwise we're minced meat."

Shadows crept in around us as the mountains that seemed far away closed in, leaving us stuck. I calmed my mind, removing any doubt and fear, and focused on casting a shield. Raising my hands, a shimmer went through the air until it covered us and the boat. Water splashed against the shield but didn't hit us.

"Impressive, now keep that up. It's going to get bumpy."

The rowboat jerked and the river dipped, tumbling down. I held on to the side, focusing on the shield around us. Large rocks blocked our path, and Callum grunted as he rowed the boat out of harm's way.

With my shield, we'd be safe.

The clear water turned white as the rapids intensified and a great roar sounded ahead.

A waterfall.

Instead of seeing beautiful sky, a rocky wall loomed ahead. "I can't protect us if we're going to crash into that!"

"Don't worry. The waterfall drops right before and flows into the cave."

Darkness replaced sunlight as the high cliff face blocked out the sun. I closed my eyes, concentrating my magic, visualizing the barrier. The boat rocked and I fell to the side losing my grip.

"Here we go!" Callum shouted over the roar of water.

The boat tipped toward the darkness and for a moment we were weightless and then we were falling. Gripping the sides of the boat, I focused every thought on keeping our shield up.

If I failed, I feared we'd both be dead.

EIGHT

CALLUM

The boat slammed into the rocks as we hit the bottom of the falls. Kelia screamed as the force lifted her up and out of the boat.

"Kelia!" I released my hold on the oars, searching for her. The river pushed us into the cave and the remaining sunlight disappeared.

"Damn it." I dove overboard into the water.

Luminescent creatures swam through the river, highlighting the area in a warm glow, the water as frigid as the lake. In the distance, I spotted Kelia kicking wildly to the surface. I swam to her, my adrenaline pumping through every cell.

She broke the surface just as I reached her, panting.

"Are you okay?" I wrapped an arm around her

waist, keeping her head above water.

"I think so. The boat?"

"It's right there." I tugged her alongside me.

When we reached the boat, she grabbed the sides and I hauled her up. She slumped against the wood.

I knelt beside her catching my breath. "You're sure you're okay?"

Her body shook. "You were right, that was very unpleasant."

Smiling, I helped her onto the bench. "We can camp up ahead."

She hugged her legs to her chest, trembling. I took the oars and guided us forward. Her face paled and she kept shivering. If I didn't get her warm, she'd freeze. All of our gear was wet, and down here, we were surrounded by rock and the occasional cave mushroom. No wood for kindling except the boat and that wasn't an option. I had to convince her to release my dampener. My fire magic could keep us warm and dry our clothes. This was no longer about tricking her into releasing the dampener. It was survival. The River of Night had an unnatural chill and one that would only be removed by fire.

The river calmed and the glow of cavern crystals and luminescent bugs illuminated the cave. I rowed, watching Kelia, eyes closed. Between the river's deadly qualities and how much power she expended, I didn't think she would be any help in this situation.

The rowboat hit against the wooden dock. One of the few places to camp. While we were still surrounded by black rock on either side, this area had plenty of space and mushrooms for a place to settle for the night.

I tied the boat to the dock then quickly went to Kelia and lifted her out of the boat.

She shivered and her teeth chattered.

"I need to get you out of these clothes and warmed up."

She nuzzled closer to my chest as I carried her over to an area near a mossy patch of mushrooms. I placed her gently on the ground and began stripping my wet clothes off then hers. No time for decency.

Undressed, I curled her into my chest wrapping myself around her as much as I could. Shivers raked her body. I rubbed my hands along her back, hoping the friction would be enough, but we were both freezing. I was so cold not even the fact she was naked in my arms could warm me up.

"Kelia," I whispered between ragged breaths. "We both need warmth. This isn't working. Remove my collar."

"It's so cold."

"I know. You have to trust me. We won't survive otherwise."

"No," she said as she curled against my arms trying to steal as much warmth as she could.

With my face in the crook of her neck, I hugged her tighter. "Unless you have firewood in that black bag of yours, we're in trouble. Using the boat will strand us here."

"I . . . I . . . can't."

"Don't be foolish. You know I'm right. Where is the key?"

She lifted a finger to the black bag tied in the boat. "Bring me my bag."

I wished I had something to cover her with, but I didn't, not until I could dry our stuff. I ripped the bag from the boat and ran back to her.

"Here." I grabbed her trembling hand.

She fluttered her eyes open, and keeping one arm curled around her chest, she put her shaking hand into the bag. She whispered an arcane word and pulled out the key.

I turned around and lifted my hair away from the back of the collar.

"If you turn on me," she chattered. "I'll kill you."

"Yes, I'm well aware. Now release me so we both can warm up."

She pushed the key in and turned. The collar fell from my neck and in a flood, I felt the course of magic return. I paused for a moment, weighing my options.

"Callum." Kelia's shaky voice finalized any doubt.

"I'm here." I pulled her back into my chest

and released the warmth from my fire magic. I moved my hands across her body, taking the time to make sure every patch of skin warmed under my touch. When I reached her chest, I carefully avoided any sensitive areas then moved on. Soon, the shaking stopped.

"I'm going to dry our bedrolls. Just hold on."

With her eyes still shut, she curled into a ball. If I didn't move quickly, she would get cold again.

The water ridden bedrolls took longer to dry, but they did. I moved hers closer and carefully picked her up and slid her on top of it then draped the blanket around her. "There. You should feel better soon. Rest."

She didn't respond or bother to cast her infamous barrier spell to keep me caged. Though now, I had my magic. I could leave her here, but the magi would hunt me forever, and I refused to go back into their prison.

No, we were in my world now and the roles would be reversed. I was no longer her prisoner, and she didn't have the ability to control me, not with my magic restored.

I would play this out, and once I understood why the queen had summoned me, I would make my move.

NINE

KELIA

Pinpricks of light dotted the walls and the ceiling, creating a soft orange glow that illuminated the dock. My eyes took a few moments to adjust to the dimly lit area. We were in the Underground, and our boat bobbed in the now calm river. To my right, a cluster of purple and green cave mushrooms, and to my left, a sleeping Callum.

His collar on the floor.

I took it off!

The magi warned me not to remove the collar, and if I did, I'd better be prepared for a fight. Callum wasn't like the other students and teachers I'd trained with, and the dark fae were loyal to their own.

Bringing my knees to my chest, I settled my thoughts, removing the panic attempting to drown me. Callum could've let me freeze or taken the boat and left me here with no way of escape. Yet, he tended to me instead of killing me which is what any captive would do.

"You're awake." His gruff voice startled me. "How are you feeling?"

"Better, thank you." Still undressed, and feeling vulnerable, I raised the blanket to cover myself. I normally didn't care about silly things like modesty, but Callum's gaze unnerved me.

Yawning, he stretched out his arms. "Fancy some roasted mushrooms?"

I glanced at the fungi in the corner. "There's nothing to create a fire."

"Not true." A flame bloomed in his palm. "And before you throw that magical lasso at me, listen."

Naked, he stepped out of his bedroll, grabbed his pants and pulled them on. The trousers hung low on his waist accentuating his muscles.

I wasn't ready for this.

With his powers restored, I wouldn't be able to easily control him like before. If I attempted to use my flame, he'd have a way to fight back. We couldn't afford a fight.

He sat back on the ground across from me with a soft smile. "Whatever you're thinking, don't."

"Are you a telepath?"

He chuckled. "No, I'm not, but I can see the

horror on your face, and normally you walk around with a blank stare. Nothing has changed."

Callum leaned forward, getting awfully close, and a warning blared through my thoughts. I should've been more careful when we went over the rapids. I still hadn't had time to process why I had become so weak. The moment I went into the water an unnatural heaviness invaded my mind and body.

I gripped the blanket around me, meeting his gaze head on. "Our agreement still stands?"

"Of course. I'm a fae of my word." With a smirk, he handed me my clothes. "I'll start on those mushrooms."

Quickly, I pulled on the pants and sweater. My mind ran with a thousand thoughts and questions on why Callum didn't turn on me. This mission was of the utmost importance, and I could not fail. I needed to do anything necessary to survive here and bring the light bearer to the magi. Yet, something about Callum had me on edge.

With every gesture, every conversation, Callum dug under my skin, making my nerves raw and chaotic. I hadn't felt this out of control since the day my family died. Flashes of the darkthings swarming emerged in my thoughts, the loud screaming from my mother, and the blood . . . so much blood.

My hands tingled and I flipped them over to see my palms glowing blue. I fisted the magic away.

"Are you sure you're feeling well?" Callum walked over holding a pile of blackened mushroom caps. "If you need to rest, you can sleep in the boat. I'll make sure we get there safe."

"I'm fine," I said, extinguishing the flames in my palms and dropping the worry from my voice. "Is that breakfast?"

His brow furrowed, but he didn't ask any more questions. "Here, they taste much better than they look."

I took a few caps from his hand and popped the fungi into my mouth. "Smoky."

"Yes, but tasty. How about a lesson before we go? It'll help lighten the mood. This one is about kissing which is important in our culture for a kiss seals most deals. Since I doubt that you've kissed before, it would be prudent of us to make sure you're comfortable. In case the need ever arises." He licked his lips, eyeing my mouth like he was hungry for something other than food.

"Is that really a good idea?"

"If you're afraid, we don't have to. I get that it scares you." Scooting closer, he placed a hand on my knee, the warmth seeping through the blanket and into my skin. "You can't be brave all the time."

"Are you calling me a coward?" My heart raced at the insult. I had fought and bled more times than I could count. How dare he speak to me as if I was a child running around with a wooden sword.

He shrugged. "I know you can fight, but some wars are won in here."

Tapping his head, he smirked, eyeing me, waiting for me to refuse, but I wasn't a coward, and though I had never kissed anyone before, I wouldn't let that inexperience give him the upper hand in this situation. "How does a kiss work when making a bargain?"

"That's an excellent question," he said, sliding over to me, his thumb rubbing a circle on my leg. "We believe that one must exchange fluids. With males, its blood, but with a male and female, it is a kiss. One of the more deadly bargains for the fae as all fae possess some levels of magic and with a kiss they exchange a sliver of that power."

"I've heard of fae bargains, but never done with a kiss."

His hand slid across my thigh, the sensation sending my heartbeat into an erratic rhythm. "The dark fae like to be a bit more dramatic and sensual about our dealings. So, are you ready?"

It's just a kiss. This is no different than learning any other battle technique.

Still . . . his mouth will be on mine.

Glancing at his lips, I noticed how full and soft they appeared and that sent my mind spinning. This was more than what I was ready for, yet if he spoke the truth . . .

As if realizing the uncertainty, he gently took my hands. "Relax and follow my lead, and you may just enjoy yourself. We'll go slow."

Too nervous to speak, I stared into his silver gaze, waiting. He moved his head closer to mine until we were barely inches apart.

"Close your eyes," he whispered, and so I did.

Smooth lips gently pressed against mine, the sensation warm and inviting. He moved his mouth, tugging at mine to open, though I didn't understand why. When I did, his tongue touched mine and a different exhilarating feeling skittered through me. He didn't taste of anything particular, but it reminded me of fire and starlight. I liked the tenderness and brush of his lips on mine and how when our mouths moved, they seemed to know exactly how to fit back together. Unsure what to do, I tried to mimic his movements until the kiss deepened and became more demanding.

Heat traveled from my chest and out to every part of me. While the warmth of my flame gave me comfort this ignited something else. I couldn't describe exactly what, but my body reacted, inching closer to his and my heart raced as if I had been running for miles. A heady daze filled my thoughts the deeper Callum kissed me and the desire to stop disappeared. I wrapped one arm around Callum's neck, this unbearable need coursing through me. He groaned against my lips, the sound a purr in my ear.

We fell back onto my bedroll, Callum landing on top of me. He grabbed my face and began kissing me in such a desperate way, my head spun. I dragged my hands across his bare back, along his sides, anywhere I could touch. Losing myself in the way he tasted.

Callum pulled back, breathing heavily, a dangerous curve to his lips. "What do you think?"

"It's nice."

"Nice?" He arched a brow, his magenta hair falling beautifully in front of his face. "I'd hoped for a bit more than nice."

"Why did you do that? Is it always like that?" I asked, truly not understanding how two people who were not together could kiss in that manner. Is that what all dark fae did and so carelessly with each other?

Resting on his elbows, he hovered closer to my face. "Sometimes," he said, his breath washing over me. "It has been known for certain deals to go further."

"What do you mean?"

With a wicked grin, he lowered near my ear and kissed right under my earlobe, the gesture making my body arch on its own. "If the deal is made between two fae with an attraction for one another much more touching will take place, but we have no more time for that lesson today, little sparrow. We have a ways to go before the river takes us to the city. We haven't even made it to the gate."

I don't care.

The moment those three words entered my

head, I froze.

I don't care?

How could I think that?

This is what Mr. Assan had warned me about. This was why I had to keep my feelings in control. I let go of Callum horrified at my thoughts. "You're right, thank you."

This game with Callum, which had been curiosity was growing into something else. The more Callum taught me about intimacy, the more I understood why my teacher forbid it.

We gathered our things and returned to the boat. Watching Callum row us out, my heart beat wildly. What was this fluttering feeling in my chest? I had a sense of longing, but why? Why did I continue to think of his hands touching me, his mouth across mine?

At least Callum didn't bother me with questions. He seemed fine to row us down the river in silence.

Take this time to meditate. Clear your mind. Remember what Mr. Assan taught you.

Closing my eyes, I crossed my legs underneath me and rested my hands on my thighs, palms up. With deep slow breaths, I emptied my mind, let the worry slip away, and imagined myself in a quiet place. A field of wildflowers, sunlight, warm and serene. The air scented with honeysuckle.

There was nothing, but me and my magic.

I focused on the magic within, the blue flame

that protected me. The only thing in all of Saol I could trust. The magic and I were one. The rocky cavern, Callum, the mission, everything disappeared, except the blue flame.

Mr. Assan called my flame a unique gift, that no one else held such a power, that the All Father himself must have granted it to me on that fateful day.

The flame was the only true family I had now.

Feeling more like myself, I opened my eyes.

Callum stared at me, no malice, no questions, but something else in his gaze. How did he feel about all this? No matter. I knew what I needed to do.

His gaze flitted behind me, and his eyes widened. "This isn't good."

I turned to see what he meant.

The air flickered red like a magical spiderweb. Red runes covered the onyx archway where the rest of the river flowed. The sides of the river had black marks and crumbled rock. A stone bridge blocked our passage through, the same red runes flickering.

"What is this?"

"Take the oars." Callum shoved the oars at me, and I switched places with him.

He stood by the front of the boat, moving his hands and chanting. The stone bridge rumbled and broke apart, chunks of it falling into the river creating waves that rocked the boat.

"What are you doing?" I yelled.

"There's no guardians here. You can't pass through unless the queen has allowed your arrival, or you pay a hefty fee—and even then, only dark fae. Something is wrong."

The magi knew trouble brewed in the Underground, but all reports were vague. Wouldn't someone have traveled here and seen this?

"Can we get through?" I asked.

"Lucky for us, I know the passphrase, otherwise those runes would obliterate us to ash." Closing his eyes, he whispered in the fae tongue.

The runes flashed bright then dimmed.

Callum grabbed the oars and we rowed under the arch and into blackness.

"I can't see anything," I said, squinting at our surroundings.

"Here." He grabbed one of my hands and pulled me toward him. "Dark fae can see in the dark. We're safe."

"I don't like this," I grumbled.

"Stay close, if you're frightened." He positioned me between his legs.

"I'm not scared. Anyone with good sense wouldn't be comfortable in this."

While there was a bit of truth to my statement, unease coiled in my belly. Without sight, I couldn't know if there were monsters nearby. I'd never been to the Underground of Saol. The stories I had heard were nothing, but nightmarish tales told to children to keep them away from caves and any entrance to the hidden world below.

Callum leaned forward a bit until his mouth came close to my ear. "If you're unsettled being in the dark, why not use that glowing ball of yours as a light?"

I sighed, wondering how I could be so unpractical and not think of that myself. Relief washed over me when the blue flame rose out of my hand. I manipulated the magic until it was round and big enough to give us a guiding light.

The blue glow pulsed and brightened the area in the boat, but barely lit the whole cavern. Moving it around, I noticed the ceiling here was higher than before, almost vanishing into the abyss above. The river expanded into a body of water resembling a lake, though I couldn't see a shoreline.

"Where are we?" I asked.

"The Lake of Sorrows."

Sliding away from Callum, I moved to the front of the boat, holding the glowing ball out over the edge. "That's an ominous name."

Callum dipped the oars in and out of the water. "For those that can't see in the dark, this is a blackness that goes on for quite a bit. The lake is large and still with no visible signs of life, even though there are creatures way below the surface. They say that the first dark queen was betrayed by her mate here and she drowned in the lake, cursing it forever."

I squinted at the water below, wondering if it was black or if that was only because this cavern had no lights, not even the luminescent bugs often found in caves.

The lake went on for an endless amount of time. I didn't like it.

Mostly, because the way back would be impossible to find. How anyone, including those with night vision, could navigate this place was a feat in itself. I'd be happy to return to the surface and see the sun again.

Soon, purple lights glowed in the distance. "Look."

"Ahh, we're almost there. The city is a bit farther in, but this docking area has a food vendor with the most delicious smoked eel."

I scrunched my nose at the thought of eating something so slimy. "I hope he has actual fish."

Callum chuckled. "I think you'll find something you like."

His laugh stopped when we got closer to the dock. Bodies lined the stony floor and a wave of putrid death hit our noses. I covered my face with my hands.

There was no food vendor, and anything that resembled a stone home or storefront had been hit with blasts that crumbled the structures to pieces. Our boat reached the long pier, but I didn't want to get out.

I grabbed Callum's arm and casted my magic over us both, creating a barrier.

"What did you do?" he said.

"Protected us. We don't know what's out there."

Callum tied the boat and climbed onto the pier then held his hand out for me. I grabbed my black bag and took his hand. He pulled me up, holding me close.

"Stay behind me," he said. "Things are worse than I thought."

"I can protect myself," I reminded him. "This is why the magi sent me."

"I don't doubt your strength, but . . ." his voice trailed off.

"What?" I tugged on his shirt.

He placed a hand on each side of my face, his thumbs rubbing my cheeks. "Be careful," he said.

"I will."

My stomach churned with an odd flutter. Not understanding Callum's motives made me nervous, more nervous than the catastrophe we were walking into.

Our steps echoed along the cavern. When we reached the end of the dock, I covered my nose, the stench of death thick in the air. Callum held out his hands, fire sparking at his fingertips. With slow steps, we maneuvered our way through the bodies, both young and old. The nearest building to our left had a display of rotting fish which made me gag, an old dark fae lay on the ground, his body covered in festering wounds.

We continued down the road, the carnage the same.

Something horrible happened here.

A figure dropped out of the darkness to land in front of us. Someone dressed in all black leathers, including a mask that covered the top portion of the face, except the eyes, and silver hair in three thick braids.

"Callum," the figure said in a feminine voice.

"Alisha?"

The fae nodded then glared at me. "I'm ordered to take you to the queen."

Alisha pulled out a thin glowing rod and made a large circle in the air. A portal appeared in front of us, the other side shimmering in what looked like an opulent room.

Callum grabbed my hand. Again, his actions were confusing. Why did he keep touching me? Before I could pull away, he tugged me behind him and through the portal.

TEN

CALLUM

The magic from the portal made my skin tingle as we entered a waiting room. I recognized the black and silver furnishings and crystal walls.

"We're in the palace," I said, and dropped Kelia's hand.

"Yes." Alisha appeared behind me. "We've been expecting your arrival. The queen is eager for you two to meet with her."

"What happened at the lake?" I asked.

"That is not my story to tell." Alisha headed for the doorway, but looked back over her shoulder at me, her nose scrunched. "Do you wish to wash the human's scent off you before you meet your queen?"

"I would never keep my queen waiting," I said

with a smile.

Kelia stayed silent, gaze flitting between me and the dark fae who looked upon her with disgust. While the queen would not harm her, others couldn't be trusted. I'd have to keep a closer eye on Kelia. There was too much uncertainty.

Alisha led us down the hall. Normally, the halls would be filled with music and laughter, but it was eerily quiet. I glanced at a passing room as a servant with a hopeless expression closed the door.

What could have everyone so on edge?

Two guards opened the throne room doors and waves of remembrance hit me. Black and deep purple curtains hung around the low obsidian tables on each side of the room. Many nights I had lounged around those tables, drinking, eating, and doing many things that went long into the night. A harpist usually sat off to the right playing, and the royal thrones had consorts and servants always tending to the royals' needs, whatever they might be.

Queen Merelda sat on her onyx throne, seven empty thrones beside her. Her white hair hung in one long braid that draped over her shoulder, a black crown on her head. One servant held her hand, cleaning her nails while another sat in front of her, holding her foot and painting her nails. The crimson gown she wore had a deep V accentuating her curves and leaving nothing to the imagination.

"Welcome, Callum, and Kelia of the magi. Your arrival is most welcomed." Her ancient voice sounded hoarse and tired and when she gazed at me with a stern look, I knew I would have to show her fealty.

"My queen." I approached the throne and kneeled before her. She lifted her foot, her dress slipping down her thighs. I took her smooth foot and kissed the top before lifting my head and gaze.

Slithering down her leg, the one I still held, was the queen's treasured pet. I stilled as the black mamba flicked its forked tongue at me. I'd never been a fan of the queen's snake, partly because its bite would kill you in a few hours if untreated—a present from the surface fae king—and one the queen used often.

Very carefully, I lowered the queen's leg, watching her pet wrap around her shin, moving closer. When I looked up at the queen there was no warmth in those eyes, no hint of nights we once spent together. Nothing but fury. She leaned over, removing my foot from her grasp and scooping her pet into her hand. The servants tending to her stilled, their expressions hidden by the black hoods they wore. She slid forward on the throne, and I bowed, keeping my head low and away from her venomous creature.

A pointed fingernail dug into my chin, raising it. "I can *smell* her on you."

I knew who she referred to but did not dare look at Kelia.

The queen's mouth twitched, and I wondered if she would kill me right here. The queen waved someone in the shadows over, releasing me from her hold. "Sit over there where I don't have to breathe in the stench of your betrayal."

Kelia and I both sat on the cushions arranged around the low tables, hesitation in our movements. We didn't come here for whatever this was. I at least expected a twist to the queen's original agreement with the magi, but I sensed much more at play.

A hooded servant brought out a decanter of wine and filled two cups, before disappearing to the shadows. I had never seen this room empty and silent and that bothered me more than the hate rolling off the queen.

Out of respect, I nodded at Kelia who reluctantly picked up the cup and sipped.

"The carnage you saw at the lake is a result of my oldest son betraying us."

"What? Prince Eldritch?" My mouth hung open in shock.

The queen held a hand up and the snake disappeared around her neck, hiding within her long hair. "As impossible as it seems, you have been gone an exceedingly long time, and things have changed in the Underground. My children don't understand our history and how we have survived so very long."

"I don't understand," I growled. "The prince loves his people."

The queen eyed the two servants who had been tending to her and they returned from the sides and began preening at the queen, another servant, this one male and uncloaked held a crystal goblet to her lips. When she was finished drinking, he returned to a spot in the shadows hiding behind the various hanging curtains and I wondered how many assassins hid within this dimly lit room.

"And that is why he believes what he is doing is right," Queen Merelda continued. "The magi have requested our aid against the growing Rift, and if we refuse they will stop all trade with the surface. King Kane has sided with the council putting us in a precarious position. The prince believes we should cut ourselves off from the surface and let the other races deal with the problem that we have survived centuries without needing a thing from those above. He does not understand the way of the life tree. If the Rift expands, the black death will continue, and we will not be safe forever."

The queen stood. "If you are to help, you should see what we face."

"Your majesty," Kelia said, standing, and my blood froze. "I did not come here to fight your war. You agreed to lend us the prodigal child in exchange for Callum's release."

Shadows moved along the walls, darkness creeping from the sides and I knew that any minute the queen's shadowwalkers would have a dagger in Kelia's throat. Yet, if I intervened the queen would question why, regardless of my agreement with the magi.

"Hmm. Yes, that was our arrangement." The queen walked toward Kelia, her long silky dress dragging on the stone floor behind her. "But you cannot return to the surface unless you do as I command. You are in my domain, human."

Kelia's eyes glowed blue, and I rushed to her side just as the shadows materialized around us. Assassins, clothed in the darkest black armor that they absorbed any light around them, surrounded us. Even I couldn't fight off this many, not to mention the queen had enough power herself to snap both our necks at once.

"Majesty," I said, and grabbed Kelia's hand to tug her behind me.

The queen's nostrils flared at my actions, and I needed to diffuse this situation quickly. "The magi are on a timeline, clearly you understand our desire to return swiftly."

"Our desire?" the queen's voice rose and even her shadowwalkers stilled. "I did not request your release so you could trollop off with a human."

I dropped Kelia's hand, recognizing my folly. "My only desire is for our world to be safe."

The queen glared at me, and I remembered

her hot and cold attitude. One moment she's whispering desires in your ear the next she would slit your throat just because your *performance* wasn't acceptable.

"You two will follow me, and not speak another word." The queen turned to where Alisha stood. "Take us to the first sector."

Alisha bowed and created another portal. This time I had the smarts not to grab Kelia's hand.

The portal took us to a smoky ruin. Dead fae lined the streets amidst rubble. More fae with solemn expressions carted off the dead and burned them in piles. The smoke made my eyes burn. Kelia coughed beside me.

"We are being sieged," the queen said. "They attacked us here first, cutting off our northern route. A calculated move that resulted in a heavy loss. They're trying to cut off all exits out of the city."

I rubbed a hand across my face, taking it all in. "Where are the others?"

"If you mean my children, Prince Dane and Prince Lato are in the southern sector preparing for another battle which we believe will happen tomorrow, and Prince Raegar has been on the surface for the past ten years on a sojourn. The attacks have been consistent in that."

"And the princesses?" I hoped they were safe, especially Lara. I hadn't seen my young mentee since I was exiled from the Underground.

"They are in our sister city getting aid and away from my son's poisonous words. Each week that goes by, he turns more to his cause. The deep fae have already aligned with him."

Kelia knelt by a youngling with an arrow sticking out of her chest. She closed the child's eyes then stood to face us. Her expression unreadable, yet I noticed how her body went rigid. She walked toward Queen Merelda. Alisha unsheathed her twin axes and I held a hand out to stop her. Kelia was not foolish enough to provoke the queen. The magi never would've sent her, and I'd seen the human hold her own, more than once.

Then before I could react, Kelia spoke. "I will aid you if it means I can leave sooner. We don't have time for this war, your majesty. The magi have a timetable that must be adhered to."

The queen folded her arms, eyeing Kelia who did not flinch or back away. "Let's return to the palace. You two may rest for the evening. Tomorrow will be a long day."

I let out a breath and Alisha sheathed her weapons. Alisha created a portal and returned us to the palace, this time in the great hall.

The queen placed a hand on my chest then leaned in by my ear, whispering so only I could here. "Do not think I have forgotten about your treachery."

I stilled, knowing anything I said would be wrong. I'd remain silent and allow her to think she had the upper hand, but once my freedom was restored, I would never kneel to the queen again.

Alisha waved us down the hallway and pointed to two doors while the queen disappeared into the shadows that seemed to slither in the space around her. "Your rooms are ready. I suggest neither of you leave them."

Kelia stopped at the door across from mine, pausing as if she had something to say, but she didn't and went into the room.

I entered my own room, wondering if the queen would kill us both or if she truly needed our help, and why mine? My hands shook and I grabbed the decanter left on a table, pouring the drink into a cup.

Why me?

It was no secret I had a special relationship with her children. I had trained them, and Prince Eldritch was my best student, but he had always been stubborn, and I doubted that seeing me would bring him to his senses.

Sleeping would be impossible, no matter how hard I tried. First, I had to check Kelia's room and make sure none of those dreaded shadowwalkers were hiding in her shadows.

I left my room and walked across the hall. I knocked on the door.

"Who is it?" Kelia asked.

"Me."

She opened, and to my delightful surprise she wore a silky black robe. "Come in."

I followed her inside, kicking the door shut on my way. "I think they gave you the bigger room."

"I'm taking a bath. Why are you here?" With her back to me, she dropped the robe and I had to hold in a groan and remember why I had come.

"I need to check the room." I started by the bed, under it, near the dressers, searching for any scent of magic. Needing to keep things light, I glanced back while I ran my fingers along the walls, searching for any grooves. "I do remember you saying that if we were to bathe, it would be in front of each other."

She stepped into the tub and settled beneath the water. "You don't need to worry. My barrier will keep away her assassins. Remember who you travel with. Bring me wine."

I dragged a chair over to the tub, grabbing the wine and two glasses off the serving tray. "Shadow magic is powerful and her—"

"I know about her shadowwalkers and I'm prepared to deal with them just as I was prepared to deal with you."

The scent of vanilla and rose wafted off the water, making me more tense. She should not be this relaxed. "It doesn't matter what you read in your history books. You can't port out of here with any magic when things get dangerous unless you plan on stealing one of the dark fae's transporter rods and I know you're smarter than that."

White petals floated on the water's surface, mixed with other oils, the varying smells making my sensitive nose tickle. Kelia sat up, twisting to meet my gaze. Bubbles clung to her skin, covering the best parts of her. "Why do you think out of all the magi, the council sent me?"

When I didn't answer, she continued, her expression hard. "My magic is a unique mutation, unlike anything else, a mixture of light and force."

"Wait," I said, my mind reeling. "You're a light bearer?"

She shook her head. "Not exactly, but almost as powerful. The shadows cower to me, not the other way around."

Sliding back into the tub, she leaned her head against the rim of the ivory tub and sighed. "It's been weeks since I had a proper bath."

I poured her a glass of wine, unsure of what else to do, my shoulders tensed and my mind raced with this new information. "Maybe I should join you?"

"I bathe alone." She held out her hand and I gave her the glass.

If one of Kelia's elements was light and force, she would certainly have an upper hand against the shadowwalkers and possibly even the queen, though I'd seen the queen pop someone's skull like a grape. Her strength terrified me just as much as her affection.

I leaned back in the chair, breathing, and trying to make sense of this situation. "Our entire journey here you refused to let me out of your sight, and you seemed fine to let me go to my own room. What's changed?"

She sipped the wine and met my gaze. "The city is under siege, and you need me alive if you want your freedom. I don't know why the queen requested your release, but she doesn't seem very fond of you."

I tipped my glass at her. "You have a point."

Once she finished her drink, she held the glass out to me.

"Another?" I asked, taking it from her.

"Just pour." She grabbed a sponge from the tray attached to the other side of the tub.

Watching her drag that soapy sponge seemed to ease some of the tension rumbling through me. Here we were in one of the more dangerous places in Saol and she was relaxing in a bath. I placed the drinks down on the floor, eager to have a distraction, even if for only a moment. "Ready for another lesson?"

"No."

"But we haven't gotten to the good part."

"Unless you are going to wipe my scent off your skin, I'm not interested." She peeked over at me. "No more touching."

Pretending that didn't break my dark heart, I leaned back in the chair. "That's fair. The queen and I have a difficult past."

Kelia's gaze narrowed and she frowned. "She seemed . . . territorial of you. If you expect us to survive, I need to know what I'm up against."

"The queen and I were lovers."

The sponge fell out of Kelia's hands, and her mouth parted in shock.

Seizing the opportunity, I dunked my hand into the water, right where it fell. Her eyes widened as I brushed against her leg, and before she tried hogtying me again, I politely handed her the sponge. "You dropped this."

Her cheeks reddened and she snatched the washcloth out of my hand. "Don't you think that piece of information would've been critical for me to know?"

I moved my chair closer until it bumped against the tub. "No, it was a long time ago and the queen stopped our relationship long before you were even born, little sparrow."

"It better not interfere with the mission." She closed her eyes and relaxed against the rim of the tub, her long blonde hair spilling over the sides like spun gold.

"I said we were lovers not that there was love between us. She will never be anything more than the queen who exiled me."

"Why were you exiled?"

Telling Kelia my past would only involve her further. The dark fae did not welcome me, not after what I had done, regardless of my good intentions. "It's safer if you don't know. You and I are outcasts here, unwelcomed and only alive because the queen needs us for something."

Kelia nodded and that was the end of the discussion. No prodding. She simply took my explanation as is. We'd only been on the road together for a few days, and yet this human had already won my approval. Cold, calculated, yet naïve and curious, powerful, beautiful and terrifying all at once. She was an enigma, and for the first time since we met, I saw her as an ally.

The door swung open, and I shot back into my seat, putting distance between us and spilling the wine all over my pants.

A servant held a tray. Her gaze flicked to Kelia then back to me, the disdain visible even with the servant's eyes shadowed by the dark hood. "Dinner is served in your own quarters."

"Of course," I said, wondering if the servant before us had poisoned the food or held a dagger beneath the folds of her dress.

The servant dropped off Kelia's food on the center table then turned to leave.

I sighed, not wanting to leave Kelia alone for the night, but I had to, for both our sakes. Picking up the plate of roasted roots and meats, I sniffed the meal, my heightened senses would scent anything dangerous. Satisfied that the food was safe, I placed it back down.

Kelia stepped out of the tub, splashing water on my clothes, and bumping my hip as she passed. "Good night, Callum." She put on the silky covering and walked over to the table, ending our conversation for the night.

I stood, taking the hint. "Good night."

She didn't turn, or say another word, and that bothered me quite a bit.

ELEVEN

KELIA

I'd been pacing in my room, thinking on everything I learned yesterday.

I knew little about dark fae, but I was sure that Queen Merelda wouldn't let me leave unless I helped her, but this thing between her and Callum added a dangerous element I didn't know how to navigate. Why did she need *him*?

The servant had left out a black leather outfit, pants, and a tight fitted shirt. I pulled at my groin area, uncomfortable with the tight clothing. Besides the outfit, no one told me of the plan or when and where we were going.

And where was Callum?

I swung the door open, needing to speak with him. He nearly fell into the room. He righted himself, his hair pulled into a top knot and a black mask covering the top portion of his face except his eyes, making his light gaze too piercing and haunting to look at, but even with the covering, he seemed tired.

"What are you doing?" I asked, holding the door open.

"Making sure you don't have any unwanted visitors," he said, leaning against the doorway. "Battle gear suits you well."

I went to close the door behind me, but he stopped it with his hands.

"What are you doing?" I asked.

His gaze darkened and he pushed me inside the room. "We're safer together. Don't ease up in this place. You're being way too casual."

Glancing down the hall, shadows danced along the ceiling, a mass that flashed a set of silver eyes before vanishing.

"We can work on your lessons while we wait."

"Our lessons are unnecessary," I stated, ignoring the excitement building inside me as Callum stalked across the room.

"There's no touching in this one. Strictly talking." He folded his arms, waiting for a response, his gaze constantly scanning the room.

"Will it be something useful?"

He moved dangerously close. "I would not waste your time otherwise. My survival is hinged on yours."

With him hovering, I pushed against his chest, creating distance. "Then speak."

"When you understand what a dark fae desires, it's easy to manipulate that want and need to satisfy your own." He placed one hand on the wall next to my head. "In the Underground the weak do not survive, and if you can't understand how to conquer, you'll be gobbled up before you leave the palace."

"I highly doubt that."

He moved to whisper by my ear, planting his other hand on the other side of the wall by my head. "Queen Merelda needs us more than we need her. Wait until she's desperate, when she shows that emotion you always try to hide, and then you strike."

My heart raced as his breath blew against my face, speaking so low I wondered if he thought the walls could hear us. "My mission here is clear. I can handle the queen."

I went to push him away and he grabbed my arm, eyeing me dangerously, and with a wicked gleam. "Don't underestimate her. You'll kill us both."

I shoved him back but not as hard as I normally would have. "Your concern is noted . . . and . . . appreciated."

His eyes widened in shock as if me giving thanks was such an unnatural thing. I wasn't without manners.

"You've taught me enough," I said in a plain tone. "Once I retrieve the child, you will have your freedom as agreed."

Callum nodded, his tense body relaxing as he rolled out his shoulders. "Well, I'm glad I've been useful."

He spun around and headed for the door, opening it and checking the corridor before waving me ahead. Only when he exited the room, did I breathe. If Callum was worried for my safety than it meant we really were in danger.

Holding my head high, I gathered my thoughts and left the room. Callum waited in the hallway, a smirk on his face as if the worry he had shown only moments ago never existed.

I wish he would've told me why the queen exiled him. It could help us. The matters surrounding his imprisonment were vague. The crimes listed were nothing short of massive theft, and desecration of a temple, but that wasn't how he was caught or why he was sent to the magi prison. Not knowing the truth about the queen's intentions unsettled me.

Alisha met us at the end of the hall, her mouth curling in disgust at the sight of me before acknowledging Callum. She twirled her rod in an oval, the air shimmering with magic. "I'll take you to the front."

The portal took us to a part of the city that seemed to be empty except for the soldiers all dressed in black. Amidst the sea of black were flashes of silver, white and varying shades of purple decorating the warriors in front of me. Alisha led us through the crowd that parted around us. The buildings in this area were crafted from a beautiful purple crystal and onyx. Some of them had balconies draped with purple hanging flowers. The high cavern ceilings were covered in glowing yellow lights, resembling stars, lighting the entire city with starlight. They twinkled, and in some areas created outlines of different creatures and plants.

It was breathtaking.

Many of the dark fae glared at me as we passed. Not only was I the only human present, but it seemed that only fae were here, their dark skin blending into the darkness and leaving only their sharp, glowing eyes. One spit in my direction and another unsheathed his sword. I knew humans weren't welcomed in this city, but they had to know I was on their side.

Someone grabbed my arm.

"Human scum," the stranger growled.

Before I could conjure my magic, Callum yanked me to his chest, a ball of fire in his outstretched hand. "The human is under the queen's protection. Touch her and die."

"It seems fitting that a traitor would align itself with the surface folk." The soldier scowled and disappeared into the crowd.

Callum moved me between him and Alisha. "Kelia should be in the palace."

"Queen Merelda seems to think the human is powerful." Alisha eyed me. "Is she?"

"The human can speak for herself, and yes, I am."

Satisfied, Alisha nodded. "We shall see, surface dweller."

The rows of soldiers ended with two tall dark fae at the front behind a barricade of jagged black spears. Past them, a large cave opening that seemed to go on forever.

Callum put a hand on my chest to stop me from going forward. His expression switched between sadness and something else. "I don't know what waits ahead, and I don't know if you're scared or very good at hiding your feelings, but I need you to know something."

I held my breath, waiting for him to finish.

His shoulders sagged and he looked at the ground instead of me. "Whatever happens today, know that I've enjoyed our time together. You do what you need to to stay alive and return to the surface."

"I don't understand."

The corner of his lip curved into a smile. "No, I don't suppose you would."

He lifted his face and pushed my hair back behind my ear. "Then let me tell you the most important part of intimacy. It's not a touch, or a physical response, but a feeling. One that can't be explained with words."

"Callum!" Alisha shouted and waved him over.

"Coming," he replied and gently stroked the side of my face. "Stay safe, little sparrow, and I hope I see you at the end."

My emotions were spinning out of control.

What was that all about?

A rumble sounded from the cave, and a dark fae shouted commands to ready ourselves. Callum stood at the front, his hands out to his sides, twin balls of fire burning from his palms.

The ground trembled causing debris and dust to fall and vibrate on the cavern's floor. My legs shook as the waves rippled in my thighs and calves. Bursting out of the darkness an enormous insectoid monstrosity emerged. Its head was covered in spikes and massive with no visible eyes in sight. Suddenly, its worm like mouth opened by way of three skin flaps, each one uncovering a wicked pincher that unfolded outward. These gigantic jaw hooks had inner bladed surface areas, serrated, and dripping a saliva that hissed as it hit the ground.

A large glob of acidic phlegm shot forth hitting a score of infantry men, dissolving their armor and flesh in its gelatinous confinement. Whipping from out of its throat, long tendrils shot forth snagging soldiers from the front ranks, pulling them back in to its esophagus that was lined with a myriad of the creature's eyes. Red hot beady orbs of hate encased in a slimy pink flesh scanned the battlefield for its next victim.

Skittering forward on a multitude of armor-plated appendages its rough epidermis was covered in sharp barbs that glowed white hot, answering who had dug out the tremendous tunnel.

The size of the monster nearly took up the entire mouth of the cave. Arrows shot over my head and into the beast but didn't pierce the tough skin covering its body. I called on my flame and shot it at the aberration. Magical chains wrapped and tightened around the creature, anchoring it just before the barricade. I screamed at the enormous amount of energy it took to hold the insect in place.

Callum ran forward, throwing fireballs at the creature who roared and thrashed. Alisha and the fae by her side sliced at the beast's side, but it didn't show any effect on the creature. Sweat beaded my brow, but my magic held. I dropped to the ground, holding out both arms and screamed. Waves of blue magic pulsed through the air, wrapping massive chains around this nightmare centipede digging into its hide, strangling it.

Die.

It roared and waved its head wildly. Callum's fireballs went off in succession flying into the creature's mouth incinerating its soft pink flesh as well as melting its eyes in the process. This destroyed the acidic saliva sacks that spat the deadly vesicant. Alisha dove under the beast, sliding near its underbelly and ripping a gash into the tough skin with her axes.

Just a little longer.

Focusing, I tightened the chains pulling it to one side, rolling the monster over. The beast went with the motion to alleviate the strangle hold, making it easier for the fae to hack away at its underbelly which didn't have the same thick coat as its top. A swirling mass of shadows ran up my magical chains, and I could barely see the lithe forms of fae within that darkness that converged on the monster. A flash of silver glowing eyes here and there swarmed the creature as slashes appeared all over the insect making it thrash wildly.

Sweat slid down my cheeks, and I continued to feed my power into the chains, feeling the insect barreling to get free from the black death. I didn't need to see what moved within those shadows to know it was the queen's shadowwalkers.

Callum reached toward the cave's ceiling clenching his fists as he pulled downward, creating massive spear like columns from the tunnels stone surface, driving their thick sharp tips through its husk. These dense stalactites punctured its hard hide, impaling it in place.

Earth magic. The second element Callum could control.

My chains wrapped around the three pinchers

and pulled the mouth open wider than it could go, ripping its flesh apart. Peeling the three sections back into a grotesque bloom of death, ending the creature's thrashing madness, the shadows around it disappearing as quickly as they had come.

I released the magic and fell forward on my hands, panting.

Shouts and yells came from in front of me. I glanced up to see a horde of similar insects only much smaller, crash through the barricades, some impaling themselves, others climbing over their dead comrades trying to reach us. Riding upon them were dark fae . . . but these fae were different. They wore no armor, only bone and cloth, white markings covering them from head to toe.

Someone grabbed me from underneath my arms. An unknown soldier helped me to my feet. "Get out of here before you're trampled."

I didn't want to leave Callum, but I was better suited for handling things from the back ranks with the ranged attackers.

Covering myself in a shield, I started searching for a better place to fight from. An explosion sent me flying forward.

My vision blurred.

When I turned to view the disaster behind me, Callum stood on a massive boulder that appeared out of the ground, his hands outstretched and waving around him. Rocks slammed into the oncoming horde of monsters.

Knowing Callum was okay, I got to my feet and ran past the charging warriors. The entire cavern shook, and I surveyed the area to find the source. Coming from the road to the left, a group of those bone covered fae pushed a massive battering ram—were they going to the palace?

But what sent my blood cold was the young fae running. A child, clutching a stuffed animal, yelling for someone.

I thought this place was evacuated!

"Stop!" I yelled, my heart lurching into my throat, memories of me being alone while my parents were killed by darkthings.

The fae turned their attention to me, snarling and smacking the cart they rode with spiked clubs.

"Kelia!" Callum shouted behind me, sprinting. "Stay back!"

I glanced at him. "She'll die!"

The little fae screamed and that was all I needed. I ran forward, knowing my shield would protect me, knowing that my flame was the one thing that never let me down, ever. I dove for the girl and gathered her in my arms as we rolled. She cried and I surrounded her with my magic.

"I've got you." I held the child to my chest.

Callum screamed and ran past, tossing fireballs at the fae. They jumped off the burning cart, too many for Callum to take on.

If it drained all my magic until death, I would not let those monsters hurt him or the fae in my arms. I held out one hand toward the bone fae, and this time instead of one magical lasso, I released a stampede of magical rhinos that smashed into the group then I morphed them into a wave and took the bone fae off the ground and raised them into the air. They shouted and dangled helplessly, once they were high enough, I slammed the wave to the ground, grinding their bodies against stone then raising them again until they slammed into the high ceiling, impaling on the stalactites, and twisting the rest until their bones were crushed into dust.

My mouth watered and white spots blinked in my vision and I rolled onto my back, breathing heavily. Callum ran to my side.

"Are you hurt?" He touched my face then my legs, inspecting me.

"No, the child."

The fae sobbed into my arms.

"She's okay." Callum carefully took the child from me.

"Are you well enough to walk?" he asked the girl.

She nodded.

"Good, stay close, I'm going to help my friend." Callum's jaw clenched. "You don't look well."

He slipped his hands under me and lifted me into his arms. I laid my head against his chest.

Alisha ran up. "Not as durable as you thought, but you did manage to help us kill the subspine and that monster is not easy to break."

"Take us back to the palace," Callum said.

Alisha opened the portal. "Go."

Her gaze paused on the child. "Mab, what are you doing here?"

Mab sniffled. "Is Nan fighting? Is she okay?"

"She's fine, go with them. The queen is not going to be pleased." Alisha grunted.

Did we win? Was that the battle? Every muscle in my body strained. I spent too much magic. The tingle of the portal tickled my skin. I wanted to sleep, and I hoped I'd be able to.

Footsteps clamored down the hallway.

"Damn," Callum whispered. His grip on me tightened as he hugged me closer to his chest.

Turning my head, I saw the reason for his discomfort. The queen stomped down the hall, flanked by guards and very sharp swords, her face fuming and the hallway behind her filled with shadows, the temperature dropping with each of her thundering steps.

"Your majesty," Callum said and gave a bow with his head.

"Get out of my way!"

Callum stumbled to the side while the queen set her fury on the child.

"Foolish child!" the queen yelled. "You were ordered to stay inside the palace. You dare defy me!"

Surprisingly, the child did not cower, but pouted. "But Nan is missing. She wasn't here. I heard the servants talk."

The queen threw her hands in the air, completely exasperated. "How am I supposed to keep you out of trouble if you insist on finding it. Your nanny is fine and fighting like everyone else."

Callum cleared his throat.

The queen shook her head. "Callum, Kelia, meet the prodigal child, Mab."

No. I forced Callum to let me go. "She's so young."

Queen Merelda glared at me. "You came for a prodigal child. We did not hide her age."

"But." My heart raced and for the first time in many years, tears burned my vision. "The Borderlands is no place for one so young."

Mab smiled at me. "I'm not afraid. I know about the big bad monsters."

"What about child did you not understand?" the queen said.

I clenched my fists, fighting back the emotion. Queen Merelda was right. I knew we were coming for a child but seeing her . . . emotions bubbled in my chest, and I was too drained to fight them back.

Mab twirled one of her white braids, the coloring almost a soft pink. "Are you taking me to the surface?"

Regaining my composure, I stood. "Yes, but not now."

"Take Mab to her room. You two need to get cleaned up. Take them to one of the suites. This war is just getting started." The Queen shook her head and stormed off.

Callum placed a hand on my elbow, guiding me to follow the guards. "That was interesting."

I couldn't speak.

If I did, the tears would cascade like a waterfall until I drowned in them.

TWELVE

CALLUM

With my arm around Kelia's waist, I guided her back to her room. Her eyes shined, and once I thought I saw a tear fall. What had changed? Did the fight drain her? Was this how she was after using so much magic? I didn't like seeing her this way.

Opening the door to her quarters, I gently helped her inside. She moved to the bed and fell facedown, dirty clothes and all.

"At least undress before you dirty those expensive sheets," I said.

"I don't care."

Half hanging off the bed, and clearly unbothered by the amount of dirt covering her body, I did the only sensible thing a fae could do. I kneeled on the ground by her feet and took off her boots.

"What are you doing," she mumbled.

"Helping a friend." With the boots off, I unrolled her socks and tossed both objects to the side of the room. "Do you need anything?"

"Some quiet."

With a heavy sigh, I grabbed her legs and made sure she was at least fully on the bed. "I'll stay close by. Rest."

Heading to the door, I shook off the uneasy feeling leaving her gave me.

"Callum," she said, curling onto her side and meeting my gaze. "Thank you."

With a nod, I left, though everything in me wanted to stay.

"The queen requests you."

"Alisha!" I jumped back as the assassin appeared out of nowhere.

"Now."

"Of course," I said with a smile. "Anything her majesty needs. Should I wake Kelia?"

"The human is not welcomed to this meeting."

A warning blared in my mind. While I didn't believe the queen would risk angering the magi, she would also lie if anything happened to Kelia, blaming it on misfortune and the hardships of war. Normally, I would think the human more than capable of protecting herself, but in the past two days the amount of magic she had expended was taking a toll, and one that would put her at risk. "I'm not leaving Kelia unguarded."

"You do not get a say."

I folded my arms, eyeing her.

With a whistle, Alisha called the shadows to her. As the queen's right hand, the shadowwalkers would listen to her. I called the fire to my palms, knowing I would need to act fast if Alisha attacked.

"Guard this room and make sure the human stays alive until we return." Alisha smiled. "Satisfied?"

"Not really," I grumbled. "Know that if anything happens to her, I will hold you liable."

Alisha turned and I reluctantly followed her down the corridor and through a massive set of doors. The queen stood over a table, staring at a raised map with onyx pieces placed strategically. Instead of her normal gowns, she wore scaled armor that covered her in a shimmering black. When I entered, she looked up and nodded at Alisha in approval.

"My queen," I said with a bow.

"Do not think I've forgotten our last encounter. Come here and greet your queen properly since you failed to do so when you arrived."

My stomach knotted at the request. I did not want to kiss her, but if I didn't it would be a sign of disrespect. "I'd think an exile would be unworthy of such an honor."

"Are you denying me?" The queen leaned over the table.

"Never, your majesty, but from your comments in the throne room, I thought it would be prudent if I followed your lead."

The queen's eyes glowed white. "Is that what you were doing when you slaughtered my daughter's husband on their wedding night?"

"That fae was a monster. I saved her."

With a growl, the queen gripped the wooden table, crushing the edge into splinters. I stepped back, thinking I may have gone too far. "You risked an alliance I had spent years building and put my daughter at risk."

I held my hands up. "I never meant to disrespect you or put her in danger. Is she okay?"

"Lara is dead."

The sudden news caught me off guard and I had no time to react to the queen's movements. In a flash, Queen Merelda had her hand on my throat, holding me off the ground as if I weighed no more than a feather. Her snake hissed an unnatural sound, reminding me that this magical familiar was more than just a dangerous pet. It had an intelligence and would strike any who posed a threat to its master.

I gripped the queen's arms, knowing my magic might save me from the queen's wrath, but Kelia would be killed before I reached her. I needed to use reason here.

"You know how important the royal children were to me. They were my students, and I had trained them since they were babes," I croaked, grabbing the arms that held me in place. "I couldn't bear to let her go to Prince Anis knowing he would rape and beat her until his sick mind had his fill."

The queen's hold on me loosened, though the black mamba slithered across my arm, ready to strike. "Do you think my decision was easy? That I don't care about my daughters?"

"No. I know you do, but you were honor bound. I had to be the one who stopped it." I didn't want to ask the next question, but I needed to know if my actions killed Lara. "Did they kill her because of me?"

"No," the queen said, her grip lessening slightly. "She married the younger brother then died during childbirth."

"Your majesty," Alisha said, breaking the tension. "Your son will not stay in this location long. We should discuss the plan."

Releasing me, I fell to the ground, the snake falling with me. I shoved the thing off and scrambled away before it came any closer. I rubbed my neck, thankful the queen decided to let me live.

"We will continue this discussion another time." Returning to the war map, Queen Merelda picked up an onyx stone. "One of the scouts found my son held up in this eastern area which is impossible to navigate with a large force. The ruins separate us and him."

"Then we'll go with a small party," I said.

"If it were that simple, we would have, except that my son in his infinite wisdom has trapped a beast infected from a darkthing in the ruins. One that is quite large."

"Wait." I stood back from the table, glancing at Alisha then the queen. "You're not suggesting what I think you are."

This time, Alisha responded. "If Mab cannot kill one creature infected with the darkness then she will never survive the Rift. The moment Mab destroys it, you may use this portal rod to bring her back to the palace."

"This is a test . . ." I took the crystal cylinder, hesitation pounding on my thoughts. "Are you not coming?"

"Alisha and the rest of our force will attack their forward camps to give your team a chance to slip away." The queen moved two more pieces on the board, her pet slithering across the table toward her hand. "If you succeed, return the child back and then move forward. I want my son captured alive."

"And this team is who, exactly?"

"You, the human, and Mab, and if you should return with one less, you will not be blamed, your past transgressions will be forgiven, and you can once again sleep where you belong."

I ran my hands through my hair, not missing

the hidden meaning. The queen would claim Kelia fell during battle and send the child. The magi would be angered, but not cut off trade. I tried not to rip out the strands of my hair, panicking about what the queen suggested and what she would do if I didn't agree. "When do we leave?"

"You may rest for a few hours. Alisha will wake you when it's time to go." With that the queen dismissed me and my concerns.

At this rate, gaining my freedom might cost me my life.

And I still had to tell Kelia.

THIRTEEN

KELIA

With my hands wrapped around his throat, I leaned over, waiting for him to fight back.

"Kelia," Callum said in a calm voice. "If you'll just listen."

"Listen? You agreed to a mission without my consent and one that includes our reason for being here."

He flipped us over and pinned my hands to the floor, the action so quick, I didn't have enough time to react. "Just. *Listen.*"

"I could kill you and leave with the child."

His expression softened. "Do you think the queen would allow that? Do you think right now there aren't eyes on us? You wouldn't make it out of the palace, and they would return your headless body to the magi with a sincere apology that you died during your service to the queen."

With a hip thrust, I bucked him off and sent my magic to lasso his hands.

"Is that what you want to do right now?" Sitting on the ground, eyeing me, the tips of his fingers flared red.

How could he do this? How could he agree to this? I was so angry!

I'm angry . . .

Realizing my emotions were taking control, I released Callum. He was unraveling me. Sliding across the floor, he moved to sit in front of me. He reached out a hand. Almost as if he was going to grab mine, but then paused.

"We are in a precarious situation, little sparrow," he said with a sigh. His shoulders fell. "We're not leaving the Underground unless we do what the queen asks, but I swear to you now, I will die before anything harms that child."

An odd sensation bubbled in my chest. A mix of sadness and fear. Pushing the wave of emotion down where it belonged, I shook my head. "Why didn't the queen ask me herself? Instead, she sends you as her messenger boy."

He scratched the back of his neck, his gaze darting away from mine. Annoyed, I stood, and he grabbed my forearm.

"Are you okay?" he asked, genuine concern in those silver eyes.

"Of course, I am." Yanking my arm out of his grip, I turned and left the room.

Alisha leaned against the opposite wall by Callum's door. Her stark white hair had been braided and looped around her head and she wore scaly tight armor in black. She played with one of her axes, the hilt going side to side in her hand. "Are you two finished?"

"We're ready for adventure." Callum laid an arm across my shoulders, smiling and causing Alisha to curl her lip in disgust.

Having him this close sent a wave of warmth to the patch of skin his hand grazed. Whether or not he realized it, he moved his thumb lazily against my neck, giving me chills. If the queen and him were lovers, I didn't think she would approve of his closeness.

"Mab is already waiting. Follow me." Alisha turned and when she did, Callum leaned over and kissed my cheek.

"Stay sharp, little sparrow," he whispered, leaving me at a loss for words.

Not having time to think on how that kiss made me feel, I rushed forward, walking fast to catch up to Alisha who headed for the throne room.

Queen Merelda sat on her throne speaking with Mab who smiled and held a raggedy white, stuffed doll in her hands. The doll was missing an arm and the red sewn on eyes gave it a very odd expression.

"Hello, again!" Mab said and ran toward us. "I hear we're going on an adventure."

Callum cut in front of me, not giving me a chance to speak, and squatted so he was face to face with Mab. "We certainly are. Are you ready to help us kill the big evil monster?"

She nodded, smiling, and making me ill all over.

I was her age when the darkthings came. How could I expect this innocent child to fight such darkness? It didn't seem fair. Though, nothing in this war was fair, and I had to remember that.

"There's no more time," the queen said. "Go now."

Alisha opened a portal and handed me the rod. "This will take you close to the ruins. Once the darkthing is destroyed, bring Mab back and then we'll return to get to the prince."

"Wait?" I said. "How do we know this isn't a trap?"

"My son will be busy." Queen Merelda stepped off her throne. The light hit her armor, making the scales shimmer. "I've sent a messenger and requested a parlay with my son. He will not miss a chance to be seen facing me in the open, raising his claim to the throne as I am acknowledging him as an equal by parlay."

"My queen," Callum interjected. "Do you think that's wise? If you're slain, the throne will fall to him. He's the eldest."

"Which is why he will accept the invitation."

"You three worry about destroying that creature," Alisha said. "We'll have a plan for handling the prince once he returns from the meeting. Just do it quickly."

Callum reached down and grabbed Mab's free hand. "Then on we go."

He walked into the portal, giving me no choice but to follow.

Stepping through, I entered a world of complete darkness.

No light, just a sea of black.

"Kelia," Callum said from somewhere in front of me. "Use that ball of yours."

"Right." Conjuring my blue flame, I held the light up high like I did in the boat.

Another, brighter white light, haloed around mine, making the area around us brighten. Callum and Mab stood in front of me, hand in hand. Mab turned back and smiled. While our combined magic gave us enough light to see, we were surrounded by black rock with only one opening and direction to go.

"The ruins are ahead," Callum said, keeping hold of Mab. "When we get close, I'll scout ahead and see what we're up against. You stay at my side until then."

Mab nodded and gripped her doll tighter.

Uneasiness and a sense of foreboding plagued my thoughts. This was wrong. I couldn't explain why, but something was off about this entire plan.

"Callum, wait."

He stopped and turned back.

Taking the portal rod, I held it up. "We should leave. Use this to take a portal right to the Borderlands."

"We can't," he said, frowning.

Callum snatched the rod out of my hand, leaning in to whisper by my ear. "Alisha would have rigged the transporter to malfunction or explode if we use it anywhere to go other than the palace."

Mab looked at me. "Are we not going to fight the monster?"

I couldn't do this. I knew the moment we entered those ruins our lives would be at risk, and I wasn't prepared to sacrifice this child to appease a mad queen. At least in the Borderlands Mab would have the full power of the magi protecting her. I didn't like going into a battle without understanding the risks and knowing how the queen felt about me, I was a liability. "There has to be another way out."

Callum shook his head. "There isn't but remember what I said."

It didn't matter what he promised. We did not know what we were up against.

Fear was ruling my thoughts. Another emotion I had trained out of me. "You're right. Let's move on."

With slow steps we ventured deeper into the

dark where the sounds of life didn't exist, and the coldness of the terrain sent a shiver across my back. Out of all the places I had ventured during my time outside the academy, none had compared to the emptiness of these caverns. Where the Starlit City hosted thousands of twinkling lights and lush colors of deep blues and purples, nothing broke through the vapidness of the real Underground.

The narrow tunnel opened into a vast area with a ceiling too high to see. Crumbling structures of various heights filled the space, the opaque stone shimmering from our light. Once, I imagined this place held beauty, but the decrepit ruins held nothing but jagged, broken steps and corners covered in spiderwebs.

Callum held a finger to his mouth and passed Mab to me. I grabbed her hand and tugged her back a bit from where we were. I nodded, informing Callum I was ready.

He took off into the ruined city, disappearing behind a stone column.

Mab gripped my hand tightly and nuzzled against my side. My heart raced, a wild panic festering, memories of the day I lost everything bubbled to the surface.

Instead of letting my emotions control me, I focused on the eerie silence, honing my hearing for anything out of the ordinary. I'd lost sight of Callum and had yet to see signs of anything else.

I was no stranger to darkthings, and they had always been weak to my magic, though the council used me to gather fighters, not fight in the frontlines. Still, I had seen various sizes and shapes of the demons from the Never. This was no different.

We can take on one creature.

The light Mab and I conjured hung above us, lighting only this section of the cavern. My sight wasn't like theirs, and I squinted trying to make sense out of the various shades of gray haunting my vision.

A set of eyes glowed from inside one of the broken buildings. The silver reflection caused me to grab Mab and push her behind me.

"That's Callum," she whispered.

"How can you be sure?"

"All our eyes look like that in the dark . . . oh, but those aren't." She pointed past the set of glowing eyes and gripped the back of my shirt, almost hiding in the fabric.

Two balls of eerie yellow flew down from the ceiling. The closer those balls came, the farther I stepped back.

A massive, winged creature landed on the top of one of the old structures. Its talons crushed the stone under its weight. The sinewy wings curled around its body which dripped with writhing shadows. Instinctively, I shielded Mab with my body, not knowing whether we should attack or flee.

A whistle to the far right caught the beast's attention. When the creature turned its head toward the sound, a fireball blasted its face.

"Now!" Callum screamed as he jumped out of the shadows, fire streaming from his hands.

With a wave of my hands, I created a barrier around myself and Mab. "Go!"

The child ran forward, still clutching her beloved doll in one hand.

The darkthing howled, a loud, haunting noise that grated on my ears. It flapped its wings, lifting off into the air and out of the way of Callum's fire attacks.

"I can't see it," I yelled, running and keeping the shield up.

We made it to the side of one of the buildings, me keeping Mab close. Callum kept his palms facing upwards, flames dancing across his fingers. I searched the darkness above him, below, around, everywhere for those glowing eyes, but nothing.

The fire vanished, removing Callum from my sight.

Focusing on the shield, I kept Mab hidden. If this beast was out there, I didn't have the capability to see it.

The earth shook, and a pillar of stone rose out of the ground. It was difficult to see anything, but a flash of silver flew from the pillar across to one of the towers.

Callum.

A blast of heat sent me and Mab forward. She fell on her face with a cry, and I twisted my body, keeping the shield tight above us. My head knocked into a rock, dazing me for a minute, causing my shield to flicker.

Mab screamed and a stream of brilliant white light shot out of her hands and directly into the blurring face of the creature. It howled as the light burned into its flesh. It took off into the air, flapping its wings and swirling dust and rock around us.

Sliding to a knee, I strengthened the shield. Part of me wanted to use my magic against the beast, but I couldn't do that while maintaining the barrier.

"Don't stop!" I urged Mab on. "I'll keep you protected."

Surprisingly brave, the young fae kept one hand aimed at the creature, the other clutched her doll. Her plum skin glowed. A massive, clawed hand, pounded the barrier. I gritted my teeth against the strain, sweat sliding down my back. Where was Callum? With both hands, the creature slammed against the shield. I couldn't maintain the barrier and also allow Mab's power to push through at the same time.

"I can't hold this!" I yelled, hoping Callum would hear.

Fire slashed in an arc, right between the two curled horns of the beast. It howled and fell forward. Snatching Mab to my side, I dropped the shield and rolled with her. The ground slanted and we tumbled down the incline way too fast.

"Kelia!" She slipped from my grasp.

We were sliding too fast, and this side of the cavern rested in pitch black, making it difficult to see where we were falling. I glanced back just to see the fear in Callum's eyes then a deep resolve as he roared and blasted fireball after fireball into the creature who flapped wildly, trying to rise.

I shot out my lasso at Mab, missing her hand.

She cried, dropping her doll to shield her head as we rolled farther away from the fight and the light. Again, I lashed out, a jagged piece of stone slicing into my cheek. My lasso grabbed her ankle, though I still needed to stop our descent.

Heart racing, blood dripping from my head and face, I focused on my power and used the last of my reserves to shoot out my blue flame and attach it to the closest stable rock. I abruptly stopped, and as Mab slid past, I tugged on the lasso, bringing her to a halt.

And just in time.

We were by the edge of a cavern cliff and Mab hung in the air, upside down.

Trembling, I slowly raised my arm, every muscle straining to save this little fae.

"Kelia!" She screamed and light pulsed from her hands. When she gazed below, her screams morphed into desperate cries. "Pull me up!"

Her struggling strained my muscles, closing my eyes, I focused on reeling her to me. I slid and opened my eyes in shock.

The rock I had attached to cracked.

No, not now.

Shaking, I tried again, pulling Mab, drawing the lasso magic back into my body. If I could just get her close enough to grab, I could save us both. I wouldn't let go, even if that action would cost me my life.

Come on. Almost there.

Reaching out, I tugged her. She held out her hands and I lifted her higher to grab her hand instead of her leg. My heart pounded, sweat covering me in a cold blanket. Finally, I yanked her forward and wrapped an arm around her waist.

And then the rock holding us split in two, sending us both over the edge.

FOURTEEN

CALLUM

Sliding down the cavern, I slapped my hands together then out, molding the stone in the cavern to bend to my will. Though I couldn't see them, the stop of their cries let me know I'd caught them in time.

A blue light bubbled to the cliff's edge, Kelia holding Mab tightly as the stone beneath them rose. Running, I jumped onto the rock, and guided the stone pillar up the slanted ground to a safer, flatter area of the ruins.

The stone thudded to the ground in the center of the ruins, right next to the dead creature.

"Let's not do that again," I said with a huff and plopped on the ground next to the trembling females.

Mab sobbed into Kelia who looked as disheveled as her appearance. Blood and dirt caked her face, but she was alive. They both were and that's all that mattered.

"There, there," I said, patting Mab's back. "The monster is dead, and we can go back home."

"Is it really dead?" Mab sat up rubbing her face, sniffling.

"It is," I said with a smile. "You did quite a lot of damage. How did you get to be so strong?"

Wiping her eyes, she shrugged. "I don't know."

Her mannerisms reminded me so much of Lara. The queen never said who Mab's mother was and I wondered which of the royal children sired such a brave child.

A dazed far off look filled Kelia's eyes. She was either in shock or hurt. Gently, I touched her arm. "And how is our human friend doing?"

She turned to me, no snark, no anger, just a void in her pale blue eyes.

"Are you hurt, Kelia?" Mab sniffled and touched Kelia's head. "I think she's got a bad cut. Can we go now?"

"Of course," I said, pulling Mab off Kelia. "I dropped the transporter. I'll find it. You two stay here." Standing, I started heading toward the area of the ruins the two females had been in when my fae senses sent a warning at my back, lighting my nerves on fire. I whirled around, my palms already ablaze.

But it was too late.

Dark fae covered the ruins, most of them hidden by their assassin gear, blending into the shadows, and right in the center was their prince. Prince Eldritch held Mab's hand.

"It's been a long time, old friend," he said at me. "You look better than expected."

A black crown rested on his long silver hair, his expression as hard as the queen's emotions. He wore black and silver scaled armor, a sign he was ready to fight.

"Prison food isn't as bad as you think," I replied with a smile, extinguishing the flames on my hands and strolling forward. "What brings you to the area?"

"You know how I fancy a good stroll through the dark," he replied with a smirk. Fae moved in closer on my flanks, weapons and magic ready to protect their prince.

My gaze went to Kelia who now stood, expression back to the stoic magi girl I knew. "I thought you were going to lunch with your mother?"

Prince Eldritch narrowed his gaze, stepping away from Mab and closer to me, his men moving in step with them. "You see, that's my mother's problem. She isn't conservative where it matters. She thinks she can read me and anticipate my reactions. She thinks I'm predictable, but I had a wise mentor who taught me to use my opponent's pride against them. She was blinded by her perception of me. She thought the status of facing her in parlay would entice my simple mind that I want to be seen as her equal. Why would I want to seem equal to my inferior?"

"Whose being prideful now?" I had taught the prince well, trained him to be king one day, and though his actions were risky, part of me filled with pride.

"At least mine is warranted. Look where you are. *Exactly*, where I wanted you so I could offer you something much more valuable than your freedom. A place by my side serving as the general of my armies. You should never have been exiled. My mother was a fool to wed Lara and an even bigger fool to send Lara's only child to a surface war."

The realization that Mab was Lara's sent a wave of uneasiness through me. While I had trained all the royal children, Lara was my favorite and I gave up everything to keep her safe, but I couldn't reveal that I cared, not now. "And if I only wanted my freedom, what then?"

Two fae warriors grabbed Kelia by the arms, another six surrounded me. Surprisingly, my little sparrow didn't have that fancy lasso of hers out and about. She either realized we were outnumbered or had spent her magic.

"Uncle E, those are my friends." Mab frowned at the prince. "You're not being nice!"

With a nod, a guard with a full face covering picked Mab up and walked into the shadows, disappearing from sight.

"Prince Eldritch," Kelia said, keeping her expression somber as Mab screamed and cried. "I want no part in this war. I am here for the child only."

"You think I'd allow my niece to be used as a pawn in some war that will affect nothing in my kingdom? I had to bring that infected creature down here by extremely hard means. The darkthings have no interest in my kingdom. They seek to destroy your world and I see that as a gift. Look at you, bringing a child to fight for you. This was a test, and you failed. I am not my mother, and we are not allies."

"You are wrong," Kelia replied. "There is a symbiosis between the surface and this kingdom. What affects my world will eventually show up at your doorstep."

"You know nothing of the Underground," he snarled, turning his anger onto her.

"No reason to fight amongst friends." I ignored the fae flanking me and moved closer to the prince. "I know your mind and your resolve. You've become a fine warrior and it seems my lessons did sink in. You have a price. Name it."

"My mother's crown."

Folding my arms, I eyed him. "You know that she is not an easy target. Even with all the preparation you have amassed. She is far more powerful than anything either of us have ever faced. To challenge her in open war is suicidal. She has not killed you because she would rather crush your spirit and make you bow at her feet. We both know exactly who she is. Come to reason, or do you no longer need my lessons?"

"Who said *I* was going to kill her? I was thinking someone who could share her bed would be better suited at the task. What would be more poetic than revenge for my father's death being administered in the same way she left him for dead."

"Your mother chose to save you that day."

The prince snarled and his eyes glowed, his power rising to the surface. "She could've saved him, instead she saw it as an opportunity. I didn't understand when I was a child, but her lies will no longer work on me. I see clearly for the first time. If anyone could understand, I thought it would be you. You have one day to return here or you two will both die. Either way, I will get what I want."

"That's rather morbid," I grumbled.

"A bargain works both ways," Kelia said. "My life is forfeit compared to the war and your threat means nothing to me. I'll get you your crown, but only if Mab comes with me to the surface as agreed. She will not be in danger. The entire Magi Council will be protecting her."

A crackle of white energy surrounded the prince, and I took a step back. I'd grown up with him and knew his innate control of lightning was nothing to take lightly.

"Kelia," I whispered in warning.

"Prince Eldritch," she said, ignoring me completely, "the queen is well fortified and protected. Without our aid, this war will continue. If you are willing to lay siege for another decade or so, then you don't need us. But if you want that crown sooner you will agree to our terms."

Fae moved with their prince, the circle of assassins surrounding us getting closer than I preferred. Prince Eldritch eyed Kelia with such hatred it drifted off in electric waves, making my hair stand up. Brave as always, Kelia held her head high, unphased by the walking death who'd set his gaze on her.

"And who are you that I should believe?" Prince Eldritch flicked a wrist and had his men step away from her. His electric energy crackled on the air. He was getting too close to Kelia, and I didn't like that.

"I am Kelia Ironstone. Great granddaughter of Phineas Ironstone and our word is our bond."

She's an Ironstone?

That revelation piqued the prince's interest and mine. Every race in Saol had heard of Phineas Ironstone. The powerful human who gave his life to create the barrier near the Borderlands, all because he made a promise to the Orc King during a game of cards.

"Regardless of your heritage," Prince Eldritch said. "Mab is royal blood and precious to me, unlike my mother who would throw her to darkness. Your price is too high."

Kelia's face softened, an unusual expression for her, but utterly gorgeous. She reached out and took the prince's hand, his guards immediately drawing their swords. The prince's eyes widened, but he allowed her touch.

A blue tendril of magic covered his hand and his gaze narrowed, but not angrily.

"Prince?" One of the assassin's moved in, but the prince held up his other hand to stop him.

The prince's jaw twitched, and he slid his hand up Kelia's arm as his white energy began circling hers in a weird dance.

Well, this conversation certainly took a different turn.

Curiosity piqued, I watched how Kelia pulled the prince closer, too close for my liking. I wasn't normally one to get jealous, but I was feeling a bit left out of the fun.

"Your magic," the prince whispered, tilting his head at her, examining her with a hungry intent. "It's . . . invigorating and . . ." He groaned and tugged Kelia tight to his chest.

"You know," I said, sliding away from the assassin on my left to get to Kelia. "Personal space is really important during a negotiation."

"If I had wanted to kill your men or you, I would have." Kelia's magic swirled with the prince's white, until the two created a burning white flame along the arm they touched. "You can feel my magic, because it is a sister to yours, an energy that few races are blessed with."

"What will you promise me, Kelia Ironstone?"

She took his hand and put both of hers on top of them. "I will protect Mab with my life, and when the Rift has been shut, I will return her here."

"And?"

"And you will have what every powerful king needs."

His mouth quirked up. "Then we are agreed."

"I'm sorry." I folded my arms, clearly not understanding this conversation. "Did I miss something? What is Kelia agreeing to besides bringing Mab back?"

Prince Eldritch turned to me, a slight smile on his lips. "You've gotten daft being stuck in that prison all these years."

He nodded at Kelia. "You bring me my mother's crown, I'll allow Mab to leave with you as agreed and when you both return, you and I will be wed."

"What?" The word came out higher than I intended, but marriage? "You can't marry a human. You're the dark fae prince. It would go against our laws."

"Right you are, old friend, but I will be king

and new laws can be made. Not only will we have a new powerful heir to the throne, but we can use it to our advantage. With our combined magic, not even you and your tricks could match us."

The prince slid his hands up Kelia's arms. "In our culture bargains our sealed with a kiss."

"A kiss?" she replied, feigning ignorance. "Is that the only way?"

I had to hide the smile. She knew it could also be done in blood. She didn't want to kiss him and that relieved me.

"No," he said to her, lowering his voice. "But if you are uncomfortable with our—"

His words were cut off with Kelia's lips.

She kissed him?

Prince Eldritch's eyes widened in shock, but only for a moment before he gripped the back of her neck and kissed her deeply, their mouths moving in such a way that I wanted to send my magic around his throat.

Pulling back with a grin, his gaze met mine and it took all my control to keep my expression slack with uninterest. With a twirl of his finger, he called his men to his flank. "Give them the rod to return to my mother. When you have the crown, return here and we will meet again."

One of the assassin's handed Kelia the rod and fell back into the shadows.

A portal to our left opened, and the prince followed by his entourage disappeared through the glowing hole.

"I think that went rather well," I said. "Except the marriage part. What were you thinking suggesting that?"

"Isn't this why you taught me?" Kelia dusted off her clothes. "Do you have a plan?"

"Better than yours to marry him."

"It doesn't matter."

"It does." I was tired of her blatant disregard of her own desires. "What you want matters and I'm not going to let you throw away your life to him."

"We're out of options, Callum."

Why did my name sound so perfect on her lips? I didn't have a plan, but I'd figure this out. I'd always been able to find a solution, even if that answer was me spending years in a magi prison— still worth it. "There is always another way."

"I don't have time for this rivalry. None of us do. I came here for a child and instead I'm thrown into a royal war and a battle of wits between lovers."

My face heated and I moved closer to her. "I am *not* her lover."

Holding her chin high, Kelia eyed me. "She still wants you, even I can sense it, and when you have your freedom, you'll run right back into her arms."

Fire heated my palms, my rage manifesting. "And what about you, little sparrow? Will I spend my newfound freedom watching the prince shove his tongue down your throat?"

She shoved me back. "I am doing *exactly* what you wanted. Keeping us both alive."

"Kelia . . ."

"Don't." Poking me in the chest, she moved forward, but I wouldn't be pushed away from her or this conversation. Not when it was the first time I sensed that she saw me as more than a prisoner.

Grabbing her hand, I gently squeezed it. "You're right. I wanted you prepared. I wanted you safe and you played the game perfectly."

Her jaw tensed as if she was holding back all the words she wanted to yell at me. When the gaze between us became too heated, she turned away. "What do we do next?"

Running a hand over my face, I loathed the idea of returning to the queen without her granddaughter and the news of the prince. "The queen will not give up her crown. She might even risk Mab's life. Our only option is to tell her the truth and find a way to locate the prince's hideout."

"They just left through a portal."

"Yes, but I have their scent." I held the rod up to my nose, picking up the fae's trail.

"Why are you sniffing that like a dog?"

Very few knew of my secret, and I had wanted to keep it that way, but it seemed I had no choice. "I'm going to tell you something, but I need to be able to trust you."

"What is it?"

"Can I trust you?"

"Yes, now get on with it. We're wasting time."

"Relax, little sparrow." I unbuttoned my shirt and tossed it to her. "Do me a favor and don't lose these."

"What?" She caught the shirt, then the boots and pants I threw next. Her face flushed red. "What are you doing?"

"And these." I picked up the sheath with the short sword. "I really like this blade. Very well balanced."

"Why are you naked?"

"Put it all in that black bag of yours." I nodded at the satchel on her waist. "I'll need them later."

Turning her head, she shoved the contents into the magical bag.

"Once I transform, get on. I'll pick up the trail and we'll find them."

"Trans—" the words ended in silence as I shifted into a wolf.

FIFTEEN

KELIA

The naked fae in front of me shifted, plum smooth skin morphing to reddish brown hair, face elongating, fangs emerging, body stretching and growing until a massive dire wolf replaced the Callum I knew.

He was a shifter.

Some fae could shift, including the king of the surface, Kane, but they were rare. The magi knew Callum controlled two elements, but none of the council knew he was a shifter.

Callum nudged my hip with his snout. Grabbing his fur, I pulled myself onto his back. Before I could ask him a question, he sprinted off into the darkness and jumped onto one of the broken ruin walls. Holding on tight, I pressed myself against him as he leaped higher and higher, bouncing from one ruin to the next. I couldn't see anything, and my reserves were low, but I couldn't stand not seeing where we were going.

Casting a soft glow above us, the light illuminated the current ruin we stood on. The old tower had pieces of its roof missing and one of the spires had been smashed in half. Callum slowed his pace as he maneuvered across the stone. Heights didn't bother me, though if he slipped, we'd both be in trouble. Could he use his magic while in that form? I'd never heard of a shifter being able to cast while in their animal form, but after meeting Callum, anything was possible.

My stomach did an odd flip, and not from the hole Callum had just jumped over. No, I had done something that I knew was risky and dangerous, which was not unusual for me, yet for some reason my stomach churned. Shaking the nervous sensation from my thoughts, I focused on the task ahead. One step at a time.

Callum backed up, and when I realized what he was about to do, I tugged on his fur. "That is too high and far for you to jump into. We won't make it."

He howled and then ran.

We soared through the air and just made the landing. Using the momentum, he continued, the rocky tunnel barely wide enough for us to run through. The ceiling only four feet from the top of my head, forced me to flatten myself to him. The tunnel split in four directions, curving upward into the dark. Callum took the far-left passage, slithering on his belly. The cavern wall closed around us, rocks scraping my shoulder and slicing through the fabric.

I cried as a jagged piece of obsidian tore at my shirt, nicking my skin.

Callum whimpered and I gripped his fur tighter, burying myself into his neck and closing my eyes in hopes I could forget the walls closing around us.

Just like that time back then.

My heart raced; my mind swirled with dark thoughts.

An image of me manifested in my head, curled into a ball with my magic cocooned around me, holding my ears to stop the screams of my family dying and the darkthings tearing them apart. Blood and black ichor splashed the magical bubble, hiding the scene playing out on the summer grass. My father fought bravely, defending me as long as he could, my sisters and mother already gone, their shredded flesh a horror I would never forget. But no matter how much magic my father expended, more of the darkthings came, drawn to the Ironstone power.

My body shook as I held in the tears.

For hours I had stayed in that spot while the darkthings slammed the barrier that kept me safe, screeching and howling and devouring the bodies of my family until flesh disappeared and only skeleton remained. By the time the magi had found me, I had gone into such a state of shock, I didn't speak for months.

Heaviness pounded against my chest, threatening to take the air from my lungs and drown me in sorrow.

I am strength, solidity, and the quiet within the storm.

I'm Kelia Ironstone.

I am unbreakable.

Over and over, I reminded myself to remove the fear and the pain, to stop the past from haunting my future. I was no longer that scared little girl. I'd proven that I can protect myself, and those beasts would not frighten me ever again.

Callum stopped.

Opening my eyes, I noticed we were high on a cliff wall in a massive cavern. Below us and toward the far left, stood two guards in front of a cave opening with glowing purple runes carved into the surrounding rock.

I slid off the wolf, my heart pounding loud in my ears. Fisting my hands, I focused on breathing in and out slowly.

"That's them," Callum whispered, suddenly back in his natural form. "Give me my clothes."

Keeping my gaze away from his body, I dug into the magical pocket and pulled out his items and handed them all over. Turning my back, I hugged myself, forcing the chill to leave my body.

The memory of that day had haunted me many times, but I'd learned to combat the fear and despair. Today, it was harder. Harder than ever before. Close spaces were the one trigger that sent my head and heart into a tailspin. Normally, I could force my emotions into submission, but not today. Everything in me felt raw and unhinged.

Warm hands grasped my arms, the sensation setting my racing heart at ease.

"You're trembling." Callum moved his hands up and down my arms, then my sides, warmth pulsating from his palms. "Are you okay?"

I wasn't.

But I couldn't let him know that. Admitting that kissing the prince was a mistake would show weakness. Talking about how the memories of my past haunted my dreams wouldn't change my future. This mission had twisted and turned me in so many directions, I could no longer hide the pain throbbing in my chest.

"Kelia." In a soft tone that threatened to tear my walls down, he turned me around in his arms. "Talk to me."

No, speaking anything right now would ruin me.

The smirk he normally wore vanished, replaced with a concerned brow and eyes that wanted answers I couldn't give. He brushed his thumb across my cheek, sending a tremor through my body. Soft hands touched my face, erasing my fear and replacing it with something else. This gentle caress broke me more than any nightmare could.

I saw no alternative motive in his eyes just a concern that reminded me of the handful of people in my life that truly cared. Before we returned to the queen, I *needed* to feel Callum and not because of a lesson.

Leaning forward, I pressed my lips to his, his eyes going wide with shock, but then those haunting beauties closed, and he pulled me closer, kissing me back and removing any doubt that the emotion between us wasn't real.

One tear fell then another.

He moved to kiss each tear away, no matter how many fell. "I won't let him take you. I swore to you we're in this together and I meant it."

His promises and featherlight strokes against my skin, opened my heart in a way that physically hurt. I didn't want to care about this fae or the way he made me feel, yet each time his lips brushed away the wetness on my cheek, I cried harder.

No one had cared for me since my parents. My mentor worked me, trained me, but never showed love and affection. It had been so long since someone held me. I had forgotten how a simple hug could bring peace to my ragged thoughts. I had spent so many years honing the emotions out of me I'd forgotten how soothing the comfort of another could be.

Callum slid his hands around me, warming my core and removing the chill of my haunted past. Each press of his soft lips reminded me that I was something more than the magi's chosen. For once, I wanted to forget about duty and let myself *feel*.

I allowed myself this moment.

The dam broke and I rode the wave out.

Keeping my cries silent, as to not alert the guards in the caverns, I dug my face into Callum's chest, letting him rub my back as I cried the past into his shirt. We sat huddled in the darkness pressed against the rock for a while. He didn't say anymore, and cradled me against his chest, holding me as if the cavern was falling apart and he was determined to shield me from it.

My life had always been dedicated to the magi and the greater quest to end the Rift. Not once since my training started had I taken a moment just for me. Callum was the sanctuary I didn't know I needed, and he would never understand how truly grateful I was to meet him. Never did I think the dark fae from the prison would be the one to set my heart free.

When my tears subsided, he slid his arms around my waist and rested his chin on my shoulder. "Whenever you're ready to go, we'll return to the queen. I'll handle everything. Now that I know where the prince is hiding, we can coordinate a plan. This will all be over soon."

"I'm ready." Wiping my face, I took a steadying breath and gazed upon Callum.

He grinned, and his eyes glowed with warmth. He leaned forward and touched his forehead to mine, cradling my face with his hands. "I'll get us through this. I promise."

Pressing his mouth to mine, he kissed me, and I let him. No matter how much I wanted this to never end, I knew the truth.

This would be the last kiss Callum and I would ever share.

SIXTEEN

CALLUM

Something extraordinary just took place and my heart raced with emotion. My little sparrow had opened her heart to me, a feat I didn't think possible. Though, I would much rather whisk her away and forget this whole Rift plan, I knew that was not an option.

The cold numbness from the wake of her leaving my arms didn't sit well with me. I wanted to hold her, assure her we would succeed, no matter the odds. I'd shared my deepest secret with her and in return she showed me hers.

She sniffled as she took the rod out of her satchel. I grabbed her hand, wanting to touch a part of her and stay connected. It seemed unnatural to separate after she had unwound in front of me. Our first days together, I thought the attraction was normal after being away from the world for so long and Kelia being a gorgeous female, but the longer I spent around this complicated human, the more I understood how dangerous my feelings were.

"Are you ready?" I asked, squeezing her hand.

She paused, taking a deep breath then nodded.

A portal opened beside us, the castle glimmering in the wavy image. With her hand in mine, we stood and stepped through.

We were in the same spot we had left in, right in the throne room, though no one was there to greet us. Keeping Kelia's hand entwined with mine, I pulled her toward the exit. "We better go find the queen."

Kelia glanced at our hands, and I stopped, already guessing what her mind was thinking. "We're in this together."

"Aren't you afraid of what they'll say?" Her gaze met mine and the softness in her eyes made me want to take her to the surface and never return. The dark fae didn't intermingled with the other races, though some of our surface kin weren't as strict. Rules didn't matter to me, they never did.

To prove that, I tugged her forward until my mouth slammed against hers, daring any who would walk in to challenge this connection. Though Kelia let me in for a moment, she quickly pulled back, her cheeks flushing red.

"What are you doing?" Her gaze darted behind me, a flash of fear in her blue eyes.

"Whatever I want." Taking her hand, I pulled her alongside me. "I told you before. I'll get us through this and anything that comes after. I'm afraid you're stuck with me, little sparrow."

Her bottom lip trembled, giving me a glimpse into her complicated thoughts. "If the queen sees us holding hands it will cause more suspicion. Right now we need her to trust us. We'll have time for pleasantries, after."

I inwardly groaned at the word pleasantries. She sounded so fancy, and I couldn't wait to see the other side of herself that she hid. "Very well."

Dropping her hand, I left the throne room and headed to the only other place I could assume her highness would be. Our footsteps echoed against the empty stone corridor. Where were the guards? The servants?

A tremor shook through the castle.

"What was that?" Kelia said behind me.

"Fighting, outside. We need to hurry."

Quickening my pace, I ran down the hall, Kelia in step with me.

Shouting poured out of the war room and a group of soldiers trailed out followed by the general. He glanced at me, face taut in a hard line before he and his entourage disappeared through a portal.

Inside the war room, Queen Merelda leaned

over the table, head bowed. I stood in the entryway waiting for her to acknowledge me. Alisha eyed me and Kelia, her brow narrowing as she could clearly smell Kelia's delicious scent all over me. It was one of the few times I wished fae didn't have such heightened senses.

"Where is my granddaughter?" The queen lifted her head, her violet eyes simmering with rage.

Thankfully for me, the queen's power rested in her fist not in magic. As long as we stayed back enough, we'd be safe. "We ran into some difficulty."

She gripped the edges of the table, her hands cracking the wood. "How many times will you fail me before I end your pitiful existence?"

"Your majesty." Kelia stepped around me like a shield. While I appreciated the gesture, I could handle the queen's wrath.

"Kelia," I whispered, eyeing her to stand down and let me handle this.

Pressing her hand to my chest, she moved me behind her, clearly determined to rescue me like a damn damsel in distress. "You were wrong. The prince had expected us. He waited until we killed the creature to show himself. He knew we were coming."

The queen's gaze flitted to Alisha. "My son has always been good at strategy which is why this feud has been dragging on for years." She sighed. "I'm assuming you know where he is. You're not foolish enough to return here with nothing."

I smiled wide and clasped my hands in front of me. "You know me well. Yes, we were able to track the prince's location and know where he is hiding out."

Alisha held out a transporter to me. "Input the destination. I'll go and investigate before we make a move. The main battle is close to the inner-city gates."

Taking the rod, I pressed my thumb into the rune. The rod heated my thumb until a flow of energy coursed up my arm, my shoulder, and to my head. I visualized the location in the caverns and the rod beeped, setting the waypoint.

"There," I said, feeling slightly relieved. "I can come with you. If—"

The atmosphere in the room changed and I wasn't quick enough to pick up why.

"Kelia . . ." my voice dropped in a whisper, half misbelief, half confusion. "What are you doing?"

Kelia stood behind the queen, her blue lasso wrapped around the queen's throat. "What you taught me to. Now give me the rod."

No, she couldn't be doing this. This was a trick of some sort. "Release the queen and we can talk about this."

Alisha shifted to the left and Kelia's magic glowed. The queen gasped and fell to her knees.

"Kelia!" Holding out my hands in a plea, I moved closer.

The black mamba shot out from the queen's robes, launching at Kelia's outstretched hand. I went to shoot fire, to stop it from biting Kelia, but she moved aside and using her power, shot out a thin blue spear and stabbed the snake to the wall.

The queen howled and moved to a knee, her power manifesting in a torrent of rage, but Kelia's grip would not loosen. She squeezed her magic around the queen's throat, forcing her back to the ground.

"What are you doing?" I said, holding my hands up in an attempt to keep things from exploding into chaos. "This is a mistake and it won't end well."

The female I thought I knew disappeared, replaced by the magi servant I remembered. There was no warmth, no empathy in Kelia's gaze just determination. "Hand over the rod or I will kill her and the two of you just like I killed her pet."

Anger pooled in my belly.

She had played me.

The wolf in me begged to be released, to take Kelia up on her promise. If she wanted a fight, I'd give her one. I was an idiot to think someone associated with the magi could be trusted. Everything she had said and done had been a trick.

"Give it to her," Alisha said.

The queen's shoulders slumped. She tried to speak, but the words came out garbled. I tossed the rod at Kelia. A blue spurt of magic released from her free hand, and she captured the rod, floating it back to her.

My chest seethed with fury.

If Kelia had any regrets in the decision, she didn't show it.

"Goodbye, Callum," she said, with no hint of emotion in her voice. Activating the rod, the portal opened and Kelia and the queen vanished through it.

I sprinted forward, slamming into the wall where the portal was only a moment ago. Screaming, I punched the smooth stone surface cracking it, knocking a painting from its veneer. My body heaved with anger and deep-down shame.

I'd shown Kelia a side of me no one had seen, and she used it against me, played me. My emotions coiled around one another, and I screamed, the sound ending in a howl as I fought back the urge to shift.

"Come on, Callum!" Alisha yelled behind me. "Get us there before it's too late."

Tossing me another transporter, I set the location, my entire body shaking with rage.

"This is what you get for playing with a human instead of one of your own," Alisha hissed.

Steadying myself, I breathed in and out until the wolf went back to sleep. Why would she kiss me? Was this all part of her plan from the start? I thought back to my lessons and wanted to kick myself for thinking Kelia was so naïve she'd never survive in my world. She reminded me again and again how powerful she was and why the magi chose her for this mission. I'd thought her true power was in that little blue flame of hers when her greatest asset was her mind.

I should've killed her.

Fisting my hands, I breathed in deep, trying to wrap my head around this situation and ignore the hurt. Kelia betrayed me and I was a fool for thinking she'd do anything else. My prison sentence had softened my resolve and that ended now.

Taking the rod from my hand, Alisha opened the portal. "You need to prepare yourself for what must be done."

Growling, I spun around. "Don't tell me what I need to do."

"I have known you all my life, Callum. You can fool yourself, but not me. When it comes time for the killing blow, you will not be able to do it. The human means too much to you." Alisha stepped through the portal, glancing back at me. "If you cannot strike, then I will be your blade."

Sickness coiled in my stomach.

Alisha was right.

No matter how much I hated Kelia, killing her was impossible.

"You make sure Mab is safe. I'll deal with Kelia."

My little sparrow was about to find out why they kept me locked up so tightly in the magi prison.

SEVENTEEN

KELIA

The guards at the entrance drew their swords the moment I appeared at the entrance with the queen. "The prince is expecting me."

"You are going to pay for this, human," the queen hissed. I had covered my lasso in thorns and wrapped it around her throat and shoulders, making it impossible for her to act on her threats.

The guard on the left waved his arm, speaking in the fae tongue, and the runes around the entrance flashed bright. "Go ahead."

Taking my hostage inside, I was surprised to see that this hideout was smaller than I expected and with less fae. The main cavern had two levels, lantern light flickering off the rocky walls.

Fae sat around sharpening blades, foraging for the glowing mushrooms that dotted the far-right area, and on the second level, cots and makeshift tents covered the area.

A throne made out of pure obsidian sat in the main area, Prince Eldritch sitting on it while talking to a guard. His gaze moved to me then the queen, his lip curving up into a wide grin.

"That was quicker than expected," he said as he rose to meet us.

The fae surrounding us grew quiet and fanned out, unsure of what to do.

"I don't think I've ever seen anyone handle my mother like this since my father died. I thought it would be Callum to enact our betrayal, but a gift is a gift. Little things go long ways." Prince Eldritch rubbed his smooth chin, his eyes glowing with excitement.

My next move had to be timed perfectly. There was no room for mistakes, especially after seeing Callum's expression. Pushing the tingle of emotion caused by even thinking his name, I focused on the task ahead. It would take all my power to pull this off. Keeping my magic wrapped around the queen, I grabbed her crown and brought it to the prince. "Our deal is almost complete."

He bit his bottom lip the closer I came, his gaze flitting between me and the crown. "It seems humans are capable of some things."

With steady hands, I placed the crown on his head. "You wear it well."

Reaching up to my face, he dragged his finger over my lips, the sensation cold and unwelcomed, so different from when Callum did it. Keeping my emotions in check, I allowed the action, and slipped my hand down the rod to the activator rune.

"Where is Mab? I will need to leave soon." Keeping the Prince focused on my face, I smiled. "Unless the fae don't keep their bargains."

Prince Eldritch's brow furrowed. "I'm insulted. You are going to be the queen of the dark fae. I keep my word. Mab is resting. I'll wake her after I deal with my mother."

Gently pushing me aside, the prince went to his mother, my magic still keeping her locked in place. The queen did not cower, or plead, she simply waited with a furious expression.

"Oh, Mother. How good it is to see you on your knees for once."

Clicking the rune, I visualized an area in the Borderlands that was close enough to see the Rift but not in an area of battle. With the way point locked, I made my move.

The portal opened, causing the queen's eyes to widen and look past her son. When the prince turned, I used the full force of my power and pushed out a stream of blue to wrap around his body, then with all my might, I tossed both of them into the portal and jumped through.

The prince growled as he landed hard on the barren land, falling onto his side.

"Do not use magic here!" I warned. "I'm going to release my magic, but if you use yours the darkthings will come in full force. Listen to what I have to say, and this will all be over soon."

Dropping my magic, I held up a hand in warning and turned to close the portal.

A giant wolf flew through the portal knocking me over, making the rod slip from my hands. The portal closed, and I swung around to face the snarling wolf.

"Callum . . ."

He pounced forward, fangs and claws ready to rip me apart.

In any other place, I would've raised my barrier and protected myself, but not here, not when one drop of magic would send out a call to the demons to the north. I cried as claws shred through my leather, ripping my skin open as he knocked me onto my back, ripping me apart, my head slamming against the ground and making me bite my lip. He thought I'd betrayed him, and that hurt more than the physical wounds he inflicted on me now.

His growls reached my soul because they were mixed with anger and pain. A deep sorrow caused by me. A snapping maw reached for my neck as if he was ready to end it all right here.

When I didn't make any move to stop the paw

swiping across my chest, he paused. I lay on my back, fire burning across my arms and chest from the open wounds. Standing over me, almost asking me why I didn't fight.

But it was already too late.

Shifters were magical creatures, more than a human with a blue flame, and the darkthings picked up Callum's scent like a rabid dog. Wails and screeches came from the north.

"Where have you taken us?" The prince grabbed his mother's arms and pulled her up from the dirt.

Staring into Callum's sad gaze I spoke. "The Borderlands. I wanted you both to see the threat we all face in order for you to end your war with one another. If we want Saol to survive, all races above and below need to work together."

Callum whimpered and nudged my side with his muzzle.

"Foolish girl," the queen spat. "Return us at once before we're all slaughtered."

Shaking the pain from my head, I searched for the rod. It had slipped from my grasp somewhere. When I went to move, the pain burned and I winced, holding a hand to my chest. Callum licked the open wound, whimpering, and I pushed his face away.

"We have to move," I said, grabbing his fur, trying to sit up, ignoring the pain.

Black shapes zipped through the sky; they

were close now. Knowing we only had a moment, I forced myself to my feet. "I'll protect us as best I can, find that rod."

The first beast soared in, wings spanning twenty feet and a mouth open in howling rage. Rows of razor-sharp teeth gnashed the air as it swooped low. The prince shot a blast of lightning through the air, igniting the darkthing up in a flash of glowing white, but that beast wasn't the only one there. Three more flew in next, black sinewy wings and triangle shaped heads with no distinct facial features screeched a vibrating sound that made my ears pop.

Callum launched through the air, grabbing the closest creature by the neck and ripping the monster's head clear from its body. Black ichor sprayed from the body that dropped to the ground. Callum didn't waste time and flung the head to the side and moved to the next creature.

Holding my left arm across my chest to staunch the bleeding, I held out my right palm, magic pouring forth. White spots blinked in my vision and when I took a step forward, bile rose up my throat.

A furry head nudged my arm. Callum had made his way back to me.

With no energy to deal with him, I ignored his bumping, until he laid on his front paws, whimpering and eyeing me with sad eyes. Taking the hint, I climbed onto his back. While it helped since I didn't have to stand, the moment he sprinted forward, my stomach hurled.

"Keep it steady," I groaned and lifted my right arm, forcing my magic out and upward.

A charging shadow came from the east, black horns curled upward, shadows rising off the tips. The bull like creature bowed its head and charged at the queen. With a quick pivot of her foot, she caught the horns with her hands, forcing the creature to a standstill.

"Today, you will see the full power of the dark fae." Her heel dug into the dirt and with a roar she flipped the massive beast onto its back. The creature had to be over two thousand pounds. Dust kicked up in the air from the movement and Callum jumped back.

On its back, Queen Merelda flipped and landed on its belly and with a massive *crack* punched the beast in its face, the sound so loud it caused the nearest darkthings to converge on the queen. Before my magic reached them, Prince Eldritch released a torrent of lightning, lighting up the sky and making it rain.

The darkthing under the queen stilled, its face indistinguishable. Black ooze covered the queen's fists and she glanced up, our gazes locking on one another—a reminder that we were not finished.

Callum moved left and sprinted across the ground, head low. He snatched the rod out of the dirt with his mouth and I patted his back. "We need distance or else those darkthings will go through the portal."

He howled, and the dark fae behind us glanced our way.

"Keep them busy while I open the portal. We'll only have a minute before more come!" The queen and prince nodded then turned to face the next wave of shadows.

Pressing my thumb on the rune, I visualized the throne area back in the cavern. When I felt the location snap, I activated the portal. The area shimmered, magic circling into a wide opening. Screeches sounded behind me as more darkthings swarmed in, flying and crawling their way. The prince and queen stepped back, but kept the fight in front of them, lighting up the sky, the queen punching and tossing creatures like feathers.

The sky cracked with thunder, lightning melding with the prince's power and calling more beasts to where we stood.

"Maema!"

Mab's scream reached me just as she dashed through the portal.

"No!" Queen Merelda yelled, turning to face her running granddaughter.

Mab's eyes widened as more creatures approached. Everything slowed and melded as Mab's scream shifted into an earsplitting cry. Light poured out of her mouth, her eyes, her hands, and shot out like a sunray. I closed my eyes, the light too bright and blinding. There were screeches, howls and then nothing.

When I opened my eyes, Mab's eyes rolled back, and she slumped to the ground.

The ground rumbled, pebbles bouncing up and down. The queen slowly moved to Mab, but a creature came up out of the ground blocking her path.

And then the dirt around us erupted with screams.

Black scorpion type creatures with wings burst from the ground and vaulted into the sky, their bodies bigger than mountain goats, their four front appendages similar to a praying mantis. Prince Eldritch used his power to blast a hole through a section while I cleared the area by the portal with my lasso.

"Mab!" the queen screamed, and I turned to see one of the creatures pick Mab up and head for the portal.

Tugging Callum's fur, I guided him to the portal. A creature slammed into my side, sending me flying off Callum's back. I groaned as I hit the ground, getting a mouthful of dirt. A growl sounded above me as Callum stood over me, ready to go after the insect. It swayed in the air along with the others as they swarmed around us, creating a barrier between us and the portal.

"No," I croaked, reaching out with my magic to steal Mab out of the darkthing's grasp.

But I was too late.

It zipped through the portal, taking Mab with it.

The queen ran forward, the prince behind her.

Callum nudged under my arm, and I grabbed him to stand and follow them back to the Underground.

The guards ran, grabbing weapons, running down one of the tunnels, in what I hoped is where the creature took Mab.

"Follow that creature!" the queen ordered.

The men looked at the prince and he nodded. "Mab is royal blood and we will not let one of our own be stolen by one of those abominations."

"I can help contain it," I said, holding my side. "If we leave now."

White spots blinked in my vision, my head spinning from blood loss, and I swayed.

"Whoa." The prince wrapped an arm around my waist. "You need to rest and be tended to."

"It got away," I huffed, my mind running through pages of history, searching for an answer as to what type of darkthing we had just encountered.

"We'll find it."

"No." I gripped the prince's shirt as my vision blurred. "We're all in danger. We're all . . ."

EIGHTEEN

CALLUM

I quickly shifted, and searched for anything to wrap myself in. One guard tossed me a pair of pants and I belted them on.

Kelia coughed and slumped against the prince who whisked her into his arms and began walking toward the second level. "You need to be stitched. Get my healer!"

"No time." She looked at her chest. Blood flowed from the wounds.

I'd never been one for regrets, but this time I couldn't ignore what I'd done. "We need you to be conscious if we have any hope of finding that creature."

Prince Eldritch headed up the incline where an area of tents had been set. He walked into one that had four cots set up, two of them occupied with wounded soldiers, most likely from the prince's last assault. He placed Kelia on one and slumped on the floor next to her, sweat sliding down his forehead.

A dark fae with her silver hair wound around her head in a braid, frowned at the prince. "Why is there a human in my tent?"

"Just heal her, Nikita. We need—" His words ended in a grunt as he gripped his left arm where his clothing was stained with blood.

Nikita kneeled on the ground and using a dagger, sliced his shirt. The annoyance on her brow vanished in an instant.

"Light crystals," Kelia groaned as she tried to sit up, holding her bleeding chest.

I ran to the opposite side of the cot and pressed on her shoulders, forcing her to lay back down. "You need to rest and get stitched."

"Callum!" the queen yelled, but I couldn't be bothered with her now, not when Kelia was bleeding out in front of me. "You need to join the search."

"Send your shadowwalkers. I need to help Kelia."

The queen grabbed my arm. "This is not a request. You and I both know you can track even better than my walkers."

Queen Merelda was one of five that knew my secret. Still, she had the resources to help Mab and I would join them later. "After I stitch Kelia."

Fingers dug into my skin as the queen forced me to acknowledge her request. "Did you know that Mab is Lara's daughter?"

I eyed the queen, frowning, and wondering why she would bring that up.

"Did you also know that Lara was *yours*."

Someone gasped and my breathing stilled. "What did you say?"

"You heard me," the queen leaned closer. "Lara was yours."

"Impossible," I whispered, my mind reeling from this absurdity. I'd always felt bonded to Lara, but to be mine . . . and Mab . . . my granddaughter?

"No time to stitch," Kelia said, interrupting the conversation. "Use your fire and seal these wounds so we can go."

My stomach dropped at the mere thought of burning her skin. Hadn't I already done enough? "But Kelia . . ." I dropped my voice to a whisper. "You'll be scarred."

That stubborn, determined gaze met me head on. "Yes, now stop wasting time and burn me."

My hands shook at her request. Between what I just discovered about Lara and what I'd done to Kelia, I couldn't focus.

Prince Eldritch grunted. "I knew you weren't loyal to Father."

Nikita lifted him up to bring him to a cot.

"Your *father* had stopped visiting my bed many years before I conceived Lara. Why do you think

Callum was around so much? Certainly, wasn't for his personality."

I couldn't deal with this right now.

"You better do as the human asks," Nikita said. "I will not waste time on her when my prince's life is in danger."

"I can stitch you," I said, glancing around for a suture and thread. A medical tent had to have one.

Kelia grabbed my wrist and yanked me toward her. "Every moment you waste puts us all in danger. Mab needs us."

Nikita ripped off the prince's shirt, revealing a black festering wound and a black spiderweb of lines expanding out and up. "If this poison reaches your heart, you'll be dead. We need a life crystal, or I must cut the arm."

"You're not cutting anything," the queen said. "If I wanted my son dead, I'd do it myself. We'll send someone to the core."

"The core? Surely, there's a less dangerous way to save his life?" Shaking my head, I raked my mind for an answer that wouldn't put us in any more danger.

"Mother's right. From this location, it's the closest. The crystals grow close to the surface, but we're not near any of those entrances." The prince hissed and laid back on the cot.

"Do it now," Kelia said, tugging on my arm. "This is our only option. Every moment you waste puts Mab in danger. She needs us."

I hated this option. Loathed it, but Kelia was right. With a silent nod, I gave into her crazy demands.

Relief washed over her face, and she began pulling up her shirt. I moved to block her from the others in the tent. While I had fantasized about her undressing, this was not the scenario I envisioned. She winced as she tried to move.

"Let me," I sighed and grabbed a pair of scissors off the nearby table. I sat on the edge of the cot and began cutting her shirt down the middle. "Cover them with your hands while I do this . . . which I still think is a ridiculous option."

Ripping the fabric free from her chest, she quickly covered herself. "Just hurry."

"I hate this plan."

Her eyes watered. "I know."

"You need to bite down on something." I took my belt off and brought it to her mouth. "Sorry, I don't have anything cleaner."

Without waiting for a countdown, I called the fire to my fingertips as she bit into the leather. "I promise to make the searing as small as possible.

She closed her eyes and then I began.

With a slow stroke, I cauterized the skin by the wound. Her body tensed, every muscle of hers clenching as the scent of burned flesh filled the tent. Muffled cries left her mouth as I closed the first wound then moved to the one that went across her chest and up toward her left breast, right by her heart. Another cry and her hands fell away as she passed out.

Dark hands came into view, followed by a piece of linen. Queen Merelda covered Kelia up, giving her privacy. The queen nodded at me to continue, and I did, knowing that these scars would always be a reminder of what I'd done. If only she had trusted me enough with her plan we could have avoided all of this.

With the wounds closed, I stepped back, shaking and feeling all out of sorts. "I need a moment."

"I'll dress the rest." Queen Merelda gazed at Kelia with almost a reverence. The queen wasn't exactly a fan of the other races, but she had a deep respect for power. "As soon as she wakes, take her with you. We don't know what that darkthing wants with Mab or why it traveled here. Did you notice how that last group maneuvered?"

"I did. Very hive like."

"Yes. Now, go rest. I need you at full power for what comes next."

Stepping out of the tent, I searched for a drink, anything to cool me down. A clay barrel sat near the side of a long table arrayed with roasted mushrooms and bloom berries—one of my favorite fruits from the Underground. The plum hued berries had a deep, robust taste. Taking the ladle out of the barrel, I drank, the water refreshing my throat and thoughts. Taking a few berries, I moved away from the noise to a quieter area of the cave where a set of smoothed out rocks had been created for seating.

I'd give the surface one thing; they had much better seating and views. My thoughts went to Mab then to Kelia until my head swarmed with questions and the pain was almost too much to bear.

NINETEEN

KELJA

When I opened my eyes, I did not expect the queen to be sitting by my side.

"You're either very brave or very stupid," she said with a slight twist to her lip. "You could have killed us all."

With a wince, I slowly slid myself up to a sitting position. Linen had been dressed around my whole chest, covering my wounds. "It was a risk I had to take."

"My duty has always been to the dark fae." Glancing over at her son, she rested back against the chair. "The surface fae have their own king and it's his duty to deal with surface problems."

"The Rift threatens all life."

"Yes, it does." Her expression softened; her gaze fixated on the sleeping prince. "How long does he have?"

"I don't know. It varies, could be hours, could be days depending on how the infection spreads." I turned and dropped my feet on the ground, catching my bearings. "How long have I been asleep?"

"A few hours."

"We need to move." I stood and wobbled. The queen grabbed my waist to steady me, her narrowed gaze showing her disapproval. "I'm fine. The bleeding has stopped."

With her hand still on my hip, she stood, and held my chin with her hand. "I have met many humans in my time, and you are unique, stubborn like them, but not selfish, a respectable quality but one that will get you killed. Though you did kill my sweet mamba."

"My life became forfeit the moment the magi saved me from death and your snake is not dead. I made sure to pin it to the wall without slaughtering it."

Releasing me, she stepped back, her eyes darkening. "If you save my granddaughter, you will have the full protection of the Underground where the magi are not welcomed. You would never have to return to the surface again."

Understanding the gravity of her vow, I bowed my head in understanding. "Thank you, Queen

Merelda, but I don't seek a reward. I will do everything within my power to save Mab and the prince."

My thoughts went to Callum who I noticed was nowhere in sight. The Queen's mouth curved into a grin. "He's out there."

Ignoring the odd flush of warmth to my cheeks, I nodded a thank you. "I'm going to see if he's ready to leave."

Quickly leaving the queen's knowing gaze, I left the medical tent. The area outside the tent was quiet. Fae sat around either sharpening swords or eating, some sleeping on black furs around campfires that held magical flames. Real smoke in the caves would be difficult to see in, but a magical fire could create the same warmth and light without the burn. Pink and azure flames casted beautiful shadows around the cavern, highlighting the unique obsidian and white crystals that made the ceiling seem like the sky of the surface.

Gazing to my left, I spotted a shaggy flash of magenta. Callum had his head down, arms folded, legs crossed, and snoring on a chair that had been melded out of the ground. A magical fire sat in front of the lone fae, the flames highlighting the sharp inclines of his cheekbones. Big, black eyelashes framed his almond shaped eyes, and it was in this moment that I realized how exquisitely handsome he truly was.

My chest rose and fell with sharp breaths as I watched him sleep, uncertain of what I should say. He would want to talk, but I didn't. The physical and mental fatigue drained my willpower and I needed more than ever to be the stoic warrior the magi trained me to be.

Callum had created a rift within my heart and the chasm left by its wake was tearing me asunder. Never would I have thought any male could change me.

How foolish I was.

With slow, shaky steps I walked over to him.

Suddenly, his eyes opened, his gaze instantly finding mine. "You're awake."

"I am."

He stared at my chest, and frowned. "And clearly not dressed properly." With a shake of his head, he pulled off his shirt and moved to put it over my head. "Really, Kelia, when this is over, we need to have a proper discussion on your etiquette."

His fingers grazed my arms and sides as he gently helped me put the shirt on. "How are you feeling? And be honest with yourself."

It was hard to deny him when he stood so close, and his breath had this dizzying effect on my thinking. "Terrible," I admitted.

Taking my face within his hands, he leaned closer. "What were you thinking?"

Pain tainted his voice and his eyes watered

with emotion. He shouldn't be looking at me like that, not now when I had to fight to keep my wits about me. "They needed to see it to understand the danger the Rift creates."

He slipped his hands down my neck to my shoulders where he gently squeezed them, his gaze moving to my wounded chest. "That's not what I was talking about. Why didn't you protect yourself? Why did you let me . . . ? You have been fighting me with that magic lasso since the day we met."

A slight tremble ran through my body. I didn't want to admit the truth that part of me deserved his wrath and in that moment hurting him was the last thing I wanted to do.

"Kelia, *please* for once will you tell me how you feel?"

"Using my magic would've been a beacon to the darkthings. It wasn't worth the risk."

He glared at me as if my answer disappointed him. "Of course. My little sparrow would always weigh the options, calculated without fault."

Placing a hand to my chest, I pressed slightly. "It's strange. I'd assume it would hurt much more, but it's tolerable."

"You can thank the queen for that. She has a magical touch with herbal remedies. She dressed your wounds and probably applied one of her healing salves."

The more I learned about Queen Merelda, the

more I realized why she had reigned for so long. "We should leave now then."

"If you two are finished chatting," Alisha said from behind us. "We need to go to the core. Our scouts sent word that the creature has gone there."

Alisha handed Callum a bundle of clothes and a short sword and he quickly changed into the leather armor. Strapping the sheath around his waist, his jaw ticked as he gazed at the queen who had just walked out of the medical tent. "I won't come back without Mab."

The queen folded her arms. "I'd expect nothing less."

Alisha opened the portal and the shimmering oval revealed nothing but darkness.

Following Callum through the portal, we walked in silence, my stomach churning with nerves. Breathing in and out, I reminded myself that I was on a mission. One that included a young fae who was now missing. There was nothing more important than closing the Rift. Yet, the truth of Mab's heritage sent a wave of uneasiness through me. How could the queen expect Callum to allow Mab to go with me? Had this been her plan all along?

Alisha walked alongside Callum, and I fell back, needing a bit of distance between them to make sense of this confusion I now felt. What would Callum do next?

And how did he really feel about the queen?

I knew this wasn't the time to be sitting here pondering his ex-lover, but I couldn't help thinking I'd been tricked, and not just me but the entire council.

Ahead, a golden light shimmered in the darkness. The narrow cavern opened up into a massive system, and one that took my breath away.

"Is that the life tree?" Carefully stepping inside and to where the level we were on curved down, I gazed at the glowing amber hued crystal.

"Part of it. It's a root. We have areas like this around the core." Callum held out his arm stopping me.

Alisha cursed and I held a hand to my mouth in horror.

Below us golden pools of steaming liquid surrounded what looked like a yellow crystallized tree, or part of it. Walkways of black mixed with fire colored glass created a spiderweb of golden beauty and right in the center sat the darkthing, its tale and body wrapped around a glowing ball that was too bright to see into. The darkthing seemed to be feeding on the ball of light, its body rippling with energy as it smothered the light orb, trying to engulf the brilliance in its clutches.

My power was a mutation of light magic which meant that if I could create a barrier around myself . . .

"Kelia," Callum whispered, crouching low,

grabbing me with him. "We have to be careful in here or the whole structure could collapse. What does that darkthing want with Mab?"

Alisha hovered close. "She's in there, isn't she?"

I nodded. "She must've subconsciously created a barrier around herself like I did once. Have darkthings ever ventured here before?"

"No," Alisha replied. "There's been no record. Creatures poisoned by them, but never one of the shadow monsters itself, and for it to come straight here . . ."

"Kelia." Callum put a hand on my arm. "When those monsters took Mab, they moved in a hive formation. Are darkthings hive mind?"

"It's possible. There's been no research to prove it, but the darkthings have been more aggressive lately and these types I've never seen before." I thought back to every text I'd read, everything I had learned about our enemy.

"Regardless," Alisha interjected, "we must kill this thing quickly. The krubera are already stirred."

Following her gaze, Callum pointed above and around us at the walls where little alcoves were carved out, some covered in a filmy yellow sheen. "Those are homes of the krubera. Mostly harmless cave ants, but they are irritable when their home is disturbed, and they have a nasty bite that can leave you paralyzed for hours."

"Those holes could fit a small child . . . that's

bigger than an ant," I said back.

"Surface ant, but not a cave ant." He turned to me, placing his hands on my shoulders. "Stay here and use your lasso to draw the darkthing away from Mab. If any of the hive starts cracking, not only could we fall into that boiling hot spring, but it'll cause all the krubera to come out and we can't fight all of them and the darkthing at once."

"I'll take care of the krubera coming out." Alisha took out a thin tube from her pocket and placed a tiny pointed object in the front. "I'll knock out any that come out while you two get Mab and destroy the darkthing."

"I can handle that shadow beast," I told them. "Let me know when you're ready."

Callum squeezed my hand. "I know you can."

With that, the two dark fae slid down the rocky cavern in different directions.

Like a spider, Callum crawled and climbed down the rock, maneuvering around the glasslike structure until his dark form disappeared from sight. Stepping back from the ledge, I sat on the ground leaning against the rock. Sweat beaded my brow as my chest ached and fatigue attacked my limbs, my injuries reminding me of my limits.

I had to be careful and strategic with my magic use because once we started, it would take all my strength to finish.

A sharp whistle sounded from my right, and I sent out my magical lasso, wrapping around the abomination's throat. Viciously, I jerked it back, pulling it off the glowing orb and dragging it directly toward me.

TWENTY

CALLUM

With the darkthing heading toward Kelia, I carefully stepped across the amber walkways, making sure each step wouldn't break the thin crystalline substance.

Deeper around the root, the steam from the pools below made my body slick with sweat, even without a shirt on. Wiping my hands off on my pants, I reached around to step on to a piece of stone to an area behind the main root.

Mab would get an earful when I found her. What was she thinking running into the portal? My heart filled with both pride and fear. She was my blood, and just like me she would protect those she cared about.

My hand slipped and I cursed, wiping the sweat

off my head. From where I stood, I couldn't see out to where I had left Kelia. I didn't like leaving her there to fight that creature alone, but she was better suited to take that shadow monster on.

I shimmied across a thin walkway to where I had seen that glowing ball of light. Quickly, and very carefully, I moved across and through the spiderweb of glass toward the side of the cavern. There, above me, sitting on a large stone piece that stuck out of the root was Mab, completely covered in glowing light.

"Mab," I whispered.

Her eyes fluttered open, and I held a finger to my lips, motioning for her to be quiet. Not too far from her sat a part of the hive, and without knowing if krubera were in there we needed to be extra careful. "Can you get down?"

She shook her head and gripped the crystal harder.

Looking around, I saw a broken piece of crystal past my feet. She must've broken a piece when climbing. I could get to her, but then we would have to find a different way out of here. "I'm coming up."

I jumped and grabbed a crystal branch above me, just catching the edge with my fingertips. My muscles strained as I pulled myself up then hopped over to another ledge and up and over, until I was close enough to Mab to grab her.

Her arms wrapped around my neck, and I

patted her hands. "Stay on my back and hold on tight. We're getting out of here."

A bunch of crystals hung from a limb, right by the entrance to a krubera hole. The hole didn't have the film over it so it could be abandoned.

"Hold on and stay quiet. We need to get some of those crystals for the prince."

"What happened to Uncle E," she whispered into my ear, squeezing my neck and holding on.

Having Mab so close, knowing the truth about her distracted me, and I had to pause to wipe the sweat off my brow. Did Mab know? Did she know that I was her grandfather?

And Lara . . . if I had known the truth, I would have done things differently. She never would've been betrothed in the first place. I would've kept her safe.

Mab squeezed my shoulder. The bunch of life crystals were close, enough to not only save the prince but protect anyone else that needed it. Sweat coated my hands, and I paused to wipe them off on my pants.

"Hurry," Mab whispered, nudging me forward.

With one step in front of the other, my thoughts spun, and my heart continued to accelerate. I reached out, my fingers just missing the bunch of life crystals.

A rustling sounded ahead.

"Callum, hurry."

Two glowing eyes appeared in the darkness.

Mab squeaked and I grabbed the bunch of life crystals just as a krubera jumped out of the hole and onto the ledge. Two long honey-colored antennas twitched in our direction. The insect was a bit bigger than I remembered, resembling the size of the dogs from the surface. It scurried forward, more curious than angry.

"Climb," I said, and slowly shifted to move Mab off my back and onto the branch above us. "Hurry."

She grabbed one of the pieces of crystal sticking out and began climbing the web back up. Once she had a head start, I moved, hoping our curious intruder did not bring its friends.

Glancing down, the krubera didn't immediately run up after us.

Instead, it rubbed its antennas together and clicked its pinchers.

All around us, glowing eyes appeared out of the hive, followed by the *clack* of insects chatting. "Keep it moving."

Mab scurried up and through the different levels, me close behind. We were still too deep into the spiderweb for me to see Kelia, and I had no idea if the krubera near her were on the move.

Something screeched from somewhere above us, a chilling noise that reminded me of nails scraping stone. The sound seemed to agitate the little bugs and they all started moving, straight toward us.

"Go, go!" I shouted, hurrying up the root to where Mab climbed.

Krubera scurried out of the hive and swarmed the root. I kicked out at the ones beside me, leaving my magic for last. My fire might melt any of the glass we climbed. A slimy antenna grazed my arms sending a shiver through me.

I hated bugs.

Mab screamed as three of the cave ants moved near her, snapping their pinchers at her clothes. I moved quicker, slicing the bulbous heads that got too close. The spiderweb widened, giving us a chance to leave the life root and move out into the cavern. To our left a massive piece of crystal created a walkway away from the root.

Alisha appeared from the other side, using her blow gun to quietly knock the ants out.

"Get to the branch," I called out.

Mab kicked one of the krubera and it fell off the root just missing my shoulder as it fell. She jumped to the wide walkway, giving my heart a drop at how close she landed to the edge. Within moments, I was behind her, stabbing at krubera crawling at us from every direction.

The walkway led out to more of the spiderweb that had pieces of pallasite and other minerals. From here, I could see the entire cavern including Kelia.

Kelia stood near the edge where I had left her, blue light flowing from her hands, one arm outstretched creating a barrier around the darkthing, her other arm, out and around the hive, covering the nearby holes. Our gazes met and I had never been more amazed. Power glowed around her, highlighting her in an ethereal aura that took my breath away.

Magnificent.

Knowing Kelia would keep us safe, I urged Mab forward. "Walk slowly."

Mab nodded. "You still have the crystals?"

"I do." Surprisingly, I had managed to keep hold of the bunch I'd been carrying.

"Good. I'm almost—"

Her words ended in a scream as the walkway in front of her broke off. I grabbed her arm, falling on to my stomach and catching her at the last minute.

"Mab!" Kelia screamed, but her and I both knew she couldn't help. The moment she moved her magic away from the rest of the hive, we'd be swarmed.

Mab dangled, the hot boiling springs below her. She gazed up at me with wet eyes as my grip slipped. I needed both hands.

"Don't!" Mab cried, almost knowing what I was about to do.

My body inched forward, closer to the edge, the smooth crystal a terrible place for saving someone's life. "I have to."

She cried. "Please."

I cared for the prince, but Mab was my blood and now that I knew that, I was never letting her go.

"I'm sorry." I dropped the life crystals and grabbed her arm with my other hand and pulled her up and over the ledge where she was safe in my arms.

There was no time for thank-yous, though. Lines appeared around us on the walkway. We had to go or we'd both die.

"Portal out!" Kelia screamed from across the cavern.

"I'm not leaving you here. I'll try and get back to the root." Looking behind me, the krubera scurried back, almost knowing that the walkway we were on was about to crumble apart.

"Go, Callum. Now! I'll be fine. Hurry!"

"Come on!" Alisha took out the rod, opening the portal.

Kelia fell to her knees just as the barrier keeping the darkthing at bay began to crack. Mab held on to me tightly and Alisha screamed at me to move.

With a growl, I turned and jumped to the ledge Alisha stood on. "I'm coming right back for you."

"I know," Kelia said, her face taut in pain as she yelled and pulsed more power.

With one arm around Mab, I ran through the portal and immediately handed off Mab to Alisha.

"I have to go back," I said and went to turn.

The darkthing broke out of Kelia's hold and zoomed toward the portal. Kelia screamed and shot her power directly at the hive.

"No!" I yelled, knowing the moment she did that the entire ceiling would crumble on top of her.

Someone grabbed my arm and threw me away from the portal. I slammed into the ground.

"Close it!" the queen ordered, standing between the portal and me.

"Don't!" I shouted, scrambling to my feet. "She'll die!"

The portal winked out, my heart going with it.

Queen Merelda took Mab from Alisha. "We are at war, Callum. Not everyone survives."

TWENTY-ONE

CALLUM

With a roar, I shifted and tore out of the cave.

I would not leave her.

The queen yelled after me, ordering me to stay, but I ignored it all.

I'm coming, Kelia. Hold on.

Running, I headed toward the core where I had left her, it was miles deep and would take time for me to reach her, longer if anything stopped me on the way, but nothing would. Pushing myself harder than I ever had, I sped through the dark, through tunnels and caverns, using my fae senses to guide me back to her.

Opening my senses, I focused on her scent,

visualizing it until her aura became a tangible entity I could track. My paws slammed against the rock, and I howled as I accepted that Kelia meant more to me than my freedom. For years, I'd dreamed about the day I would be free. That reality seemed hazy without her in it.

Speeding down a deep incline, I ran, hating myself for leaving when I did. I could've tried to reach her, to port out together. Keeping her close to my thoughts, I focused on getting back to the life root, believing that my little sparrow would not die so easily.

Though my heart wanted to hope, logic told me there was no way.

Howling, I ran faster, not once stopping, panic setting in.

What if she was dead?

Pain raced through my heart, lancing out in every direction until my mind hazed over. She couldn't be gone. She had to survive. She had to . . .

Sliding to a stop, I froze.

Rock and glass covered the ground, the cave-in had spread out into the cavern I came from where the entrance to the core used to be.

No.

Shifting, I climbed over the debris, ignoring the bits of rock that sliced into my feet. The darkthing was gone, the hive destroyed but the root still stood, glowing and unbreakable. She'd brought the ceiling down, knowing it would crush her along with everything else.

"Kelia?" I called out, digging through the rubble. "Kelia!"

Tears splashed my cheeks as I used my earth magic to shove rock away. "I'm here. Just tell me where you are!"

My vision blurred, one of my nails ripped off as I continued to dig through the rubble. My chest heaved, my breaths coming faster, and I yelled, the pain shredding me from the inside. Throwing rocks, I screamed in defiance, sobs breaking through my chest in a violent tornado.

My fingers grazed something soft, and blue light peeked through the wreckage.

On my knees, I dug deeper, easing the rock away carefully.

Three fingers, then a hand, her arm . . . bit by bit, I removed the debris until I could wrap my hands around her and pull her out.

She lay limp in my arms, her body still warm. I held her close to my chest, the tears falling against her face. With shaking hands, I adjusted her so I could press my ear against her chest.

Thump . . . thump . . . thump.

Gripping her tight, I sighed. She was alive.

I knew it.

I laughed, my voice cracking with emotion. Wiping the dirt off her face, I kissed her forehead. "You're too stubborn to die, and I've never been more grateful."

Gathering her in my arms, I stood, kissing her cheek, and inhaling her scent. "I'll get you out of here. Hold on."

With her passed out, I couldn't put her on my back and shift into my wolf form which meant I was about to walk through the Underground, naked, carrying a sleeping human. Walking would take much longer to return, but I was ready for whatever lay ahead. She was alive, and that's all that mattered.

Heading back the way I had come, I hummed to myself, singing a song that Lara had sung as a child. She was my daughter, though I should have realized the similarities. Lara had always been like me, even our sense of humor had been the same.

The queen would need to answer a few of my questions. I deserved that much after this fiasco. Then there was the prince. We had never been close, but I didn't want to see him die. If I hurried back, maybe we could try again, or go to a different life root.

Kelia stirred in my arms. Her skin warmed, getting hotter. Soon, we'd be in a somewhat safer area where we could rest. If I veered right, back toward the city, it would be a slight detour but there was an oasis with soft moss and fresh water where we could rest. Readjusting her in my arms, I ran, heading toward the safe haven.

The more I held this female, the harder it was

to deny the bond. It pulled and tugged me closer, making me realize that leaving her would be near impossible. She wasn't fae and worse, she was a magi, beholden to an ancient sect who would not see her marry or bond with anyone.

Leaving was no longer an option for me, but I had no idea how Kelia felt. Did she care or had I been the one tricked the entire time?

Yellow and white lights shone in the cavern as I reached the oasis. A slow-moving river rushed along a mossy green embankment. The luminescent worms creating a natural skylight. I placed her on the soft moss, running my hand across her warm forehead.

Looking around I tried to find something to use to carry water. Big white and blue mushrooms dotted an area by the river. Plucking one of the large caps off, I scooped up water and brought it over to Kelia. Sliding under her, I rested her head against my chest and brought the water to her lips. "Drink."

Drops of water trickled down her mouth and neck. I wiped them away with my hand then held her close. She would be fine. A few hours of rest and I'd move her again. For now, I'd keep her safe and warm.

Gently moving her back on the ground, I went to drink water and wash my face then I shifted. My fur would keep her warm. Curling around her, I nuzzled onto her lap and shut my eyes, fatigue finally winning.

"I've been porting around everywhere, and you're here taking a nap?"

Opening my eyes, I yawned, seeing Alisha standing by us. Her gaze went to Kelia, and she kneeled beside the sleeping human. "I see the human still lives."

She patted the top of my head.

I let out a low growl and Alisha smiled.

"Don't be a grump," she said and stood. "We need to return. Prince Eldritch is not doing well. We moved him back to the palace. We think he'll pass tonight."

Instantly, I shifted. "The queen has to have life crystals somewhere."

Unphased by my nakedness, like most fae, she continued speaking. "We tried. She found a few in the vault, but nothing worked, and she did try. Not because she wants peace with the prince, but because Mab is inconsolable, and the queen has always had a soft spot for her. He'll seem okay after we use one and then within minutes the blackness spreads again, like a vicious root."

"We need to go." I bent down to lift Kelia up. Alisha held out a hand to stop me.

"I'll take the human. If she wakes, I'd expect she wouldn't be pleased that you were naked."

"Humans and their odd quirks . . . fine but be careful." I held out my hand. "Give me the rod."

Alisha handed me the rod then gently lifted

Kelia.

One of the cave butterflies fluttered by. The big jade wings as beautiful as I remembered. I wished Kelia was awake to see it.

Visualizing the palace, I clicked the rune and opened the portal to the room Kelia had been staying in. The air shimmered and a wavery image of the bedroom appeared. Alisha stepped through first, I followed.

Once back in the palace, I sighed. "I'm going to get changed. Make sure someone tends to her."

Alisha nodded and began walking toward the bed.

Leaving, I shook the unease from my mind.

Heading toward the room I was staying in, I tried to ignore the pull to run back to Kelia, knowing she was injured, but I couldn't. I needed to clear my head and have a strong drink. Inside the quiet room, I went toward the table that held the wine I'd left from when we were here last. Taking the decanter, I drank, drowning out the mess in my mind.

Kelia barely accepted me as her friend, and I expected her to want me hanging around her forever? I slammed the decanter on the table, sloshing the rest of the red liquid, the desire to go to her making me mad. With a resigned breath, I stood and headed to the wardrobe where I got dressed. Slipping on a clean shirt, I thought back to when Kelia first arrived at the prison. She'd been fierce and demanding and breathtaking. I should've known from the moment that magical lasso wrapped around my neck my attraction to her was more than physical.

Remembering how she mounted me by the fire, ready to prove her power, I chuckled. Stubborn and dominating, yet so naïve about her beauty. Tugging on a pair of black pants, a slow ache formed in my chest at all the moments we shared, and how I thought she betrayed me . . . and then what I'd done. In my anger I'd torn her up, and I'd never been more disgusted with myself.

Bile rose in my throat, and I faced myself in the mirror. Looking at my somber features, the heaviness of my heart reflecting in my eyes made me feel like I was viewing an unknown entity. It felt so strange being in a familiar setting yet so out of touch with it. I wasn't the fae who had once wandered these halls. Prison and my time with Kelia had forged me into something more. And just like I had sacrificed my life for Lara's, I would accept the fate and the future that laid outside the door.

Someone knocked.

"Enter."

The door opened, and an exhausted Kelia stumbled in.

I was by her side within seconds. "What are you doing? You should be resting."

Leaning against the door, she nodded then

glanced to her left.

"Mab?" I moved the door fully open and knelt in front of the young female.

She sniffled and grabbed Kelia's hand. "I'm sorry. I know she's hurt, but Uncle E . . . he's . . ." Tears sprang forth and I pulled her into my arms.

"It's okay. Alisha told me." Holding Mab tight, I looked up at Kelia who's eyes watered.

"I thought . . . if anyone could help Uncle E it would be her." Mab rubbed her face with her sleeve. "Please, there has to be a way."

My chest ached with Mab's sorrow. "Is there?"

"Bring me to him," Kelia said and moved, standing straighter, the magi warrior replacing the bruised human. "We will do all that we can. I promise you that."

Mab took her hand and the emotion running off sent a wave of sadness through me. Fae were always sensitive to emotions, but shifting fae . . . everything was heightened and right now I could feel Mab's pain, the grief and fear so thick it was almost tangible. Taking Mab's other hand, we walked, silent and determined.

Scrvants busied around us, now that there was no army at the door. Silent hushes followed everyone as if the entire palace knew the prince laid at death's door. Mab guided us through the quiet halls. Halls I used to run around, play in, a home that I didn't deserve but had been allowed.

Two guards stood outside the prince's

chambers. Seeing Mab, they moved, one of them opening the door. A few lanterns had been lit in the dark room. The queen sat next to a four-post bed with black silk curtains that had been drawn back. She held the prince's hand who slept on the bed, covered in a mass of black bedding. Dark lines, like cracks, appeared all around his skin. The closer I came, the more my heart broke.

The scent of death wafted around the room like a pallid nightmare. Mab gripped my hand tighter, and I pulled myself together for her, not wanting to show her the depth of sadness pounding against my chest.

It was Kelia who broke away first, moving toward the edge of the bed. She lifted the blanket, exposing the prince's arm. The area where the darkthing had bitten, an angry black, festering wound oozed. Mab gasped and leaned into me. I wrapped an arm around her, rubbing her shoulder.

Kelia sat on the chair, examining the wound.

"Is there anything you can do?" Queen Merelda asked, her voice soft and low.

"I can't, but Mab might."

"Me?" Releasing my hand, she walked to Kelia. "What can I do?"

"Do you know what it means to be a light bearer?" Kelia asked, giving Mab a faint smile who shook her head no. "Light bearers only came into existence after the Rift. They are said to be an answer from the All Father to defeat the darkthings and have the power to remove all darkness."

"All darkness?" Mab stepped closer.

"Yes, all." Kelia reached out and took Mab's hand. "You destroyed those shadow monsters with your light. This wound is darkness manifested."

"So . . ." Mab's gaze went to the queen then back to Kelia. "Are you saying I could help Uncle E?"

"You can do anything, if you believe it." Kelia brought her and Mab's joined hand over the wound. "Close your eyes, and search for the darkness, find the root, and destroy it."

With a fervent nod, Mab closed her eyes.

I held my breath, not knowing what was happening. Kelia's gaze stayed on Mab, her hand never leaving hers. At first nothing happened, and then light glowed from Mab's palm hovering over the wound and then the unexpected happened.

The darkness began lifting.

"I don't believe it," I gasped, turning to look at the prince. The black lines on his face began retreating. "I think it's working."

"Just like that, Mab," Kelia said. "You keep pulling it out like a splinter, slow, steady, taking all of it. I'm right here, keeping you safe. There's no monsters just the dark and the light."

The queen's other hand went to her mouth and one tear slid down her cheek. I'd known the queen for hundreds of years and I only saw her cry once—the day she exiled me. The black lines continued to retreat and Kelia created a blue ball of her magic around the area of darkness being lifted from the wound. Black smoke like tendrils pulled out of the prince's side, gathering in a mass right under Mab's hand.

I couldn't believe it was working.

A groan sounded from the prince and the queen leaned by his head, wiping his forehead with a cloth. "This is almost over."

Mab whined and I went to her. Sweat slipped down her forehead. I placed my hands on her shoulders. "What can I do? How can I help?"

Kelia met my gaze. "You're doing it."

The oozing black floated in the air, contained by Kelia and Mab's magic. When the last drop had been pulled, and all the black gone, Kelia motioned me over.

"It's out, Mab, good job. Open your eyes because now we need to be very careful."

Kelia slid away from the prince, keeping her magic around the ball of darkness that writhed like a mass of moving shadows.

"Wow . . ." Mab stepped back. "Is that all of it?"

"Yes," Kelia said. "Callum, I need you to surround my magic with your fire magic, keep it contained, and when I release mine, the fire will destroy the rest of the darkthing."

Finally, something I could do. I hated standing and watching. "Tell me when."

Calling the fire to my hands, I wrapped my flames around her barrier, surprisingly my flames didn't destroy her magic, they joined creating a purple flame that flickered and pulsed.

Her eyes widened and her gaze met mine.

The moment our magic intertwined, something switched inside me and I knew she had to feel it too.

I didn't just care for her.

She was my mate.

I could feel the bond snapping into place as our magic swirled and created something entirely new, an orb of glittering violet as dark as my plum toned skin.

While I couldn't revel in this wonderful discovery, I focused on the little problem floating in the room.

"On my count," she said, returning to her more demanding self.

Keeping her gaze, I watched as she counted.

"1 . . . 2 . . . 3."

On three, she stepped back, and I slammed my hands together, crushing the ball of death in a fiery slap.

We all went silent, looking at each other than the prince. Kelia went back to the wound, smiling. "No lines."

"That means?" The queen's hand shook as she gripped the edge of the bed.

"He'll live."

Mab threw herself around Kelia's legs, crying and muttering a million thank-yous.

My gaze locked onto Kelia's, and I had never been more in awe of anyone.

She was more than my mate. She was everything.

TWENTY-TWO

KELIA

The prince groaned as he slid into a sitting position, holding his head. "That was very unpleasant."

"Uncle E!" Mab ran and jumped on the bed, causing the prince to stumble back onto the pillows with a laugh.

"I'm fine," he chuckled.

"You need to rest, and we should leave." The queen stood, giving Callum and me a firm look.

"Really, I feel fine." Prince Eldritch kissed Mab's forehead. "In fact, I think we should celebrate."

"Don't be ridiculous," the queen replied with a frown, but the prince was already moving . . .

directly toward me.

"My mother keeps the best wine in her chambers." He held out his arm for me. Though his steps were slow, the natural color had returned to his face. "Shall we?"

I glanced at the queen who rolled her eyes, but behind the annoyed expression there was a tenderness there. "Very well."

"I want to come too!" Mab dashed forward, grabbing my hand.

"You are going to bed. Alisha!" the queen called out, taking Mab and walking past us.

The prince cleared his throat, drawing my attention back to him. Looping my arm around his, we stepped into the hallway. Glancing back over my shoulder, Callum watched me, his jaw in a hard line. I turned around, unsure of how to react to the fire brimming in his piercing eyes.

Alisha took Mab who waved as she said goodbye while we followed the queen.

"What you've done simply amazes me," the prince said with a curl to his lips.

"I've done nothing."

His shoulder brushed against mine. "You helped save my life, and that is more than nothing."

Not wanting to talk, I smiled instead, keeping my gaze forward. When the queen stopped at a room, her guards flanking the door, I used it as an excuse to break away from the prince's embrace and head inside after Queen Merelda.

Fatigue filled my steps, and I eyed the big, cushioned couches arrayed in the sitting room. If this was where the queen slept, it must've been in a separate area behind the massive purple curtains that created a wall at the back of the room.

Someone stepped beside me, brushing my arm, and I knew it could only be one person. "Care for a drink?"

"I'm fine, thank you."

"My offer still stands, and I'm certain mother would approve of our union." He slipped his hand around mine. I was too tired to deal with his advances. After everything I'd been through, I would need sleep and rest.

"Thank you," I replied, removing my hand from his grasp. "My life is on the surface and with the magi. I need to return and quickly. If those darkthings had a hive mind then they will now know where the largest cache of life crystals are and will come here. The council must know of this."

The prince leaned over, and I thought I heard a low growl come from Callum who had moved closer to us. "Don't dedicate your life to an ancient society when you and I could herald in a new race."

"Let's not get ahead of ourselves," the queen interrupted, glaring at her son enough for him to break away from me. "You are still royal blood, and our line must stay pure, now all of you leave.

I wish to speak to the human alone."

Callum shoved past the prince who laughed and followed him out. Once the door was closed, the queen motioned to me to sit with her on the long velvet couch.

"When I was young, I had many suitors requesting my hand, including Callum." She unfastened her leather bracers and placed them on the table. "But unlike you, I am not free to love whomever I wish."

Relaxing into the soft couch, I watched as the queen unbuttoned her leather vest and tossed it to the ground then untied her braid. Her hair fell around her shoulders in long, silvery waves. It was the first time I had seen her this way and she was breathtakingly beautiful.

"The prince thinks our combined power would produce a powerful heir," I said, ignoring the comment about Callum.

The queen grabbed a decanter of wine off the low obsidian table next to us and poured two glasses. She handed me one. "You could. Your power is unique, very similar to a light bearer. It seems you have a strong effect on our males."

Taking a sip of wine, I thought on my next words carefully. The queen was being very casual with me, and I didn't want to misspeak. "They see my power that's all."

The queen laughed, her head tilting back. "Oh, to be young again. My dear, power is one thing yes, but that does not illicit desire. I would allow the marriage if my son is the one you want. Is he?"

Between her words and the wine, I felt vulnerable, something I didn't like. Callum and I had never discussed our feelings, though I sensed he cared, but after I tricked him to take the queen, I really didn't know how he felt about me. Mab had said he was the one to save me from the cave-in, but what if he did that to secure his freedom?

"I have a gift for you." The queen smiled and whispered a word in her fae tongue. The black snake slithered on to the couch and I froze. "Relax, if I wanted to kill you there are more entertaining ways. This is not an ordinary snake, and yes while its bite will kill you; it can also do something else."

The queen took out a black box with silver etching along the sides. She opened the lid and inside were six vials filled with green liquid. Taking one out, she smiled and held it up. "Drink this and after you are bitten it will counter the poison instantly."

"Why would I do any of that?"

Dragging a fingernail along the snake's back she smiled. "Because once you are healed, you are impervious to any type of poison."

Seeing the shock on my face, she continued. "You are taking my granddaughter to the surface and I need you powerful in all ways. I already know you can fight, and your intellect is impressive, but even the strongest fighters can fall to a single drop of poison."

"And how do I know that isn't some poison that will kill me outright?"

"Here," she said. "I'll show you."

Taking the vial, she drank then held the snake to her wrist. "*Bìdeadh.*"

The black mamba bit into the queen's wrist drawing blood then quickly retracted. "See? Nothing to fear."

She handed me a vial, taking my glass from me. I held it, counting in my head, waiting for any sign that the queen felt ill. When more than a minute had passed with no change in her expression, I drank the vial. The queen commanded the snake again and it bit into my wrist.

My stomach churned from the liquid and my mouth watered.

"You'll feel out of sorts as the poison and the tonic work through your system."

I gripped the side of the couch, my tongue feeling like sandpaper and my head spinning. Closing my eyes, I breathed deeply, wanting to throw up what I just drank. Another minute passed and my stomach clenched.

"Let's chat while we wait for you to recover. Do you know why Callum was imprisoned?" the queen asked, dragging a finger along the rim of her glass.

"No, the record is sealed," I replied, my voice hoarse and pained. Opening my eyes, I breathed slowly, using my training to steady the panic festering under my skin. "Not even my superior told me."

The queen drank before speaking. "I sent him there."

"Why?"

With a smile, she handed me back the wine. "The wine will help. Callum is stubborn, arrogant, and fiercely loyal."

Her gaze darted to a portrait on the wall of a group of dark fae, two I recognized as the queen and a young Prince Eldritch. "Callum never knew Lara was his, even though their bond was unlike any of his other students. When he discovered that her betrothed had very unfavorable tastes, he slaughtered the fae on his wedding night. I, of course, understood why he had acted so rash but could not speak it. The king was unfortunately still alive at that time and though he assumed Lara wasn't his, he never denied her station."

"Why would you exile him then?"

The queen sipped her wine, drumming her long fingernails against the top of the couch. "What he did nearly risked our alliances. He had to be punished and exile was easier than killing him."

Holding the glass in my hand, I thought on everything I'd learned. "Why are you telling me this?"

"I am no fool. Callum will not return to my bed when his heart belongs to another."

"What . . . ?"

A knock on the door interrupted the conversation. Followed by a deep voice. "My queen, we must speak."

"Enter," she said, sipping her wine and glancing at the door with a smirk.

The general entered; his eyes widened at the sight of me. "I'm sorry, your majesty, I didn't know you had company. I can return later."

"No need, Kelia and I are finished." She handed me the decanter. "Take this to Callum. It's his favorite."

Taking the wine, I stood and bowed my head. "Thank you."

"We will discuss arrangements for you to leave. I have a feeling you won't be going alone." She flicked me away, returning to her cooler approach. Leaving, I closed the door behind me.

"I'm sorry, I didn't know she was here," the general whispered, but loud enough for me to hear.

"Shut up, Daviti, and come serve your queen."

Laughter followed as the rustle of fabric and whispers sounded inside. I smiled, holding the wine to my chest. If the queen could find happiness after everything she'd endured, maybe I could too. Leaving the pair, I headed toward the room Callum stayed in, across from mine.

I lifted my hand to knock and paused. What was I going to say? I had no idea if what the queen said was true, and if it was, what did that mean? I still had to return to the surface and help in the last battle, and Callum had won his freedom.

Draining the glass in my hand, I let the liquid soothe my throat. Not only was I feeling off from what the queen did, but seeing Callum sent a different sort of panic through me.

He at least deserved a goodbye. I could grant him that. I knocked on the door.

"Who is it?"

"Kelia, the queen sent me with plum wine."

"It's open."

The moment I entered the room, I regretted it. Callum sat on a bench, shirtless, carving a piece of wood. He glanced at me beneath dark lashes, his expression conflicted.

Ignoring the stare, I walked to the table near him and placed the wine on top of it. "The queen said this is your favorite wine."

"It is." He returned to his carving, whittling away at the wood.

"What are you making?"

"A figure for Mab."

"Oh. That's nice." I was never good at small talk, it seemed unnecessary, but now I wished I had some idea of what to say. There were many things I wanted to discuss with him and struggled to even start.

He continued carving, not speaking and when the silence was enough to drive me out the door, I knew it was time to say goodbye.

"I'll be leaving in the morning, and as agreed you are free. I just wanted to thank you. Without you this mission wouldn't have been a success."

He stopped, his knuckles lightening as he gripped the knife. "That's all you have to say?"

"Aren't my thanks enough?"

With an angry huff, he abruptly stood, sending the chair backward. "No, Kelia, it's not enough."

His chest heaved as he eyed me across the table, attempting to pull my secrets forward with his gaze. "I desire an explanation."

"For what? You've got your freedom. There's nothing else to discuss."

Pushing away from the table, he stormed toward me, furious. "Was this all a game to you? The magi who cares for nothing but her mission. I'm not a toy, nor do I care for being played with."

"If you think I'd waste my time on such frivolous things you don't know me at all."

"Get out."

"Excuse me?"

"Get out!"

He screamed and instead of getting upset or leaving, I returned his anger with my own. "How dare you."

He laughed, shaking his head. "How dare I? You're an idiot."

With a snap of my fingers, I shot my blue flame forward, wrapping it around his neck. His gaze darkened.

"Not this time, little sparrow."

Ice crawled along my magic, freezing me to my core. I released him and was slammed against the wall, shock coursing through my thoughts.

"Tri-mage," I whispered, shocked at that revelation. There were only two others in all of Saol who held the same power, and one was on the Magi Council. No wonder Mab was so powerful.

"Among other things." Ice coated my wrists as he locked me in place. His face contoured in an angry expression. The cold seeped into my skin causing me to shake.

"Let me go," I chattered.

"No." He leaned closer. Looking down at me and pressing his hands on the wall beside me. "Not until you and I talk."

I kneed him in the groin, but he quickly blocked the move, releasing one of my hands. With a right hook, I plowed into his face. He took the punch with a growl and grabbed my arm, slamming me against the wall and using his ice magic to lock me in place.

My blue flame rose from my arms as the rage inside turned into an inferno. Ultimately, thawing the ice around my wrists. "Release me or I will show you how powerful I am."

"Then at least you'd show me something," he

spat back and grabbed my arms, pinning them to the wall.

It was then I realized the emotion in his gaze wasn't anger it was pain.

"You know," he said, his voice deep and low. "At first, I thought you were crazy. Mostly from the magic and being raised by a bunch of heartless magi."

My heart raced.

"But then there were these moments during the journey when something else flashed in your eyes, a rawness that wasn't always there."

Stop talking. Please.

"But that emotion would disappear, and I just assumed it was part of your eccentric behavior. Until you cried in my arms."

I knew what he referred to, yet I was powerless in that moment.

Using my magic, I focused on thawing the ice locking me in place and not the beating of my racing heart. Turning my head, I ignored the pain in his eyes, the hurt and confusion I knew was from me. I had buried my feelings for so long, it was almost hard to recognize them at all.

"Give me the decency to look at me when I speak." The authority in his voice forced me to turn.

Slowly, I faced him. His vibrant magenta hair hung around his face and the seriousness in his gaze made my stomach knot.

"This," he said, pointing a finger at me. "Is just

a mask. You got what you wanted, no matter how it affected me."

"You're wrong," I said, keeping my voice even.

"Am I?" His jaw twitched. "I'm not a fool, yet you've made me feel like one."

I couldn't find the words, so I sent my magic at him, wrapping my blue flame around his neck.

"No more games." His eyes darkened and his voice growled. "How would you feel if you were me? Allowing those moments and kisses?"

My chest tightened at the hurt in his eyes. "Did you enjoy yourself?"

A low growl left his lips and he slammed ice shards around my body, sending a chill up my spine. "I think it's clear how I felt."

In a quick movement, he took my arms and planted them above my head just like I had done to him. Emotion I hadn't felt since I was little rolled through me: fear, panic, desperation.

Cold ice reformed around me, the cold making me shiver.

"You used me," his voice trembled.

"That's not true."

"It is. I thought . . ." He shook his head, almost as if he was struggling with what to say.

Meeting his charged gaze, I reminded him of the only truth that mattered. "You have your freedom. That was the agreement and the only thing you wanted."

My voice trembled on the words, and I felt

myself breaking because I knew what he wanted from me and why he was angry. His forehead scrunched together as he read my reaction, understanding dawning in those beautiful light eyes.

"Don't run from this," he said in a soft voice as his grip on me loosened, bringing my arms down by my sides. "Don't run from *me*."

"We can't." The response recklessly flew out of my mouth before I could stop it.

Those two words were enough to melt the anger between us, and Callum leaned his forehead against mine. "I spent decades in a prison with no chance of release. You showed up and not only set me free but gave me hope." Taking my hand, he placed it on his chest. "Do you feel that? That's what my heart does every time you're near."

"What are you saying?" The queen's words played over in my mind.

"I'll follow you straight into the Rift if you let me in here." He tapped my chest, right where my heart beat a vicious rhyme.

Tears welled in my eyes. "I don't know how."

A lazy smile formed on his lips. "We'll figure it out together if you give us a chance, and you're crazy if you think I'd let you take the only remnant I have left of my daughter to face those monsters without me there to help you protect her. I'm going whether you like it or not. But this is more than that. I want you to stop hiding from what is between us. If I'm wrong and you feel nothing, then you tell me right here and now."

Could I? What would happen when we arrived on the surface? What would the magi say? There was no time for fun or love.

Love . . . did he . . . no one loved me, not since losing my parents and siblings. Was I even capable of love? "I don't know how to be anything other than myself."

"I don't want you to change. I love you exactly how you are."

"Callum . . ." The tears fell freely, and when he leaned over to kiss me, I pressed against him, diving into the unknown. His hands slipped to my thighs, and he lifted me up and into his arms, holding me with ferocity and kissing me as if separating me would be the death of him. When I pulled back to breathe, he righted his grip on me and kissed my cheek.

One tear fell then another, and another, and another until I could no longer see. The emotion spilling out into an uncontrollable wave of agony. Thirteen years of pent-up emotion tumbled out in a wail. Callum brought us to the ground, taking me into his lap, his hold steady and warm.

"You're right," I sobbed. "I do pretend. It's how I survived. Do you know what it's like to watch your family be eaten by darkthings?"

Callum's silver gaze widened. I wiped the tears off my cheeks.

"I was seven when it happened. At the same time the darkthings killed everyone I loved; my powers emerged. I had created a barrier around myself, and it only saved *me*."

"You were just a child." All anger and hubris had left his voice as he rubbed my back.

"I was in shock for weeks. The magi forced me to secrecy, and I didn't have anyone . . . not a friend, nothing. I stopped caring. It was the only way to stop the pain and control the wild magic inside."

"Kelia . . ."

"People respect those they fear. Acting the way I do protects me from ever being hurt . . . until you."

Meeting his gaze, I forced out the confession. "I heard stories about you. Callum Deathstrike is a monster, trickster. Be on guard. I was ready. You were just a mission. Until I saw you."

He went to speak, and I stopped him. "Let me finish."

He swallowed, nodded, then gently placed his hand on my foot.

I recalled the moment I saw him. "You were beyond handsome, mystical almost . . . everything from your voice to your swaggering walk. I had never seen anything like you before. I had to ignore the emotions and when we went into the woods those odd emotions kept festering, and I couldn't allow myself to feel."

"Yet, you kept pretending." There was no more anger, and I felt guilty for all the lies.

I nodded and wiped my face, feeling too open and raw to speak.

He wrapped me in a hug. "I'm sorry about your family."

He stroked my hair and I leaned against his shoulder and held on to him. There were many things I wanted to say and explain, but I couldn't. After we got Mab out of the city, Callum would be free to go where he wanted with or without me. Would he really come to the surface? Gripping the front of his shirt, I tried not to think of the after and focus only on the now.

Callum slid his arm under my legs and lifted me up. He carried me to the bed. "Rest."

I grabbed his arm, feeling vulnerable for the first time in my life. "Stay, please."

A soft smile spread on his face. "Of course."

He settled in behind me and wrapped the blanket around us. I rolled over so I laid against his chest. With his arms around me, a calmness washed over me, and I knew that somehow, everything would be okay.

When I woke sometime later, I didn't move away from Callum. Having his arms wrapped around me brought me a sense of peace and rightness.

A soft groan left his lips as he curled into my side. "Morning already?"

"Yes, but we don't need to get up right now."

"I don't want to." He tugged at the bottom of my shirt. "I'm sorry for the way I treated you yesterday. I was angry and having Prince Eldritch remind me of that idiotic proposal didn't help." He rolled me under him. "Would you really have married him?"

"No, I would've found a way out."

Satisfied, he hovered closer to my face. "I'm coming with you."

"To the surface?"

"Yes, and anywhere else."

"You mean that?"

"I meant what I said yesterday, and it makes sense now why the queen released me. She knew I would never let Mab be taken by the magi and I wouldn't have, but I understand what we all face and together, we can win." He trailed kisses down my neck.

"What about the queen?"

He nibbled behind my ear. "Is my little sparrow jealous?"

Ignoring the rush of heat left by his lips, I continued. "You two had a child together and I know the queen would take you back if you wanted her to."

"I'd rather go back to prison," he grumbled. "Besides, I'm not leaving my mate."

"Your mate?"

Nodding, he pulled back, leaning over me, his

hair covering part of his face. "I know you felt the bond when our magic combined."

"It was unlike anything I'd experienced before."

"Kiss me with your magic."

"What?" I thought I'd heard him wrong, but he repeated himself.

"Do as I do, little sparrow," he purred then opened his mouth just an inch above me, a puff of cold breath washing over my face. "This is my bargain with you that as your mate my heart will never stray to another's and you will have all of me, forever."

His confession made me smile from the inside out. I pulled my blue flame up from my core, bringing the familiar magic to my mouth. He moved, pressing his lips to mine, and opening himself up. Closing my eyes, I brought down the barriers I'd created and let him in. When our lips collided, a spark ignited in my chest, a warm energy that flowed back and forth between us, connecting us in a way that surpassed all understanding.

He groaned against my lips, his hands sliding everywhere at once. "You're mine and I want to feel you all the way down to your soul." He continued kissing me until our magic blended into one, creating a flame that was the same shade of the deep violet orb we had made, a beautiful blend of both our powers.

When I pulled back, needing to breathe and

stop my shaky thoughts, he rolled onto his side with a grin. I didn't know how this was going to work or what the magi would say, but I couldn't ignore my feelings or what I wanted anymore.

Taking a strand of my hair with his fingers, he sniffed then scrunched his nose.

"What?" I asked, yanking my hair back from him.

Without a response, he swung off the bed and to my side.

"What are you—"

Lifting me off the bed, he walked toward the door, snatching the wine with one hand as he passed the table.

"Where are you taking me?" He kicked the door closed behind us and headed across the hall to my room.

"You need a bath."

"Now?"

He laughed, his smile wide and refreshing. "I'm sorry, but we both need a wash. Darkthing blood reminds me of rotten mushrooms."

"It is not that bad . . ." I said, sniffing a piece of my hair. We hadn't stopped to rest or clean ourselves since we fought the darkthings in the Borderlands.

"I love you, but you deserve a proper kiss with no holding back. The stench on both of us is becoming a bit rancid."

Love.

He said he loved me and in such a casual way, I didn't feel awkward or uncomfortable. In fact, warmth caressed my chest and tingles filled my belly.

Ignoring his scrunched nose, I looped my arms around his neck and tugged him closer. "If you hurry, this time I may let you do the washing."

A low rumble sounded from him. "Don't tease me, little sparrow."

"No, seriously, I need help with these bandages. I don't think I can untie them all by myself."

Callum growled and nibbled my ear as we entered the room. "If I wasn't sure, I'd think you were jesting me, but my little sparrow doesn't know how to tell a joke."

"No, but I'm willing to learn."

With that one declaration an understanding passed between us. My emotions were a mess I buried long ago, but each day with Callum the girl who existed before her family died started to re-emerge. He claimed I saved him when it was reversed.

Tomorrow, we would leave for the surface and straight into an uncertain war. I didn't know what would happen or if any of us would survive, but for today, I would leave duty at the door and let myself fall headfirst into love.

I deserved that.

And so did he.

The end.

Thank you for reading!

Make sure to sign up for my newsletter where you can get sneak peeks, prizes, and much more.
http://eepurl.com/ghabvr

To continue the adventure grab the next story in *The Shifting Fae series: The Eternal Sea*

A powerful runaway princess and a fae pirate will discover there's more than scandalous emotions churning in the sea.

Havana flees an arranged marriage to run to the Oasis where human, fae, and every other race of Saol live in opulent paradise. To get there, she'll have to board a ship called the Ravager which is just as deadly as its dark fae captain.

It doesn't take long for the sea to capture Havana's heart, and it takes even less for her to fall for the silver-haired Leon who is just as dangerous as the wild sea he navigates.

But Havana isn't just running from a marriage.

The secret she harbors will set war upon the Ravager and its crew, and she's the only one who can stop it.

If she's willing to tell the truth.

The Eternal Sea is a stand alone Fantasy Romance within the Shifting Fae world. Perfect for readers looking for epic fantasy, slow-burn romance, fast-paced action and a happily ever after.

Follow this link to read more!

https://buy.bookfunnel.com/p7ap1txp7w

ABOUT THE AUTHOR

USA Today Bestselling author Eliza Tilton graduated from Dowling College with a BA in Visual Communications. When she's not arguing with excel at her day job, chasing after four kids, or playing video games, she's writing fast-paced young adult fantasy and paranormal tales. Check out www.elizatilton.com for more of her books or follow her on tiktok @elizatilton where she shares tons of bookish stuff.

Milton Keynes UK
Ingram Content Group UK Ltd.
UKHW021052020524
442115UK00014B/488